CW01238014

Love Secrets and Olives

Lea Winslow

© 2024 Lea Winslow. All rights reserved.

A Will, a Way, and a Whisker

Eleni

I slump into my chair, the same one I've been sitting in for the past three years, and stare at my computer screen. Another day, another mind-numbing series of marketing reports to analyse. I'm good at this, I remind myself. I can crunch numbers and spot trends with the best of them. But as I open yet another spreadsheet, I can't help but wonder if this is really all there is.

This office is a maze of cubicles and fluorescent lights, a sterile and suffocating environment that seemed to suck the life out of everything within its walls. The room has a distinct scent of stale coffee, printer ink, and a hint of musty air. Occasionally, the smell of someone's microwaved leftovers drifts through the space. Inside, there is a low hum from the computers and printers, interrupted by the occasional ringing of phones and the constant clacking of keyboards. Outside, the distant sounds of traffic and construction can be heard through the windows.

"Good morning, Eleni!" chirps Sarah from the next cubicle. "Ready for another exciting day of consumer engagement metrics?"

I force a smile. "Oh, you know me. I live for pivot tables." As I dive into the data, my mind wanders. There's got to be more to life than this, right? I'm capable of so much more, but here I am, trapped in a sea of cells and formulas. My phone buzzes, startling me out of my existential crisis. Dad's name flashes on the screen. Great. Just what I need to brighten my day.

"Hello, Father," I answer, trying to keep the sarcasm out of my voice.

"Eleni," he says, his tone already making me brace for impact. "I'd like you to join me and Margaret for dinner tonight. There's something we need to discuss."

My stomach does a little flip. "Sure, Dad. Sounds... great."

As soon as I hung up, I let out a groan. "Fantastic. Another evening of 'Why Can't You Be More Successful?'" I mutter to myself. "I can't wait to hear how I've disappointed the family legacy by choosing marketing over... I don't know, discovering a new species of bioluminescent jellyfish or becoming a finance guru."

I lean back in my chair, imagining the impending lecture. "Oh Eleni," I mimic my father's voice, "Why waste your potential on such frivolous pursuits? When I was your age, I was already my company's top financial analyst for emerging markets."

Sighing, I turn back to my computer. At least I have a few hours to prepare my defences. Maybe I'll even come up with a witty comeback this time. Who am I kidding? I'll probably just sit there, nodding and smiling, while secretly plotting my escape to a remote island where I can live out my days as a humble goat herder.

But for now, these consumer engagement metrics aren't going to analyse themselves. I take a deep breath and dive back in, trying to ignore the knot of anxiety forming in my stomach. Just another day in the thrilling life of Eleni Katsaros, disappointment extraordinaire.

***

As I stare at the mind-numbing spreadsheet, my thoughts drift back to the funeral of my grandfather from 3 weeks ago. I had always promised myself that I would visit more often, and spend more time with my grandparents while they were still here. But life always seemed to get in the way - work, commitments, excuses. And now it was too late. With only a couple weeks of vacation each year, I didn't want to spend them all in Seranos, the small village where I had spent all my childhood summers. It was my favourite place on Earth and the only place I truly felt at home.

George was never the same after my Grandma passed away 5 years ago. The light in his eyes seemed to dim, and the infectious laughter that used to echo around the grove became a rare sound. He threw himself into the work with an intensity that was both inspiring and heart-wrenching. I watched as the man who used to take long, leisurely walks through the olive groves, sharing stories and wisdom, now laboured from dawn till dusk with a steadfast, sombre determination. The joyful spark that had ignited countless family gatherings and community celebrations seemed to flicker and wane. As a child, he was my hero, larger than life and endlessly cheerful. But the loss of Grandma carved a quiet sorrow into his face, etching deep lines that spoke of silent grief and unspoken loneliness.

The morning of Grandpa George's funeral dawned clear and bright, the Greek sun casting a golden glow over the whitewashed stones of Seranos. I stood at the entrance of the small, centuries-old church; its doors flung wide open as if embracing all who came to mourn. The air was scented with a mix of incense and the briny sea breeze, a familiar smell that brought memories flooding back.

As I stepped inside, the murmur of hushed conversations filled the church, villagers mingling in their Sunday best, exchanging nods and gentle pats on the shoulder. The wooden pews were packed, and the overflow of mourners spilled out into the courtyard, where chairs had been hurriedly set up. It felt less like a sombre occasion and more like a family gathering where everyone knew each other's names and stories.

The service was a tapestry of old village traditions and heartfelt tributes. The local priest, who had known George since he was a boy, gave a tender eulogy that painted him not just as a community pillar but as a man of laughter and kindness, whose generosity was as abundant as the olive groves he tended. His voice wavered as he recounted anecdotes that drew soft chuckles and teary smiles from the congregation.

After the service, the procession to the cemetery was a slow, meandering walk through the village. Children darted between adults, too young to understand the sorrow but feeling the day's solemnity. We passed by familiar landmarks, each a chapter from my summers here— the old fountain, the village square, and finally, the dusty path leading to the small cemetery overlooking the sea.

As the ceremony concluded, the mood shifted subtly from mourning to remembrance. Tables laden with food appeared as if by magic, covered with dishes prepared by the village's women. People started to eat, talk, and even laugh as stories about my grandfather began to weave through the crowd, each tale bringing him vividly back to life in the village's collective memory.

Standing there, amidst the laughter and tears, the warmth of the community enveloped me. I realized that in Seranos, funerals were not just about saying goodbye; they were about affirming life, the enduring bonds of community, and the threads of shared memories that connected us all.

I can't help but chuckle bitterly as I recall Dad's impatience to leave.

"We should head back to London tomorrow," he'd said, barely waiting for the last mourner to leave. "No point in staying here any longer."

No point? I wanted to scream. It was George's funeral, for crying out loud. But then again, when had Dad ever wanted to stay in Seranos?

I close my eyes, transported back to those endless summers of my childhood. The whitewashed walls of our family home, the salty breeze carrying the scent of wild herbs. Mum would drop me off, her eyes sparkling as she chatted with Grandma and Grandpa. She'd stay for weeks, basking in the warmth of family and tradition.

"Remember when we'd count the days until we could go back?" I mutter to myself, a lump forming in my throat. "Before everything changed."

After Mum died, those summers became... different. Dad would fly me there, his jaw set in a hard line as if the very act of returning to Seranos pained him. He'd barely at the door before saying, "I'll pick you up at the end of August," and zooming off in a cloud of dust.

Even now, I can feel that hollow ache in my chest, the mixture of excitement for the summer ahead and crushing disappointment that, once again, Dad wouldn't be part of it.

"Thanks for that, Dad," I mutter sarcastically. "Nothing says 'I love you' quite like dumping your kid in a village and hightailing it back to the big city."

I shake my head, trying to dispel the memories. It's no use dwelling on the past, especially with tonight's dinner looming. Speaking of which...

Glancing at the clock, I let out a dramatic sigh. The inevitable moment has arrived. While I start collecting my belongings, Mrs. Patel, the nurturing figurehead of our accounting department, peeks into my workspace.

"Off to a hot date, dear?" she asks, her eyes twinkling mischievously.
I snort. "If by 'hot date' you mean 'dinner with my father where he'll inevitably list all my life choices he disapproves of,' then yes, absolutely scorching."
Mrs. Patel clucks sympathetically. "Oh, fathers. They mean well, but..."
"But they have a funny way of showing it?" I finish, raising an eyebrow.
She pats my arm. "Just remember, you're a wonderful girl. Don't let anyone make you feel otherwise."
I force a smile, touched by her kindness. "Thanks, Mrs. P. I'll try to channel your optimism."
I step into the elevator, my stomach churning with a mixture of dread and determination. "Here we go," I mutter to my reflection in the mirrored walls. It's time to make the Katsaros family proud—or at least not to royally embarrass myself. Baby steps, Eleni. Baby steps."

***

I stand before my father's imposing townhouse, frozen in place like a Greek statue - only less dignified and infinitely more neurotic. The manicured hedges and pristine white facade are a far cry from my dingy basement flat. Even the air feels different here - crisp and refined, carrying the faint scent of roses from Margaret's prized garden.
"Come on, Eleni," I mutter, willing my hand to move. "It's just a doorbell, not a detonator."
My finger hovers uncertainly. I could still make a run for it. Claim food poisoning. Or maybe temporary amnesia. I can almost hear the lecture about to unfold. Eleni, when are you going to take life seriously? I playfully rehearse my comeback: "Oh, I am serious, Dad—seriously

considering becoming a professional cat herder. It's a growing field, you know." I chuckle quietly when the porch light flickers on, startling me. Great, now I'm loitering suspiciously outside my own father's house. Wouldn't that just be the cherry on top of this anxiety sundae?

The door swings open just as I muster the courage to ring the bell. There stands Margaret, her warm smile easing the tight knot in my stomach. She entered my life when she married my dad and, I was just 13. Margaret has been a steadfast stepmother—always there, consistently caring, and sincerely loving towards my dad. I was part of the package deal, and she embraced that with a by-the-book dedication that has always commanded my respect. I've always appreciated her, and I believe she cares for me in her own structured way. We never ventured into the warm waters of a mother-daughter relationship, nor did she try to fill the gaping maternal void left by my mom. Don't get me wrong, I'm deeply thankful for her—especially for managing my father all these years. In truth, it was Maria, my childhood best friend Callie's mom from Seranos, who offered those fleeting maternal summers. She provided the kind of nurturing that lingered in my heart, even if just seasonally.

"Eleni, darling!" she exclaims, enveloping me in a hug that smells of cinnamon and comfort. "We were starting to worry. Come in, come in."

I step inside, the familiar scent of lemon polish and old books washing over me. "Sorry, got held up at work," I lie, hoping my voice doesn't betray me.

Margaret's eyes soften as she takes my coat. "Oh, sweetheart. I know how much you miss George. He adored you so."

A lump forms in my throat. "Thanks, Margaret. I miss him terribly."

Margaret leans in, her voice lowering conspiratorially. "Your father's in his study. Why don't you freshen up while I coax him out? Dinner's almost ready." I nod gratefully, desperately needing a moment to collect myself.

***

Dad takes his place at the head of the table. I can't help but notice how his tailored suit contrasts sharply with the cosy domesticity of the dining room. It's as if he's perpetually ready to dash off to a board meeting, even on a Tuesday night. His hair, though greying at the temples, is meticulously combed back, and his glasses sit precisely on the bridge of his nose, adding to his perpetual air of being prepared for serious business. His presence, with a posture rigid as the back of his chair, seems to command attention, asserting a formality that feels almost out of place among the warm earthy tones of the room.

I bite back a sarcastic retort, reminding myself that picking a fight within the first five minutes would be a new record, even for us. Instead, I sit at the table, smoothing my napkin over my lap with exaggerated care.

"The roast smells wonderful, Margaret," I say, desperately grasping for a safe topic.

Margaret beams as she bustles in from the kitchen, a steaming platter in her hands. "Oh, thank you, dear. I hope you're hungry!"

"So, Eleni," he begins, his voice carrying that familiar note of disapproval, "how's work?"

I take a sip of wine, buying myself a moment. "Oh, you know," I say lightly, "same old, same old. Spreadsheets, meetings, the occasional office drama over who stole whose yogurt from the fridge. Honestly, the highlight of my week was choosing between plain and fruit yogurt. Went with fruit. I like to live on the edge."

Margaret chuckles, but Dad's frown deepens. "I see. And you're... content with that?"

The weight of unspoken expectations hangs heavy in the air. I nearly hear the wheels turning in his head: 'All that education, all those opportunities, and she's making jokes about yogurt thieves.'

"It pays the bills," I shrug, stabbing a roast potato with perhaps more force than necessary. "And I'm good at it."

"Being 'good' at something isn't the same as excelling, Eleni," Dad says, his tone maddeningly patient. "You have so much potential—"

"Petros," Margaret interjects gently, "why don't we talk about something else? Eleni, dear, have you thought about taking a holiday soon? You work so hard; you deserve a break."

I shoot Margaret a grateful look. "Actually, I've been thinking about that..."

My mind drifts to Seranos, sun-drenched olive groves, and waves' soothing rhythm against the shore. For a moment, I allow myself to imagine a life there – one filled with purpose and connection, so different from the grey monotony of my London existence.

Dad's voice snaps me back to reality. "A holiday? Now? Eleni, this is precisely the kind of short-term thinking that—"

"Petros," Margaret says, a hint of steel beneath her gentle tone. "Let's just enjoy our meal, shall we?"

I hide a smirk behind my wine glass. Margaret may be soft-spoken, but she's the only person I know who can get Dad to back down with a single word. As she deftly steers the conversation to safer waters, I can't help but wonder how different our family dinners would be without her calm presence as a buffer.

The rest of the meal passes in a haze of stilted small talk and meaningful glances. With every bite, I feel the weight of unspoken words pressing down on me, threatening to crack the veneer of polite conversation at any moment.

As I push the last bite of roast potato around my plate, Dad clears his throat. Here we go, I think, bracing myself for the inevitable lecture.

"Eleni," he begins, his voice taking on that familiar patronizing tone. "I've been thinking about your... situation."

I can't help but roll my eyes. "My situation? You mean my life, Dad?"

He ignores my sarcasm, pressing on. "You have so much potential. That degree from LSE, and yet you're wasting away in that dead-end job. When are you going to start taking your career seriously?"

"Oh, I don't know," I quip, unable to resist. "Maybe when the job market starts taking my CV seriously? Or when nepotism becomes an Olympic sport?"

Dad's jaw tightens. "This isn't a joke, Eleni. You need to be more motivated and push yourself. You can't keep drifting like this."

I bite back a more biting retort, instead muttering under my breath, "Because your constant disappointment is such great motivation."

"What was that?" Dad asks sharply.

"Nothing," Actually, Dad wasn't always this way; things just seemed to get tougher as he got older. When Mum was still around, everything felt gentler, smoother somehow. After she died, I guess Dad just didn't know how to handle raising a ten-year-old girl on his own. He thought he'd have done his job perfectly if he equipped me with all the right tools for success—like a nice home, private schools, a solid education. But I wasn't one of his business projects; life isn't a simple equation where a good house plus a good education automatically equals a high-flying corporate star.

I sighed, then decided to go for broke. "Look, Dad, I know you mean well, but have you considered that maybe, just maybe, your definition of success isn't the only one that matters?"

His eyes narrow.

"And what's that supposed to mean?"

I take a deep breath, steeling myself. "It means that success isn't just about having a high-paying job or climbing the corporate ladder. Success can be about being happy, finding joy in the little things, or just being content with who you are and where you are in life."

Dad's expression softens slightly, but he's clearly struggling with the concept. "Contentment? Happiness? Those are subjective, Eleni. They don't pay the bills."

Okay, here we go again. Before he launches into another tirade, I decide to cut to the chase.

"So," I say, forcing a lightness I don't feel into my voice, "was there something specific you wanted to discuss tonight? Or was this merely our usual 'Eleni falls short' dinner appointment?"

***

Dad's face tightens, and for a moment, I think I've pushed too far. But then he straightens, clearing his throat.

"Actually, yes. There is something we need to discuss." He pauses, his eyes flickering to Margaret, who gives him an encouraging nod. "It's about your grandfather's estate."

My heart skips a beat. "George's estate? What about it?"

Dad's lips press into a thin line. "He's left you his shares at the grove in Seranos."

The words hit me like a punch to the gut. I blink, certain I've misheard. "What?"

"The grove, Eleni. The house, the groves, the business, everything." Dad's voice is clipped and controlled. "And the cat. He's yours now, too."

"Ari?" I stammer, my mind reeling not just from the shock of the inheritance but also from the unexpected addition of a pet. "Grandpa left me... his cat?"

"Yes, Aristotle."

This dialogue was getting more and more surrealistic.

My mind reels. The grove, the house, Ari? Mine? I open my mouth, but no words come out.

"And Aristotle," I murmur, almost to myself, a smile tugging at my lips despite the gravity of the situation.

Dad leans forward, his eyes intense. "Eleni, listen to me. This isn't an opportunity; it's a burden. Do you have any idea what it takes to run an olive oil business? The work, the expertise, the sheer manpower?"

A memory flashes through my mind: Dad, much younger, his face twisted with frustration as he argued with Grandpa George. "This place is dying, Dad! There's no future here!"

I blink, coming back to the present. Dad's still talking, his voice urgent. "We left that life behind for a reason, Eleni. Don't throw away everything we've worked for on some... romantic notion of village life."

I can see it in his eyes – the fear, the desperation. He's not just worried about me; he's reliving his own past, his own choices.

But as I sit there, absorbing the news, a riot of emotions swirls through me. Surprise, of course – I never expected this. Fear, because holy crap, a grove? What do I know about olives beyond putting them in my martinis?

And yet... there's something else. A tiny spark of excitement, of possibility. Images flash through my mind: sun-drenched groves, the scent of the sea, laughter echoing through whitewashed streets.

"I... I need to think about this," I manage to say, my voice barely above a whisper.

Dad's eyebrows shoot up. "Think about it? Eleni, there's nothing to think about. We sell, we move on. It's that simple. I already contacted a solicitor who is ready to deal with everything. You don't even need to go."

But it's not simple—not at all. As I sit there, I realize that for the first time in years, I feel something I'd almost forgotten—a spark of something thrilling, a sense of adventure that I thought I had lost. Maybe, just maybe, this could be the start of something beautiful.

Hope.

"Well, Aristotle, looks like it's just you and me—and a few olive trees," I murmur to myself as Dad continues to argue his points. It's almost laughable, this sudden shift in my life. From mind-numbing spreadsheets to... what? Olive oil mogul? Cat whisperer? The idea would be absurd if it weren't so terrifyingly real.

And there's Dad, looking like he's ready to march into battle against this absurd twist of fate. Poor guy, he's got his own ghosts, and now here I am, potentially stirring them all up with talk of embracing our roots. Roots that are tangled in soil and family history he'd rather forget.

Yet, as I sit here, listening to him, something strange bubbles up inside me—a mix of defiance and determination. Who knew the prospect of dirty fingernails and cat fur could feel like... freedom? Freedom from the predictable, from the monotony that has coloured my London life in the drabbest shades.

As the words hang in the air, mixing with the scent of Margaret's roast and the underlying tension, I realize this isn't just about inheritance, obligations, or even making monumental life decisions on a Tuesday evening. It's about the possibility of life being something more than what it's been so far. And that thought alone, despite the

fear, makes me smile genuinely for the first time in a long while. And hey, if I fail, at least I'll fail spectacularly, with a philosophical cat by my side to judge me."
Maybe it's madness, maybe it's a mid-life crisis a few years too early, or maybe, just maybe, it's the beginning of a story I'd actually want to read.

***

Back in the familiar yet now strangely distant feel of my London flat, I sink onto the couch, the conversation with Dad still echoing in my head. Staring at the ceiling, I can't shake the image of some solemn solicitor, clad in a sombre suit, rifling through George's vibrant life. The very thought sends a shiver down my spine. "Not on my watch," I mutter, grabbing my phone with a newfound determination. I should make the trip, even though it mainly involves clearing out Grandpa's house and handling the legal matters myself.
"Janet? It's Eleni. I need to cash in on those vacation days, like, all of them. Three weeks should cover it." The words sprint out before doubt can reel them back. After the call, I flop back, a ridiculous smile plastering my face. I picture Dad's reaction when he hears I'm hopping the next flight out. "He's going to need a very strong drink," I chuckle to myself, imagining him explaining to his golf buddies why his daughter chose olive pits over profit margins.
The room feels smaller already, as if it's shrunk in response to my mind's expanding horizons. "Here's to trading in spreadsheets for olive branches," I toast to the empty room, lifting an imaginary glass. Who knows? This might just be the craziest, most brilliant thing I've ever done.
With that, I start making lists—what to pack, what to sort, what to dream. Because if I'm going to do this, I'm not

just going to dip my toes in. No, I'm diving in headfirst, ready to swim in the deep end of life. And who better to do it with than Aristotle, the cat philosopher? "Hope you're ready for company, old boy," I say into the quiet, my heart fluttering with a cocktail of nerves and excitement.

The following day, I find myself pulling a suitcase out from under my bed, the wheels sticking a bit as I drag it across the floor. As I start packing, I mutter to myself, "Alright, Eleni, what does one pack for a potentially life-altering adventure? Sunscreen, check. Courage, um... rain check?"

I toss a few sundresses into my suitcase, then pause, holding an old, faded T-shirt I used to wear. The fabric, soft from years of salt and sun, transports me back to lazy summer afternoons in Seranos.

Suddenly, I'm twelve again, perched on a gnarled olive tree branch, my legs swinging freely as Grandpa George's laughter echoes below.

"Eleni," he calls up, his eyes twinkling, "come down before you turn into an olive yourself!"

I giggle, "But Grandpa, I want to see the whole village from up here!"

"Ah, but the real treasure of Seranos isn't in what you see," he says, his voice warm and wise. It's in what you feel—the earth beneath your feet, the sun on your face, the love in your heart. That's the inheritance I want to leave you."

The memory fades, leaving me clutching the t-shirt to my chest, tears pricking at my eyes. "Oh, Grandpa," I whisper, "I hope I'm not too late". I shake my head, trying to clear the sudden flood of emotions. "Get it together, Eleni. You're packing for a trip, not auditioning for a Greek tragedy."

"Christ," I mutter, zipping up my overstuffed suitcase. "Well, here's to discovering myself—or confirming this is my most nostalgic mistake yet. Fifty-fifty chance, really."

***

When I step outside, I am welcomed with a typical London drizzle, the city seemingly crying on my behalf—or maybe it's just mocking my attempt at a dramatic exit. As the taxi merges into the morning traffic, I lean back, the reality of what I'm doing starting to sink in. I'm leaving. Maybe I am leaving, not just on a holiday or a brief escape from work deadlines, but for something more permanent. The thought both thrills and terrifies me. I stare out the window, watching the familiar streets blur past, each one a thread unravelling from the fabric of my London life.

At the airport, the hustle and bustle swallow me whole. I navigate through security, clutching my passport and boarding pass like they're lifelines. Around me, people chatter in a dozen languages, some excited, some tired, all in motion. It strikes me then, how we're all just stories in transit, each of us with our own destinations and dramas.

Waiting at the gate, I pull out my phone and scroll through photos—one of the last summers in Seranos, with me grinning beside Grandpa George, his arm around my shoulders. My heart clenches.

As I settle into my window seat on the plane, I can't help but feel like I'm starring in my own personal dramedy. The kind where the hapless heroine makes a life-altering decision and hilarity (hopefully) ensues.

"Excuse me," a voice interrupts my internal monologue. It's the man assigned to the middle seat, looking apologetic.

"Excuse me, could you please grab your bag for me?" I suddenly remember that I had left my handbag on the seat next to me.

"Oh, sure," I say. As he settles in, I catch a whiff of expensive cologne. Great. I'm going to smell like a duty-free shop by the time we land.

"First time flying to Greece?" the cologne man asks, clearly trying to be friendly.

I turn, mustering a polite smile. "No, but it's my first time flying there to potentially throw my life into chaos, so that's exciting."

He blinks, taken aback. "I... see. Business or pleasure?"

I snort. "Neither. Unless inheriting an olive business from your grandfather and running away from your corporate job counts as either of those. And let's not forget the cat," I add.

"Sounds like the plot of a romantic comedy," he says with a chuckle.

"God, I hope not," I mutter. "I don't have the wardrobe budget for that."

As the plane begins to taxi, I close my eyes, my stomach doing somersaults that have nothing to do with take-off. This trip is so different from my last visit to Seranos. Then, I was weighed down by grief, saying goodbye to Grandpa George. Now? Now I'm... what? Chasing a dream? Running from reality?

"Maybe both," I whisper to myself.

"Sorry, did you say something?" Cologne Man asks.

"Just giving myself a pep talk," I reply. "It's a long flight. Plenty of time to second-guess every life choice I've ever made."

He laughs, a warm, genuine sound. "Well, for what it's worth, I think inheriting an olive business sounds pretty amazing."

I smile, surprised by the sincerity in his voice. "Thanks. I just hope I don't mess it up spectacularly."

As the plane lifts off, I can't help but grin. "Well, Eleni," I think to myself, "your life might be a mess, but at least it's an interesting mess now. A sense of adventure fills me, I don't know what awaits me in Seranos, but I'm ready to find out. Ready to face whatever challenges and changes come my way. Because sometimes, to find what truly makes us happy, we have to venture far from where we started—geographically, emotionally, completely. Move over, Mrs. Papadopoulos' soap operas; there's a new drama in town - starring me, a bunch of olives, a cat, and probably a lot of embarrassing mishaps. Opa!"

From Poseidon with Love

The taxi lurches around another hairpin turn and I clutch the door handle, my knuckles white. "Is this how all Greek men drive or just you?" I ask the driver, who merely grins and honks his horn as we careen past a donkey cart. "Almost there," the driver announces, jerking to a stop that nearly sends me through the windshield.

The Aegean sparkles below, impossibly blue. Each wave reflects the sunlight, casting playful glimmers that dance across the undulating waters. The crisp, salty air rushes in as I open the window, mingling with the scent of wild herbs from the surrounding hills—scents that evoke memories of long, sun-drenched days. A surge of excitement courses through me, tinged with an undercurrent of doubt. What exactly am I doing? Is this a bold adventure or have I completely lost touch with reality?

Stepping out of the taxi, the warmth of Seranos wraps around me, and my legs feel unsteady—not just from the long ride, but from the wave of memories stirred by the dazzling Aegean sun. The village unfolds like a familiar painting, every detail vivid and alive. The air carries a mix of sea salt and the earthy scent of olive groves, a fragrance that instantly takes me back to carefree childhood summers.

Narrow cobbled streets wind through Seranos, flanked by whitewashed houses glowing in golden light. Blue shutters swing gently in the breeze, adding splashes of colour to the scene. As I walk, the worn stones underfoot seem to hum with the stories of generations, while the soft sounds of life drift from open windows—old songs, the clink of spoons against coffee cups, and murmured conversations.

The village square opens up, alive with the rhythm of daily life. Ancient olive trees offer shade to a group of elderly men playing backgammon, their laughter rippling through the air like music. For a moment, I'm a child again, skipping barefoot across the sun-dappled stones, chasing shadows between the trees.

Heading toward the water, the streets burst with bougainvillea, their bright magenta flowers standing out against the deep blue sky. At the edge of the village, the small beach and its pebbles greet gentle waves, while a wooden pier stretches into the sea. Fishermen mend their nets on its edge, their boats rocking softly in the water. The salty tang of the sea mixed with the faint smell of fish feels timeless, as if the village and the sea have been locked in this quiet dance forever.

Above this small cove, the rocky coast ascends into hidden alcoves accessible only by weathered steps cut into the cliffs—secret havens from the outside world. Despite Seranos' tranquil isolation, it's just a short drive to Navagos, a bustling town where modern life buzzes in contrast. Here, the young and restless can experience the wider world without ever straying too far from the roots that anchor them here.

This village, cradled by hills and caressed by the sea, is a tapestry of old and new, tradition and the quiet promise of tomorrow. As I absorb the sights and sounds, the familiar and the forgotten, I can't help but wonder if this place, frozen in time yet whispering of change, might still hold a place for me.

Hefting my suitcase, I stumble, nearly face-planting. The cobblestones are just as treacherous as I remember. So much for making a graceful entrance.

"Need help with that, Eleni?" Theo, owner of the fisherman's shack, the only restaurant in Seranos, calls from the café where he is playing backgammon with his friend.

"No, no, I've got it!" I insist, dragging the suitcase behind me like an uncooperative toddler. It catches on every bump and crevice.

I pass the old olive tree where Callie and I used to play. A memory flashes - us hanging upside down from the branches, shrieking with laughter as Andreas tried to knock us down with a broom. My cheeks warm at the thought of Andreas.

"Eleni! My daughter!" A wrinkled face beams at me. It's old Sophia, one of my late grandmother's best friends. "You are back!". I smile and stop to hug her.

By the time I reach the steep hill to George's - my - house, I'm sweating and panting. Maybe I should have accepted Theo's help after all. But I'm determined to prove I can handle this.

"You can do this, Eleni," I mutter. "It's just a suitcase. And an olive grove. And your entire future. No pressure."

The handle comes off in my hand as I give the suitcase one final tug. I stand there, momentarily stunned, staring at the broken handle. "Well, that's one way to make an entrance," I sigh. Welcome home, Eleni.

***

I finally manage to haul my rebellious luggage to the front door of George's house. My hands tremble slightly as the door creaks open, and a wave of memories washes over me.

Stepping into George's house, the familiar sweet fragrances of rosemary and jasmine immediately wraps around me, transporting me back in time. I can almost hear the echoes of my laughter as a child, darting through these rooms in a dripping swimsuit, with Grandma's joyful laughter chasing after me.

I pause in the doorway, the air holds a hint of moisture, a subtle reminder of the sea's proximity. As I close my eyes, a wave of emotion swells within me, the joy of memories clashing with the pang of loss.

"Well, here we are," I announce to the empty house, my voice wavering. "Just me and-"

A disdainful meow interrupts my melodramatic moment. I turn to see Aristotle, or Ari as George called him, perched regally on the back of George's favourite armchair. His piercing green eyes seem to stare directly into my soul, judging every life decision I've ever made.

"Good to see you too," I say, reaching out to pet him. Ari responds by haughtily turning his head, tail flicking in clear disapproval. "Still the life of the party, huh?"

With his sleek grey tabby fur, Ari sits with an air of authority that reminds me irresistibly of George. I can't help but smile as I say to him, "You know, Ari, if reincarnation is real, I'm pretty sure you're my grandfather, returned to keep a watchful eye on me."

The cat fixes me with a look that seems to say, "And you've given me plenty to watch."

"Oh, come on," I protest, laughing despite myself. I'm not that disastrous, am I?" Ari simply blinks slowly, a master of nonverbal judgment.

I sigh and sit down beside him, reaching out again in hopes of a truce. Ari deigns to allow a brief scratch behind his ears this time before sauntering off with feline dignity.

"Guess that's progress," I murmur, watching him disappear into the next room.

The front door swings open with a bang. "Eleni!" rings out a voice I'd know anywhere.

Suddenly, I'm enveloped in a whirlwind of floral perfume and wild curls. Callie, my childhood best friend, has me in a bear hug so tight I struggle to find air.

"Cal—can't...breathe..." I manage to gasp out.

"I missed you so much! It's only been three weeks, but what was that last visit? You were here less than a day, then zoomed back to London like you were escaping a horde of zombies!" she exclaims, releasing me just enough to let me catch my breath.

"It wasn't exactly my choice," I reply, rubbing my ribs where she squeezed. "Dad made us leave. He's pretty good at pulling a disappearing act."

"So, you're here to stay this time? Taking over the business, diving into the glamorous life of wrestling goats, and oh—reminding my stubborn brother about his priorities?" Callie says with a twinkle in her eye, referring to Andreas, who, it dawns on me, is now technically my business partner.

A laugh escapes me, tinged with a hint of nervousness. "Partners with Andreas, huh? I always miss the practical details in my grand plans."

Callie nods, her curls bouncing. "Yeah, big time partners. Welcome to the real world, where it's not just about picturesque sunsets and old family stories."

The reality hits me like a cold splash of water. "I... I'm just here for three weeks initially," I start, trying to organize my thoughts. "I need to sort through George's belongings, handle some legal stuff, and just...say goodbye to him properly. As for the estate, I'm going to take some time to think it over and weigh my options."

Callie gives me a stern look, her eyes narrowing slightly in mock severity. "Look at Eleni Katsaros, all reserved and British now!" she exclaims, her voice lilting into an exaggerated imitation of my own. "'I will weigh my options, Callie,'" she mimics, a playful smirk dancing on her lips before giving me a soft, understanding smile. "We'll figure it out, Eleni. And hey, getting to boss Andreas around might not be so bad, right?" She nudges me playfully, lightening the mood.

"Right," I laugh, the weight of my decisions lingering, but eased by the familiar comfort of my friend's presence.

"How's Andreas these days? It's been ages since I last saw him," I ask, attempting to sound nonchalant, though my voice betrays a hint of eagerness.

Callie shrugs, a wry smile flickering. "He's hanging in there. One day he seems fine; the next, he's showing up on our doorstep at 2 AM, too drunk to make it back to his place. But you'll see for yourself soon enough."

Callie's eyes twinkle with mischief as she changes the subject. "Oh, by the way, my mom practically filled your fridge to the brim. She's convinced you'd starve without her intervention."

I laugh, picturing Maria's well-meaning invasion of my kitchen. "That sounds just like her. I bet I won't need to shop for food for a month!"

"Try two!" Callie grins. "She's packed your fridge so full, I think she's planning to feed the village if there's ever a siege. Mom's practically a one-woman emergency service."

She hops up, already backing towards the door. "Anyway, I've got to dash. There are about a hundred things I need to sort out before dinner—you know, ensuring the village doesn't fall apart without my supervision. We'll have heaps of time to chat later. Love you, Leni-bean!" She wraps me in another tight hug, then whirls out of the door with the same whirlwind energy she entered.

Callie has been my best friend since our childhood summers in Seranos, continuing even as life took us on different paths during university. Our friendship endured through monthly marathon calls, covering every small and significant detail of our lives. I was her right hand at her wedding to Nikos, and I even managed to prevent her from bolting at the last minute—a favour Nikos hasn't forgotten. Callie, the granddaughter of Stavros—who started the olive business with my grandfather—grew up more like my sister than just a summer friend.

Callie's beauty is the kind that doesn't conform to the usual standards pushed by social media. It's unique and natural, marked by her always sun-kissed skin sprinkled with freckles and her deep, warm brown eyes that are quick to express joy or empathy. Her chestnut hair flows in lively waves, and she carries an energetic, engaging aura. Her presence is a force, magnetic and genuine, drawing all eyes to her the moment she steps into a room. With Callie's laughter still echoing in the house, I turn to face the clutter and chaos of cleaning, thinking, "From emotional baggage to dusty shelves, it's time for some heavy lifting."

***

"Well, Ari, I suppose we should make this place habitable again," I mutter, grabbing a broom from the corner. L lounging on the windowsill, Ari gives me a look that clearly says, "You're on your own."

"Oh, come on," I groan, sweeping vigorously. "You could at least pretend to help," as Ari yawns dramatically.

As I clean, I take in the familiar details of George's—now my—house. The air smells of sea salt, old books, and a hint of lavender from the sachets my grandmother used to make. The walls are adorned with faded family photos and colourful abstract paintings my grandmother created. With its sun-faded rugs and mismatched cushions, the living room still houses the hefty wooden bookcase brimming with dusty novels and encyclopaedias.

George's old armchair commands the corner, flanked by a small table cluttered with his reading glasses and an open crossword puzzle.

The kitchen smells faintly of rosemary and garlic, remnants of countless family meals. I wipe down the aged oak countertops and open windows to let the breeze dispel the mustiness. A row of spice jars on the window sill, their labels faded, line up like sentinels.

The bed is unmade in the bedroom, the linens tangled—a silent testament to its sudden abandonment. I straighten the sheets and pause at the dresser, touching the delicate lace doilies my grandmother so loved. The closet door creaks as I open it, revealing rows of old coats and a jumble of shoes.

I tackle the study, where George spent countless hours. The desk is a scatter of papers, pens, and an ashtray brimming with pipe tobacco. Bookshelves line the walls, filled with well-thumbed volumes on philosophy and history, the titles gold-leafed and grand. As I dust, I imagine my grandfather here, lost in thought, a silent conversation between him and his books.

Lastly, my bedroom, a nostalgic capsule of my childhood summers, remains almost untouched. Sea shells and starfish hang whimsically from the ceiling, swaying gently with each breeze that slips through the open window. The bed, a cosy enclave, is draped with a mosquito net delicately embroidered with mermaids by my grandmother—a testament to the countless stories she spun beneath its gauzy folds. The soft, sandy tones of the walls, adorned with faded photographs of seaside escapades, evoke the tranquillity of the beach just a short walk away. As I clean, I'm not just tidying up but reconnecting with the family legacy housed within these walls.

"You know, Ari," I say, pausing to wipe sweat from my brow, "back in London, roommates help with the cleaning. But clearly, you're exempt from such mundane tasks, aren't you?" Ari blinks slowly, his gaze oozing disdain, clearly affirming, "Of course, I am."

After slogging through an hour of dusting and sorting, I push open the door to the terrace for a well-deserved break. I step out onto the terrace, and my breath catches. The view never fails to stun me—the endless blue of the Aegean stretching to the horizon, dotted with small islands in the distance. The terrace itself is lined with potted geraniums; their bright red blossoms vibrant against the sun-bleached white walls of the house. A few wicker chairs and a table sit neatly arranged, offering a perfect spot to soak in the scenery. Though weathered by the salty air, the railing still stands strong, enclosing this small outdoor retreat.

"Ah, look who's sailed back to us," Yiannis calls out, his voice raspy like the pull of the tide, his white beard unkempt as the sea foam.

I turn to see him, propped against his usual spot by the railing.

"Yiannis!" I greet, grinning back. "Scaring away the fish with your tales, are you?" He gives a hearty laugh, his eyes squinting with mirth.

"Me and the fish have a deal—they listen to my stories, I let a few go. Seems fairer than what those city nets offer. Are you back then to take over George's inheritance?"

"Guess I can't argue with that logic," I chuckle, leaning on the cool stone of my balcony. "I came for just three weeks to deal with everything personally."

"Just three weeks…" he says, smiling. "Out here, time might as well stand still," Yiannis retorts, gesturing

expansively. "You city folks rush too much. The olive trees, the sea—they don't hurry for anyone."
"Is that your subtle way of advising patience?" I ask, amused by his roundabout wisdom.
"Patience, persistence," he corrects with a knowing look, "like the sea against the cliffs. Keeps pushing, never asking if it should.
Laughing, I nod. "I've missed your sea-worn wisdom, Yiannis."
"And I've missed giving it," he says, his voice softening. "Now, go catch your sunset. The sunset won't wait, and it's got its own stories to tell—if you're still keen to listen."
After our brief encounter, I lean against the railing, smiling to myself. Yiannis hasn't changed a bit—still part philosopher, part sea-worn fisherman, with that knowing twinkle in his eye. He's always been a fixture of my summers here, his presence as constant as the tides. His life by the sea has shaped him into something like a living legend around Seranos, his stories woven into the fabric of the village. Even his appearance speaks of a life intimately connected with the Aegean: the sun-etched lines on his face, the sea salt in his beard, the relaxed strength in his shoulders accustomed to years of casting nets and pulling in vigorous catches. He represents a piece of Seranos that feels both timeless and deeply comforting. As I watch him shuffle back into his house, I think it's reassuring to know that some things, like Yiannis's steady presence, don't change, no matter how long you've been away.
I settle into the old wicker chair on the terrace, completely worn out after another couple of hours cleaning and sorting. The day's work has taken its toll, leaving me looking as weary as I feel. My clothes are wrinkled and dusty from cleaning, and my hair, which I'd

hastily pulled back, has escaped into a mess around my face. I pour myself a generous glass of wine, hoping it will help ease the fatigue. As I take my first sip, I let the calm of the early evening soothe me, enjoying the peace of the familiar surroundings and the gentle breeze. The sun is beginning its descent, painting the sky in a riot of colours.

Each sunset here feels like a personal performance that never fails to captivate. I can't help but smile, remembering the game George and I used to play, debating whether tonight's display would lean more toward the fiery oranges or the serene purples. "What's your bet, Grandpa?" I murmur with a chuckle, toasting the empty chair next to me. "Oranges or purples tonight?"

***

As I lift my glass for a sip, a sudden movement at the water's edge draws my attention. I nearly choke on my wine as a figure rises from the sea—holy, dripping Poseidon! Under the blaze of the setting sun, he strides from the sea, a harpoon slung over his shoulder and fish swinging from his belt like trophies. Well, isn't Seranos full of surprises?

"Okay, either I've drunk myself into a mythological fantasy," I whisper to no one in particular, "or the village just rolled out its latest tourist attraction." He looks like the sea itself sculpted him—waves and salt crafting every muscle with care, like a tribute to the old gods.

As he gets closer, the details become clearer—the chiselled jaw, the careless toss of wet hair, and that smirk. Oh, that smirk! "Seranos, since when did you start casting gods in your sunset shows?" I murmur, fanning myself with one hand while gripping the wine glass like a lifeline with the other.

Despite the fatigue pulling at my limbs, a jolt of adrenaline—or is it amusement?—courses through me. Is this a hallucination? If so, bravo, brain, bravo! Maybe it's the wine talking or the lack of sleep, but as he approaches, I can't help but think, "Should I pinch myself or just keep ogling?"

My pulse quickens as the figure from the sea starts heading towards my house. I jump up, a reflex to try and tame my windswept hair and straighten my wrinkled clothes. "Come on, Eleni, make this work," I plead with my tangled hair. But it's a lost cause. I look like I've been through a wind tunnel, different from the image I'd hoped to project.

A wave of recognition washes over me as he nears, squinting in the dimming light. Oh no. No, no, no. It can't be. But it is.

Andreas Papadopoulos. The almighty Andreas. My childhood crush and the unwitting star of my most cringe-worthy moments.

Memories come flooding back, particularly a mortifying one: me, ten years old, trying to show off my diving skills to impress him. The dive ended not with applause, but with a spectacular belly flop, a missing swimsuit top, and years of teasing.

"Get it together," I whisper fiercely, hoping my cheeks aren't as red as they feel. "You're an adult now. You can handle seeing Andreas without making a complete fool of yourself."

Yet, as Andreas closes the distance, his familiar smile in view, doubt creeps in. My hands are clammy, my heart's racing, and I have a sneaking suspicion I'm about to prove myself very, very wrong.

I can't help but chuckle, remembering the ridiculous lengths I went to as a child to win Andreas's heart. At nine years old, convinced of our star-crossed fate, I had crafted what I thought was an unbreakable contract—a 'marriage certificate' plastered with rainbow hearts and clumsy cursive.

"Oh, Eleni," I whisper to myself, shaking my head at the memory, "you were quite the determined romantic, weren't you?"

I had solemnly handed the certificate to Maria, Andreas's mother, demanding with the utmost seriousness, "Please make sure he signs this." Maria had stifled her laughter, patting my head with gentle amusement.

That "certificate" became a running joke in both our families. Every time I visited, Maria would ask with a wink, "So, Eleni, shall we plan the wedding now?" while Andreas, ever the big brother figure, would call me 'little Leni' and ruffle my hair.

As Andreas approaches, with a smile on his face and the sunset lighting up his features, my heart skips a beat—out of nostalgia more than anything.

"Well, well," he says with a grin, "if it isn't my little Leni, all grown up."

I mentally wince at the nickname but manage a smile. "Andreas," I reply, my voice steadier than I feel, "you emerging from the sea with a harpoon kind of makes the Poseidon comparison hard to avoid."

He laughs, the sound warm and familiar. "You haven't lost your touch with words, I see. Still the spirited Leni." He then shifts to a more serious tone. "We're expecting you at dinner. Mama's almost ready."

"Dinner?" I respond, slightly thrown off.

"Yes, you, me, Callie, Nikos — it's all arranged. Just waiting on these fresh catches," he nods towards the fish strung along his belt. "Better hurry, or you'll never hear the end of it."

His casual mention of the plans reminds me of the lighter, carefree days of our past, but I can't help noticing the slight fatigue in his eyes—a hint that life hasn't been all smooth sailing for him.

"Alright," I reply, striving to keep the mood light. "I wouldn't dare upset Maria. I'll try to make myself look presentable." A part of me worries about the changes I see in him. What stories lay behind his tired eyes? And why, despite the years and distance, does my heart still flutter at his familiar, affectionate call of 'Leni'?"

As Andreas starts to walk away, I suddenly remember my finicky feline guest. "Wait, Andreas!" I call out, perhaps a bit too eagerly. "What does Ari eat? He won't touch anything I've tried."

Andreas pauses and turns back with a hint of a smile. "Aristotle? Only the freshest catch will satisfy his royal palate."

"Of course," I sigh, rolling my eyes at the cat's gourmet tastes.

My brain, still reeling from the earlier spectacle of Andreas emerging from the sea, impulsively drives me to ask, "Could I snag one of your fish for him?"

Cringing at my awkward phrasing, I mentally kick myself. Smooth, Eleni. Real smooth.

Andreas laughs, his mood lightening. He unhooks a small fish from his belt and tosses it to me. I catch it deftly, and can't help but joke, "Going full hunter-gatherer, are we?"

He grins and shakes his head, then continues on his way.

Watching him leave, I'm struck by the changes in him. It's been seven years since our paths last crossed—he was a newlywed then, bright-eyed and optimistic. Now, there's a heaviness to his stride, a subtle shadow beneath the surface. Once the playful teen, his features have settled into the rugged lines of manhood, his hair now flecked with silver—a stark contrast to the vibrant youth who once dominated my teenage dreams.

Callie told me about his difficult divorce during one of our phone calls. His ex-wife, a wealthy Athenian who used to have a lavish lifestyle, never truly adapted to our quieter village life, leading to a split marked by bitter disagreements over lifestyle and values.

As I stand there, holding a raw fish and watching Andreas disappear around a corner, I can't help but feel a mix of emotions. Nostalgia for the carefree boy I once knew, curiosity about the man he's become, and an unexpected flutter in my chest that I thought I'd long outgrown.

I stroll back into the kitchen, my thoughts still buzzing with images of Andreas. Ari perches on the countertop, eyeing the fish in my hand with the focus of a world-class marksman.

"Here you go, Ari boy," I say, placing the fish on a small plate. Ari dives in without hesitation, and I can't help but chuckle. "At least one of us knows what we want."

Leaning against the counter, I tousle my already unruly hair. "So, Ari, should I try to dazzle him or just stick with the hot mess theme?"

Ari pauses his feast to shoot me a look that could only be described as 'judgy.'

"You're probably right," I concede with a nod. "The dishevelled look is quite the statement. Very avant-garde."

Eyeing my ensemble—Grandma's old slippers and an oversized t-shirt—I ponder aloud, "But perhaps I should aim for something a bit less 'rolled out of a laundry basket' and more 'effortlessly chic' for tonight?"

Ari, clearly disinterested in my wardrobe woes, resumes his dinner.

"Oh, come on," I plead, "work with me here. You're supposed to be my fashion guru. What would you wear if you were trying to impress a fish-god?"

Ari pauses, a bit of fish dangling comically from his mouth, and our eyes meet. I burst into laughter.
" Of course, you're right. When in Seranos, accessorize with seafood. It's definitely the way to go."

Ties that Bind

With the image of Andreas emerging from the sea still in my mind, I step out into the soft golden light of evening, the warm air brushing against my skin as a familiar welcome. The village hums with life around me; children's laughter bursts from a nearby alley, and the clatter of dinner settings echoes from open windows, layered with the occasional ripple of laughter. The sun dips lower, casting a rosy glow on the whitewashed walls, transforming the village into a canvas of pink and gold—a stark contrast to the often-dreary backdrop of my London flat.
As I turn the corner onto Maria's street, the rich fragrance of jasmine from her garden weaves through the air, blending seamlessly with the smells of dinner preparations. A knot of longing and nerves tightens in my chest—it feels like returning home, but home isn't without its pressures.
I pause at her gate, smoothing my hair and drawing a deep, steadying breath. I step into Maria's courtyard, and it's like entering a secret garden oasis. Terracotta pots overflow with vibrant geraniums and fragrant basil while fairy lights twinkle lazily overhead. The centrepiece is a massive old olive tree, its gnarled trunk a testament to years of family gatherings beneath its sheltering branches.
The dinner table nestles under the protective boughs of the olive tree, beautifully set with gleaming dishes and flickering candles, echoing the countless family meals of my childhood here. Memories flood back of evenings spent under these very leaves, where Callie and I would eventually doze off, lulled to sleep by the blend of adult laughter and the rhythmic clinks of ouzo glasses.

"Eleni, my daughter!" Maria's rich and warm voice cuts through my reverie as she approaches with open arms. "Come, come! You're just in time!"

I'm enveloped in a hug that smells of home, and for a moment, I'm that little girl again, seeking comfort in Maria's embrace after scraping my knee.

"Maria," I manage, my voice thick with emotion as I pull back, the edges of my vision tinged with tears. "Everything looks just beautiful."

She looks at me, her hands—still strong despite the years—cradling my face. "And so do you, my child. Now, sit down! The table's laden with all your favourites."

Laughing, I glance over the spread—an array of traditional Greek dishes that tug at both my heartstrings and my hunger. "Are you planning to feed an army, or just me?"

"Pah!" She dismisses with a hearty wave of her hand. "You've gotten too thin. London doesn't feed you like we do here. But don't worry, we'll fatten you up soon enough. And you're so pale! Make sure you get some sun and soak up your vitamin D."

As we walk to the table, the rich flavours of dolmades, spanakopita, and grilled fish weave a tapestry of aromas that evoke vivid memories. I pick up a slice of freshly baked bread, its warm, yeasty scent enveloping me.

"You know," I begin, my voice thick with nostalgia, "Grandpa and I used to come here after a long day in the farm, and Maria, you'd always have a special treat waiting for us. He'd wink at me and say, 'Maria makes the best lemon cake in all of Greece, just for us.'"

Maria's eyes soften, a mist of memories and affection lighting them up. "George always had a soft spot for you," she says, her voice tinged with nostalgia. "He'd be so proud to see you back, taking over the grove."

I nod, my eyes tearing up, a mix of nerves and resolve building within me. "I hope so. I just... I hope I won't disappoint him, you know?"

A deep, familiar voice breaks through the gathering emotions as I grapple with my doubts. "If you're half as stubborn as your grandfather, the grove is in good hands."

I then notice Nikos weaving his way through the crowd toward me, his smile as wide and genuine as ever. Before I can even say hello, he greets me with a joke.

"Eleni! Without you, that wedding might have just been me, a priest, and an empty aisle," he says, his voice warm and teasing. I laugh, shaking my head at his dramatic flair, but there's no mistaking the gratitude in his tone. It's not every day you get credited with saving a wedding, but apparently, my little chat with Callie had worked wonders.

Nikos looks effortlessly sharp, as always—casual, but with that unique mix of rural charm and intellectual sharpness that seems to define him. We fall into conversation, and it doesn't take long before he steers it toward his work.

"We're trying some new techniques on the farms in the region," he explains, his enthusiasm lighting up his face. "Integrating more sustainable practices. It's about finding that sweet spot where tradition meets a bit of modern science."

I nod along, genuinely interested. There's something infectious about how Nikos talks about farming—not as a chore, but as something worth preserving and perfecting. Andreas joins us before I can ask more, and that familiar playful smirk is already in place.

"He's trying to make a tech enthusiast out of me," Andreas says, clapping Nikos on the back. "Imagine that—computers monitoring olive groves."

Nikos laughs, his tone light but persuasive. "It's not just computers, Andreas. It's about preserving what we have for future generations, making sure we're not just surviving but thriving."

I listen, intrigued by Nikos's ability to navigate their differing views. His words are gentle but firm, and I can tell he's trying to nudge Andreas toward seeing the bigger picture. Watching the two of them, their camaraderie evident despite their different approaches, I can't help but admire Nikos's ability to balance progress with preservation. He makes it all sound so vital, so possible.

Just then, Callie emerges from the kitchen. "Alright, enough shop talk, you three. Dinner's ready, and if I know my mother, no one's leaving this table hungry or without a lecture on eating more vegetables," she declares with a laugh, ushering everyone towards the dining table.

The dinner table is a vibrant display of Maria's culinary prowess, with every dish more inviting than the last. I find myself seated between Callie and Andreas, the familiar clatter and chatter of a Greek family meal enveloping us.

" Remember when Callie and Eleni decided to 'help' with the harvest? Oh, the trouble you two caused! " Maria asks, her eyes twinkling.

"Oh God," I groan, covering my face. "We knocked over an entire crate of olives trying to carry it ourselves."

"And then tried to hide the evidence by stuffing as many as possible into your pockets! Your jackets were sagging down to your knees by the time you were done." Andreas adds with a smile.

Callie nudges me, her eyes shining with the joy of the shared memory. "Yeah, and remember how we tried to walk normally past Maria, pretending nothing happened, olives dropping out with every step?"

As the stories flow, I can't help but notice Andreas. While everyone else is animated, his smile fades slightly. His attention drifts back to his own thoughts, and a hint of distance creeps back into his gaze.

I lean closer, dropping my voice to a soft murmur. "You seem a bit out of it tonight. Is everything okay?"

Andreas jolts, seemingly yanked from a distant train of thought. He offers a quick, somewhat strained smile. "Yeah, I'm fine," he replies. "Just got a lot on my mind about work."

I nod, observing him more closely. An unmistakable tension marks his features and a certain weariness shadows his eyes—signs of stress that seem to go beyond the day-to-day worries of work. As laughter and chatter fill the background, I notice that the youthful, carefree Andreas I used to know now seems overshadowed by layers of responsibilities and a more profound, more personal burden that remains unspoken.

Just then, Callie's exuberant voice cuts through my contemplation. "Eleni, earth to Eleni!" she calls out, her tone playful yet insistent. "We need your expert opinion here— We're debating the best flavour of Maria's homemade ice cream, and we need your tiebreaker!"

Caught off guard, I chuckle, momentarily setting aside my concerns. "Oh, apologies, I drifted off there. But honestly, how can anyone surpass Maria's cherry? It's like she managed to bottle up the essence of summer into every scoop."

Laughter ripples around the table, drawing me back into the circle of warmth and shared memories.

***

As I stroll back from Maria's, the warm night air caresses my skin, carrying the lingering scent of dinner and laughter. I'm reflecting on the joyful chaos of the dinner when a gentle giant ambles up to me.

"Well, hello there," I whisper, my pace slowing as a large, golden-haired dog with floppy ears approaches. His soulful eyes meet mine, his tail wagging energetically.

"You look like a giant, lovable mess," I laugh softly as he tilts his head, listening attentively before issuing a gentle "boof."

"Very intimidating," I jest, grinning at the harmless giant before me. His response is to roll over, inviting a belly rub, which I happily provide.

"You're just a big softie, aren't you?" I coo, scratching his belly. His joyful demeanour makes me smile even wider. I rise and resume my walk, the dog trotting alongside me like an old friend. "Looks like you've chosen to tag along," I comment with a smile.

As we wander through Seranos' tranquil streets, the dog's quiet companionship enhances the sense of returning home.

As I approach my house, the evening still clinging to the last bits of light, I notice Yiannis lounging on his terrace. A mischievous grin spreads across his face as he notices my new, shaggy companion trotting at my side.

"Well, well, if it isn't Zeus, the gentle giant," Yiannis calls out, his voice rich with amusement. "Seems like you've made a new friend."

Chuckling, I pat Zeus gently. "Is that his name? Despite the slobbery kisses, he's certainly majestic in his own way."

"Indeed," Yiannis laughs. "We villagers named him Zeus more for his thunderous bark than his divine demeanour. He's quite the beloved figure around here."

"Seems like he's charmed everyone already," I reply, scratching Zeus behind the ears.

Yiannis nods, shifting comfortably in his chair. "And speaking of charm, how are you feeling?"

I sigh, a mixture of emotions swirling inside. "Honestly, I feel tired, confused and emotional. Too much for one day…"

"Ah," Yiannis says, his tone turning reflective. "Zeus here might have some lessons for you then."

Curious, I ask, "Oh? Like what?"

"Zeus doesn't overcomplicate life," Yiannis explains with a smile. "He lives in the moment, responds to kindness, and doesn't dwell on the past. Maybe that's something you need too. Look after your surroundings, be present, and they'll support you back. And this big fellow," he gestures towards Zeus, "will teach you about finding joy in the simple things."

"I suppose there's wisdom in that," I concede, feeling a bit of tension ease.

Yiannis chuckles. "Don't be fooled by my casual philosophizing—I'm just an old man who enjoys a good sunset. But remember, Eleni, taking care of what's around you, whether it's a stray dog or your own well-being, starts with nurturing yourself."

His words resonate with me, their simplicity touching a chord. "I'll remember that, Yiannis. And perhaps Zeus can help keep me grounded."

"He'll stick by you, no doubt," Yiannis assures me. "And he might just show you that life doesn't always have to be a series of tasks to manage, but moments to be enjoyed."

Smiling, I look down at Zeus, who seems perfectly content with our companionship. "Thanks, Yiannis. Here's to taking things one step at a time."

"Exactly," Yiannis replies, raising his glass in a toast. "To new friendships and fresh starts."

"To new chapters," I echo, feeling lighter as Zeus and I head inside, prepared to face whatever lies ahead, together.

***

As the morning light peeks through the small window of the old storage shed, I wrestle with the rusty latch, my makeshift sidekick Zeus eagerly wagging his tail beside me. "Sorry, pal, this fishing expedition isn't for you," I chuckle, glancing at his expectant eyes. "We're on a quest for the resident tyrant cat." Ari was already there the moment I woke up, staring me down with a look that clearly demanded, "Where's my fish?". I sighed, getting out of bed to tackle the unlikely task of fishing to please a particularly finicky cat. Now, here I was in the old storage shed, rummaging through dusty shelves for whatever fishing gear I could find to fulfil my morning's unexpected adventure.

The air inside the shed is thick with the scent of old wood and lingering memories. As I step further in, a shaft of sunlight illuminates the corner where George's fishing gear has been gathering dust. The sight of the neatly arranged rods, each handle polished smooth from years of use, brings an unexpected lump to my throat, memories flooding back.

"Come on, Eleni" Grandpa's voice echoes in my mind. "You can't catch fish by willing them onto the hook."

I'm suddenly twelve again, gangly and impatient, huffing dramatically as my line remains stubbornly fish-free.

"Patience, little one," he chuckles, his weathered hands steadying mine on the rod. "The sea gives her treasures to those who respect her rhythms."

"But Grandpa," I whine, "what if the fish are on strike? Maybe they formed a union!"

His belly laugh rumbles through me. "Ah, there's that imagination of yours. Tell you what, let's make a game of it. For every minute you wait quietly, I'll tell you a story about the stars."

And just like that, my restlessness melts away, replaced by eager anticipation of his tales.

Blinking back to the present, I swipe at my eyes. "Right," I mutter to Zeus, who's peering up at me with concern. "No rods for me. I'm sticking to the basics."

I emerge from the shack clutching a simple line and hook, feeling both ridiculous and determined. Zeus dashes ahead, leading the way to the rocky outcrop where I plan to try my luck at fishing. He flops down beside me with the thud of a dropped sack, looking back with a wagging tail. I'm still in my oversized nightgown, the giant yellow smiley face on it seeming overly optimistic for the task at hand.

"Okay, Zeus," I mutter, threading a bit of bread onto the hook. "Let's see if I can channel some of that Grandpa magic"

After some failed attempts and considering to give up, I see Andreas approaching, his presence as familiar as the sea itself. He's always been an early riser, choosing to swim in the calm morning waters off the rocks in front of George's house, where the depth allows for easy diving.

He pauses, a hint of surprise on his face as he takes in my makeshift fishing setup—me in my nightgown, Zeus wagging his tail wildly, and my amateurish fishing attempt. "Morning, fish whisperer," he teases, his eyes glinting with amusement. "Trying to feed the village with your new friend?"

I roll my eyes, feeling my cheeks warm under his gaze. I yank at my fishing line, only to find the bread bait has dissolved. "And how do you propose to catch anything without bait?" he asks, clearly enjoying the moment too much. "Just curious."

I glance at my empty hook and reply jokingly, "I thought I'd try manifesting them into existence." His deep and infectious laughter fills the air.

I shoot him a playful glare. "Andreas, much as I enjoy your company, I've got a high-maintenance cat who expects a fresh catch," I say, trying to keep the mood light despite my failing fishing attempt.

He chuckles heartily, the sound echoing off the rocks, and then joins me, stretching out leisurely next to me. "No need for early morning fishing, Eleni. Ari has his daily routine down," he informs me, still amused. "He's at the pier for breakfast with the returning boats, and at Theo's by dinner. Your feline overlord is well taken care of."

"Of course he is," I sigh, half in jest. "Living the high life better than most of us ever will." We fall into a comfortable silence, the only sound the gentle lapping of waves against the rocks. Andreas leans back, eyes closed, soaking in the sun's warmth. For a brief moment, his features relax, the worry lines smoothing out, and he looks content, unburdened.

It's a stark contrast to the reserved, almost sombre man at dinner last night. Watching him, I'm struck by the fleeting peace in his expression. But the quiet moment is short-lived. As he shifts to stand, his arm brushes against mine. The brief contact sends a tingling warmth through me, more startling than the cool morning air. It's an innocent touch but sparks a flurry of sensations I hadn't anticipated, stirring a mix of familiarity and new, electric awareness that pulses quietly beneath my skin.

Still reeling from the brief brush of his arm against mine, I watched as Andreas began to pull off his shirt, clearly preparing to dive into the sea. Before I could stop myself, the words tumbled out: "Andreas Papadopoulos, don't you dare take that shirt off and dive into the sea in front of me!". The moment the sentence escaped my lips, a wave of mortification crashed over me. Heat rushed to my cheeks as I froze, my brain frantically replaying the scene. *Oh no. I did not just say that out loud. Did I?*

He paused mid-motion, shirt half-off, looking genuinely baffled. "And why would that be?" he asked, a smirk beginning to form as he caught the flush creeping up my cheeks.

"Because, it's... it's," I stammered, desperately grasping for any remotely sensible excuse. He raised an eyebrow, clearly waiting for a logical explanation. "Because it's very inappropriate!" I blurted out, instantly cringing at my own words. Great, Eleni, since when did you appoint yourself the modesty police?

His rich and unabashed laughter filled the air. "Okay, then I'll wait until you're inside. Would that be appropriate enough for you?"

Mortified, I stood up and hurried towards the house, calling over my shoulder, "Yes, you do that!" His amusement was evident, and just before I escaped completely, he added, "Oh, and don't forget, Monday morning, you first go to the solicitors, and then we meet at the facility. Don't be late, Leni!"

Great job, Eleni, you've just set a world record for embarrassment. I chastised myself all the way back to the terrace, my face burning. This was all Ari's doing, somehow. That cat had manipulated me into this ludicrous situation with his imperious demands for fish before I'd even had my coffee.

Reaching the terrace, I spotted Ari luxuriating in a patch of sunlight, thoroughly cleaning himself. "You little tyrant, you're grounded for a week!" I announced.

He didn't so much as glance my way, completely unperturbed by my threats. His indifference only added to my frustration, but as I watched him bask in the warm glow of the morning, I couldn't help but laugh at myself. Eleni, you've really outdone yourself this time.

***

The rest of the day unfolded serenely. I enjoyed breakfast on the terrace, soaked up the familiar embrace of the sea during a long swim, and continued tidying around the house. In the afternoon, I indulged in a nap on the living room sofa, lulled by the soft symphony of village life—the gentle murmur of waves, the distant chatter of neighbours, and the rhythmic chirping of crickets in the sun. A gentle breeze wafted through the open window, carrying the scents of my childhood. It had been years since I felt so relaxed.

Later in the afternoon, Callie's voice broke through my tranquillity with a phone call. She proposed a dinner at Theo's, suggesting it was the perfect chance for a proper catch-up. "A girls' night out with the faithful companion of ouzo," she said.

As the evening sun had painted the sky in strokes of pink and orange, I made my way to Theo's. Theo's fisherman's shack was a weathered wooden structure that seemed to have grown organically from the beach itself. Strings of fairy lights twinkled along the eaves, and mismatched tables and chairs spilled out onto the sand. The smell of grilled fish and lemon wafted, drawing me in.

I saw Callie sitting there, bathed in the golden light of the sunset. Her face lit up as I approached, and she sprang up to hug me.

"Eleni!" she said, embracing me tightly.

"I've missed you," I replied, returning her hug with equal fervour. We laughed as we sat down, and almost immediately, Theo appeared, placing a bottle of ouzo on our table with a knowing wink before heading back to the grill.

Settling in, Callie's expression turned tender. "So," she started, leaning forward, "how have you been coping, really? We haven't had the chance to really talk since George's passing."

I paused, taking a deep breath, feeling the weight of the question and the cool glass of ouzo beneath my fingertips. "It's been tough, Cal," I admitted, the words releasing some of the tension I'd been carrying. " Losing him... it's left a hole, not just in my life but in my heart."

Callie reached across the table, her hand covering mine, squeezing gently. "I can only imagine, Eleni. He was such a big part of this place, of all our lives. But seeing you here, taking steps to connect with everything he loved... it's what he would have wanted."

I nodded, the comfort of her understanding washing over me. "That's why I'm here, isn't it? To connect, to heal, to figure out my path forward."

The conversation flowed more easily after that, diving into memories of George, both bitter and sweet. Each recollection was a shared piece of our intertwined lives, bringing both laughter and tears. As we talked, the sun dipped lower, the sky deepening to a rich, velvety blue, and I felt a profound sense of connection—not just to Callie, but to George, to Seranos, and to the life I started to forget some time ago.

"So how is life in London?" Callie inquired, shifting the conversation.

I let out an exaggerated sigh. "Oh, the usual glamorous life," I said sarcastically. "If by glamorous you mean getting buried under endless spreadsheets and trying to meet family expectations."

Her laughter filled the air, easing the tension in my shoulders.

"But honestly," I continued as I filled our glasses with ouzo, "London was okay. It's busy, and often pretty lonely. I was just going through the motions, hoping it would eventually lead to something worthwhile. And somehow, those motions brought me back here, sharing ouzo with you by the sea. Not too shabby, right?"

Callie's face softened with empathy. "Yeah, we're all just trying"

I took a sip of ouzo, grimacing slightly at the sharp burn. "What about you? How's married life treating you?"

A fleeting shadow crossed Callie's face, almost too quick to catch. "It's good. Nikos is... well, he's Nikos, as always."

I raised an eyebrow. "You don't sound too sure about that."

Callie exhaled slowly, her fingers playing absently with her glass. "It's just... sometimes I think I might have settled down too soon. Don't get me wrong—I love Nikos, but there are moments when this village feels a bit too small."

"Oh, Cal," I said, reaching out to squeeze her hand. "Have you talked to Nikos about how you're feeling?"

She nodded. "Yeah, we've had a few talks. His work is really fulfilling for him; he's passionate about what he does. And me, somehow, I ended up as the village event planner—I can't even recall how that happened. I love this place, truly, and I can't imagine growing old anywhere else. But sometimes, I just wonder what else might be out there. Maybe we could just explore a bit, live somewhere else for a few years, and come back later. But Nikos, with all his enthusiasm for his work here, isn't too keen on the idea of 'exploring'."

I understood her dilemma all too well. "It's ironic, isn't it? I came back here to find myself, and you're thinking you should leave to do the same.". As we sat silently for a while, immersed in our thoughts, I decided it was time to shake off the heaviness. "So, Callie, what's the over-under on me tripping over something and face-planting in front of half the village? Place your bets."

Callie burst out laughing, her shoulders shaking. "Oh, I don't think you'll need to trip. You're already a hit. Eleni Katsaros is back, and everyone's thrilled."

I gave her a mock-serious look. "Thrilled as in 'it's nice to see her,' or thrilled as in 'let's see what chaos she stirs up next'?"

"Definitely the first one," Callie said, still grinning. "But, don't let me stop you from keeping things interesting."

I laughed, shaking my head. "Well, good to know I've got an audience. Maybe I should start practicing my bow for when I inevitably provide some unexpected entertainment."

Callie's expression grew more serious as the laughter died down and we savoured the last bites of our meal. She leaned in slightly, her voice lowering as if to share a confidential matter.

"Eleni, I need to talk to you about the business—and Andreas," she started, her gaze searching mine for understanding. "Things haven't been going well, and I'm really worried."

I set down my glass, my attention focused. "What's been happening?"

Callie sighed, fiddling with her napkin. "It's just... the business is struggling more than anyone wants to admit. The market's been tough, and some bad harvests have really set us back." She paused, her eyes filled with concern. "And Andreas, he's been taking it all on himself. After his divorce, it's like he lost his spark."

I nodded, recalling the distant look in Andreas's eyes earlier in the evening. "Has it been really bad?"

She leaned back, her eyes sad. "Yeah, and for Andreas, it was a blow to his pride too. He's been trying to hide it, but I can tell he's burned out. He keeps pushing himself, trying to keep everything afloat."

"And the pressure's just building," she continued. "He won't talk about it much; he just buries himself at work. I'm scared he might just walk away from it all one day."

Callie sighed deeply, her eyes reflecting a mix of concern and frustration. "That divorce took a lot out of Andreas too, more than any of us realized," she began, her voice tinged with a hint of anger. "It wasn't just the end of his marriage but the sense of failure that really shook him. From the start, it was clear that she wasn't cut out for life here. She never really left Athens behind, not mentally. They even got a place at Navagos marina, thinking it might bridge the gap between her world and his."

She shook her head, disdain flickering in her eyes. "Andreas was too optimistic, trying to please her, hoping it would work. But she had no concept of the struggles here, how hard he worked for every euro. She just kept spending, living like she was still under her rich father's wings. And the worst part? When they visited Seranos, she'd flood her social media with posts about how quaint and perfect everything was—'peace and harmony,' 'home sweet home.' It was all for show. The minute they arrived, she was counting down until they could leave. It was complete hypocrisy."

Leaning back, Callie's expression darkened. "He never talks about the details, but the divorce was messy. She drained him, not just financially but emotionally too. It's like she took parts of him we'll never get back."

I reached across the table, squeezing her hand. "Thanks for telling me, Cal. I had no idea it was this bad."

"Yeah," she breathed out, managing a weak smile. "Just thought you should know what you're walking into. I know you're dealing with a lot, coming back and all, but Andreas might need more help than he'll ever ask for."

***

I hustle to the village's small resident parking area Monday morning, navigating the quaint cobbled streets with cautious steps to avoid a clumsy stumble. Reaching the parking lot, I pause before George's old car, touching the faded blue paint. A wave of sentiment washes over me.
"Well, old girl," I whisper affectionately, "it's just you and me today."
The engine comes alive with a comforting rumble, echoing with memories of George teaching me to drive right here in this car. "Slow and steady, Eleni," he used to say. "The car responds to your energy. Be calm, and she'll be calm too."
Drawing in a deep breath, I embrace that tranquillity he always preached as I start the car and head out to Navagos—the bustling town that marks a sharp contrast to Seranos' tranquil pace. As the landscape shifts from sleepy village charm to the dynamic pulse of town life, I weave through a mix of traditional charm and modern hustle, the streets a lively maze of tourists and locals, shops, bars and restaurants. My nerves tighten as I approach the lawyer's office, the weight of the day settling firmly on my shoulders.
I reach the law office in a building where polished wood and sleek leather dominate the decor. The lawyers, representing both the company and George's private matters, convene in a conference room that epitomizes corporate austerity.
As they begin to outline the complexities of estate laws, clauses, and company liabilities, their words blend into a monotonous hum, and I struggle to maintain focus. My gaze drifts to the window, catching my own reflection.
"Ms. Katsaros?" The sharp tone of one lawyer snaps me back to reality. "Do you understand the terms as we've laid them out?"

I jerk slightly, blinking away my distraction. "Yes, of course," I reply, though my mind scrambles to piece together the details of the last ten minutes.

The lawyers resume, their dialogue a labyrinth of financial terms and legal stipulations. With each passing moment, I feel more and more constricted in this office. "If you could just sign here, Ms. Katsaros..." One of them slides a document toward me with a practiced smile. Exiting the building, the vibrant life of Navagos greets me with open arms. I inhale deeply, the salty air mingled with the distant cries of seagulls reorienting me. As I approach the Seros Olive Oil Manufacturing Facility, affectionately shortened to "the facility" within our family, the familiar contours of its structure awaken a swell of nostalgia. Nestled closer to Navagos, its strategic location optimizes our shipping and receiving operations, connecting the deep-rooted traditions of our groves with the pulse of modern infrastructure. The facility stands as a testament to efficiency clad in rustic charm, embodying the legacy of George and Stavros's vision.

Pausing at the entrance, I draw in a deep breath. The robust scent of freshly pressed olives envelops me, laced with the sharp tang of brine and the warm embrace of sun-heated stone—a fragrance steeped in memories of sun-drenched summers, darting through the groves with Callie, our laughter mingling with the cicadas' song. Inside, the facility buzzes with the rhythmic hum of advanced machinery, a stark contrast to the hand-operated presses of my childhood memories. Sleek stainless-steel tanks reflect the overhead lights, casting a modern glow on the walls that seem to whisper stories of past generations. Despite the upgrades, the place retains an inherent warmth, as if the very air pulses with the dedication of the Katsaros and Papadopoulos families who have tread these floors through the decades.

Making my way towards the office area, my hand brushes against the cool, rough texture of the stone walls. Each corridor is lined with expansive windows framing views of bustling roads leading to Navagos. As I step further into the heart of the facility, the familiar sense of purpose solidifies my resolve to bridge the old with the new, honouring my heritage while steering us towards a sustainable future.

As I reach the meeting room, I hesitate at the threshold, my heart skipping a beat at the sight of Andreas. He is deeply engrossed, bent over a sea of disarrayed papers, his expression etched with intense focus. I find myself captivated, noticing nuances of his presence I had previously missed.

Was his hair always touched by that rebellious curl at the nape? Observing how his strong hands navigate the documents—firm yet tender—sends an unanticipated thrill through me. Mesmerized, I watch him manipulate a small pebble, his thumb caressing its smooth surface in a thoughtful, rhythmic motion. This small act reveals his habit: Andreas often gathers stones outdoors, habitually smoothing them between his fingers as a way to centre his thoughts. It's a practice rooted in childhood, born from days spent collecting pebbles by the seaside, a personal ritual to steady his restless mind amidst turmoil.

"Are you going to just stand there all day, or are you going to help me sort out this mess?" Andreas's voice, laced with a playful undertone, jolts me from my trance.

My cheeks burn with embarrassment as I'm caught in my observation. "I was just... admiring the, uh, efficient use of space in here," I reply awkwardly, gesturing vaguely at the chaotic room.

Andreas quirks an eyebrow, the corners of his mouth twitching into a knowing smirk. "Right. Because nothing screams 'efficiency' like being buried under an avalanche of invoices," he teases.

***

Stepping into the room, I respond with a light chuckle, my attention immediately captured by Andreas. He exudes a quiet confidence, even surrounded by the disarray of papers covering the table. He stretches, easing the stiffness in his broad shoulders, and for a moment, I can see the traces of his former athletic life beneath his now slightly heavier frame. His shirt stretches a bit across his chest, hinting at the physical demands of his past.

As he refocuses on the paperwork, the intensity of his concentration is apparent. A slight crease forms between his brows, a small sign of his challenges. "Need a second pair of eyes?" I ask, stepping closer. Andreas looks up, his eyes, a striking grey or dark blue depending on the light, meet mine with an intensity that momentarily takes my breath away.

"Wouldn't say no to that," he responds, his lips curving into what almost resembles a smile. I pull up a chair next to him, and as our hands accidentally touch, a spark of warmth shoots through me. His presence is subtly magnetic, drawing me in more than I had anticipated.

"I was hoping you'd say that," I say quietly, focusing on the paperwork while still very much aware of him beside me. As we work together, his scent—a combination of the outdoors and something uniquely his own—surrounds me, both comforting and compelling.

Our collaboration is smooth, marked by small interactions—a touch, a glance—that weave an increasingly complex tapestry of connection. Each moment reveals more of Andreas: not just the stoic figure from my past, but a man of depth and subtle complexities, irresistibly real.

As we delve into the financial reports, a familiar face pops her head into the office. It's Areti, the facility's long-time receptionist, her warm brown eyes lighting up as she spots me.

"Eleni! Is that really you?" she exclaims, rushing over to envelop me in a tight hug. "Look how you've grown! You were just a little thing always trailing after your grandfather."

I can't help but laugh, feeling a rush of affection for this motherly figure from my childhood. "It's great to see you too, Areti. I hope I've improved my ability to stay out of trouble since then."

"Oh, I wouldn't count on it," Andreas mutters, but there's a hint of amusement in his voice that makes my heart skip a beat.

As word spreads of my arrival, more staff members drop by to welcome me. Each face brings a flood of memories—Nicholas from accounting, who always had a candy for me, and Katerina from quality control, who taught me how to taste olive oil properly. Their genuine warmth chips away at the anxiety I've been carrying since this morning.

"Alright, enough of the reunion," Andreas finally says, his tone gruff but not unkind. "We've got work to do."

As the others file out, I turn back to the spreadsheets before us. "So, walk me through our current financial situation," I say, determined to prove I'm here to contribute.

Andreas raises an eyebrow. "You sure you're ready for that? It's not exactly light reading."

I meet his gaze head-on. "Try me."

For the next few hours, we dive deep into the business's intricacies. Andreas explains each aspect with surprising patience, and I find myself hanging on his every word. The numbers tell a story of struggle but also resilience, and I'm struck by how much this place means to him.

"What if we try to restructure our distribution channels?" I suggest, pointing to a particular set of figures. "It looks like we're losing efficiency here."

Andreas leans in, his shoulder brushing mine as he studies the numbers. "Hm. That's... actually not a bad idea," he admits, a note of surprise in his voice. "We could potentially cut costs without sacrificing quality."

The small compliment sends a warm flush through me. "I may be new to olive oil, but I do know a thing or two about business," I say, trying to keep my voice steady despite the butterflies in my stomach.

As we continue working, I notice a shift in Andreas' demeanour. His initial scepticism gives way to genuine engagement, and he starts actively seeking my input on various issues. It's subtle, but I can feel the professional respect growing between us.

"You know," Andreas says during a brief coffee break, "I wasn't sure what to expect when you showed up. But you've got good instincts, Leni. Your grandfather would be proud."

The compliment, delivered in his matter-of-fact way, means more to me than I care to admit. "Thanks," I reply, hoping he can't see the blush creeping up my cheeks.

As the day wears on, I find myself increasingly drawn to Andreas. It's not just his rugged good looks (though those certainly don't hurt), but the passion and dedication he brings to his work. Every decision he makes is carefully considered, always with the groves' and people's best interests in mind.

The sun is setting by the time we wrap up, casting a warm glow through the office windows. I stretch, feeling both exhausted and exhilarated. "We make a pretty good team," I say, surprising myself with my boldness.

We start walking towards the parking lot, our footsteps echoing off the walls of the facility. The air is thick with the scent of the day's work.

"So, city girl," Andreas teases, breaking the comfortable silence. "Still think you can handle village life?"

I roll my eyes, fighting a grin. "Please. I was born for this. You're the one who looks like he needs a nap."

"A nap?" He clutches his chest in mock offense. "I'll have you know I could outwork you any day of the week."

"Is that a challenge, Papadopoulos?" I quirk an eyebrow, finding myself enjoying our playful exchange a little more than I should.

As we reach the car park, Andreas fumbles with his keys, which clatter to the ground. We both bend to retrieve them at the same time, our hands brushing briefly. A spark of electricity surges between us, and I hastily retract my hand, my pulse quickening. "Sorry," we both mutter simultaneously, and I notice a brief flash of something—maybe surprise, maybe attraction—in his eyes before he conceals it with his usual reserved expression.

I clear my throat, suddenly conscious of our proximity. "Well, um, see you tomorrow?" Andreas nods, his smile gentle and almost brotherly. "Take care until then, Katsaros."

Watching his car pull away, I'm left with a tingling sensation where our hands touched, and the slow realization that my feelings for Andreas might still be there, this time no longer a childhood admiration but are shaping into something far deeper and more complex. This realization leaves me both excited and apprehensive about what lies ahead.

Back home, I collapse into a chair on the terrace, Zeus plopping down beside me with a contented sigh. The sky has shifted into a tapestry of twinkling stars. "What am I doing, Zeus?" I muse aloud, scratching behind his ears. Zeus tilts his head, giving me a look that seems to say, "You're asking the wrong species, lady." I chuckle, shaking my head. "You're right. Maybe I should be pondering simpler mysteries, like 'who's a good boy?'" His tail thumps enthusiastically against the terrace tiles.

As I gaze out at the moonlit sea, I can't help but wonder if I've made the right choice. "Am I brave for taking this leap, or just spectacularly foolish?".

"What do you think, Zeus? Brave or bonkers?" He lets out a soft "woof" in response. "Both, huh?" I laugh, scratching under his chin. "Yeah, that sounds about right. Welcome to the Eleni's life choices extravaganza. Hope you brought popcorn."

As I head inside to eat something, I can't shake the feeling that I'm happy where I am right now despite the challenges ahead and the confusion swirling in my heart.

Olives, Ouzo, and Other Dangerous Temptations

"Okay, Eleni, deep breaths. It's just Andreas. The same guy who used to smash your sandcastles with a football. No big deal," I mutter to myself, pacing beside my car in the village square parking lot. The morning sun casts a gentle warmth on my skin as I fidget with the strap of my leather satchel, trying to steady my nerves.

The past week had been a whirlwind. I'd spent most of it at the facility, diving into the ins and outs of the business and getting to know the core team. Andreas was mainly at the grove, but we'd crossed paths enough for our connection to deepen in ways I hadn't quite expected—or fully processed.

And now here I was, waiting for him to pick me up for a tour of the grove, my stomach doing little flips like it was auditioning for a gymnastics team.

A rumble of an engine makes me whip around. Andreas' pickup rolls into view, kicking up dust. My heart does a little flip as he parks and hops out.

"Good God," I murmur, my eyes trailing over him. His dark, wavy hair is a tousled mess from the wind, and his faded t-shirt clings to broad shoulders with an effortless precision that borders on cruel. "Morning, Leni," he calls, striding over. "Ready for your grand tour?"

I plaster on a casual smile. "Sure thing, Farmer Andreas. Just try not to bore me to death with olive trivia, okay?" He chuckles, a rich sound that does funny things to my insides. "No promises. Hop in." I sneak glances at Andreas' strong profile as we drive towards the groves. His jaw is clenched slightly, and I notice him absently rubbing a small stone between his fingers.

"Everything okay?" I ask.

He startles slightly. "Yeah, fine. Just... thinking."

We lapse into silence as the familiar landscape rolls by. When the groves come into view, my breath catches. Row upon row of gnarled olive trees stretch towards the sea, their silvery leaves shimmering in the sunlight. Memories wash over me – picnics with Grandpa, chasing fireflies at dusk. "Oh," I breathe, tears pricking my eyes.

Andreas glances at me, his expression softening. "Welcome home, Leni."

As we step out of the truck, the briny sea air mingles with the herbal scent of sun-warmed leaves. I close my eyes, overwhelmed. "You okay?" Andreas asks quietly. I nod, not trusting my voice. After a moment, I manage a wobbly smile. "Just... a lot of memories, you know?". He nods, looking out over the groves. "Yeah, I know."

I take a deep breath, squaring my shoulders. "Alright, Papadopoulos, show me what you've got. And if you start waxing poetic about soil pH levels, I reserve the right to stuff olives in my ears."

Andreas laughs, the sound echoing across the peaceful groves. He gestures for me to follow, his feet crunching on the ground as we weave through the rows of trees. The sun filters through the silvery leaves, dappling the ground with shifting patterns of light and shadow. I trail a few steps behind, letting the calm of the grove wash over me. The air smells alive—earthy, herbal, and kissed with salt from the nearby sea.

"First lesson," Andreas begins, his voice steady and practical, "these trees aren't just plants—they're history. Some of them are over five hundred years old. They've seen wars, storms, droughts... survived it all."

I glance up at one particularly twisted trunk, its bark a labyrinth of cracks and ridges. "I know, kind of like the people here," I say softly, running a hand over its rough surface. Andreas stops and turns, his gaze unreadable. "Yeah. Like the people."

There's a weight to his words I can't quite place, and for a moment, we stand in silence, the breeze rustling the leaves around us. I force myself to look away, focusing on the landscape instead. The grove stretches endlessly; it's achingly beautiful and makes me feel... small. Not insignificant, but part of something vast, something timeless.

"Come on," Andreas says, breaking the spell. He leads me to a low stone wall, where he crouches to pick up a handful of soil. "The secret's in this," he says, holding it out for me to see. "This dirt's been feeding these trees for centuries. Get the balance right, and it's magic. Get it wrong, and—"

"Let me guess," I interrupt, trying to lighten the mood. "It's a disaster of biblical proportions?"

Andreas grins, the serious edge slipping away. "Not quite, but close. You'd be surprised how fussy these trees can be. They make Londoners look laid-back."

I snort, the sound startling in the quiet grove. "Okay, Farmer Andreas, impress me. What's the secret to olive-growing perfection?". He leans back on his heels, his gaze narrowing playfully. "Patience. And maybe a little luck. Kind of like dealing with you." I roll my eyes but can't help the smile tugging at my lips. "Charming. Really."

Andreas clears his throat, "Come on, I'll show you how we prune." He leads me to a nearby tree, demonstrating the precise cuts needed to keep the branches open and healthy. As we work, my mind wanders to childhood memories. "Remember those picnics your mom and Grandma used to organize?" I ask, a smile tugging at my lips. "Down by the beach while George and your dad worked?"

Andreas chuckles, the sound warm and rich. "How could I forget? You'd always steal my dessert when I wasn't looking". "Excuse me," I retort, playfully indignant. "I was simply redistributing resources. Besides, you always got the biggest piece of baklava". "Only because I was faster," he teases, his eyes crinkling at the corners.

The banter feels easy and natural, like slipping into a favourite sweater. But there's an undercurrent, a tension I can't quite name. I find myself hyper-aware of Andreas' movements, the way his hands move confidently through the branches, the flex of muscles beneath his shirt.

"Oh! And those ridiculous breath-holding contests in the sea," I say, desperate to distract myself. "I swear, one day I thought we'd both drown from sheer stubbornness." Andreas grins. "You were a worthy opponent, Leni. Still are, I'd bet."

"Well, I've had years of practice holding my breath through boring meetings. I'd probably destroy you now."

"Is that a challenge?" His voice is low and playful, with an edge that makes my pulse quicken.

I meet his gaze, chin lifted in mock defiance. "Maybe it is. What are you going to do about it, Papadopoulos?"

For a moment, the air between us feels electric. Then Andreas laughs, breaking the tension. "Save it for later, city girl. We've got work to do."

As we continue through the grove, I'm caught between the warm glow of nostalgia and the confusing tangle of my present emotions. Every shared memory, every casual touch as Andreas shows me pruning techniques, leaves me more off-balance. I came here to save my grandfather's legacy, not to... I shake my head, trying to clear it. Focus on the trees, Eleni. They're the only roots that matter right now.

***

When we break for lunch at the farmhouse, I'm sweaty, tired, and strangely content. The farmhouse sits quietly among the ancient olive trees. Its stone walls, weathered by time, are steeped in history, connecting past generations to my presence here. The terracotta roof bathes in the warm glow of the midday sun, while the open windows offer generous views of the expansive groves stretching toward the sea.

Inside, the farmhouse exudes the simple charm of rural life. The kitchen, where Andreas and I prepare our lunch, is compact, centred around an old wooden table, and surrounded by mismatched chairs that seem just right for this setting. The shelves hold an array of ceramic pots and pans.

A sense of belonging washes over me as I slice tomatoes and cucumbers for a salad. The aroma of basil and oregano mixes with the fresh scent of the vegetables, the atmosphere is thick with nostalgia, and I'm keenly aware of every glance Andreas throws my way, every smile that dances on his lips. As we settle at the table with our sandwiches, Andreas stretches out, his long legs brushing against mine under the table. It's casual, unintentional—or at least, that's what I tell myself—but the contact sends a little thrill through me.

"Not bad for your first day," he says, watching me with a faint smile.

"Not bad?" I feign offence. "I'm practically a pro. Admit it—you're impressed."

He leans forward, his eyes glinting with amusement. "Alright, I'll give you this—you've got potential, Leni."

His tone is light and teasing, but something in his expression feels heavier, like he's seeing more than just the little Leni. I swallow hard, breaking the moment by focusing on the view of the groves. The trees sway gently in the afternoon breeze, their leaves whispering secrets I wish I could decipher. Andreas follows my gaze, his voice quieter now. "You know, this place… it has a way of getting under your skin." I nod, the weight of his words settling over me.

He looks at me then, and for a moment, the teasing, the banter—all of it falls away. There's something raw in his eyes, something unguarded that makes my chest ache. Breaking the moment, he then continues, his voice softening to a more sincere tone. "Really, Leni, these trees could tell a thousand stories. Maybe they'll share some with you if you're willing to listen."

I smile, touched by the sentiment. "I think I'm starting to hear them already," I reply, glancing around at the sprawling branches. "It's a lot to take in, but I'm learning." "That's the spirit," he nods, picking up a fallen olive and rolling it between his fingers. "It's not just about keeping the traditions alive. It's about understanding why they matter." I watch him closely, noticing the gentle way he handles the olive as if it's a precious relic. "And do you always talk to your olives like that?" I ask, a playful note creeping back into my voice. Andreas laughs, a sound that seems to clear the air between us. "Only the ones that listen. The rest, I leave to fend for themselves." I chuckle, the tension easing between us. "Considerate of you. I hope they appreciate your efforts." "Well, they haven't complained yet," he quips, winking at me. "But there's always a first time for everything."

I laugh, feeling a warmth spread through me at our easy back-and-forth. "Well, I appreciate their hospitality," I say, looking around at the grove. "And yours. Today has been... more enlightening than I expected." He meets my gaze again, something flickering in his eyes before he holds the look a moment longer than necessary. With a hint of a smile playing at the corners of his mouth, he says, "There's a lot more to show you. And I'm glad I'm showing it to you, Eleni."

I gave him a playful glance: "Just make sure it's the olive groves you're showing me, Andreas, and not just your expert olive-picking technique." As Andreas started to laugh, I spotted Nikos approaching the farmhouse. His arrival shifts the atmosphere, and I can feel my mind switching gears from our playful banter to business mode. "Hi Nikos!" I call out, waving him over. "Perfect timing. We were just wrapping up our olive whispering session." Nikos chuckles as he joins us, his green eyes warm with amusement. "I hope the olives had some wisdom to share," he says, settling into a chair at the rustic wooden table.

I lean forward, excitement bubbling up inside me. "Oh, they did. And I've got some ideas I can't wait to run by you both." I tuck a wayward strand of hair behind my ear, my hands already starting to gesture as I speak. "I was checking George's notes while cleaning up his study. What if we introduced a limited edition of single-grove olive oil? We could market it as a premium product, highlighting the unique characteristics of each section of the farm. He was considering that option seriously."

Andreas shifts in his seat, his thumb idly brushing over a small stone he's picked up. "Eleni, that sounds... ambitious. But we have to be realistic about our resources. George and I discussed this several times but decided to wait until…"

He trails off, the words hanging in the air. I lean forward slightly. "Until what?" I prompt, my voice is quieter but insistent.

"Until the finances improve," he says firmly, though there's a subtle unease in his tone that he can't entirely hide.

I feel a flicker of frustration at his hesitation. " Andreas, this could be a game-changer for us. We have the quality; we just need to showcase it properly."

"It's not that simple," Andreas says, his voice clipped. "We need to consider the costs and the logistics. And honestly, I've been thinking... maybe it's time to consider other options. Like finding an investor."

The word 'finding an investor' hits me like a punch to the gut. "You mean selling? Are you serious? This business is your family's legacy, our legacy. We can't just give up on it!"

Andreas' jaw tightens. "It's not about giving up, Eleni. It's about facing facts. The business isn't what it used to be."

I can feel my cheeks flushing with emotion. "But it could be! If we just put in the effort, try new things-"

"Effort isn't always enough," Andreas cuts in, his voice sharp.

Nikos clears his throat, his calm presence a balm to our rising tempers. "Let's take a step back," he says, his tone measured. "Eleni, your idea has merit. Andreas, your concerns are valid. Why don't we look at this as a potential long-term goal? We can start small, perhaps with a test run, and see how it goes."

I take a deep breath, trying to rein in my frustration. "That... that sounds reasonable," I concede, though I can't quite keep the disappointment out of my voice. Andreas nods slowly, some of the tension leaving his shoulders. "We can look into it," he says, not quite meeting my eyes. As the meeting wraps up, I'm left feeling a mix of hope and confusion. Andreas' words about selling the farm echo in my mind, leaving me unsettled.

The week passes in a flurry of activity. I split my time between the production facility and the groves, throwing myself into learning every aspect of the business. Each day brings new discoveries, from the intricacies of the cold-pressing process to the subtle differences in flavour between olives from different parts of the grove.

Finally, as the sun sets on Friday evening, I find myself on my terrace, a glass of wine in hand and Zeus curled up at my feet. Ari lounges nearby, his tail swishing lazily.

"Well, boys," I say, taking a sip of wine, "what a week it's been." Zeus lifts his head, giving me a look that seems to say, 'Do tell.'

I laugh softly. "Oh, you know. Just your typical city girl turned olive oil tycoon story. Complete with a stubborn, frustratingly handsome partner and more spreadsheets than I care to count."

Ari looks totally uninterested and starts to have an urgent cleaning session.

"Thanks for approving Ari, " I say, "But you know what's weird guys? Despite the arguments and the long hours... I feel more at home here than I ever did in London."

I take another sip of wine, my gaze drifting over the sea and upcoming sunset colours. "It's like... every minute I spend at the grove, every villager I chat with, every sunset I watch from this terrace... it's all weaving itself into my heart."

Zeus lets out a soft woof, and I smile down at him. "Yes, you're definitely part of that too, you big softie."

As the last rays of sunlight paint the sky in shades of pink and gold, I find my thoughts drifting to Andreas. His resistance to change, his hints about selling, or finding an investor as he outs it gently... they frustrate me to no end. And yet...

"Is it crazy," I muse aloud, "that even when he's driving me up the wall, I still want to be around him? To figure him out?"

Ari gives me a look that seems to say, 'Humans are weird.'

I laugh, raising my glass in a mock toast. "To complicated feelings and stubborn Greek men," I declare. "May we survive them both."

***

The warm sand shifts pleasantly beneath my feet as I navigate down to Seranos beach. The morning sun is bright against my squinting eyes. Spotting Callie's familiar silhouette near the water's edge, a grin spreads across my face.
"Oi! Manos!" I shout, bringing us back to our teenage days "Ready to relive our glory days or what?"
Callie spins around, her face breaking into a wide smile. "Katsaros! You finally made it. I was beginning to wonder if you'd chickened out."
I roll my eyes theatrically as I approach her. "Please, as if I'd miss a chance to remind you who really rules the water."
"Oh, it's on," she declares, her eyes twinkling with the promise of mischief. With a sudden burst of energy, she dashes toward the water, sand flying behind her.
"Hey! No fair!" I call out, laughter bubbling up as I sprint after her.
We dive into the refreshing embrace of the Aegean, our shrieks of laughter mingling with the splash of the waves. Swimming out further, the weight of the past week dissolves with each stroke.
Eventually, after a spirited debate and a fierce but friendly competition, we declare our swimming race a tie and collapse onto our towels, breathless but still laughing.
"God, I've missed this," I exhale contentedly, tilting my face up to bask in the sun's warmth.
"Me too," Callie responds, her voice tinged with a soft nostalgia. "It's terrific to have you back, Eleni."

I turn to her, feeling a surge of affection for my lifelong friend. "It's good to be back," I affirm, my heart anchored in the truth of those words.

As we start to dry off, a loud rumble from Callie's stomach breaks the serene moment, and I can't help but burst into laughter. "Guess some things never change, right? How about we head to Sweets and Beans?"

"You read my mind," she says with a grin as we pack up our beach gear.

With spirits lifted and old times revisited, we make our way to the café, ready to indulge in some well-deserved treats and continue our day of catching up, just like the old days.

We stroll towards the welcoming facade of Sweets & Beans, the café's clean white walls, and large, inviting windows standing out in the quiet street of Seranos. As we step through the door, the rich aroma of freshly baked spanakopita greets us, mingling with the scent of strong coffee and sweet pastries—a sensory invitation to linger.

"Ladies!" Fotini, the owner, exclaims from behind the counter with a broad smile. "My, my, it's like stepping back in time. You two haven't changed a bit!"

I laugh, shaking my head. "Fotini, your eyesight must be going. We're practically ancient now."

"Speak for yourself," Callie retorts, giving me a playful elbow nudge.

We make our way to our favourite corner table, which feels like stepping into a cosy time capsule. The café's interior is bright and airy, with a touch of rustic chic—exposed wooden beams overhead, chalkboard menus offering today's specials, and potted plants adding a splash of greenery. Faded postcards and local artwork line the walls, each piece telling a story of the village's vibrant community life.

"Remember when we used to come here after swimming?" Callie asks, her voice tinged with nostalgia as she glances around.

"How could I forget?" I reply, the memories flooding back. "You'd always con me into sharing my baklava."

"Hey, I was doing you a favour! Saving your waistline and all that," she jests, her eyes sparkling with mischief.

Our laughter fills the café, drawing amused and familiar glances from other patrons who also remember us. Chuckling, Fotini comes over with our order—spanakopita for me, tyropita for Callie, and a shared plate of loukoumades because some habits die hard. As we dig in, the flavours are as delightful as the memories; each bite is a reminder of our youth and the unbreakable bond we've carried through the years.

Sitting here, with the buzz of conversation around us and the occasional villager stopping by our table to joke about "the good old days," I feel an overwhelming sense of contentment. It's as if no time has passed at all, yet everything is different. This warmth, this sense of belonging, it has everything to do with being home.

Back at the beach, Callie and I found a welcoming patch of shade under an old tree. Its branches spread wide above us, providing a cool respite from the sun's embrace. I pulled out a deck of cards, the edges soft and worn from years of use—our designated "beach deck" since our teenage years when we weren't allowed to bring the new ones to the beach.

"Ready to lose spectacularly, Cal?" I asked, shuffling the cards with a smirk.

Callie snorted, her back comfortably against the tree trunk. "In your dreams, Leni. I've been sharpening my skills with Nikos."

"Ooh, sharpening skills with Nikos," I teased, waggling my eyebrows suggestively. "Is that what we're calling it these days?"

She swatted at me playfully, her laughter mingling with the gentle rustle of the leaves. "Oh, please, get your mind out of the gutter! But speaking of gutters..." Her voice lowered to a mischievous whisper. "What's the real scoop between you and Andreas? Come on, spill!"

My cheeks felt suddenly warm, betraying my calm demeanour. "There's no 'scoop.' We're just... reconnecting, that's all."

"Uh-huh," Callie said, a knowing smirk playing on her lips as she took her hand of cards. "And I'm the Queen of England."

As we played, the conversation meandered from Andreas to other juicy bits of village gossip, each story punctuated by bursts of laughter and exaggerated expressions of disbelief.

"Did you hear about old man Christos?" Callie asked casually, placing a card on our makeshift table of sand.

I shook my head, curious. "No, what's he been up to now?"

She leaned closer, her voice dropping even lower, her eyes gleaming with mischief. "Well, rumour has it he's taken to nude sunbathing. On his rooftop, no less."

I sputtered, nearly spilling my drink. "You're joking!"

"Not at all," she chuckled. "Poor Mrs Ariti got quite the eyeful when she was hanging her laundry. Swears she's never seen such a sight!"

We collapsed into giggles, the cards temporarily forgotten as we imagined the scandalised neighbour's reaction. The laughter was easy and natural, and as the afternoon stretched lazily before us, I felt a weight lifting from my shoulders. Here, with Callie, under the dappled light filtering through the leaves, the pressures of London and the complexities of my new life in Seranos seemed miles away. It was just like the old days, only better because now I realised how much I had missed this and needed it. Later, we're sprawled on my terrace, watching the sun dip towards the horizon. The wine in our glasses is crisp and cool, perfectly complementing the warmth of the evening air. We chat idly, savouring the tranquillity that only a sunset and good wine can bring.

"I've missed this," I murmur, the words slipping out with a wistfulness that surprises even me.

Callie turns to me, her expression softening in the fading light. "And I've missed you, Eleni."

I take a sip of wine, letting the flavours linger on my tongue as I consider her words. "I didn't realise just how much I missed it here until I came back. It's like… I've been sleepwalking through my life in London, and now, suddenly, I'm wide awake."

Callie reaches over and squeezes my hand, her touch grounding. "It sounds like you've been given a second chance here. So, what are you going to do with it?"

I look out at the sea, now painted in stunning shades of purple by the setting sun. The waves gently lap against the shore, a rhythmic sound that's as comforting as the wine is invigorating. The answer, startling in its clarity, rises unbidden to my lips. "I'm seriously considering staying," I confess, the words feeling right as they fill the space between us. "This is home. It always has been, hasn't it?"

Callie nods, her smile tinged with a quiet joy. "I think you've known that deep down, even when you were miles away."

As the last rays of sunlight fade, casting long shadows across the terrace, a sense of peace settles over me. With the gentle sea breeze and Callie's easy companionship, I feel anchored, as if all the paths I've wandered have led me back to where I began.

"So, you're really considering it?" Callie asks after a moment, her voice tinged with playful curiosity. I catch the underlying tease but choose to overlook it.

"I think I am", I reply.

Callie raises her glass, the wine catching the last light. "To finding home, and to new beginnings," she toasts.

I clink my glass against hers, the sound sharp and clear. "To home," I echo as night settles over us and the stars begin to twinkle in the velvet sky. I know that this day has changed something fundamental in me. For the first time in a long time, I am exactly where I want to be.

***

Andreas

I rub a smooth pebble between my fingers, its cool surface soothing as I stand among the gnarled olive trees. The grove unfolds around me, a mosaic of silver-green leaves whispering in the breeze. It's been nearly three weeks since Eleni arrived. This morning, she's busy at the facility with Nikos and the accountants, immersed in spreadsheets and projections, while I'm out here, managing what she playfully refers to as the "real business." She mentioned she'd come to see me this afternoon, and that time is now.

Her energy is infectious. She dives into the operations with a zeal that's both admirable and, frankly, a bit unnerving. She's bursting with ideas, talking about increasing productivity and expanding capacity and sketching out business plans on the back of used envelopes. Her ambition seems boundless, and it's starting to thaw the numbness that had settled over me after years of fighting losing battles alone.

But there's so much she doesn't know, so much I've kept from her. After my divorce, I was financially ruined. To salvage what I could, I took out massive loans against my shares of the farm—decisions made in desperation. I discussed it with George; he was as supportive as a father could be, telling me, "Son, do whatever you need to do. We're family and we'll find a way to pay it back." Neither of us could have anticipated the bad seasons that followed, compounding the disaster.

George's passing left me resolved to sell the business—it seemed the only way out. I was certain I couldn't rebuild alone. When I learned that Eleni, not Petros, had inherited George's shares and planned to come back for a few weeks, I was convinced she'd be overwhelmed and flee back to her life in London. I saw her as a spoiled city girl on a brief escapade into her past, soon to realise that life here was no fairytale.

That's why I never shared the true extent of my financial woes; I thought it irrelevant. I was also ashamed. Only George knew the full depth of my despair. Moreover, there was something selfish in my silence: when Eleni looked at me, I felt seen as the man I used to be—confident, vital, someone of worth. Her presence and belief in me were healing wounds I hadn't even admitted were festering.

But now, watching her throw herself into this venture, seeing her so dedicated, so full of hope and determination, I'm starting to regret my decision to keep her in the dark. As our connection deepens, the burden of my secret grows heavier with each passing day. The last thing I want is to see her face fall when she learns the truth, to watch the light in her eyes dim. I dread the disappointment I might see there, a reflection of my own failures.

Out here, among the ancient groves, I wrestle with these thoughts. I know I need to tell her, and soon. The longer

I wait, the harder it will become. I owe her that much, especially if there's any chance that together, maybe, just maybe, we can turn things around…

I turn my head to the sound of footsteps and see Eleni approaching with a broad smile, calling out, "You look deep in thoughts, Papadopoulos! What are you up to, saving the world?" I return her smile and reply, "Actually, I was just figuring out how to handle your antics for the afternoon, which, believe me, can be just as challenging as saving the world. " My words are light with humour to mask the darker undertones of my mood.

Previous thoughts about telling Eleni everything still on my mind, I find myself unusually attentive and keenly aware of the implications of our growing closeness. The warmth of the mid-morning sun beats down on us in the grove as I show her how to prune the suckers sprouting aggressively at the bases of the olive trees.

"Alright, you see these shoots here?" I say, pointing to the small branches growing low on the trunk. "These are what we need to remove. They sap energy from the tree but don't actually bear fruit."

Eleni nods, kneeling down to inspect them closer, her V-neck shirt dipping forward slightly. I quickly avert my gaze, but not before I catch a glimpse of her bra. Heat rushes to my face, and I force myself to focus on a nearby tree.

"Got it, Chief," she replies, her tone playful. "So, these are the freeloaders of the tree world?"

"Exactly," I laugh, relieved by the change of subject. "They take resources without giving anything back. Kind of like that one roommate I had at university."

Eleni grins, pulling at a stubborn shoot. "I bet he didn't make for good olive oil, though."

As she bends again to tug at another sucker, the same view presents itself. I chastise myself silently and turn to

check on another tree, but the image lingers in my mind. When she straightens, she catches me quickly shifting my gaze.
"Are you checking on me, Andreas?" she asks with a mischievous smile.
"Why would I do such a thing, Leni?" I try to keep my tone light, masking the turmoil inside.
She bends down again deliberately, teasingly. "I don't know. Maybe you're checking your calculation skills, say if you can guess my bra size in one go?"
I laugh, attempting to keep the mood jovial. "Oh, don't worry, I don't need to check my skills in that department; they are perfect."
"Jerk," she chuckles and turns back to her work, leaving me grappling with a mix of amusement and sudden longing.
Standing there, watching her effortlessly joke about something so personal, sends an unexpected shiver down my spine. *Stop it,* I reprimand myself. *You're treading dangerous waters here.* Eleni isn't just a fleeting distraction; she's here to help—to possibly save this farm that means so much to both of us. She's my business partner, part of the family, and, most importantly, she's still little Leni. I remind myself firmly, doing my best to push down the feelings bubbling up, threatening to complicate everything.
Resolved yet unsettled, I focus on instructing her, putting aside personal turmoil. We continue through the grove, the sun climbing higher, casting long shadows that weave around us like silent witnesses to the tension and laughter that fills the air.
The late afternoon, as I steer the pick-up along the winding road back to Seranos, beside me, Eleni sits with the window rolled down, her hair catching the breeze and tossing in soft waves. The sunlight seems to cling to her,

accentuating the warm tones of her skin and the slight flush on her cheeks from the day's work in the grove. Her hazel eyes catch the light, revealing flecks of amber that I'd never noticed before. Her scent—something faintly floral with a hint of earthiness—lingers in the car.

I glance over at her as she leans her elbow on the window frame, her fingers absently brushing her lips. She looks relaxed, but there's a quiet intensity about her as if her mind is turning over a dozen thoughts at once. There's something magnetic about the way she's both present in the moment and distant, lost in her own world.

"Long day," I say, breaking the silence.

She turns her head toward me, a small smile playing on her lips. "Productive, though. Don't you think?"

I nod, keeping my eyes on the road. "Not bad for someone who thought suckers were just freeloaders this morning."

She laughs, warm and infectious. "Hey, I caught on, didn't I? You should be proud of your student."

"Proud, sure," I reply, a smirk tugging at my lips. "But let's not get ahead of ourselves. You're not exactly ready to take over the grove just yet."

Eleni rolls her eyes with dramatic flair, though her smile doesn't waver. "Give me time, Andreas. Rome wasn't built in a day."

I chuckle, the weight of my earlier thoughts lifting, if only for a moment. "We'll see about that."

As we near the village, the familiar rooftops of Seranos come into view, I find myself reluctant to end our day, and before I can overthink it, I ask, "How about dinner at Theo's before you head home?"

She looks at me, surprised but intrigued. "Dinner at Theo's? Are you trying to bribe me with food after all that hard labour you made me do?"

"Maybe," I say with a shrug, keeping my tone light. "Or maybe I just think you deserve it."

She considers for a moment before nodding. "Alright, but only if you let me order dessert."

I grin. "Deal."

Eleni and I sit at a wooden table under string lights, a carafe of ouzo between us. I ordered her favourites—grilled octopus, fried zucchini, and, of course, a plate of Theo's famous cheese-stuffed peppers.

"You really do remember," she says, her eyebrows raised in mock suspicion as the food arrives. "Trying to win me over with my favourite dishes? Sneaky."

"What can I say?" I reply, leaning back in my chair. "I'm a man of strategy."

"Mm-hmm," she hums, spearing a piece of zucchini with her fork. "Next thing I know, you'll be offering me the last loukoumade to really seal the deal."

"That would be taking things too far," I deadpan, earning a laugh from her.

As the evening unfolds, the ouzo flows, and so does the conversation. We fall into easy banter, the kind that feels natural and nostalgic all at once.

"Do you remember that summer your grandparents had the big barbecue here, and you spilled red wine all over Maria's white dress?" I ask, grinning at the memory.

Eleni groans, burying her face in her hands. "Ugh, how could I forget? I was mortified! Maria looked at me like I'd committed a capital offence."

"To be fair," I tease, "that dress didn't deserve to survive. It looked like it belonged to a wedding cake."

She swats my arm playfully. "You're awful! And anyway, you weren't so innocent that day either. If I remember correctly, someone decided it would be a great idea to jump into the sea fully clothed."

"Only because someone dared me," I counter, pointing my fork at her.

As we pick at the last remnants of our meal, the tone shifts slightly, the playful teasing giving way to something softer.

"You've changed," she says quietly, studying me over the rim of her glass. "But not as much as you think."

I meet her gaze, unsure how to respond to the sincerity in her tone. "And you… you're not what I expected. Not in a bad way," I add quickly.

She tilts her head, curious. "What did you expect?"

I pause, searching for the right words. "I thought you'd be more… distant. Detached. But you're—" I stop, realising how much I'm about to reveal.

"I'm what?" she prompts, a playful but gentle smile on her lips.

"Still you," I say simply, taking a sip of ouzo to hide the emotion behind the words.

The conversation ebbs and flows as the night deepens, the stars shimmering above us. By the time we leave, there's a lightness in the air that wasn't there before. As we walk back to her house, the sound of the waves following us, I feel a strange and unexpected sense of contentment.

***

Eleni

The dinner at Theo's ends in a blur of laughter, shared memories, and the warm haze of ouzo that lingers pleasantly in my veins. My cheeks hurt from smiling, my stomach aches from laughing, and yet, a small knot of anxiety tightens as I glance at Andreas across the table. The way he looks at me—warm, amused, attentive—it's messing with my head.

Am I reading too much into this? Or is there something there? I replay every glance, every smirk, every fleeting touch from the evening like a desperate detective piecing together a case. His jokes felt softer tonight, his teasing less sharp. Or was that just the ouzo talking? God, Eleni, get a grip. You're acting like a teenager.

As we step out into the cool night air, Andreas moves beside me naturally, his arm brushing mine as we begin the short walk to my house. The breeze carries the scent of the sea, mingling with the faint citrusy tang of his cologne. It's intoxicating, or maybe that's the ouzo again. Either way, I feel like I'm floating.

We walk in comfortable silence at first, the quiet punctuated by the occasional laughter of distant villagers. I feel his fingers graze mine for the briefest moment, and a shiver runs through me. Before I can overanalyse, he does it again, his touch lingering slightly longer this time. I glance up at him, trying to gauge his expression in the dim light. Calm, unreadable—classic Andreas.

When we reach a narrow path, he places his hand lightly on the small of my back to guide me, the touch sending electricity down my spine. Oh, no big deal. Just your entire nervous system lighting up because of a casual gesture. He removes his hand quickly, almost as if he's trying to avoid making me uncomfortable, but my skin hums where his fingers had been.

"Thanks for dinner," I say, trying to sound casual and not like I'm overanalysing every step he takes.

"Thanks for the company," he replies, his voice steady but warm. I want to read more into it, but I don't trust myself right now.

When we finally reach my door, I turn to face him, suddenly hyper-aware of how close we are. The street is quiet, the air still, and everything else seems to fade away for a moment. Andreas holds my hands lightly but firmly, his thumbs brushing against my knuckles.

His eyes meet mine, and something in his gaze shifts. It's softer, deeper—like he's trying to say something without words. My heart pounds so loudly that I'm convinced he can hear it. Is it longing? Is it curiosity? Oh my God, is he going to kiss me? He's totally going to kiss me.

I tilt my face up ever so slightly, my breath catching, my entire body waiting. The moment stretches unbearably, and then—he moves.

His lips press against the corner of my mouth, barely brushing my cheek. It's tender, fleeting, and utterly confusing. Pulling back, he smiles faintly, his expression now unreadable again.

"Sleep well, Leni," he murmurs before turning and walking away, leaving me rooted to the spot.

I stand there, staring after him, my mind a chaotic swirl of emotions. What just happened? Was that nothing? Was that everything? Did I imagine the whole thing?

As I close the door behind me, leaning against it for a moment, I let out a long, shaky breath. My fingers instinctively brush the spot on my cheek where Andreas's lips barely touched. The faintest hint of a smile spreads across my face despite my confusion. What was that, Papadopoulos? A kiss or a well-placed detour?

I glance over at Zeus, sprawled lazily in the corner, wagging his tail as if he already knows my secrets. "Well, Zeus," I mutter, crossing the room, "apparently, your new job is to help me figure out if Andreas is a cryptic genius or just a master at driving me insane."

Zeus thumps his tail in agreement—or mockery, who can tell?—. Ari, perched on the armrest of the sofa, lifts his head just enough to judge me before closing his eyes again.

In the quiet of my bedroom, I sink onto the bed, my head spinning with thoughts of Andreas's gaze, his restraint, his lingering touch. What am I doing? What is he doing? Is this…something? Or am I completely out of my depth?

Despite my internal interrogation, the thrill of it all leaves me grinning like an idiot.

I flop onto my back, staring at the ceiling, and blurt out to the room, "That's it. I'm staying." The words surprise me, but they feel undeniably true as soon as they're spoken. I sit up and look at Zeus, who's already curled up at the foot of the bed, and then at Ari, who's now watching me with what I swear is feline scepticism.

"You heard me, boys," I say with mock solemnity. "This is home now. Whatever happens, I'm not leaving." Zeus wags his tail as if to seal the deal, and Ari yawns, clearly unimpressed. "You two better get used to me."

***

The following day, sunlight filters softly through the trees as I sit on the terrace with my coffee. The air is cool and fresh, carrying a hint of salt from the nearby sea. I take a sip, the warmth grounding me, and glance at Zeus, stretched out beside me in his usual relaxed sprawl.

Yiannis appears, his fishing cap slightly askew, as if he's just woken up. He gives a casual wave and makes his way over, leaning comfortably on the garden wall between our terraces.

"You look like a squid caught in a net, Eleni," he remarks, his eyes twinkling. "Waving around but not actually going anywhere."

I roll my eyes and set my mug down. "Thanks for that brilliant insight. Why don't you go back to terrorising fish?"

Yiannis smirks, leaning back with a contented sigh. "I'm retired, remember? My terrorising days are behind me. Now, I terrorise you."

"Lucky me," I mutter, but the corner of my mouth twitches with a smile.

He studies me for a moment, his expression softening. "You've got that look again. The one your grandmother used to get when she was deciding between olive oil or butter for her cookies. Big decisions ahead, eh?"

I laugh despite myself. "Oh, just the usual—whether to sell the grove, stay in the village, or, I don't know, move to a remote island and start a crab cult."

Yiannis chuckles, scratching his chin thoughtfully. "Crabs don't take kindly to leaders. Too many legs to march in the same direction. Now, tell me, what's actually bothering you?"

I take a deep breath, swirling my coffee in its mug as I consider how to answer. "It's not bothering me, exactly. I just…" I pause, searching for the right words. "I've decided to stay. Here. In Seranos. Whatever happens with the grove, this is where I want to be."

Yiannis raises an eyebrow but doesn't look surprised. "Well, it's about time. Took you long enough to figure that out."

I laugh softly, shaking my head. "It feels… right, you know? But now comes the hard part."

"And what's that?" he asks, though I get the feeling he already knows.

I sigh, setting my mug down. "Calling my boss in London to quit, for one. And then calling my dad to tell him I'm staying. That'll be… interesting."

Yiannis nods, leaning forward slightly. "Your boss will survive. And your father? He might grumble and sigh, but he loves you. He'll come around. You Katsaros are as stubborn as olive roots. Once you make up your mind, there's no budging."

I smile, his words filling me with a strange sense of reassurance. "Thanks, Yiannis."

As he ambles off, I watch him go, feeling a mix of nerves and certainty settle in my chest. I glance down at Zeus, who's now fully awake and watching me with his head tilted, and Ari, who's sauntered out onto the terrace, looking predictably unimpressed.

"Alright, boys," I say, grabbing my phone. "Time to get it over with."

I take a deep breath, fingers hovering over my phone. The call to Janet goes surprisingly smoothly - she's disappointed but understanding. I take a deep breath, staring at the phone in my hand. Okay, Eleni. You can do this. He's just your dad. The same dad who spent your childhood convincing you that a B+ was the same as failure. No big deal.

The dial tone barely finishes its first ring before Dad answers. "Eleni." His voice, clipped and business-like, sets my nerves on edge instantly. "I wasn't expecting a call from you today."

"Well, brace yourself," I say, trying for lightness. "I've got news."

There's a pause on the other end, the kind that comes when Dad is shifting into 'prepare-for-disappointment' mode. "I'm listening."

I settle deeper into my chair, holding my coffee mug like a lifeline. "I've decided to stay in Seranos. For good."

Silence. The kind that could suck the air out of a room.

"You're staying?" he says finally, his voice careful. "In Seranos? Eleni, this isn't another impulsive decision, is it? You've barely been there three weeks. Do you even know what you're committing to?"

"I know exactly what I'm committing to," I say firmly. "The grove, the business, the community—it's where I'm supposed to be."

He exhales, the sound heavy with scepticism. "Eleni, you've never run a business before, let alone a grove. It's not like managing a group project at university or planning a marketing campaign. This is real work. Hard work. And let's not even get started on the financial risks."

His words sting, but I steel myself. "I know it's not easy, Dad. But maybe that's the point. I want to do this. I want to build something meaningful."

There's a soft sound, like he's adjusting his chair. "Eleni, this isn't about wanting. It's about being realistic. You're not equipped for this. And frankly, I don't understand why you'd give up your life in London for—what? A romanticised dream of village life?"

"It's not romanticised," I snap, unable to keep the frustration out of my voice. "I've been here long enough to see the challenges. And you know what? That doesn't scare me. What scares me is going back to London, sitting in an office, and realising I wasted my chance to do something that matters."

His sigh is sharp, the kind that signals he's digging in for a lecture. "Eleni, happiness isn't a career strategy. You can't just chase feelings. You need stability, security—"

"Don't you think I know that?" I interrupt, my voice rising. "I've spent years chasing stability. It hasn't made me happy, Dad. And if staying here, working my ass off, and maybe failing is what it takes to feel alive, then that's what I'm going to do."

There's a long pause, and for a moment, I wonder if he's hung up. Finally, his voice comes through, quieter this time. "This business… George poured everything into it and got so little in return. I don't want that for you."

My heart softens at the hint of concern in his tone. "I'm not George, Dad. And I'm not you, either. I need to figure this out for myself. Even if it's hard. Even if I fail."

Another long silence. Then, with an almost palpable heaviness, he says, "I suppose I can't stop you."

I smile faintly, though my throat feels tight. "No, you can't."

"But don't think I'll be here to pick up the pieces when it all goes wrong," he warns, the sharpness returning to his tone.

"I wouldn't expect you to," I say evenly.

There's a slight pause before he adds, almost begrudgingly, "If you're staying, make sure you're practical about it. Keep records, hire good help, and don't make emotional decisions."

"Of course, Dad. Practicality is my middle name," I say, unable to resist one last jab.

His sigh comes through the receiver loud and clear. "I doubt that. But… take care, Eleni."

"I will," I reply softly.

When the call ends, I set the phone down and let out a breath I didn't realise I was holding. The conversation wasn't perfect, but I felt like I'd held my own with him for the first time in a long time.

"Here's to starting something new," I mutter to myself, raising my coffee mug in an imaginary toast to Zeus and Ari, who watch me with varying levels of interest.

Whatever comes next, I'm ready. Or at least, I think I am.

Realizations and How Not to Handle Business Talks

After hanging up with my dad, it felt like a massive weight had been lifted from my chest. That's when it hit me—aside from our brief chats in passing around the village, I hadn't properly visited Sophia since I returned. Now seemed like the perfect time; I could definitely use a dose of her wisdom. Sophia had been one of my grandmother's closest friends, a lifelong resident of the village, and the unofficial keeper of Seranos' collective secrets. If anyone could offer perspective, it was her.

As I walked through the winding streets toward Sophia's house, Zeus trotted happily beside me. His tail thumped in a steady rhythm, somehow soothing and mildly irritating at the same time. At some point, he'd discovered a stick. He was carrying it proudly, pausing every so often to glance back at me, his tongue flopping out in pure, uncontainable joy.

I, on the other hand, was a mess. My hair was sticking to my forehead, the sun felt like it was actively trying to cook me, and my thoughts were an overcomplicated web of Andreas' cryptic behaviours and my growing self-doubt.

"What is it with men and their ability to be completely unreadable, huh?" I muttered, kicking a stray pebble. Zeus tilted his head at me, stick still firmly wedged in his jaw. "No, seriously. Do you think he's trying to annoy me on purpose, or is he just naturally talented at it?"

Zeus let out a sharp bark that startled a flock of birds into a flurry of wings. I sighed. "Appreciate the insight, Dr. Zeus. Always so profound," I muttered, shaking my head.

He bounded ahead, pausing a few steps later to glance back at me, his mouth stretched in a goofy grin, complete with a dangling string of drool that sparkled in the sunlight. It was hard to stay frustrated with that face, even if he had no idea what I was saying.

"You know," I continued, as much to myself as to him, "you're not exactly the world's greatest conversationalist. You don't give advice, you can't argue back, and let's be honest—you'd sell me out to Andreas for a treat without a second thought." Zeus barked again, the sound suspiciously like agreement. "Figures," I muttered. "Traitor."

The path narrowed, and Zeus, as if determined to prove he was part of the landscape, flopped into the dirt and began rolling with abandon, his golden fur turning into a tapestry of twigs, leaves, and... was that a beetle?

"Zeus, really?" I groaned, planting my hands on my hips. He popped back up, looking immensely pleased with himself and thoroughly accessorized by the countryside. With an enthusiastic shake, he sent a spray of dust and debris flying in all directions—mostly mine.

"Fantastic," I said, brushing bits of olive grove off my dress. "You're lucky you've got that face. Otherwise, this would be a very different conversation." Zeus, oblivious to my grumbling, trotted ahead with his usual carefree bounce, leaving me to laugh despite myself.

We passed a low stone wall that marked the edge of Sophia's property, her small cottage just visible through a tangle of flowering vines and herbs. "Okay, here's the plan," I said, stopping just short of the gate and crouching to meet Zeus' big brown eyes. "Sophia is like... the Oracle of Delphi, but with more cats and less formal seating. She will tell me what to do about Andreas, and you'll sit quietly and not knock over any jars of mystical herbs, okay?"

Zeus licked my face in response, his tongue catching my nose and leaving a trail of slobber behind.

"I'll take that as a yes," I said, wiping my face with my sleeve. "You're really nailing this supportive sidekick thing."

As I pushed open the gate, the hinge let out a creak that sounded oddly like a groan of warning. If anyone could untangle the mess in my head—or at least make me laugh while trying—it was her.

I step into Sophia's cottage, and the scent of herbs envelops me like a comforting hug—rosemary, thyme, and something earthy and slightly citrusy I can't quite place. It starkly contrasts the stale air of my life back in London, where "fresh" meant opening a package of pre-cut fruit from the shops.

"Sit, sit," Sophia urges, her hands fluttering toward a worn armchair adorned with a colourful crocheted throw. As I sink into its lumpy cushions, my eyes wander over the room's every nook and cranny. It's a treasure trove of trinkets and memories—hand-painted plates, sepia-toned photographs, and a string of dried peppers swaying slightly in the breeze from an open window. A cat eyes me suspiciously from its perch on a windowsill, flicking its tail in disdain.

"You look like you've seen a ghost, child," Sophia chuckles, her blue eyes twinkling as she bustles with an ancient copper kettle.

I let out a short laugh, the tension in my chest easing slightly. "I wish it were that simple, Sophia. I'm just... overwhelmed. Andreas. The grove. Everything."

"Ah, yes," she says, nodding sagely as she sets two mismatched mugs on a tray. "Life's two great mysteries: men and the land. Both as stubborn as a mule in the summer heat."

I can't help but smile. "That sums it up pretty well, actually."

She pours steaming water over fragrant herbs, the steam curling like an invitation to let it all out. "Start at the beginning, child. What's weighing on you?"

I take a deep breath, struggling to put my thoughts into words. "It's Andreas. One minute he's charming; the next, he's as closed off as a padlocked shed. I feel like he pulls away every time I try to get closer. And then there's the business..." My words falter, and I stare into the steam rising from the cups. "What if I mess this all up? I don't even know where to start."

Sophia clicks her tongue, setting the kettle down with a gentle clang. "Ah, my dear, you're trying to solve the wrong riddle. The grove doesn't need to be 'managed' the way one manages accounts or employees. It needs to be understood."

I frown. "Understood? I'm not sure I even understand myself right now, let alone a grove full of stubborn, ancient trees."

She chuckles warmly, the sound wrapping around the room like sunlight through an open window. "The olive trees hold wisdom far older than our fleeting worries. The soil, the wind, the rhythm of the seasons—they'll guide you if you're willing to listen."

I sip the tea she hands me, the complex, earthy flavour grounding me somehow. "Listening to trees... That sounds poetic, but what does it even mean? How do I start?"

Sophia's eyes crinkle with a smile. "There's no manual for this, child. It's in your blood. Spend time with the land. Run your fingers through the soil. Let the seasons teach you what no ledger or consultant ever can."

I exhale a laugh. "It sounds peaceful, but what about the practical side? The harvest? The finances? And let's not forget Andreas. He's a walking contradiction. Half the time, I can't tell if he's testing me or just waiting for me to fail."

"Men like Andreas are like olive trees themselves," Sophia muses, leaning back in her chair. "Deep roots, but slow to show their fruit. He carries burdens he's not ready to share, but that doesn't mean he isn't willing to stand strong beside you when the time comes."

I lean forward, gripping the mug tightly. "So what am I supposed to do? Just wait for him to figure himself out?"

Sophia's gaze sharpens, pinning me in place. "You don't wait. You lead. Your instincts are stronger than you give them credit for, and your voice is needed—not just for the grove but also for him. Andreas doesn't need someone to fix him. He needs someone to remind him who he was."

Her words settle over me, heavy yet oddly empowering. "And what if I'm wrong? What if I mess it all up?"

She leans closer, her voice dropping to a near whisper. "Do you know how many times your grandmother doubted herself? She was terrified when she started tending this land. But she didn't let that fear stop her, because she knew the grove needed her just as much as she needed it. The same spirit runs through you, Eleni."

I blink, a warmth blooming in my chest. "You really think I can do this?"

"I know you can," she says firmly. "And as for Andreas... well, the roots of the olive tree run deeper than you think."

I blink, trying to piece together her cryptic words. "What does that mean?"

Sophia winks, a sly smile playing on her lips as she turns to tend a pot bubbling softly on the stove. "You'll see. Trust me, child. All in good time."

As I watch her bustling around her tiny kitchen, the doubts in my chest seem a little lighter. Maybe, just maybe, she's right. Maybe I can do this after all.

After our talk with Sophia, her words stayed with me all week, propelling me to stop doubting and start doing: "There's no manual for this, child. It's in your blood."

That's how I ended up marching into the facility on Monday morning, a shaky determination pushing aside my imposter syndrome—barely. Looking back, the week was a rollercoaster, a constant pendulum swinging between "You've got this" and "What in the world are you doing?"

I spent most of the week immersed in logistics, quality control, and working closely with Nikos. I like to think I picked up more than a few things. Keeping my interactions with Andreas to a bare minimum definitely helped my focus. I only saw him briefly during his fleeting visits to the facility, and our exchanges were limited to polite "How are you doing?" and not a single hint of acknowledgement about that evening.

Of course, that didn't stop me from thinking about him. Every free moment, my mind replayed those fleeting interactions—the brush of his hand, the way his eyes lingered, the tone of his voice. It was maddening how easily my thoughts spiralled, turning small moments into something much larger, much more complicated.

Was I falling in love with him again? *If you can even call my childhood crush "love."* No, I decided firmly. Don't even say the word. You're here on a mission—a mission that does not involve descending into the emotional chaos of unrequited love. That's the kind of messy, energy-draining business you absolutely cannot afford. Nope, steer clear of the L word, thank you very much.

Thankfully, Nikos became my guiding light this week—my personal olive oil Yoda. He patiently walked me through the ins and outs of production, from quality control to sustainability strategies. His calm, steady confidence was a welcome contrast to my constant internal chaos. We were also discussing ways to make the farm more sustainable.

"What if we install solar panels to power the facility and use the surplus energy to offer charging stations for e-bikes in Navagos?"

Nikos paused, a thoughtful smile spreading across his face. "That's an excellent idea, Eleni. It shows you're thinking not just about the business but also about integrating it with the community."

I'd tucked his praise away like a treasure, replaying it every time self-doubt crept back in. Now, standing here on the terrace, I let those thoughts swirl in my mind. The warmth of determination mingled with the inevitable undertone of self-doubt.

***

Andreas

I spot Dimitris before he notices me, his tall frame and sharp suit making him stand out like a peacock among pigeons in the bustling taverna. He's leaning casually against the bar, flashing his signature grin at a waitress who seems utterly captivated. Some things never change. Dimitris and I grew up together, practically inseparable. We were the so-called "hit boys" of Seranos and Navagos, always getting into harmless trouble. He's the son of a local politician and was obsessed with political science from a young age. After university, he returned to Navagos to work with the town's mayor, quickly carving out a name for himself in local politics. Now, he's an influential figure in the region but still carries the air of the 16-year-old charmer who couldn't resist flirting with anything that moved.

"Breaking hearts again, Lekas?" I call out as I approach, unable to resist interrupting his little show.

He turns at the sound of my voice, his green eyes lighting up with genuine warmth. " Look who's finally crawled out of the olive grove." He strides over and pulls me into a manly hug that feels more like a wrestling move, nearly knocking the air out of me.

We settle into a corner table, the chatter of the taverna buzzing around us like background music. As I glance at him, perfectly put together with his styled hair and carefully trimmed stubble, I can't help but feel distinctly scruffy by comparison.

"So," I say, raising an eyebrow, "how's life treating Navagos' most eligible bachelor?"

Dimitris leans back in his chair with an easy grin. "Ah, you know me—keeping busy with local politics during the day and... appreciating the finer attractions of Navagos by night."

He smirks, signalling the waitress to bring over a bottle of ouzo and a spread of meze. "And what about you? Still carrying the weight of the world on those broad shoulders?"

I sigh, running a hand through my hair. "The business is in trouble, Dimitris. Really bad trouble. I don't know how much longer we can keep it afloat."

His playful expression sobers instantly. "That bad? What are your options?"

"Selling," I admit, the word tasting bitter on my tongue. "But the idea of letting go of all that history... it feels like cutting off a part of myself."

He nods, a flicker of sympathy crossing his face. "And Eleni? How's she handling all of this? I heard our little Leni has grown into a very determined—and beautiful—woman." A mischievous smile plays on his lips.

The mention of her name sends an unexpected jolt through me. Dimitris calling her beautiful adds a sting of jealousy I don't know what to do with. I clear my throat.

"She's... determined, all right. Stubborn as hell. She insists we can turn things around."

"Sounds like someone else I know." Dimitris smirks knowingly before adding, "And what about her 'I'm going to marry Andreas when I grow up' crush? She's not exactly 'little Leni' anymore, is she?"

Heat creeps up my neck. "She's... Look, it's complicated."

Dimitris leans forward, eyebrows raised in surprise. "Complicated, huh? Complicated like you're falling for her?" His grin widens, and a little laugh escapes him despite his attempt to hold it back. "Papadopoulos, this was the last thing I expected to hear tonight."

"Christ, Dimitris," I mutter, pouring myself a hefty glass of ouzo. "It's not – I mean, I'm not – "

"Relax," he says, holding up a hand, though his amusement is impossible to miss. "I'm just teasing. But seriously, Andreas, I haven't seen you this worked up about anyone since... well, you know."

I throw back the ouzo, but the burn down my throat is not enough to drown out the memories. "That's exactly what scares me. I told myself I was done with all of that."

Dimitris leans forward, his voice softening. "Andreas, I get it. You were burned. But you can't let one bad experience shut you off forever. Maybe Eleni is exactly what you need—someone to remind you of who you were, who you still are." He grins, adding, "Which would be great for me too. I could finally get my cocky, funny friend back."

I snort. "That's rich, coming from the guy who's never been in a relationship longer than a week."

"True," he concedes, tapping his temple with a smirk. "But I know happiness when I see it. And you, my friend, have that look—the one that says you're scared out of your mind but also more alive than you've been in years."

I open my mouth to argue, but the words catch in my throat. Damn him, but he's not wrong.

Dimitris leans back, satisfied. "Here's my advice, take it or leave it. Don't fight it. Let yourself feel something real again. And as for the grove..." He pauses, the mischief giving way to thoughtfulness. "Navagos is growing. Why not think outside the box? Agrotourism is huge these days—there's money to be made there. There are also new government grants for sustainable agriculture."

I blink, caught off guard. "That's... actually not a bad idea."

"Of course it's not," he says with mock indignation. "I'm not just a pretty face, you know."

I laugh, feeling lighter than I have in weeks. "No, you're also a massive pain in my ass."

"And you wouldn't have me any other way," he retorts, clinking his glass against mine.

As the ouzo flows and the conversation shifts to lighter topics, I find myself grateful for this infuriatingly perceptive friend who always knows how to say exactly what I need to hear—even if I'd never admit it.

Once the dinner concluded, Dimitris, being Dimitris, had insisted on dragging me out to a new club in Navagos, declaring it a test of whether we still had the chops to live up to our old "hit boys" reputation. The moment I stepped inside, the pulsing bass hit me like a physical blow, a visceral thrum that settled in my chest. Neon lights cut through the darkness, painting the crowd in vivid, surreal hues—a sea of youth, abandon, and raw energy.

I slipped my hand into my pocket, fingers brushing the smooth stone I always carried. It grounded me, a small reminder of something real amidst the sensory assault.

"Now this," Dimitris shouted, his voice barely audible over the music, "is more like it!" His green eyes gleamed with a mischievous light as he scanned the dance floor like a predator assessing his prey.

I forced a thin smile. "Great," I muttered, knowing full well he couldn't hear me.

In true Dimitris fashion, he wasted no time, sliding seamlessly into the crowd. Within minutes, he was surrounded by a group of laughing tourists, already halfway into some animated story that was likely exaggerated beyond recognition. He had a way of charming everyone in the room—something I admired, even if it exhausted me.

I made my way to the bar and ordered a beer, leaning against the counter as I took in the scene. The stone in my pocket felt heavier with each passing minute. This world no longer felt like mine; I wasn't sure it ever had.

A blonde woman sidled up next to me, her smile all coy confidence. "Buy me a drink?" she asked, her voice laced with invitation.

For a split second, I considered it. It would be easy to slip into something meaningless, to act like the carefree guy I used to be. But the thought was hollow, leaving a bitter taste in my mouth.

"Sorry," I said, shaking my head. "I was just leaving."

I caught Dimitris' eye from across the room and gestured toward the exit. He raised an eyebrow in question, but I just shrugged and walked out.

The cool night air was a relief, the faint scent of the sea cutting through the neon haze still lingering in my senses. I took a deep breath, letting it steady me as I headed back to my flat.

The condo was perched on the top floor of a modern building at Navagos Marina, floor-to-ceiling glass offering a panoramic view of the darkened sea. It had all the trappings of luxury—sleek lines, expensive furnishings, and a prime location surrounded by designer boutiques and upscale restaurants. I'd bought it after my marriage, a desperate attempt to create some semblance of happiness for my ex-wife and stay close to Seranos. It didn't work. When the marriage ended, she left everything behind, including the flat. I ended up with it, not out of choice, but because she didn't want it. And believe me, I'd paid for it—five times over.

Now, the place served as little more than a convenience. I stayed here sporadically, mainly when I needed to be in town for business; most of the time, I stayed at the farmhouse.

I unlocked the door, the hollow sound of it swinging open echoing in the pristine space. "Home sweet home," I muttered, tossing my keys onto the glass coffee table.

Catching sight of myself in the full-length mirror, I paused. I looked as out of place here as I felt. I always had.

I sank onto the edge of the bed, the weight of the day settling into my shoulders. Pulling out my phone, I scrolled through my contacts, thumb hovering over Eleni's name. I was tempted to call her for a moment—just to hear her voice. But it was late, and what would I even say? I had no right to stir up her life when I hadn't even sorted out my own.

"Get it together, mate," I muttered, dropping the phone onto the nightstand.

The truth was, Dimitris had a point. I hadn't felt this alive in years, and the reason was as clear as the late-night silence of the flat around me. Eleni. Every moment with her, whether it was a fleeting glance or how she furrowed her brow in concentration, seemed to ignite something inside me I thought had been long extinguished.

It wasn't just her beauty, though God knows that was enough to leave me breathless. It was the way she moved, with purpose and grace, as if the whole world could fall apart around her and, she'd still be there, determined to make it right. There was a way she tucked her hair behind her ear when she was deep in thought, the smallest gesture that somehow felt monumental. Or the way she tried to gather her hair into a makeshift ponytail when she was focused on the endless papers in front of her. Her fingers would fumble for a hair tie she didn't have, and with a frustrated huff, she'd let it fall back around her shoulders, a cascade of waves that made my chest ache. It wasn't deliberate—she wasn't trying to be alluring. But that's what made it so captivating. She was just... herself.

And her eyes—those deep hazel eyes—lit up like embers whenever she talked about something that mattered to her. Whether she was brainstorming ideas or passionately defending the grove's future, her voice would quicken, her hands gesturing wildly to punctuate her thoughts. And I couldn't look away. The energy radiating from her was magnetic, her presence filling every inch of the room.

Even in quieter moments, she had a way of getting under my skin, like when she chewed the end of her pen absentmindedly while studying a chart or sighed with exaggerated exasperation after failing to make sense of some overly complicated report. She'd mutter to herself, too quiet for anyone to hear, but I'd catch the words and feel my lips twitch with a smile I couldn't suppress.

Then there were the times she caught me staring—those fleeting seconds when our eyes met across a room. She'd tilt her head, her lips curving in a half-smile, and I'd feel like she'd just reached into my chest and squeezed my heart with her bare hands. Every detail about her drew me in; even her frustration was a kind of poetry. She had a fire in her, a passion I'd forgotten existed in people, let alone myself. It stirred something in me, not just desire but admiration, a longing to be worthy of standing beside someone so fiercely alive.

Dimitris was right. I hadn't felt this alive in years—not since I was young and foolish enough to think I had the world at my feet. And now, here she was, making me feel all over again.

"Fuck," I whispered, the realization hitting me like a punch to the gut. "I'm in love with her."

The words hung in the air, raw and undeniable. It was terrifying and exhilarating all at once. I thought of the way Eleni challenged me, how she saw past my gruff exterior to the man I used to be—the man I wanted to be again.

I ran a hand through my hair, staring into the darkened room. "What are you going to do about it?" I asked myself, but no answer came. Just the lingering weight of the truth and the faint glimmer of hope that maybe—just maybe—I could figure it out before it was too late.

***

Eleni

I stride into the meeting room, my pulse thrumming with anticipation and unease. The air feels thick, charged with an unspoken tension that tightens when my gaze meets Andreas'. For a fleeting moment, I see the boy I once knew, but then his jaw sets, his face hardening into that closed-off mask he's perfected, and the memory slips away like sand through my fingers.

Nikos' voice breaks the silence. "Let's get started. Eleni, I believe you wanted to share some ideas?"

I clear my throat, forcing my nerves down as I straighten in my chair. "Yes. I've been researching sustainable energy solutions—ways to reduce our production costs without compromising the business' future. One of the best options is solar panels. If we—"

"Solar panels?" Andreas cuts in, his voice laced with incredulity. "You want to gamble on solar panels when we barely keep the lights on? Do you even hear yourself?" The heat of his dismissal ignites something in me, and I shoot him a glare. "It's not gambling; it's investing in a long-term solution. Or is thinking about the future too much of a stretch for you these days?"

His eyes flash, a warning. "I call it being realistic. Someone has to be since you're more interested in playing visionary than dealing with the real problem."

I grip the table's edge, my frustration bubbling to the surface. "At least I'm doing something! Your solution seems to be giving up and selling off everything our families worked for. How's that for realism?"

The room falls silent, every eye darting nervously between us. Nikos looks like he's about to interject, but Andreas leans forward, his tone cutting as he speaks.

"You think I want to sell? That it doesn't kill me to even consider it? But sometimes, Eleni, you must know when to cut your losses. Better that than clinging to a sinking ship out of sheer stubbornness."

His words sting, but not as much as the defeat I see simmering behind them. "That's just it, Andreas," I say, my voice quieter now, trembling with something more profound than anger. "You're so afraid of sinking that you've forgotten how to swim. You've forgotten how to fight for something—anything—beyond just surviving. You've forgotten how to hope."

For the briefest moment, his expression cracks, and I glimpse the vulnerability hiding beneath his gruff exterior. The uncertainty. The fear. It's gone as quickly as it appeared, replaced by his impenetrable mask.

"Hope," he says, his voice cold, "doesn't keep the business running. It doesn't pay debts. Maybe you've forgotten that not all of us have the luxury of failing."

His barb cuts deep, but I refuse to let it show. "And maybe you've forgotten that failure isn't the worst thing," I counter, my words sharper now. "The worst thing is never trying. Never risking anything because you're too scared of what might happen if you lose."

There's a flicker of something in his eyes—guilt? Regret?—before he looks away, jaw clenched. "Not all risks are worth taking," he says quietly, the words heavy with unspoken meaning.

"Not all risks are failures," I fire back, my voice softening. "And not everyone is out to hurt you."

The double meaning in my words hangs between us, electric and undeniable. I think he might say something for a moment, but instead, his hands tighten on the table until his knuckles go white. His silence is louder than any argument.

Nikos clears his throat, a nervous cough that feels like a jarring intrusion. "Let's take a break," he says, glancing between us. "We can revisit this once we've all had a chance to reflect."

The room empties quickly, the other department heads practically sprinting for the door. I stay seated, staring at the table, my heart pounding in my chest. My mind replays the argument, the weight of his words clashing with the raw emotion simmering beneath them.

When Andreas finally stands, he hesitates by the door. I feel his gaze on me, but I don't look up. A second later, he's gone, leaving the tension of our unfinished fight lingering in the air.

What just happened? My breath comes out in a shudder. The argument wasn't just about solar panels or business strategy. It was about us, about everything we couldn't say but somehow managed to lay bare. And now, I have no idea where that leaves us.

Later that evening, I sit cross-legged on the floor of my childhood bedroom, surrounded by dusty boxes of my grandfather's belongings. The familiar scent of old paper wafts up as I sift through the chaos. Zeus lies sprawled beside me, his golden head resting on my thigh, watching my every move as though I'm performing the most fascinating magic trick. Ari, on the other hand, perches on the windowsill, his green eyes half-lidded.

"Real smooth today, Eleni," I mutter, glancing at Zeus. "Nothing screams 'competent professional' like picking a fight in front of the entire management team. What do you think? Should I add it to my already impressive résumé of life choices?"

Zeus thumps his tail once, a comforting rhythm that makes me smile despite myself. Ari lets out a low, dismissive meow, as if to say, don't ask me. I've already resigned myself to your questionable decisions.

"Thanks for the vote of confidence, you two," I say, rolling my eyes. I reach into another box, pulling out a stack of photos bound with a faded ribbon. As I untie it, a single image slips loose and lands face-up in my lap.

My breath catches. It's a photo of two children—a six-year-old girl and a thirteen-year-old boy—sitting beneath the sprawling branches of an ancient olive tree. Andreas and me, our faces glowing with sunshine and freedom, his arm draped casually over my shoulders.

"Look at this, Zeus," I whisper, holding the photo up for him. He sniffs it curiously, his nose twitching before softly huffing. "Yeah, that's us. Back when things were... simpler."

Ari hops down from the windowsill and pads over, his tail flicking dismissively before settling a few feet away. He regards the photo with what I can only interpret as mild interest. However, it's likely annoyance at being excluded from whatever is taking my attention away from him.

I trace the edge of the photo, my fingers brushing over our sun-kissed faces. "What would you say, Grandpa?" I murmur. "If you could see us now? Fighting like two overgrown kids in front of everyone you trusted to keep this grove alive. I can almost hear you laughing at how ridiculous we've become."

Zeus nudges my arm with his nose, and I scratch behind his ears absentmindedly. "I know, I know," I say softly. "It's complicated. Life's complicated. But still..." I glance at Ari, "What do you think, Aristotle? Would you bet on us figuring it out?"

Ari blinks once, slowly. If that isn't the feline version of "I wouldn't hold my breath," I don't know what is.

I close my eyes, letting the memory of that day under the olive tree wash over me—the feel of the rough bark against my back, the summer heat on my skin, and the solid, comforting weight of Andreas' arm on my shoulder. The boy in the photo had a quiet determination, a spark that drew me in even then. It's still there, buried beneath layers of fear and frustration, but it's there.

Opening my eyes, I study the photograph again. The years have changed us both, but at this moment, I can still see that boy in him. The same intensity in his eyes, the same set to his jaw when he believes in something—or someone.

"Maybe we're both a little lost," I murmur, stroking Zeus' head.

I prop the photo up on my nightstand, next to the seashell, which was a birthday present from Andreas when I was eight. My gaze lingers on it as I lean back against the bed. Zeus lets out a soft whine, resting his head on my knee again, his eyes filled with unwavering loyalty. "You're right, Zeus," I say, smiling despite the lump forming in my throat. "If I can keep going, maybe Andreas can too. Maybe we both can."

The photograph sits there like a silent promise—a reminder of what once was and a glimmer of what could still be. Not just for the business but for us. If only we're brave enough to try.

***

I nearly jump out of my skin when I hear my name called from the terrace. My first thought is that I've finally lost it—too many late nights and too much olive oil-related stress. But then, I hear it again. Andreas' voice.

I scramble to my feet, scattering the photos I'd been sorting; my heart pounds as I inch toward the door. Andreas? Here? Now? It feels surreal, like the kind of thing that only happens in a half-dream state after too much wine.

Pinching my arm as I push open the terrace door, I whisper to myself, "If this isn't real, my subconscious owes me an explanation."

The cool night air rushes over me as I step outside, and there he is, leaning against the railing, shoulders hunched, looking like he's holding the weight of the world. His usual self-assured stance is gone, replaced by something raw and uncertain. It's almost disarming.

"Eleni," he says, his voice rough, as if dragged over gravel. "I… I need to talk. If that's alright."

I blink, my brain working overtime to process the scene. "Wait. Andreas Papadopoulos voluntarily showing up to talk? Am I dreaming? Should I alert the media, or is this a private event?"

The corner of his mouth twitches, but it's not quite a smile. "It's just me," he says.

"That's exactly what Dream Andreas would say," I counter, crossing my arms as a half-joke, half-shield against the way my pulse has started racing. But I step closer, my humour softening as I take in his face. He looks tired, his eyes clouded with something vulnerable.

"I've been thinking," he begins, his voice measured but hesitant, as though he's testing the waters. His fingers fidget with a small stone in his hand.

"Thinking is good," I say, trying to coax him on. "Some people should try it more often." My attempt at humour earns me a small huff of amusement, but his expression quickly turns serious again.

"About my marriage," he says, and just like that, the air around us changes.

I swallow hard, unsure of what to say. This isn't the kind of conversation I expected when I walked out barefoot, but I nod, letting him continue.

"It was doomed from the start," he says, his voice low and even. "We were too different. She wanted something I could never give her, and I thought... I thought I could make it work through sheer stubbornness."

"But sometimes stubbornness isn't enough," I say gently, finishing the thought for him.

His gaze flickers up to meet mine briefly, and then he looks back at the stone in his hand. "I let everyone down, Eleni. The community, my family... myself."

The vulnerability in his words hits me like a wave, and I fight the urge to reach out and touch his arm. This feels like walking on a tightrope—one misstep, and he might retreat into himself again. "Andreas," I say, trying to keep my voice light but steady, "you can't be everything to everyone. You're not a superhero. Or... okay, maybe a slightly grumpy one, but even superheroes need a break."

That earns me an honest reaction—a quick glance, a ghost of a smirk—but it fades as quickly as it came.

"I can't help it," he says, his voice cracking just slightly. "This place, these people—they're counting on me. On the Papadopoulos name. If I fail..."

"You won't," I interrupt, surprising myself with the intensity of my own voice. "And do you know why? Because you're not alone in this, Andreas. You have people who want to help, who want to see you succeed. If you'd just let them in for once instead of trying to do everything on your own."

He looks at me then, really looks at me, his dark eyes filled with something I can't quite name. It's raw, aching, and so very human. For a moment, I think I've gone too far—that he'll shut down completely. His jaw tightens, and I brace myself for him to brush me off.

But then his shoulders sag just slightly, and he says, almost inaudibly, "Maybe. Anyway, I came to apologize for today."

"You know, for a guy who never talks, you're pretty good at it when you try," I say, attempting to lighten the mood again. "Not bad for a first effort. Gold star for participation."

Andreas shakes his head, a faint smile playing at the corner of his lips. "Thank you," he says abruptly, standing straighter, like the conversation has drained something from him. "For listening."

"Anytime," I say softly, though I'm not sure if he hears me as he turns toward the door.

As Andreas reaches for the terrace door, his hand hovers just above the handle, hesitating. He turns back to me, his gaze meeting mine, holding a mix of uncertainty and—could that be hope?

"Eleni," he says, his voice quieter, gentler than I've ever heard it. "Would you… I mean, if you're not too busy… maybe we could meet at the grove tomorrow? For lunch?"

My heart does an ungraceful flip, but I force myself to play it cool. "Oh?" I ask, tilting my head. "What's the occasion?"

He shrugs, "No occasion. Just thought we both could use a break. Clear our heads a little. No business talk—just Andreas and Eleni. Maybe even having… silly fun."

I blink. Did he just say silly fun? Andreas Papadopoulos? Serious, brooding Andreas? My lips twitch as I try not to laugh. "Silly fun, huh? That's a bold proposal."

His smile softens, just a flicker of warmth, but enough to make my chest tighten. "It's been known to happen," he murmurs, then glances away as if suddenly unsure of himself.

I nod, probably more enthusiastically than I mean to. "Sure, that sounds nice. I'd like that."

He lingers for a second as though there's more he wants to say, but instead, he nods and disappears into the night, the soft click of the terrace door echoing in his wake.

I exhale, leaning against the railing as my thoughts race. This is good, right? A chance to spend time with him away from the weight of the village, the business, and all the responsibilities bearing down on us. Maybe out there, in the quiet of the olive grove, under those ancient, knowing trees, we'll finally find the space to—

I catch myself before the thought runs away from me. Because even as I indulge in this flicker of hope, that familiar doubt creeps in. Andreas is still holding back. I can feel the unspoken truths hovering just beneath the surface, threatening to break through but never quite making it. His honesty about his failed marriage and the crushing weight of expectations was a start, but I know there's more.

"Oh, Andreas," I mutter into the night, resting my chin in my hand. "Why is trusting me so hard for you?"

The frustrated part of me wants to grab him by the shoulders and demand he tell me everything, every last hidden fear and secret. But another part—the part that understands the quiet, unyielding strength he wears like armour—knows better. After all, I'm guarding my heart too, in my own way. Aren't we all?

I sigh, my gaze drifting to the moonlit sea, the waves shimmering like quicksilver in the distance. Tomorrow at the grove. It's a start. And maybe—just maybe—amidst the serenity of trees, we'll find the courage to drop our guards, to stop dancing around what we're afraid to admit.

"At the very least," I say to the cool night air, a wry smile tugging at my lips, "it'll be a pretty backdrop while we tiptoe around our feelings."

An Olive Grove Affair

By mid-morning, I found myself pacing the village square, waiting for Andreas to pick me up. I'd been so excited about our plan that I'd skipped work entirely—today was about relaxing anyway, right? My mind had been buzzing since I woke up, and choosing what to wear for this so-called "silly fun" had turned into a full-blown crisis. It wasn't exactly a dress code I was familiar with, especially considering the person who coined it was Andreas.

With him, "silly fun" could mean anything. We could end up playing football at the beach, or he might decide to throw me into the sea, clothes and all, just for his own amusement. After much deliberation and a few failed outfits, I settled on a trusty pair of denim shorts and a V-neck t-shirt—the kind I knew Andreas had a tendency to peek at when he thought I wasn't paying attention. If we were doing "silly fun," I figured I might as well come armed. A girl needs every advantage she can get.

When his car pulled up, I barely had time to take a deep breath before I hopped in. Andreas leaned over, his proximity sending my heart into overdrive, and greeted me with a casual peck on the cheek. It was brief, unassuming—and far more nerve-wracking than I wanted to admit.

We set off in silence, the warmth of the sun spilling through the windows as a soft sea breeze filled the car. Andreas' expression was relaxed, his body language easy, and I found myself mirroring his calm demeanour despite the flutter of excitement in my chest. He wore khaki shorts and a linen shirt with the sleeves rolled up to his elbows, his sun-tanned arms resting casually on the steering wheel. Of course, his shirt had far too many buttons undone for my peace of mind. The tan skin and hint of muscle peeking through were impossible to ignore, and when I stole a glance, his lips quirked into a knowing smirk.

He knew I was checking him out. Jerk.

Desperate to regain some semblance of control over my racing thoughts, I shifted my gaze away from him, and that's when I spotted it—a picnic basket perched on the backseat. It was neatly packed and clearly brimming with food. The sight sent a little jolt of surprise through me. Andreas and preparation weren't two words I often associated together.

"Now, now," I teased, trying to suppress my smile. "Isn't that basket lovely?"

Andreas glanced at me, his smirk growing into a full grin. "Oh, that. It's great, isn't it? In a way I can't even begin to comprehend, my mum somehow found out about our little grove lunch escapade. She decided that I'm incapable of feeding you properly and might tarnish the family name, so she took matters into her own hands."

I laughed, shaking my head. "In this village, information travels faster than light."

"Clearly," Andreas replied dryly, glancing at the road ahead. "And before you ask, yes, those are your favourite feta, tomato, and cucumber sandwiches in there."

I turned to him, feigning shock. "No. With the drizzle of olive oil, thyme, and basil?"

He nodded, the corner of his mouth lifting in amusement. "Exactly the way you like them. Mum made sure of it."

"I love her so much," I said enthusiastically, practically beaming.

Andreas chuckled, a deep sound that sent a pleasant warmth through me. "Do you remember how you used to squeeze the sandwiches before eating them? You'd crush them in your hands until the bread soaked up all the olive oil and tomato juice. They looked disgusting."

I snorted, shaking my head. "I was a child of exceptional culinary standards, okay? Sophisticated gastronomic palettes demand proper technique."

"Sure," he said with mock seriousness.

We both laughed, the sound filling the car and mingling with the soft rustle of the wind. The conversation shifted to easy small talk, a playful back-and-forth that felt as natural as breathing. It wasn't heavy or loaded with the weight of unspoken emotions—just light, peaceful chatter that set the tone for the day ahead.

As the car wound its way through the familiar roads toward the olive grove, I leaned back in my seat, feeling more at ease than I had in weeks. The sun danced on the dashboard, the breeze carried the faint scent of salt and wildflowers, and the promise of a simple, carefree afternoon stretched out before us. Whatever this day held, I couldn't help but think it was already off to a perfect start.

***

The sun was high when we reached the farmhouse, casting a golden haze over the olive groves. The air was warm, but a gentle breeze carried the coolness of the sea, and crickets sang their steady chorus.

While Andreas began unloading the car, watching him in his element—comfortable, at ease—felt oddly soothing. For a moment, I stood there, absorbing the scene. This place, this man... it all felt so achingly right, even if my emotions were still a mess.

He straightened, catching me watching him. "How about we go down to the beach for a picnic?" he suggested, his voice casual, though his eyes held that familiar spark. "I'll grab some towels and beers. I've got cold ones in the fridge."

I snorted, unable to hide my grin. "Of course you do. You'd never be caught unprepared without your precious beer. Yeah, let's do it—I'm already sold on the idea."

But as soon as I said it, reality hit. "Uh, Andreas," I said hesitantly, "I didn't bring a swimsuit. Kind of a crucial picnic-at-the-beach item, don't you think?"

His smirk was instantaneous, and the mischievous glint in his eyes made my stomach flip. "That's fine. You can swim naked. I promise I won't find it… 'inappropriate.'" His tone dripped with amusement, throwing my own snarky comment from weeks ago right back at me. It felt like a lifetime ago, yet the memory still flushed my cheeks.

I rolled my eyes. "Yeah, I'm sure you'd love that. But seriously, what am I supposed to do?"

Andreas leaned against the car, still grinning. "Go to the bedroom," he said, pointing inside. "Top drawer of the chest. Callie leaves a few swimsuits here for when she visits."

"Convenient," I said while heading inside, leaving Andreas to gather the rest of the supplies.

The bedroom felt like it belonged to another era, with mismatched furniture and decor dominated by our families' relics. The chest of drawers had clearly seen better days, its surface worn smooth by years of use. Yet, amidst all the nostalgia, the room unmistakably felt like Andreas. A t-shirt was draped over the back of a chair, the bed was haphazardly made, and his cologne's faint, woodsy scent lingered in the air. It was intimate, in a way that made my heart thud uncomfortably in my chest. I also couldn't stop asking myself: does this man ever sleep at his own place? Judging by the state of the room, it looked like he practically lived here. The farmhouse didn't just feel like a stopover for him; it felt lived in, claimed.

I found a simple, comfortable swimsuit in the top drawer, pulling it out quickly before my brain could overanalyse the fact that I was standing in Andreas' bedroom, surrounded by his things. As I changed, I caught myself glancing at the t-shirt on the chair. For one ridiculous moment, I was tempted to bury my nose in it, but I shook the thought away, giving myself a stern mental lecture. Get it together, Eleni.

When I stepped back outside, Andreas was waiting, with the picnic basket in one hand and two packs of beer dangling from the other. He looked up as I approached, his expression unreadable for a split second before it morphed into a grin.

"Do you think we have enough beer?" I teased, raising an eyebrow. "Are you trying to get me drunk, Papadopoulos?"

He laughed, the sound rich and unrestrained. "Stop talking, Katsaros," he said in mock seriousness. "Pick up those towels and follow me."

"Yes, sir," I replied with a dramatic salute, scooping up the towels as instructed.

***

He started walking toward the path that wound down to the beach, the muscles in his arms flexing slightly under the basket's weight. I trailed behind, watching the easy way he moved. The sound of the waves grew louder as we neared the beach with the soft hiss of the breeze through the trees. The day had already been promising, but with Andreas leading the way and the prospect of a quiet afternoon by the water, it felt like something more—a memory in the making.

The beach was exactly as I remembered it—a quiet, unspoiled stretch of sand shaded by the familiar olive tree that had seen its fair share of our childhood picnics. The sun bathed everything in gold, casting rippling reflections across the water. Andreas set the basket down with an easy familiarity, settling under the tree as though no time had passed since we'd last done this.

He popped the caps off two beers with practised ease, handing me one as he leaned back against the trunk. I let the cool bottle rest against my palm for a moment before taking a sip, savouring the crisp bitterness that paired perfectly with the salty breeze.

"This spot hasn't changed," I said, glancing at the lapping waves in the distance. "Except maybe the boats. There seem to be more of them now."

Andreas followed my gaze, his expression softening. "It used to be my dream to be on one of those. A skipper, sailing the Aegean, maybe even beyond."

I turned to him, surprised. "Really? I don't remember that."

"I didn't talk about it much," he admitted, his lips curving into a faint smile. "It was more of a fantasy than a plan. I always thought about it—feeling the wind, the freedom."

I chuckled, imagining a younger Andreas with sun-bleached hair, a captain's hat too big for his head, steering an imaginary boat. "What stopped you?"

He shrugged, taking another swig of his beer. "Life. The grove. Responsibilities." He paused, then added with a smirk, "And the fact that I may get seasick sometimes."

I burst out laughing, nearly choking on my sandwich. "Captain Andreas, ruler of the high seas… until the waves get choppy."

We shared a smile, the kind that comes from years of shared memories and easy familiarity. For a moment, it felt like we were kids again, sitting under this same tree with no idea how complicated life could get.

Andreas nudged me with his elbow. "Come on," he said, setting his empty beer bottle down. "Let's go swim."

The sea shimmered invitingly, but I shivered as I dipped my toes in. "It's freezing!" I complained, inching forward reluctantly.

Andreas, however, had other plans. He bolted past me, the water splashing around him as he ran, laughing like a teenager. Before I could react, he turned, cupped his hands, and sent a wave of cold water directly at me.

"Ah!" I shrieked, trying to shield myself. "Andreas! Stop it—"

But he wasn't done. With a wicked grin, he grabbed me by the waist. He unceremoniously shoved me deeper into the water, his laughter echoing across the beach.

"Unbelievable!" I sputtered, wiping salt water from my face as he doubled over with laughter, so clearly proud of himself. "You're such a child!"

"You love it," he teased, backing away just as I lunged for him.

A full-blown water war followed—splashing, shouting, and more laughing than I'd done in years. We tried to drown each other in jest and recreated our old favourite game: me climbing onto Andreas' shoulders to attempt a "graceful" dive into the sea. It was far from aesthetic, but the laughter that followed was worth it.

By the time we stumbled out of the water, our bodies were chilled to the bone, our fingers shrivelled like prunes, and our cheeks aching from smiling. We collapsed onto the sand, neither of us bothering with the towels. The warmth of the sun and the grains of sand beneath us felt familiar.

Lying on my back, I stared at the clear sky, feeling the sun dry the saltwater on my skin. Andreas was beside me, close enough that our shoulders touched. Neither of us spoke; there was no need to. The sound of the waves, steady and unchanging, filled the silence like a soothing lullaby.

Then, without a word, I felt his hand brush against mine in the sand. Slowly, deliberately, he slid his fingers between mine, interlacing them with an ease that felt so natural, so right, it took my breath away. I turned my head to glance at him, but his eyes were closed, his face relaxed in the sun. It wasn't a gesture meant to be noticed or commented on—it simply was.

And so I didn't speak. I didn't pull away. I just stayed there, letting the moment wrap around us like a warm blanket. We lay like that for what felt like hours, our hands intertwined, our shoulders touching, the world narrowing to the soft rhythm of the waves and the sunlight drying our skin.

***

Once we were dry and the sun started to feel less like a warm hug and more like a full-blown roasting, we retreated to the shade of the tree. Andreas popped open another beer bottle—because, of course he did—and rummaged through the picnic basket until he found the box of cherries his mum had packed. He wasted no time devouring them, eating them with the kind of reverence usually reserved for sacred rituals.

"You and your cherries," I teased, watching him.

"What can I say?" he replied, shrugging. Then, without warning, his expression shifted, his eyes sharpening as they fixed on mine. "What about you, Eleni?" he asked, his tone curious but sincere. "How was life in London? What were you up to all these years?"

The question caught me off guard but in the best way. Andreas rarely steered conversations toward me, and his sudden interest made me sit up a little straighter. "Well," I started, brushing some sand off my knees, "after school, my father decided it was his mission to launch my career. He arranged a couple of 'dream job' interviews—his dreams, not mine. Unsurprisingly, they didn't go well."

Andreas snorted, already amused. "Classic Petros," he commented, his tone dripping with sarcasm.

I laughed. "Eventually, I settled into a decent marketing job. It wasn't thrilling, but it paid the bills. My dad, ever the pragmatist, bought me a small flat as a 'kick-start' in life. Of course, it came with a side of guilt-laden responsibility. You know, 'improve your circumstances if you want more luxury,' that sort of thing."

Andreas shook his head, his lip curling in mock disdain. "Nice. Very Petros again."

I grinned. "I thought so, too. Anyway, my life revolved around that flat, work, a couple of weeks of yearly holiday, and the occasional night out with friends. When I talk about it now, it feels like it happened a million years ago, but really, it's been—what? Less than two months?" The realisation hit me like a gust of wind, and I trailed off, glancing around. The olive trees swayed gently in the breeze, their silver-green leaves glinting in the sunlight. The sea shimmered in the distance. It all felt so surreal compared to the routine monotony of my life in London.

Apparently noticing I'd drifted off into my thoughts, Andreas broke the silence with a pointed question. "No boyfriends?"

I blinked, startled. "Right now?"

"Well, yeah. Right now... and before," he clarified, amused by my reaction.

I hesitated for a moment before answering. "Right now, no. But I've had my share of... disappointments."

He raised an eyebrow, his curiosity piqued. "Callie mentioned you had a serious relationship a few years ago. Nearly got engaged?"

"Ah, Archie." I let out a dry laugh. "That's a sad one. He was this upper-middle-class boy, all polished and proper, working in finance in London. We were quite a match—on paper, anyway. My dad was over the moon, naturally. I think it was the first time he really believed I'd achieved something significant. Archie ticked all his boxes."

Andreas snorted, rolling his eyes. "I bet he did."

"To be fair, Archie wasn't a bad guy," I continued, my tone softening. "He was handsome in his own way, charming enough. And his mother? Oh, she was a gem. I even thought I loved him for a while—or maybe I just loved how happy he made my dad. Either way, it was easy. Comfortable. Everyone expected a proposal, even me. But then... well, then I found out he was cheating on me with someone from his office."

Andreas stiffened, his jaw tightening. "Bastard," he muttered, anger flashing in his eyes. "Please tell me you slapped him. Or threw something heavy at him."

"Sadly, no violence was involved," I said with a rueful smile. "But if it helps, I later found out he'd cheated on me a couple of times before that, so I ended things pretty quickly."

"If he were here," Andreas said darkly, "I'd drown him in two minutes flat."

"Tempting as that is, I think I'll pass," I replied, shaking my head. "Besides, I got my closure. Long story short, that relationship ended, leaving me with a stellar self-confidence level and an unwavering trust in men. Obviously."

Andreas looked at me then, his expression softening in a way that made my chest tighten. "Hence, here you are now," he said quietly. "And for what it's worth, I'm glad for that."

His words hit me harder than I expected, their warmth melting away the lingering bitterness of the memory. I smiled, feeling a little lighter.

The rest of the afternoon passed in a blissful haze of swimming, chatting, and teasing each other about anything and everything. We were both ravenous again when the sun dipped lower in the sky, painting the horizon in fiery hues.

Andreas turned to me as we packed up. "How about I whip up something back at the farmhouse? You can't tell me you're ready for this day to end just yet."

I didn't even hesitate. "Absolutely not," I said, grinning. "Lead the way, Captain Cherries."

His laugh echoed over the waves, and I couldn't think of a better way to close the day.

As we neared the farmhouse, I noticed Andreas' pace quicken. At first, I didn't think much of it. Maybe he was eager to drop off the basket or craving another beer—classic Andreas priorities. But then, his steps turned into an outright sprint, and for a good ten seconds, I stood there like an idiot, blinking after him, completely baffled. And then it hit me. Oh no. Oh no, no, no. Rookie mistake, Eleni.

I broke into a run, shouting as I tried to catch up, but the odds were stacked against me. Andreas had a head start, considerably longer legs, and, most importantly, the unbridled determination of a man chasing victory. My protests were as effective as throwing pebbles at a tank.

"Andreas, don't you dare!" I yelled, my voice rising in panic. "I swear, I'll kill you! And then I'll tell Mama Maria what you did so she can kill you again! Andreas! Don't be a jerk!"

But it was useless. He'd already reached the outside shower and turned the water on, the victorious laugh of a 12-year-old trapped in a grown man echoing across the yard.

"You can always join me, Eleni!" he shouted, his voice dripping with amusement.

"In your dreams!" I fired back, stopping in my tracks and crossing my arms, simultaneously furious and resigned.

I stomped over to the wooden picnic table. I sat down with a dramatic huff, sulking as I listened to the sound of water cascading and—oh, because of course—Andreas singing. Loudly. Off-key. It was all so aggravatingly familiar.

The thing about the farmhouse was that we had this outdoor shower—more like the ones you find at beaches, really, with a simple spout and no privacy. The "luxury" came from the solar-heated water tank on the roof. After spending the whole day soaking up the sun, the water would reach the perfect temperature for a shower. It wasn't endless, though. Once the hot water was gone, you were stuck with icy cold until the tank reheated the next afternoon.

Growing up, this system was a battleground. Maria and Grandma, the household enforcers, had a strict no sand in the house policy. And trust me, they were like bloodhounds when it came to finding even a speck of sand. So after a trip to the beach, showers were mandatory before we could step foot indoors. The tank usually had enough hot water for all three of us—Callie, Andreas, and me. But Andreas, being the opportunistic menace that he was, always made sure to outrun us, monopolising the hot water and leaving Callie and me shivering under the cold tap. Maria would yell at him every single time, threatening to ground him or ban the beach, but nothing ever deterred him.

Now, nearly two decades later, here I was again, sitting on the same picnic table, listening to his ridiculous shower antics and silently begging the universe to spare me a few drops of warm water.

When Andreas finally stepped out from behind the shower curtain (if you could even call it that), he was still grinning like the smug idiot he was. Water dripped from his hair, and his grin widened when he saw the glare I was sending his way.

"Don't cry, Leni," he said, tilting his head in mock sympathy. "I left you some hot water. But you'd better be quick." His tone was so unbearably proud of himself, it was almost impressive.

I narrowed my eyes at him, pointing accusingly. "You're the cruellest of them all, Andreas. A bad, bad boy. Don't think I won't tell Maria. She'll ground you for life!"

He laughed, utterly unbothered by my threats. "And how is she going to do that?"

"Don't kid yourself," I shot back, unable to keep the corner of my mouth from twitching. "She'll find a way."

He chuckled, running a towel over his hair as he walked toward the house. "Good luck with your shower, Katsaros," he called over his shoulder.

***

Andreas

Inside the farmhouse, the air was cooler, the sunlight filtering through the weathered shutters. I grabbed a towel and dried myself absentmindedly, a self-satisfied grin still plastered across my face. The faint sound of Eleni's grumbling drifted through the open windows as she finally took her turn in the outdoor shower. If I knew her at all—and I did—she was cursing me under her breath for hogging the hot water.

I moved toward the kitchen, pulling open the fridge to inspect the possibilities for dinner. A jar of olives, some feta, some tomatoes... Maybe some pasta? Eleni always loved her pasta after a long day at sea. My hand hovered over the olives, but my thoughts were far from food.

The day at the beach played back in my mind like a favourite movie reel. Her laugh—the way it rang out, unrestrained and infectious—still echoed in my ears. We'd fallen into an effortless rhythm, the kind that comes from years of shared history. But it wasn't just the nostalgia that got to me. It was her.

Seeing her so carefree, her guard down, was intoxicating. Watching her splash and play in the sea, her hair a wild mess, and the sun turning her skin golden did something to me. It wasn't just longing; it was something deeper, more consuming. Every smile, every teasing remark, and every stubborn challenge she threw my way only drew me in further.

Eleni had always been a force to be reckoned with, even as a child. But now? She was luminous and magnetic, making it impossible to look away. And when she'd perched on my shoulders, wobbling dramatically before flopping into the water with all the grace of a falling olive branch, I'd felt more alive than I had in years.

The sound of her voice pulled me out of my thoughts, soft at first, then rising into an exaggerated monologue. It wasn't directed at me—no, Eleni was talking to someone else entirely.

"Well, my feathered friends," she said, towel in hand as she rubbed it through her damp hair, "you've witnessed it first-hand. The true villain of this story is Andreas Papadopoulos." She paused for dramatic effect as though expecting applause—or bird chirps of agreement.

"This," she continued, gesturing vaguely toward the outdoor shower, "is the kind of man who hogs all the hot water. I mean, is this fair? Is this gentlemanly behaviour?" She looked up at the olive branches as if seeking judgment from the local wildlife. "No. No, it is not."

I couldn't help but grin, leaning against the doorway where I had a perfect view of her little performance.

"And do you know what makes it worse?" she went on, flipping her hair dramatically and waving the towel like a prop in some tragic play. "He's not even sorry. Not even a little! A true menace."

I couldn't hold it in any longer. A low chuckle escaped before I could stop myself. Stepping out of the doorway, hands tucked into my pockets, my breath hitched.

She was standing on the patio, towel in hand, rubbing it through her hair with quick, frustrated movements. The sunlight kissed her damp skin, making her shimmer like something out of a dream. Her bare shoulders glistened as she tilted her head, drying her hair; that ridiculous V-neck t-shirt she'd worn earlier was clinging to her in places now, her denim shorts slightly darker at the edges where the fabric hadn't dried yet.

The little things about her were holding me captive. The curve of her neck, the subtle tilt of her head, and the small smile playing on her lips as she talked to no one in particular—all of it stirred something in me that was both familiar and completely new. It wasn't just desire, though that was undeniably there, humming under the surface, a constant that pulled at the edges of my resolve and left me wondering how I'd managed to keep my distance this long. It was the ache of wanting more—more of her laughter, more of her wit, more of her. And it wasn't just about how stunning she looked in that moment; it was about how she made me feel like myself again.

She caught me staring, of course.

"What?" she called, narrowing her eyes but clearly amused. "You've got something to say, or are you just going to stand there smirking like the villain you are?"

I stepped out of the doorway, leaning casually against the frame. "I was just enjoying the show," I said, grinning. "You always were a little dramatic, Leni."

I started the pasta inside the farmhouse and poured two glasses of wine. Eleni wandered in just as I placed hers on the counter, her towel now hanging over one shoulder. She accepted the glass without a word and took a long sip before suspiciously eyeing me.

"Pasta?" she asked, lifting her glass and taking a sip. "Is this your attempt at seduction, Papadopoulos? A man and his signature dish?"

I raised an eyebrow. "Seduction requires effort. This is survival."

She grinned, watching as I rummaged through a drawer for a pot. "I hope you're better at survival now than when we were kids. Your survival skills back then included eating cherries until you nearly made yourself sick."

"Worked, didn't it? Still alive." I filled the pot with water, setting it on the stove. "And if I remember correctly, you were the one who nearly burned down the farmhouse trying to make toast."

"One time," she said, holding up a hand, "and I still maintain that toaster was defective."

I smirked, grabbing a handful of salt and tossing it into the water. "Of course. Nothing's ever Eleni's fault."

When everything was ready, I topped the pasta with feta before sliding her plate across the counter. She inspected it as if it were a work of art, her fork hovering in mid-air.

"Well?" I asked, leaning against the counter. "What's the verdict?"

She took a bite, chewing slowly before nodding once. "Not bad," she said. "Better than your usual fare."

"High praise," I muttered, taking a bite myself. "Coming from someone whose cooking repertoire includes toast and microwave soup."

Her eyes gleamed as she pointed her fork at me. "Careful, Andreas. Keep this up, and I might start thinking you're trying to impress me."

I didn't reply immediately, letting the moment hang between us. Instead, I raised my glass to hers in a silent toast. She held my gaze for a moment longer before clinking her glass against mine, the faintest hint of a smile playing at her lips.

The tension broke as she turned back to her plate, the banter fading into a quieter rhythm as we ate. The conversation may have slowed, but the air between us crackled just the same. As always, with Eleni, it was never just about the words.

***

Eleni

I would never say it out loud, but that pasta was incredible. Every bite was a revelation and the fact that Andreas had made it? That only added to the experience. But as good as the food was, watching him cook had been even better. The way he moved—calm, deliberate, yet somehow effortlessly confident—kept my attention locked on him.

The earlier ease between us, the laughter and teasing, had shifted into something else entirely. The air between us felt charged, humming with an unspoken tension that neither of us was ready to name. Every glance he sent my way seemed to linger a fraction too long. Every smile I gave him felt like a risk. And though neither of us acknowledged it, we were both circling the inevitable.

After we ate, Andreas cleared the plates and stood, announcing that he'd handle the dishes. "A peace offering for the shower," he said, smirking.

I hopped onto the counter near the sink and settled in to watch him work. The room was quiet, save for the soft clinking of dishes and the rush of water. He was focused, his expression thoughtful, his jaw tightening occasionally as though he was wrestling with something unsaid.

My gaze kept drifting to him—how could it not? The muscles in his arms, the faint shadow of stubble on his jaw, the way a stray lock of hair fell across his forehead. Even in this mundane act, he seemed entirely magnetic. My chest felt tight, the tension between us curling in the pit of my stomach and spreading outward.

When he finished, he turned off the tap, drying his hands slowly with a towel. His movements were unhurried, almost too deliberate. I set my glass down, feigning composure I didn't feel. In the name of being a responsible adult—or perhaps out of fear of what might happen if I stayed any longer—I cleared my throat.

"I think it's time for me to go," I said softly, trying to keep my tone light.

He stilled, towel in hand, turning toward me. His brow furrowed slightly, and for a moment, he just looked at me—too long, too intensely. The seriousness in his eyes made my breath catch, and I felt the full weight of that unspoken something we'd both been avoiding all day.

He set the towel aside and stepped closer, the floor creaking softly under his weight. When he reached me, he placed his hands on either side of my thighs, leaning in until his face was so close that I could feel the warmth of his breath against my cheek.

"Is it, Eleni?" he asked, his voice low and quiet. "Are you sure?"

His proximity scattered my thoughts. The heat radiating from him, the intensity of his gaze—everything narrowed to this moment. A soft, involuntary sound escaped my lips, somewhere between a sigh and a plea.

"Maybe not?" I managed, though my voice was barely more than a whisper.

His hands gently came up to cradle my face, his fingers brushing softly along my jaw. His eyes locked onto mine—dark, searching, and intent—as though he was looking for an answer I wasn't sure I had to give.

"Not yet," he murmured, his voice as soft as the space between us.

The words hung suspended between us, charged with possibility. His thumb traced my cheekbone, a touch so gentle it sent electricity racing through me. I wanted to close the distance, to bridge every unspoken thing between us. Still, something held me back—a delicate balance of desire and restraint.

He leaned closer, his lips nearly brushing mine—a whisper of a touch that felt more like a question than a kiss. My heart thundered, every sense heightened, waiting.

When his lips finally met mine, it was nothing like I'd imagined. Soft yet urgent, tender yet consuming. His hands slid to my waist, pulling me closer until there was no space left between us. My fingers tangled in his hair, anchoring myself in this moment.

Effortlessly, he lifted me, setting me on the edge of the dining table. His hands were on my hips, strong and steady, as his lips left mine and began a trail of slow, deliberate kisses along my jaw, down to the hollow of my throat. Each touch felt like a promise, a claim, as though he were tracing a map of me, memorising every inch.

My hands explored him in turn, running over the hard planes of his shoulders and the taut strength of his back.

It was overwhelming, this closeness, this intensity that felt like it might consume us both. When his hand slid beneath my t-shirt, his fingertips skimming the curve of my waist, I gasped, my head falling back, giving him access to more of me.

He paused, his forehead resting against mine, his breathing ragged. "Eleni," he said, my name a plea, a question, a reverence all at once.

I cupped his face, my fingers brushing against the stubble along his jaw, forcing him to meet my gaze. "Don't you dare stop now, Andreas," I said, my voice trembling but resolute.

A soft, breathless laugh escaped him, and his eyes burned with something that felt like both longing and relief. "I wasn't planning to," he murmured before his lips found mine again, fiercer this time, as though every argument, every unspoken feeling, every hesitation had melted into this moment, poured out through the press of his body against mine.

Right here, right now, nothing else mattered. Not tomorrow, not next week, not the uncertainty of everything outside this room. All I knew was how he made me feel—the way his breath sent sparks across my skin and his weight pressed against me, grounding me and igniting me all at once. His fingertips left tingling trails as they moved with purpose, learning every curve, every edge of me. I needed him. I not just wanted but needed to feel his touch, to have him close, to lose myself in him in a way I never had with anyone else.

My hands explored him with growing urgency. I felt the rhythm of his heartbeat through his shirt, rapid and wild. When my fingers clutched the fabric, pulling him closer, a sound escaped him—part growl, part surrender.

His lips traced a path down my jaw, each kiss leaving a trail of heat. I gasped at the sensitive curve of my neck, my hands clutching his shoulders. When he pulled back, our foreheads together, his breathing ragged, his eyes asked a question words couldn't capture. I brushed my thumb against his chest, a soft smile playing on my lips. "What are you waiting for, Andreas?" The words came out steady, despite the fire consuming me.

His lips twitched into a warm, unguarded, and devastatingly tender smile. Without a word, he guided me toward the bedroom, his steps deliberate but unhurried, as though every second carried its own weight. When we reached the edge of the bed, he started to undress me, every touch sending shivers all over my body. His hands moved to my waist, firm but gentle as he eased me down onto the soft mattress.

I barely had time to adjust before he was above me, his body hovering, his presence overwhelming. His touch was a study in restraint, achingly gentle as his fingers explored every curve and hollow of my body. He started at my shoulder, the warmth of his hand trailing down to my collarbone, gliding along my ribs before resting on my breast. His thumb brushed over my hardened nipple with deliberate softness, and I arched into him instinctively, a quiet moan spilling from my lips. He paused, his eyes gleaming with mischief, a hint of a smile betraying his teasing intent.

Slowly, as if savouring every moment, Andreas bent his head, his lips grazing the sensitive skin of my collarbone. The featherlight touch ignited a ripple of heat that spread through me, making my pulse race. He kissed the hollow of my throat and the swell of my breast, his mouth lingering just enough to tease before moving lower, leaving a trail of heat in its wake. Each kiss, each touch was unhurried, like a sculptor committing every detail of his masterpiece to memory.

"Andreas," I whispered, my voice breaking on his name, equal parts plea and surrender. My hands found his shoulders, desperate for something to hold on to as the ache inside me grew unbearable.

He responded with a soft hum, his lips curving against my skin as if he took pleasure in my unravelling. His tongue flicked over a sensitive peak, and my body arched of its own accord, chasing the sensation. His hand drifted lower, skimming the sensitive skin of my inner thigh, his fingers just shy of where I craved him most. I parted my legs instinctively, my body answering a call I could no longer resist.

He paused, lifting his head to meet my gaze, his eyes dark with desire yet tempered by an aching tenderness. "Tell me what you want," he murmured, his voice thick and heavy with the promise of what was to come.

"You," I breathed, the word barely more than a whisper. "I want all of you."

At my admission, something shifted. His restraint cracked, giving way to a raw, consuming passion, though he still moved with infuriating patience. His lips claimed mine, the kiss deep and searching, as his hand found the heart of my need. His touch was both a torment and a balm, his fingers stroking with an exquisite precision that had me trembling beneath him.

The tension inside me built to a breaking point, my every nerve alight, my body arching to meet his. When he finally positioned himself above me, his hand bracing my hip, I held my breath, the moment suspended in perfect anticipation. He finally joined us slowly, agonisingly, the sensation a rush of exquisite relief and overwhelming fullness. A gasp escaped me as we became one, our bodies fitting together in a way that felt inevitable, destined.

And then we moved, our rhythm unhurried yet impossibly consuming, a perfect dance of bodies and souls. Every thrust, every sigh, every whispered word of love etched itself into my very being, the longing now a profound connection that anchored me to him completely. Time ceased to matter, the world dissolving until only this—only us—remained.

The Olive Grove Drama Society

Andreas
The first rays of sunlight crept into the room, bathing it in soft light. Eleni was still asleep beside me, her breathing steady and calm. She lay on her stomach, her head turned slightly, her hair spread out across the pillow. The sheet had slipped down her back, revealing the gentle line of her spine. She looked peaceful, entirely at ease, and I couldn't look away.

I thought back to last night. The way she moved with me, trusted me felt like nothing else existed in the world but us. It wasn't just the physical connection—it was how she looked at me, how she reached for me. It was so much more than I'd ever hoped for, and I realized how deeply it had changed something inside me.

Careful not to wake her, I leaned forward and pressed a soft kiss to her shoulder, savouring the warmth of her skin against my lips. She stirred slightly but didn't wake. I pulled back and stood, dressing quickly, and made my way to the kitchen.

As the coffee brewed, the steady sound of the machine filled the quiet farmhouse. Once I poured myself a mug, I stepped out onto the porch, letting the crisp morning air wrap around me. The olive trees swayed gently in the distance, their branches catching the first light of the day. I slipped a hand into my pocket, my thumb tracing the familiar smooth surface of the pebble I always carried. The events of last night replayed in my mind, vivid and inescapable. Alongside the warmth of those memories came a pang of unease, sharp and unwelcome.

Do I know how to do this anymore? The question lingered, heavy and insistent. After everything I'd been through, could I allow myself to hope, to risk something so fragile? The fear of dragging Eleni into my chaos, of hurting her, twisted inside me. She deserved more—so much more than I could be certain I could give her.

And yet, the thought of stepping away, of letting this end before it even began, felt unbearable. My chest tightened at the very idea. Every moment with her last night—her laughter, her touch, her unwavering belief in me—was etched into me, too powerful to ignore.

I drew in a deep breath, willing the racing thoughts to slow. The day stretched ahead, quiet and full of possibility.

And so, it seemed, did everything between us.

I don't know how long I stood there, lost in my thoughts, the coffee cooling in my hand as the morning stretched on. The sound of footsteps broke through my mental fog, and I turned to see Eleni coming into the living room.

"I can smell the coffee. Is there enough for me too?" she asked, her voice light, almost casual, like this was just another morning. But her eyes betrayed her. There was a quiet anticipation there, laced with anxiety, worry, and something that twisted my chest—hope. Hope mixed with a deep, unspoken fear that I might treat last night as if it didn't mean anything.

She looked so vulnerable standing there, trying to keep herself steady, so afraid I might let her down. That fragility, that trust she had placed in me, hit me harder than I expected. I could see it clearly now—she was in love and she was terrified. Realizing what she might think and be bracing herself for broke me in ways I hadn't thought possible.

I couldn't let her carry that fear. I didn't know where this would lead or if I was capable of being the man she deserved, but I knew one thing: I couldn't let her think, even for a moment, that she meant less to me than she did. She wasn't a fling, and this wasn't casual. It was something I hadn't even dared to name yet, but it was real, and it was hers.

Setting aside my doubts, I forced a warm smile and stepped toward her. My hands settled lightly on her waist, pulling her closer. I kissed her softly—a quick, gentle reassurance that I hoped would say everything I couldn't yet put into words.

"Of course there is," I said. "Captain Andreas is at your service, milady."

The corners of her mouth twitched into a smile, and then she laughed—a light, genuine laugh that softened the tension in her face. It wasn't everything, not yet. But there was relief in her eyes, a flicker of trust that hadn't been there a moment ago. Not complete, but enough to remind me how much she was willing to believe in me, in us.

"Captain Andreas, huh?" she teased, the playfulness returning to her voice. "I hope you're as good at pouring coffee as stealing all the hot water."

I chuckled, stepping back just enough to grab her a mug. "You might be pleasantly surprised," I said, handing it to her.

She took it, her fingers brushing mine briefly, and neither of us moved for a moment. It wasn't perfect, it wasn't certain, but it was a start. As her smile grew, reaching her eyes, I felt a small, quiet certainty settle in my chest: I couldn't imagine not being the person who made her smile like that.

***

Eleni

We were in the car, Andreas driving me back to the village, and I was doing my best not to stare at him too much. But honestly, could you blame me? Last night was... let's just say I learned much about myself. For starters, I discovered I can be loud. And apparently, I can talk dirty while being loud, a skill I didn't even know I had. Add that to the list of unexpected talents.

I also learned a few things about my body I wasn't aware of before, though just thinking about them now was enough to make my cheeks heat. Last night wasn't just amazing—it was life-changing. I didn't know it was possible to feel that alive, that wanted, that utterly undone.

But the morning? That was a different story.

I woke up alone, and naturally, my first thought was that Andreas had made a run for it. I expected to find some scribbled note on the table: "Sorry, urgent business, see you around." Typical dramatic me, right? But then I found him on the porch, standing there with a mug in his hand.

At first, I thought, ok, not bad, he's still here. But then I saw the look on his face—distant, like his mind was a million miles away in some dark corner of his thoughts. And that's when I freaked out. I was ready to pack my bags for Heartbreak Hotel.

When he heard me coming and turned around, it got worse. His expression was so guarded, so unreadable, that my stomach dropped. But just as quickly, he shook it off, like flipping a switch. He smiled, handed me coffee, and started acting like I was some delicate piece of porcelain that might shatter if he even breathed wrong.

Honestly, I didn't know what to make of it. The whole morning had me spinning. On the one hand, I was terrified by his initial reaction—had last night been too much for him? On the other, this over-the-top carefulness wasn't exactly reassuring either. Why do men think women are made of glass? I mean, sure, I have my insecurities, fears, and doubts. But I'm not looking for someone to shield me from the world. And Andreas? He needs to get that. We both have our baggage, but isn't that the whole point of this? To figure it out together?

By the time we got in the car, though, things had settled. The awkwardness of the morning seemed to have faded. Andreas was more relaxed, holding my hand occasionally as he drove, and the easy warmth between us from last night starting to creep back in. I still had questions—lots of them—but for now, it felt ok.

Until we pulled into the village square. That's when it hit me.

"Shit!" The word flew out of my mouth before I could stop it.

Andreas looked at me, startled for a second, before bursting into laughter—actual, genuine, full-on laughter.

I stepped out of Andreas' truck and immediately felt the weight of a thousand invisible eyes lock onto me. The door slammed shut behind me with an incriminating clang echoing across the quiet square. Andreas, of course, didn't help. Leaning out the window, he waved goodbye, his smirk smug enough to make me want to throw my bag at him.

"Jerk," I muttered as the truck disappeared down the road. And so began the walk—no, the walk of shame—down the winding cobblestones to the house. The path had never felt so exposed or so long.

I adjusted my bag over my shoulder, wishing I had something more substantial than oversized sunglasses to shield me from the village's laser-focused attention. The Committee of Early Morning Judgments was already full force, strategically stationed on balconies and benches. They were pretending to water plants or read newspapers, but their heads turned just enough to track my every step. Great. They've got front-row seats.

A pair of elderly women perched on a bench giggled behind their hands, their whispering just loud enough to ensure I heard them.

"Good morning, Eleni!" one of them called out, her voice far too bright and cheerful. The glint in her eyes was unmistakable: We know.

"Good morning," I replied tightly, forcing a smile that felt more like a grimace as I quickened my pace.

As I walked, my treacherous mind decided to serve up a highlight reel of last night. Andreas' hands on my waist, the press of his mouth on mine, the husky way he murmured my name like a secret meant only for me. My face heated as I remembered his low chuckle when I knocked over the lamp in a frenzy of... enthusiasm.

"Focus, Eleni," I hissed at myself just as I stumbled over a loose cobblestone and nearly collided with a stray chicken. That was it—I officially looked like a mad woman, alternately grinning and scowling to myself as I trudged through the village. Nothing says 'completely innocent' like smiling at nothing like a lunatic.

I finally reached the narrow alley leading to the house, relief flooding me as I realized I was almost there. Just a few more steps, and I could collapse into the safety of my own space.

But, of course, the universe wouldn't let me off that easily. A cluster of men sipping coffee and reading newspapers outside their homes glanced up as I passed.

"Hi, Eleni," one of them drawled, his tone laced with a mix of politeness and barely hidden amusement.

"Hi," I muttered, keeping my head down and walking faster.

I should've taken the goat path, I thought bitterly. I'd rather deal with an actual goat than endure this parade of smirks.

Finally, the terrace door came into view, and I slipped inside with a dramatic sigh of relief, vowing to never again leave the house without a proper escape plan. But, of course, peace wasn't in the cards for me yet.

Sitting there, sipping a steaming cup of coffee and smirking like the cat who swallowed the canary was Callie. She was perched on one of my chairs like a queen holding a court, clearly waiting for me.

"Good morning, sunshine," Callie drawled, her eyes sweeping over me in one slow, deliberate pass. "Or should I say… good morning, storm survivor?"

I froze, my stomach dropping. "Callie, don't."

"Oh, but I must," she said, leaning forward with a grin that widened as she took in my dishevelled state. "Look at you! Hair like a bird's nest, looking like you've wrestled a tornado? You're a walking masterpiece of chaos. Glorious, glorious chaos."

"How did you even know I was coming home?" I asked, narrowing my eyes.

Callie laughed. "The moment Andreas' car left the farmhouse, one of the guys texted me. I have my contacts."

"Unbelievable," I muttered, running a hand through my tangled hair. "I thought I was their boss."

"Oh, you're definitely the boss, alright. The naughty boss." Callie burst out laughing, her laugh carrying through the terrace. I poured myself a cup of coffee, trying to tune her out. "I invoke my right to remain silent," I said, clutching the mug like a lifeline.

Callie nearly choked on her coffee. "Silent? Eleni, you must've hit your head. This is Seranos. You don't have rights here. They were revoked at the town hall years ago—right around the time the Committee of Judgments formed."

"I can and will ignore you," I muttered, taking a sip.

"Go ahead," Callie said breezily. "I'll just fill in the blanks myself. Let's see…"

"You're insufferable," I cut her short, covering my face with my hands.

"And you're glowing." She leaned back, smirking. "Honestly, I don't even need to ask. That grin says it all. Oh, and that look Andreas gave you when he dropped you off? Chef's kiss. The entire village probably needs to hose themselves down."

Peeking through my fingers, I shot her a glare. "I'm not even going to ask how you know all this. Honestly, I wouldn't be surprised if old Katerina WhatsApped you the moment I stepped out of the car."

Callie laughed, holding her hands up in mock surrender. "But just one more thing—"

"No," I said firmly.

"I didn't even say it yet!"

"I know that look. Whatever it is, the answer is no."

Callie's smirk grew. "Alright, alright. Just this: Was he as good as you imagined when you were thirteen?"

"Callie!" I gasped, my cheeks flaming.

She dissolved into laughter, clutching her stomach. I groaned, grabbing my coffee and heading for the shower. "Maybe I'll just move back to London. Andreas can keep the damn business. And the village. And you. I'll live where no one knows what I look like post-sex."

As I walked away, Callie called after me, still laughing. "Don't think you're getting out of details, Eleni! Wine at my place tonight! Bring snacks and the whole story!"

I closed the bathroom door behind me, leaning against it for a moment as my cheeks cooled. But despite myself, a small, traitorous smile crept across my lips.

"Fine," I muttered to the empty room. "Maybe I'll give her some of the story. But I'm skipping the part where my sandals were on the wrong feet."

***

The following week is a blur of routine—or at least the closest approximation of routine my life can manage right now. Most of my time is spent at the facility, staring down spreadsheets and business plans like I'm trying to bend them to my will. Spoiler: they aren't cooperating. I've convinced myself that if I focus hard enough, I can drown out the thoughts circling in my head. Thoughts that mostly involve Andreas, who keeps popping up at the facility like some kind of irritatingly handsome jack-in-the-box. A meeting here, a casual stop-by there. He leaves this lingering effect each time, like the smell of fresh olive oil—hard to ignore and impossible to forget.

I chew on the end of my pen, glaring at the screen before me as if sheer hostility will make the numbers behave. Solar panels, high-quality olive oil lines, rebranding—it all looks good on paper, in theory. The problem is the theory part. Can we actually pull this off, or am I just slapping fancy buzzwords on a sinking ship and hoping no one notices?

"Eleni? Hello? Earth to Eleni!" Nikos waves a hand in front of my face, his grin equal parts amused and exasperated.

I blink, jolted out of my spiral, and quickly set the pen down. "Sorry, got lost in the glamour of cost analysis," I say, as if I haven't just spent the last ten minutes mentally spiralling about Andreas. Again. Nikos leans back in his chair, eyebrows raised. "Thinking about business plans or a certain someone with an impressive talent for brooding?"

My face goes warm, and I instinctively reach into my pocket, my fingers brushing against the smooth stone Andreas gave me. "Business plans," I say, my voice a little too high-pitched to be convincing. "Obviously. Anyway, about those solar panels…"

Thankfully, Nikos lets it slide. He starts talking about energy savings and efficiency.

"Right, that's good," I say quickly, trying to sound like I've been paying attention. "And the high-quality olive oil line?"

Nikos leans forward, clearly in his element. "I think it's solid. We can market it as a premium product. Maybe even get a celebrity endorsement."

I snort. "Sure, because nothing says 'high-end olive oil' like an influencer holding it up next to a giant pool float."

Nikos laughs. "You'd be surprised. Stranger things have happened."

Like me and Andreas, apparently. Like the other day when he kissed me, pulling me into that empty meeting room like we were teenagers sneaking away at a school dance. The way his hands held my face, his words—"I missed you"—mumbled against my lips like a confession. And then, the very next day, he barely looked at me. A quick "Hi, Eleni," followed by a faster exit, mumbling something about an urgent errand.

It's not like this is easy for me either. I mean, I'm in love with the guy, for goodness' sake. And yes, I'm freaking out. How could I not? But at least I know what I want: to try. To see where this thing—whatever it is—could go. To deal with all the "issues" life throws our way, together. Because that's the point, isn't it? Facing things with someone instead of constantly tiptoeing around the possibility of something real?

Andreas, though? He's, as usual, a mystery wrapped in a riddle and tied up with one of those frustratingly tight knots you can't undo no matter how hard you pull. I don't know if he's scared or confused, or both. Honestly, it's exhausting. I can't keep playing this guessing game, trying to decipher his every move like it's some kind of emotional Sudoku puzzle.

I need to talk to him. Really talk to him. The problem is that Andreas isn't exactly the poster boy for heart-to-hearts. But I can't keep living in this constant back and forth limbo. It's draining. Maybe we could figure this out together if he'd just let me in. But there's something he's holding back, I'm sure of it. Every time it feels like he's about to say it, he pulls away, shutting down before I can reach him. And it gets to me—this wall he keeps between us, this refusal to trust me completely. After everything, how can he not see I'm here for him?

"Eleni?" Nikos' voice cuts in again, his expression softening. "You ok?"

"Fine!" I say a little too loudly. "Just, uh, excited about all these new ideas. Rebranding, right? Let's talk about that." My voice betrays me, though. I sound as convincing as a tourist trying to haggle at the Saturday market.

I sigh and run a hand through my messy bun, "Do you think I'm crazy for trying to change so much at once?" I ask, the question slipping out before I can stop it.

Nikos tilts his head, considering. "Assuming we are still talking about the business, no," he says, smiling. "I think you're brave. Change isn't easy, but it's necessary. And honestly? You're doing this for the right reasons. Your grandfather would be proud."

His words hit me in a way I wasn't expecting. I nod, managing a small smile. "Thanks, Nikos."

"Anytime," he says, returning to his usual, easy-going demeanour. "Now, let's figure out how to make these numbers work without selling your soul."

As we bend over the laptop together, I take a deep breath and force myself to focus. Whatever happens with Andreas, I have work to do. The grove isn't going to save itself, and I'm not about to let it—or myself—fall apart.

Still, as I stare at the spreadsheets, one last thought sneaks in before I can stop it: Andreas better figure out what he wants soon. Because this in-between is driving me completely insane.

***

Andreas
As I drove toward the farmhouse, the engine hummed steadily, a sound I usually found comforting, but tonight, it grated on my nerves. Maybe because it was too steady. Too consistent. Unlike everything else in my life, which seemed to be spinning just slightly out of control.
Eleni's face flashed in my mind—how she'd looked at me earlier, her eyes searching mine for... something. An answer, maybe. A clue. And I'd done what I always do. Made up some excuse about deliveries, mumbled a quick goodbye, and left her standing there. Again.
I am an idiot.
What the hell am I thinking? The morning after that night at the farmhouse—after seeing her so vulnerable, so open—I promised myself I wouldn't let her think she was just a fling. I decided I'd set aside my doubts, do whatever it took to make her smile, and not mess with her head. And what am I doing now? Kissing her one day, like some lovesick teenager who can't keep his hands to himself— because, let's be real, I can't. I so fucking love her. Then, turning around the next day and running like my life depends on it. Brilliant, Andreas. Really top-tier work. Too much for not messing with her head. Gold star.
She's trying. That's the part that makes it worse. She's trying to be patient with me, to meet me where I am, even when I keep shutting her out. I know she's frustrated. I see it in the way her shoulders tense when I avoid her and hear it in the clipped edge of her voice when she asks if

I'm "too busy" to talk. She hasn't said it outright yet, but I know she's waiting for me to stop running.

The problem is, I don't know how.

I ran a hand over my face, dragging my fingers through my hair. I'd told myself I was taking things slow. That I needed to be sure. For her sake, for mine. But if I were honest—and maybe it was time I started being honest—it wasn't about going slow. It was about fear. Fear that I'd mess this up like I'd messed up everything else. My marriage, my finances, my life outside this village. I couldn't fail her too.

And then there was the debt. Just thinking about it made my stomach twist. How was I supposed to tell her that my business shares weren't even mine anymore? That they were tied to a bank loan I'd taken out to pay for my divorce. And now Eleni was caught in it, whether she knew it or not.

I could still see the way she'd looked at me when we kissed. Like she trusted me. Like she believed in me. And every time I think about that, I feel like the biggest fraud in the world.

"This isn't working," I muttered to myself, the words cutting through the quiet hum of the car. It wasn't just about the business. It was this whole charade I was playing—pretending I could keep her at a distance, that I could somehow shield her from the wreckage of my life while also holding on to whatever was growing between us. All I was doing was creating more distance. And she deserves better than this. Better than me dodging her like a coward.

The farmhouse came into view, its silhouette framed by the fading light. I slowed the car as I pulled into the gravel driveway, the crunch beneath the tyres grounding me for a moment. Normally, this place felt like a sanctuary. Tonight, it felt like a reckoning.

I stood there for a moment, staring at the house. I'd avoided this for too long, telling myself that silence was a form of protection. But it wasn't, not for her, and definitely not for me. She needed to know the truth—about the debts, about why I kept pulling back, about everything. And if I couldn't face that, then I didn't deserve her at all. With a deep breath, I returned to the car and drove back to Seranos to see her.

***

Eleni
The evening air still carried some of the warmness of the day as I sat on the terrace watching the sunset, trying to clear my head and cradling a glass of wine. Zeus lay sprawled at my feet, his tail occasionally thumping against the floor, while Ari perched on the chair beside me, his green eyes fixed on the horizon like he was contemplating the secrets of the universe—or maybe just judging me for not sharing my wine. Probably the latter.
I let out a sigh, leaning back in my chair as the sky turned shades of pink and gold. "Honestly, Zeus," I began, swirling the wine in my glass. "Is it so hard for a man to act like an adult? One moment, he's staring at me like I'm the centre of the universe. The next, he's brooding like some tragic Greek hero. And don't even get me started on those fingers. It's like he's weaponizing them!"
Zeus's ears perked up at my voice, his big, soulful eyes fixed on me like he actually understood. Meanwhile, Ari flicked his tail with a pointed air of disapproval, clearly unimpressed with my rant.
 "Weaponizing my fingers? That's a new one," came a familiar voice, cutting through the quiet.
I jumped, nearly spilling my wine as I whipped around. There he was, standing at the edge of the terrace with that

proud, crooked smile on his face like he knew exactly how to throw me off balance. Which, of course, he did.

"How long have you been standing there?" I demanded, heat rushing to my cheeks as I sat up straighter.

"Long enough to know I'm apparently some kind of Greek tragedy," Andreas said, stepping onto the terrace with an easy confidence that made me want to throw my wine glass—preferably in his direction. "Mind if I join you?"

I hesitated, caught between annoyance and the inconvenient fact that even when he was being infuriating, I still wanted him around. With a reluctant sigh, I motioned to the chair opposite mine. Ari let out a soft huff, hopping down from his seat as Andreas approached, clearly deciding he didn't want to share his perch.

"Looks like I'm not the only one who's annoyed with you," I muttered as Zeus thumped his tail in enthusiastic welcome.

Andreas smirked, lowering himself into the now-vacant chair. "Good to know I'm making friends everywhere I go."

I rolled my eyes but said nothing, trying not to notice the way the setting sun caught the faint streaks of grey at his temples. He leaned back, stretching his long legs out in front of him, and for a moment, we sat in silence. The tension between us lingered in the air, unspoken but heavy, as I stared at the horizon and pretended not to notice the way his gaze flicked toward me.

"So," Andreas said finally, his voice quieter now, "what exactly makes me a Greek tragedy?"

I glanced at him, raising an eyebrow. "You don't already know?"

"Enlighten me," he said, leaning forward slightly. His expression was teasing, but there was something in his eyes—something softer, almost hesitant—that made my chest tighten.

I tilted my head, a small smile playing on my lips despite myself. "You're not as tragic as you think, Andreas. The brooding thing? It's a bit much sometimes. But you've got your moments."

He chuckled, settling back in the chair. "Moments, huh? Not exactly glowing praise."

"Well, you're no Zeus," I quipped, gesturing toward the dog, who had rolled onto his back, paws in the air, perfectly content. "But you've got potential."

Andreas smirked, shaking his head. "High bar."

As the sun dipped lower, the conversation shifted into an easy rhythm. We swapped stories about the grove, about the villagers and families. The evening felt lighter, freer, as though we'd both let our guards down. It wasn't forced or complicated—just... simple. And for a while, I forgot about the back-and-forths, the frustrations, and the unanswered questions.

But then the conversation softened, the laughter fading into a quiet that felt intimate, unspoken things lingering in the air between us. Andreas shifted in his chair, his fingers drumming lightly against the armrest, his gaze fixed on the horizon.

"I don't want to mess this up, Eleni," he said suddenly, his voice low, almost hesitant. "I'm not always good at this. I'm trying, and so far... I'm failing spectacularly."

He let out a nearly painful smile at his own words, the kind that didn't quite reach his eyes.

I watched him carefully, setting my glass down and leaning forward slightly. "That's dramatic, even for you," I said lightly, swirling my wine.

"I'm scared that if I let you get too close, I'll hurt you. I'll disappoint you," he said, his voice low and hesitant.

"And?" I asked, my voice sharper than I intended.

He blinked, clearly surprised by my question. "And what?" he asked, his brow furrowing.
That was it. I could feel the floodgates breaking. All this overthinking, hoping, and being whiplashed between the highs and lows, and the wine, of course—it all came crashing down in one furious wave. My grip on the stem of the glass tightened before I set it aside completely, afraid I might actually throw it.
"Ok, so we get close and you hurt me," I said, my voice rising. "Let's recap, just to clear things up. You plan that amazing day at the beach, sleep with me, and then don't call me for two days. Then you kiss me in empty rooms and tell me you miss me, only to avoid me like I don't exist. And now you show up at my house, unannounced, to what—give me this tired, 'Oh, I don't want to hurt you' line?"
I was fuming now, the words tumbling out before I could stop them. "What are you saying, Andreas? You're already hurting me. One day, I'm over the moon; the next, I don't even know if you think about me. And all of this, apparently, is because you don't want to hurt me?"
I barely took a breath, the heat of my own words driving me forward. "I really don't want to know what it would look like if you did want to hurt me, because this? This is torture. You know very well what I want, Andreas. But now it's your turn. What do you want from me?"
The terrace fell utterly silent in the wake of my outburst. Even the insects seemed to have paused, the stillness so complete it felt like the world itself was holding its breath. The moment stretched, and for the first time, I truly registered the weight of what I'd just said. This wasn't me—not the one I knew, anyway. I didn't do this. I didn't lay everything bare, raw and vulnerable, like a declaration of war and a plea for peace all at once. But I couldn't bring myself to regret it. I'd done it because I deserved clarity.

I deserved to know. The relief of saying it all out loud, of claiming my emotions without shame, was exhilarating.

When I looked at Andreas, his expression mirrored my own shock. But there was something else there too, something I couldn't name yet. His eyes locked on mine, and for a moment, neither of us moved, the silence between us heavy with everything unsaid.

Andreas' expression shifted, his shock melting into something else entirely. Something I couldn't quite define—a mix of amusement, softness, and something wild that sent a shiver down my spine. If it was even possible to look like that all at once, Andreas somehow managed it.

He leaned back in his seat, the faintest curve of a smile tugging at his lips as his dark eyes locked on mine. The intensity in his gaze was enough to make my pulse skip, but I refused to look away. The silence stretched between us, charged and electric, until he finally spoke.

"Eleni Katsaros," he said, his voice low and steady, the weight of his words landing like a thunderclap. "You have no idea how much I am in love with you."

The world seemed to tilt, everything else fading away as his confession settled over me. For a moment, I couldn't breathe, couldn't think, couldn't process what I'd just heard. He said it so simply, so matter-of-factly, like it wasn't the single most life-changing thing he could've said.

"Well," I said finally, blinking as the words sank in. "Eleni, you asked for clarity… here you go."

The words escaped before I could catch them, hanging in the air like a neon sign. My cheeks warmed as I realized I'd said it out loud. The corners of my mouth twitched into a stunned smile, unsure of how he'd react.

Andreas chuckled, the sound low and rich. "What can I say? I aim to please."

***

It broke something in the tension, and I couldn't help it—I laughed. A real, full laugh that seemed to lift the air around us. Andreas leaned back, watching me with a small, satisfied smile that was softer than his usual smirks, and for the first time that evening, everything felt lighter.

The terrace table, set with a simple spread of bread, olives, and a bottle of wine that had been meant just for me, became a place to share. Andreas poured us both a glass, raising his in a mock toast that earned him an eye-roll and another laugh from me.

As we ate, the conversation ebbed and flowed with an easy rhythm. As the evening wore on, Andreas reached across the table at one point, his fingers brushing the back of my hand as he leaned closer, his voice low and warm as he shared a memory of his father teaching him to prune the olive trees. His thumb grazed over my knuckles absentmindedly, and I let it, the small, tender gesture sending warmth through me. I leaned closer to him, resting my chin in my hand. "Is this how you fix all your messes?" I teased softly. "A love declaration and a few charming stories?"

He grinned, his expression easy and unguarded in a way that made my heart ache. "Only for you."

The conversation slowed, and we fell into a comfortable silence, the kind where words weren't necessary. Andreas reached out again, his fingers brushing the inside of my wrist before his hand settled over mine. I turned my palm up, letting his fingers interlace with mine as we sat there, the stars bright above us.

At some point, he kissed me. It wasn't hurried or planned; it simply happened as natural as breathing. He leaned in across the table, his lips brushing against mine softly at first, then with more certainty when I kissed him back. The warmth of his hand in mine and the solidness of his presence made everything else feel far away.

By the time the evening began to wind down, it felt like the terrace had become its own little world, separate from everything outside us. Together, we cleared the table, gathering empty wine glasses and plates in an unspoken rhythm.

When we stepped inside, the house felt different somehow—warmer, quieter, as though it had absorbed the softness of the night. We didn't say much as we walked toward my room, but there was no need for questions or invitations. He followed, not with hesitation or assumption but with a natural ease that made it feel like we'd done this a thousand times before.

Inside my room, his gaze fell on the bedside table. The seashell he'd given me as a birthday present when we were kids sat next to the childhood photo of the two of us that I found in George's boxes. He reached for the shell, holding it delicately in his large hand. "I remember this," he said, his voice softer now, as if he were speaking more to himself than me. "I had to dive deeper than I ever had to get it. The moment you saw it in my hand, you demanded I give it to you. Of course, I said no. Then you went crying to my mum, and she forced me to give it to you as a birthday present."

I couldn't help but laugh, his expression still faintly annoyed after all these years. "You know me," I said lightly. "Always a lady." He chuckled, shaking his head as he set the shell back in its place before picking up the photo. He studied it for a few minutes, his lips curling into a smile that seemed to carry both nostalgia and fondness. By then, I'd already slipped into bed, watching him quietly as he sat on the edge, his movements unhurried. He pulled off his shirt, set it aside, and lay back against the pillows, his arms tucked behind his head, staring at the ceiling as though lost in thought. I turned toward him, resting my head against his chest, my arm wrapping around his waist as if it were the most natural thing in the world.

His hand found my hair, his fingers moving through it absentmindedly, the sensation so soothing I could've stayed like that forever. The steady rhythm of his breathing beneath me, the faint scent of the sea still clinging to his skin—it felt like home.

After a moment, his fingers grazed my jaw, the warmth of his touch sending a shiver down my spine. Gently, he tilted my chin upward, and when our eyes met, he leaned in, brushing his lips against mine. The kiss was soft, deliberate—nothing rushed, nothing to chase. Unlike the fire of that first night in the farmhouse, this was something different, something steady and sure. It deepened gradually, the world around us dissolving into the quiet rhythm of shared breaths. His hand slid down my back, pulling me closer, and a sigh escaped me, unbidden.

My fingers tangled in his hair, relishing its familiar softness, and he shifted, guiding us as we lay back together. Hovering over me, his gaze locked with mine—gentle, yet searing in its intensity. His thumb caressed my cheek as he murmured, "Is this ok?" The tenderness in his voice unravelled me. Unable to speak, I nodded, my heart swelling with an emotion too big to name.

Andreas moved with care, his reverence evident in every touch as he slowly unwrapped the layers of my clothing. Each movement felt like a vow, his calloused hands reverent as they grazed my skin. When nothing remained between us, he paused, his gaze lingering as if memorizing every detail. "Never forget how much I love you," he whispered, his voice rough with emotion.

His lips travelled down my neck, each kiss leaving a trail of warmth in its wake. I shivered as the soft rasp of his stubble teased my skin, and a quiet gasp slipped from my lips. His hands explored gently, one sliding up to cup the curve of my breast.

"Andreas," I breathed, arching instinctively into his touch. He glanced up at me, his eyes dark with longing but tempered by the softness of love. Slowly, his lips descended, brushing my skin with featherlight precision until they found their way to my nipple. The first touch sent a spark straight through me, and I clutched his shoulders, anchoring myself as he teased, his mouth skilled and patient.

His other hand drifted lower, tracing a path along my thigh. As his fingers brushed higher, I parted my legs, surrendering to the inevitable. When he touched me intimately, we both let out a low, shared groan, the sound reverberating through the quiet space between us. His touch was slow and deliberate, a rhythm that built steadily, drawing me higher with every stroke.

I pulled him back up, capturing his mouth in a kiss that was both desperate and tender, craving the closeness of his body against mine. When he entered me, he did so with exquisite care, our bodies aligning in perfect harmony. A sigh escaped us simultaneously, a testament to the relief and wonder of finally being one.

Our movements were unhurried, every motion deliberate and full of meaning. His gaze never left mine, and our connection seemed to deepen with each moment. The intensity in his eyes, the silent assurance of his love, made my heart race as we moved together.

And just like that, the day faded, the space between us disappearing as our bodies moved together under the quiet glow of the moonlight spilling through the window.

It was simply us—connected, unspoken, natural—like the rise and fall of breath.

***

I woke the next morning with a sense of quiet contentment. The room was bathed in the soft light of early morning, and for a moment, I stayed where I was, savouring the stillness. The memories of last night flickered through my mind—his touch, his kiss, the way everything between us had felt so easy, so right.

The scent of coffee drifted faintly through the air, pulling me from my thoughts. I climbed out of bed, throwing on a light robe as I padded toward the living room. The house was quiet, save for the faint clink of a cup on the terrace. I followed the sound, and as I stepped into the living room, I spotted Andreas outside, standing with his back to me.

Shirtless.

Of course.

I stepped outside, the morning sun warm against my face, and crossed my arms. "Very subtle, Papadopoulos," I said, my voice dripping with sarcasm. "Shirtless on my terrace at 7:30 in the morning. Now we certainly guaranteed to be the talk of the village for the next ten years."

Andreas didn't turn around. Instead, he raised a hand, his fingers splayed in a quick "one-minute" gesture, his posture unusually rigid. His head tilted slightly to the side as he listened, and the way his hand gripped the edge of the terrace railing made something in my stomach twist. Whatever conversation he was having, it wasn't casual.

My humour fizzled out as curiosity took its place. I stayed where I was, trying to make out his words, but his tone was low and clipped, each word too muffled to decipher.

His free hand ran through his hair, his fingers lingering at the back of his neck in a way that only made him look more tense.

When he finally hung up and turned to face me, the look in his eyes made my heart lurch. My earlier lightness was gone in an instant, replaced by a gnawing panic. Something was wrong—I could feel it.

"Who was that?" I asked, my voice coming out sharper than I intended as my pulse quickened.

Andreas hesitated, his hand brushing the back of his neck before falling to his side, the weight of whatever he'd just heard clearly still pressing on him. For a second, I thought he might brush it off, but then he sighed, his gaze steady but heavy.

"Your dad," he said finally. "Petros."

The words hung in the air between us, heavy and loaded, and I felt the floor tilt slightly beneath me. A dozen questions surged forward, but none of them found their way out. All I could do was stare at him, the implications of that one revelation swirling in my mind.

High Stakes, Higher Spirits

Andreas
The moment I walked back inside, I barely had time to brace myself before Eleni started.
"Why did he call you? What does he want? Is he dying? Does he know about us? How could he know about us? I didn't even know about us until yesterday!" Her words spilt out in a panicked rush, her eyes wide and blazing, her arms flailing as she paced the living room.
"Eleni." I tried to interject, but she was already on her next thought.
"And why didn't he call me directly? Oh wait, of course, I'm just his clueless daughter. Why bother when he can call you? And what were you even talking about? Don't just stand there, Andreas, tell me!" She whirled on me, her voice rising as she planted her hands on her hips.
"Eleni." My voice was firmer this time, and she stopped mid-rant, her chest heaving, her eyes locked on mine. "Take a deep breath."
"I'm not breathing until you tell me what's going on," she snapped, but there was a crack in her voice, a flicker of vulnerability behind the fire.
I stepped closer, placing my hands gently on her shoulders. "You need to calm down first. Sit. I'll make you some coffee, and I'll tell you everything. But I need you to breathe."
"Too late for coffee and too late for breathing," she shot back, shaking her head. "Just tell me, Andreas. Now."
Knowing she wouldn't settle until I ripped off the band-aid, I sighed and guided her to the couch, sitting beside her. Her eyes bore into me, and I knew I had to get this right.

"Alright," I began, keeping my voice low and steady. "Your dad called me because he knows you'd never consider what he's about to propose. Some investors are interested in buying the whole business. Petros thinks it's worth hearing them out, and he asked me to talk to you because he didn't think you'd listen to him."

Eleni's mouth opened, but I held up a hand. "Let me finish. They want to come next week to visit the grove and the facility. It's non-binding; it's just a preliminary meeting to see what they have to offer. Nothing has been decided, and nothing will be without you."

For a moment, she just stared at me, her expression unreadable. Then she blinked, her lips parting, but no sound came. Her wide, dull eyes met mine, and I saw the shock sinking in.

"Eleni?" I prompted gently, reaching for her hand. She stayed silent for another beat before the rant began.

"Oh, that man," she spat, her voice rising. "He never fails himself, does he? Undermining me at every turn! Going over and over me like a bulldozer, always thinking he knows better!"

I held her hand, my thumb brushing over her wrist in slow circles as I let her vent.

"And I hope you told him where to go—somewhere I can't mention to my father, but you definitely can," she snapped, her frustration still palpable.

"I told him that I'd talk with you," I said calmly.

She turned on me, her tone sharp now. "You think this is ok? You're just going along with him like some—some mesmerized acolyte of his shiny London investor talk?"

"This isn't about sides, Eleni," I said calmly, squeezing her hand. "This is about the grove and what's best for it."

"What's best for it?" she shot back. "What's best is not selling it off to a bunch of strangers who wouldn't know an olive tree from a telephone pole!"

Her anger was spilling over now, but I didn't let it faze me. I leaned in slightly, my voice gentle but firm. "Eleni, our problems at the grove are real. You know that. All I'm saying is we listen to them. Let them visit. Treat it like an outside audit—get an objective view of where we stand. That's it. If we don't like what they say, we send them packing. No harm done."

Her expression was still furious, but I saw the cracks forming in her resolve. "I don't trust them," she muttered. "Then don't trust them," I said simply. "If they're not the right fit, I'll drive them to the airport myself and put them on the first flight back to London."

Her lips twitched, almost like she wanted to smile but refused to let herself. "You promise we'll do this together?" she asked, her voice quieter now but still edged with suspicion. "You're not going to ghost me halfway through this and leave me to deal with them on my own?"

Her question was so unexpectedly earnest, so disarmingly cute, that I couldn't help but smile. I pulled her into a hug, wrapping my arms around her tightly. "We're in this together. Promise." I murmured against her hair.

She didn't say anything, but I felt her relax slightly in my arms, the fight in her still there but less.

***

I waved goodbye to Eleni, trying to keep the morning's tension from settling back over me. "See you tonight," I called over my shoulder, forcing a smile that felt more genuine than it had a few minutes ago. She nodded, a faint smile touching her lips, giving me a semblance of peace as I turned to head for the grove.

The village square was lively as usual, and I couldn't help but chuckle when old Mr. Giorgos called out from his usual spot outside the café. "You dodged a bullet there with that 'I love you,' son," he said with a wink. "That was a good move. We thought little Katsaros was going to feed you to the fish!"

Grinning, I replied, "Well, I learned from the best how to navigate these waters!" The laughter that followed felt warm, a testament to the close-knit community that had become a part of my life.

"Keep that up, and she'll have you dancing to her tune before the olives are picked," another villager teased as I passed by, her voice carrying over the morning bustle.

"I'm working on it!" I replied, my response earning a round of good-natured laughter.

Finally reaching my car, I slipped inside and shut the door, the familiar space giving me a momentary bubble of solitude. As I started the engine, the humour of the morning faded, replaced by the gnawing weight of the other secret I was carrying. The one about my credit debts that I couldn't tell her.

Sitting there, keys in hand, I found myself at a crossroads. If the investors bought the grove, maybe I wouldn't need to reveal my financial mess. It was a tempting thought, delaying the inevitable. The idea of selling the land broke my heart—I loved this place, its soil, its soul. And I hated hiding anything from Eleni, especially something that directly affected our future.

But the thought of looking weak in Eleni's eyes, of her seeing me not just as flawed but as a failure, gnawed at me. I was in an impasse, caught between my love for the land and the pragmatic need to secure its future—and ours.

The drive to the grove was quiet. As I covered each mile, I wrestled with the gap between being honest and doing what was necessary. Selling might be our only option, but what would that mean for my integrity, for our relationship?

When I parked the car, I paused to take a deep breath and gather my thoughts. Tonight, I had planned to tell her everything. But as I stepped out into the crisp morning air, a sense of pragmatism took over. The decisions I faced were intertwined with our futures, complex and deep.

And so, as I walked towards the grove, I made a silent resolution: to hold my secret close just a little longer, at least until after the investors had come and gone. Maybe this delay could spare us both some unnecessary pain. Perhaps, if the sale went through, I wouldn't need to reveal the depths of my troubles at all.

***

Eleni

After Andreas walked out, I lingered by the door, watching him head through the village toward his car. With a sigh, I turned to Zeus and Ari, my ever-loyal audience.

"Alright, you two," I began, stepping into the room. "What do we think about this investor situation? And don't just sit there looking smug, Ari. I know you have opinions."

"It's not that simple, is it?" I muttered, pacing the room. Zeus's ears perked up, his tail giving a soft thump. "Dad always has some kind of angle. Always. And Andreas—" I stopped, shaking my head. "I trust him, but the fact that he went along with this? That he didn't immediately shut it down? What am I missing here?"

Zeus let out a low whine, his soulful eyes fixed on me as if he had the answer I was looking for. "And selling the whole business? Everything? That's just—" I threw up my hands. "No. Not an option. Right, Zeus?"

His tail wagged harder, and I sighed, crouching down to ruffle his ears. "At least someone around here agrees with me."

"And you," I said to Ari, trying to ignore the lump forming in my throat, "would probably sell the grove for a crate of fresh fish." He blinked slowly, his tail flicking once in that dismissive way that always reminded me of George. It was exasperating but also... comforting. Ari wasn't warm or openly affectionate, but his presence was steady, grounding—like George's had been. I sighed, the tension in my chest easing ever so slightly. "Fine," I muttered, a reluctant smile tugging at my lips. "I get it. You're Switzerland."

The smile faded as my thoughts turned back to my father. "It's just so... him, isn't it?" I muttered, shaking my head. "Going over my head like this, as if I'm not capable of making a decision for myself. It's like he still sees me as a kid who can't handle responsibility."

Zeus whined softly, "Maybe I'm being too hard on him," I admitted. "Maybe he's just worried. But does he have to make me feel like I'm constantly failing? Like I'm not enough?"

Ari jumped down from the windowsill, brushing against my leg as he passed. I watched him go, "At least you two don't judge me," I said softly before standing up. "Okay, enough of this. Time to face the day."

As I grabbed my bag and stepped outside, Andreas's parting words echoed in my mind, "I'll see you tonight." Those casual yet promising words sparked a tiny flutter of warmth in my heart. I paused, a smile creeping across my face. "So, we're really doing this, huh? We're an item now," I whispered to myself, the idea lifting the heaviness from my shoulders slightly. Inspired by this new personal revelation, I walked out feeling a bit more buoyed.

***

By the time I reached the facility, I was braced for another hectic day, though my thoughts still circled around the morning's events. Nikos was there, talking to the quality control department.

"Nikos," I said, walking in. "We need to talk."

He looked up, raising an eyebrow at my tone. "That's never a good way to start a conversation."

I ignored his quip and we walked to an empty meeting room. "Investors are coming next week. Dad and Andreas arranged it."

That got his attention. "Investors?" he asked, setting down his pen. "What kind of investors?"

"The kind who want to buy the whole business," I said, my frustration bubbling to the surface again. "Not partners. Not supporters. Buyers."

Nikos leaned back in his chair, crossing his arms thoughtfully. "I take it you're not thrilled about the prospect?"

"Thrilled? This isn't what I signed up for!" I snapped. "We're supposed to be saving the grove, not selling it to some suit who'll probably turn our artisanal olive oil into some mass-produced travesty."

He nodded slowly as though weighing his response. "I get it. But don't you think you should at least hear them out?"

I frowned. "Why? So they can tell us how much they'll pay to destroy everything?"

"So you can understand what they're offering," he countered. "Look, I'm not saying you agree to anything. But what's the harm in listening? If you don't like what you hear, you walk away. But what if there's an opportunity here—something we haven't thought of?"

"They want to buy the business," I said again, emphasizing the word. "Not inject cash, not become partners."

"And that's exactly why you need to meet them," Nikos replied evenly. "To talk, to negotiate. Maybe there's a way to make it work in your favour. If they're serious, you can try to shape the terms. But we'll never know if you don't even meet them."

I stared at him, the fight draining out of me bit by bit. As much as I hated to admit it, he made a good point. If Andreas and Nikos were both saying the same thing, maybe I was being too emotional about all this. Maybe I was overreacting.

"Fine," I said reluctantly. "But if they try to replace our olive trees with some genetically modified super-olives, I'm holding you responsible."

Nikos chuckled, leaning back in his chair. "I'll be there with you both during the meetings, don't worry. We'll face the super-olives together."

As he left the meeting room, I felt a strange mix of frustration and cautious acceptance swirling in my chest. For now, at least, I could live with that.

***

The next couple of days passed in a blur of quiet productivity and tentative calm. To my surprise, I was beginning to get used to the idea of the investors' visit. Not that I liked it, mind you—I was still sceptical—but the initial sting of betrayal and frustration had dulled. It helped that Andreas took charge of dealing with them. I flat-out refused to handle the logistics, and he didn't push me. He took their calls, arranged their itinerary, and promised to keep me in the loop without making me feel cornered.

I focused my energy on what I could control. Most of my time was spent at the facility, poring over spreadsheets, working on presentations, and trying to come up with the most compelling way to showcase the grove and our operations. If these people were going to come all the way here, they'd better be impressed. At least, that's what I told myself.

It hit me how much had changed since I first set foot in Seranos. Back then, I was a mess—panicked, unsure what to do or even where to start. A few months ago, the thought of taking a three-week holiday felt impossible, let alone quitting my job and settling here with a cat, a dog, and—somehow—a brooding boyfriend. (A very, very handsome one, I might add.) But now, as frustrating as everything was, I realized I was facing it with a sense of purpose I hadn't known I had. I wasn't just reacting anymore—I was stepping up and taking ownership, even if it still scared me.

Meanwhile, Andreas was at the grove most of the day, handling the hands-on work that I still struggled to wrap my head around. It was a good balance, in a strange way. We both had our roles to play, even if they weren't exactly what I'd imagined when I first came here. Maybe that was part of the lesson—I couldn't control everything, but I could adapt, and sometimes that was enough.

The evenings, though, were another story. Something shifted after the night he told me he loved me—not in a dramatic, earth-shattering way, but in a quiet, natural one. Andreas started staying over, and it wasn't something we talked about or planned. It just happened. He'd be there when the day ended, and neither of us saw the point in him leaving.

Our nights were easy and light, a welcome escape from the weight of the work and the looming investor visit. We didn't talk about strategies or financials. Instead, we watched the sunsets together from the terrace, Ari perched nearby with his usual air of superiority and Zeus sprawled out like the oversized puppy he was.

Sometimes, we'd go for a swim in the early mornings, the water cool and crisp as the sun rose over the horizon. Other times, Andreas would cook dinner while I hovered nearby, pretending to help but mostly just getting in the way. "You're worse than Zeus," he'd say with a mock sigh as I snuck a bite of whatever he was chopping. "At least he waits until I've turned my back."

"Quality control," I'd reply with a grin, earning a pointed look that made me laugh every time.

There was laughter, too—so much laughter, like when Zeus knocked over a chair trying to chase Ari, who leapt onto Andreas's lap with all the indignation of a king forced to mingle with peasants. Or the time Andreas tried to teach me again how to skip stones at the beach; I was never good at this, even as a child. "It's all in the wrist," he'd said, demonstrating with effortless precision as his stone hopped across the water. When I tried, my first stone sank like a rock, and the second went wildly off course, startling a seagull.

"Remind me never to take you to a skipping competition," he teased, watching me glare at the water like it had personally wronged me. "You're a menace to both physics and wildlife."

It was easy. It was fun. It was everything I hadn't realized I'd been missing until it was right there in front of me. And for now, I let myself enjoy it. It wasn't just about the grove or the investors anymore—it was about embracing the moments in between, the simple joys that made everything else feel worthwhile.

I still had doubts, of course, about the investors, about my father's motives, about whether I was making the right choices for the grove. But I was starting to see that I didn't have to have all the answers. I wasn't that scared, uncertain woman who stepped off the plane a couple of months ago. I was learning to trust myself—to trust Andreas—and that, more than anything, felt like progress.

***

By the time I got home, the gossip mill in the village had reached a full boil. Someone had something to say about the investors' visit everywhere I went today. Speculation ranged from the ridiculous—"They're going to replace the olive trees with hotels!"—to the absurdly specific—"I heard they're from a secret royal family in London. That's why they're coming here in disguise!" Needless to say, I was relieved to shut the door behind me and escape the noise, though it didn't stop my mind from spinning.

Maria had invited all of us for dinner tonight—me, Andreas, Callie, and Nikos. Andreas had texted earlier to say he'd meet me there directly, leaving me pacing my house, debating what to wear and what to say when I saw Maria. This wasn't just a dinner. This was the first one since Andreas and I became an actual… thing. If that wasn't enough, Callie would undoubtedly be armed with a thousand teasing remarks, ready to pounce the moment I walked through Maria's door.

"You're awfully quiet, Ari," I muttered, glancing over at the tabby. He blinked at me in a slow, deliberate motion that somehow conveyed both boredom and judgment. "Oh, don't look at me like that. It's not like I planned this whole thing with Andreas. You were here; you saw how it just… happened."

Ari stretched lazily, his tail flicking once before he tucked his head beneath his paw, clearly uninterested in my spiralling thoughts. Zeus, on the other hand, sat at my feet, his tail thumping against the floor, an endless rhythm of encouragement.

"At least you're listening," I said, scratching Zeus behind his ears. "This dinner... it's important. Maria's been like a second mother to me, and she's always been in my corner, but this feels... different. What if she thinks I'm rushing things with Andreas? Or that I haven't thought it all through? She always worries about me, and the last thing I want is to disappoint her."

"And then there's Callie," I continued, laughing softly despite my nerves. "She's going to tease me mercilessly. I can already hear her making jokes about us naming olive trees after each other or something equally ridiculous."

Ari let out a soft, rumbling meow as if to remind me he had no patience for my overthinking.

I smiled faintly. "You're right. Maria's never been anything but kind to me, even when I've been a mess. But still... this is new territory. She's seen me grow up— through all my awkward phases, all the times I came running to her for advice or just for one of her hugs that made everything seem okay. And now, walking into her house as someone who's... with Andreas? It's a lot. I just want her to see that I'm not some starry-eyed kid anymore. That I can be someone worthy of the people who matter to me."

Zeus barked softly while Ari stretched with the regal indifference only a cat could pull off.

"Alright, alright," I said, brushing my hands over my dress to smooth out imaginary creases. "I'll just be myself. What could possibly go wrong?"

I stepped out of the house; the sun had begun its slow descent, casting the village in hues of gold and amber while the faint scent of thyme lingered in the breeze. The Aegean stretched out in the distance, shimmering like a restless jewel, its familiar tang filling the air with memories of endless summers.

The cobblestone streets were quiet now, the day's bustle giving way to the easy rhythm of the evening. I could hear the faint murmur of voices from the open windows, mingling with the occasional clink of glasses and the distant hum of cicadas. It was the kind of moment that could only belong to Seranos—simple, unhurried, and impossibly beautiful.

This village had a way of calming me, of reminding me to breathe, even when my thoughts threatened to spiral out of control. Tonight, whatever happened, I told myself I could handle it. Maria's house, her table, her warm presence had always been a place of comfort. Surely, even with all the changes, that hadn't disappeared.

By the time I reached Maria's gate, the scent of blooming jasmine mingled with the aroma of something rich and savoury wafting from her kitchen. The familiar sounds of clinking pots and pans carried through the air, underscored by Callie's laughter echoing from the courtyard. I paused for a moment, taking it all in, before pushing open the gate and stepping into the glow of lanterns that had begun to light up the evening.

***

Once I stepped into the courtyard, the first thing I saw was Andreas, Callie, and Nikos, who squeezed onto the corner sofas, shouting and laughing as they slapped cards on the table. Slapjack. Seriously? Am I the only one stressed here?

The sound of my footsteps must have caught their attention because they all froze mid-game, turning toward me like a trio of mischievous children caught red-handed.

Callie was the first to recover, practically launching herself off the sofa and wrapping me in a dramatic hug.
"Now I know you're avoiding me," she whispered at lightning speed, her voice dripping with mock accusation. "But mark my words, I'll corner you somewhere tonight, and you'll spill everything." She leaned closer, her voice dropping to a conspiratorial whisper. "I heard about the L-word. Is it true?"
"Callie, I missed you too," I replied, laughing as I gently pried her off me.
Nikos was next, enveloping me in one of his easy, good-natured hugs. "Good to see you, Eleni," he said warmly before stepping aside.
Then it was Andreas' turn. He stood back for a moment, grinning like an absolute idiot, before strolling over and pulling me into a hug that felt all too comfortable and familiar. Before I could say anything, he planted a loud, unapologetic kiss on my lips, the kind that could probably be heard all the way to the café.
"Andreas!" I hissed, pulling back so fast I nearly stumbled. I smacked his arm in mock indignation. "Seriously? We're at Maria's house! Behave!"
He didn't even flinch. "Relax," he said, smirking as he leaned closer, his voice low and teasing. "She's in the kitchen. She can't see us. Want me to show you my room?"
This time, my slap landed a bit harder. He let out an exaggerated "Owww," clutching his arm like I'd done serious damage. Then, to my absolute horror, he turned toward the kitchen and shouted, "Muuummm! Eleni's here, and she's slapping me!"
Before I could murder him on the spot, Maria's head appeared in the doorway, her expression equal parts amused and unimpressed. "Oh, I'm sure you deserved it," she said dryly, her eyes twinkling.

"In your face, Papadopoulos," I muttered under my breath, smirking triumphantly.

Maria, of course, had perfect timing. "Eleni, dear," she called sweetly, her voice carrying the weight of a hundred unspoken expectations. "Can you come to the kitchen and help me?"

I could feel my face turning crimson as I glanced around for support. Callie, Nikos, and Andreas were all watching, their smirks practically identical as their eyes silently screamed, You're on your own.

With a deep, steadying breath, I plastered on a smile and walked toward the kitchen, all too aware of the laughter bubbling behind me. This is going to be a long night, I thought, but a small part of me couldn't help feeling... happy.

Once I stepped into Maria's kitchen, the familiar atmosphere began to work its magic, calming my nerves bit by bit. The space was a comforting chaos of warmth and life—the scent of oregano and simmering tomato sauce filled the air, mixing with the faint sweetness of fresh bread cooling on the counter. The countertops were cluttered in the best way: bowls of freshly picked lemons, jars of preserved olives, and a small pile of handwritten recipe cards that looked as though they'd been used a thousand times over. This wasn't just a kitchen; it was Maria's heart, poured into every corner.

Maria gave me a warm smile as she glanced over her shoulder. "Eleni, dear, would you mind preparing the salad? The vegetables are washed and ready for you."

It didn't escape my notice that everything was washed, laid out, and clearly foolproof. Maria knew better than to take risks with my questionable cooking skills. I nodded, grateful for the straightforward task, and set to work.

For a while, we worked in companionable silence. I watched Maria move masterfully around her kitchen, stirring a pot here and seasoning something there, her hands as confident and steady as if she were conducting an orchestra. The rhythm of it all—the soft chopping of vegetables, the occasional clatter of utensils, the soothing hum of the evening breeze—started to settle me. But, of course, the silence didn't last long.

"So, Eleni," Maria said suddenly, her voice carrying that distinct mix of warmth, reassurance, and just enough edge to make you brace yourself. She was the only person alive who could make "So, Eleni" feel both comforting and terrifying. "How is my boy treating you?"

My cheeks flared hot, and I froze mid-chop. For a moment, I felt like I was eight years old again, caught doing something I very much shouldn't have been. "Uh... fine," I stammered, focusing intently on the cucumber in front of me.

"Just fine?" she asked, raising an eyebrow. "If he's only treating you fine, then I've failed as a mother. He clearly doesn't know how to treat an amazing woman who's in love with him—and who he loves very much too, as every living soul in the village says!" she said, laughing.

Her laugh was warm and infectious, but I was too busy wishing the ground would open up and swallow me whole. My mental preparation for this exact moment? Gone. Out the window. Vanished. I stood there, gaping like a fish, unable to form a single coherent thought.

Maria, clearly enjoying herself far too much, stopped what she was doing, walked over, and pulled me into a hug. That was all it took. The floodgates opened, and I melted into her arms. The scent of her—soap, herbs, and something uniquely Maria—wrapped around me, and I felt the weight of the past few weeks pressing down all at once. The anticipation, the stress, the emotions I'd been holding onto—they all poured out as I sobbed into her shoulder.

She didn't say a word, just held me tightly, her hands stroking my back in that steady, motherly way that said, "I'm here. I've got you".

Finally, when the worst of it had passed, she pulled back and cupped my face in her hands; her eyes filled with so much love it made my chest ache.

"Eleni," she began, her voice gentle but firm, "he is my son, and God knows I love him more than words can ever say. We've been through our share of difficulties, especially after their father passed. Andreas had to grow up in an instant, taking on responsibilities no boy should have to shoulder. Not because I asked him to, but because that's who he is. And I want him to be happy—more than anything. During that divorce, when he was trying so hard to hide his misery from us, it shattered my heart. All I wanted was to take away his pain.

"But now... now I see his eyes shining again. I see glimpses of the carefree, happy boy he used to be. And I know that's because of you. You've brought that light back to him, Eleni." She paused, her expression softening even further. "But I need you to know something. Yes, he's my son, but you are my daughter. You always have been, and you always will be. Whatever happens between the two of you, you'll always have a shoulder to cry on, someone to turn to for advice. Him being my son doesn't change that. You are and will always be my little feisty, sweet Eleni. Okay?"

By the time she finished, I was crying again, but this time, the tears felt lighter, cleansing. I wrapped my arms around her, holding her as tightly as she'd held me moments before.

Oh, how I loved this woman. How stupid I'd been to stress over this dinner, to think for even a second that this was new territory. This wasn't new territory. This was Maria—my Mama Maria.

***

The dinner was in full swing, and the courtyard buzzed with the warmth of shared stories, clinking glasses, and the kind of laughter that came easily when surrounded by family. Maria's food was, as always, beyond perfection—platters of roasted lamb, crisp golden potatoes, and salads bursting with colour covered the table.

Everyone seemed to be talking at once; Callie was recounting a particularly chaotic event she'd organized, Nikos chimed in with his deadpan commentary, and Maria interjected occasionally with her own sharp humour. Even Andreas seemed lighter tonight, leaning back in his chair with a rare, easy smile as he listened to his sister's story.

I was mid-sip of my wine, completely relaxed, when I felt it—Andreas' hand on my leg under the table. My heart leapt, and before I could even react, his hand slid higher, his fingers teasing the edge of my skirt. My entire body froze in disbelief.

What. Was. He. Doing?

Instinct took over, and I kicked him hard on the leg. The sound of his muffled grunt should've been satisfying, but it was too late. I choked on the wine I'd been drinking, coughing violently as I tried to swallow and breathe at the same time. My eyes watered, and I was vaguely aware of Andreas laughing like an idiot as he rubbed his shin.

Callie, of course, was the first to notice. "What happened, Eleni? Too many mosquitos under the table?" she asked with a wicked grin.

That was all Nikos needed to join in, his deep laugh booming across the courtyard. I shot them both a deadly glare that, unsurprisingly, didn't do much to stop the teasing. Instead, Callie nudged Nikos and said, "I bet it was one of those stealth mosquitos. You know, the really persistent ones." They both dissolved into more laughter, and I knew I was doomed.

Turning to Andreas, who was now openly smirking, I hissed, "You are a dead man, Papadopoulos."

But before I could follow through on my threat, Maria swooped in to save the day—or, more accurately, to restore order. "Andreas!" she barked, her voice carrying the authority of a seasoned mother. "You either behave or go to your room and eat there alone!"

The table fell silent even though her eyes were twinkling with amusement; Maria's tone was so serious that none of us dared challenge her. All four of us suddenly found our laps very interesting, clearing our throats like guilty children caught misbehaving.

Still staring at his lap, Andreas muttered, "Sorry, Mum. Won't happen again."

That did it. The tension broke, and the table erupted into laughter. Even Maria couldn't keep a straight face, her stern façade melting into a smile as she shook her head. Andreas, however, was decidedly less amused. He sat there with the chastened expression of someone who knew better than to risk further wrath.

As the laughter subsided and we resumed eating, Maria's voice cut through the conversation with an unexpected seriousness. "So, what is it with these investors?" she asked, setting down her fork and folding her hands neatly on the table. "I want to know everything. Every detail."

The sudden shift in tone caught us all off guard. I exchanged a confused glance with Andreas, who looked just as puzzled as I felt.

Maria continued, her gaze sweeping over each of us. "Who are they? When are they coming? How long will they stay? Where will they stay? When will they come to the facility? When will they go to the grove? Will they come to the village? I want everything detailed now."

Her rapid-fire questions left us momentarily speechless. It wasn't just the quantity of information she demanded—it was the intensity with which she asked. It was as if she was preparing for a military operation, not a simple investor visit.

Andreas, ever the brave soul, attempted to reassure her. "Mum, you don't need to worry about any of this," he said, his voice unusually soft.

Maria, of course, pretended not to hear him.

For the next half-hour, the interrogation continued, with Maria pressing for every last detail about the investors' visit. None of us dared question why she needed to know so much. By the time the dinner ended, we were all exchanging puzzled looks, silently agreeing that whatever Maria had planned, it was best not to get in her way.

As I hugged Maria goodnight, I couldn't help but laugh inwardly at how the evening had turned out. Andreas' antics, Callie's teasing, and Maria's mysterious determination—this was Seranos in all its chaotic, wonderful glory.

As I was about to leave, I noticed Andreas lingering just behind Maria, shifting from one foot to the other like a kid waiting for recess. Then, out of nowhere, he blurted, "It's late. I better walk Eleni home."

It was, without a doubt, the most ridiculous thing I'd ever heard. We were in Seranos, for God's sake—a place where you could leave your front door open, and the biggest nighttime danger was stepping on a stray cat.

From the corner of the room, I heard Callie and Nikos burst into laughter. Callie, of course, couldn't resist. "Very creative, Andreas. Gold star!"

Maria chimed in without missing a beat. "I agree. You should walk her home, son. I've heard reports of wild goats attacking lone women at night in Seranos. We wouldn't want that, now would we? Perhaps you should even sit at her terrace and keep guard till morning."

Her words were met with another round of laughter as I stood there, half-embarrassed, half-amused, while Andreas tried to maintain his dignity. Without further delay—and with Maria's blessing—we left.

The moment we turned the first corner onto the quiet, moonlit street, Andreas' demeanour shifted entirely. Gone was the awkward, overgrown teenager I'd just witnessed at his mother's house. He placed a hand on my shoulder, pulling me gently closer, and kissed the top of my head. His hand slid into mine, his grip firm and steady as we walked together under the soft glow of the moonlight.

Breaking the silence, Andreas spoke, his voice suddenly serious. "Did you find my mum's questioning normal?"

"No," I replied without hesitation. "I'm as puzzled as you are."

We walked a bit further in companionable silence until Andreas spoke again. "I hope she's not up to something."

I couldn't help but laugh. "Well, even if she is, are you brave enough to confront her?"

He paused, then grinned, his voice low with mock seriousness. "Hell no."

His laughter mixed with mine, and as we continued down the narrow street, hand in hand, I realized that whatever Maria was plotting—and let's be honest, Maria was always plotting—I wouldn't trade this moment for anything.

Investors, Goats, and Other Disasters

I found myself growing increasingly restless. The night before the investors' arrival, I tossed and turned in bed, unable to quiet my racing thoughts. The room felt both too hot and too cold, the sheets tangling around my legs. Beside me, Andreas slept peacefully, his chest rising and falling in a steady rhythm that only served to highlight my own agitation.

I stared at the ceiling, counting imaginary cracks, before finally giving up. With a sigh, I slipped out of bed, careful not to disturb him, and padded softly to the kitchen. Zeus, who had claimed a corner of the room as his own, lifted his head groggily, his tail thumping once against the floor. "It's okay, baby," I whispered, crouching to pat his head. "I'm just losing my mind. Go back to sleep."

I poured myself a glass of water and stepped out onto the terrace. The cool night air raised goose bumps on my arms, a welcome contrast to the suffocating weight in my chest. The moon hung low over the sea, casting a silvery path across the gentle waves. It was beautiful, peaceful—everything I wasn't feeling inside.

I took a sip of water and closed my eyes, willing the calm around me to seep into my soul. I could do this. I had to do this.

"Can't sleep?"

I jumped at Andreas's voice, turning sharply; I found him leaning casually against the doorframe, his silhouette outlined by the soft glow from the kitchen. His hair was mussed, shirtless as usual, and there was an amused tilt to his mouth that made me want to simultaneously kiss him and throw my glass at him.

"Do you always sneak up on people like that?" I hissed, clutching my glass tightly.

"Only when they look like they're about to spiral," he said, stepping onto the terrace. His voice was soft, but his eyes gleamed with that infuriating mix of concern and amusement. "You're talking to Zeus at midnight. That's never a good sign."

"He's a better listener than you," I shot back, though my voice lacked real venom.

Andreas chuckled and leaned on the railing beside me, his arm brushing mine; the warmth of his skin seemed to calm me slightly.

"Alright, what's going on in that head of yours?" he asked, his tone softening. "Is this about tomorrow?"

I sighed, the tension knotting in my chest finding its way into my voice. "I don't want them here, Andreas. I never wanted them here. These people don't care about the grove, or Grandpa's legacy, or any of this." I gestured vaguely at the sea. "They just want to pick it apart and turn it into something it's not."

He was quiet for a moment, his gaze fixed on me. "I know," he said finally. "I know this isn't what you wanted. But maybe—just maybe—it's not as bad as you think. Meeting them doesn't mean you're agreeing to anything. It's just… listening."

I shook my head, staring down at the glass in my hands. "What if they say all the right things? What if they convince you or the whole village, and I'm the only one standing in the way? What if I'm wrong?"

Andreas reached out, his hand warm and solid as it curled around mine, steadying the glass I hadn't realized was trembling. "Eleni, if it doesn't feel right to you, then it's not right. Simple as that."

I looked up at him, the sincerity in his eyes cutting through the storm of doubt in my head. "You make it sound so easy."

"It's not," he admitted, a soft smile tugging at his lips. "But nothing worth fighting for ever is."

The warmth of his words and the quiet confidence in his voice made my chest ache. He squeezed my hand gently, then tugged me toward him, wrapping an arm around my shoulders. "Come on," he said softly. "Let's go back to bed. You'll need your strength tomorrow to tell those investors where to shove their spreadsheets."

A laugh escaped me, light and unexpected, and I leaned into him, letting his steadiness soothe the edges of my anxiety. "You're impossible, you know that?"

"I've been told," he said, pressing a kiss to my temple. "But I'm also right."

***

The hum of machinery filled the air as we walked through the production floor, the rhythmic clinking of bottles on the assembly line oddly soothing. The facility gleamed under the morning light streaming through the large windows, each surface spotless in preparation for our visitors. Nikos paced ahead, clipboard in hand, his crisp shirt and blazer making him look every inch the rural development professional.

And then there was Andreas.

Gone were his scuffed boots and rolled-up sleeves, replaced with a light linen suit paired with a perfectly pressed white shirt, the top button undone for just the right amount of casual charm. His dark hair, which usually stuck out in unruly waves, was smoothed back in a way that looked unfairly good on him. He didn't just clean up well; he transformed.

I trailed a step behind, trying not to stare. How was it that the man who'd fallen asleep on the sofa yesterday with Zeus drooling on his shoulder could now look like he belonged on the cover of Modern Mediterranean Elegance?

He caught me looking and raised an eyebrow. "What?" he asked, a smirk tugging at the corner of his mouth.

I blinked, snapping out of it. "Nothing," I said too quickly. "You just—you're really pulling out all the stops, huh? I didn't even know you owned a suit."

"Surprises keep life interesting," he said smoothly, adjusting his cuffs. "Besides, you've got your business goddess thing going on today. Had to step up my game."

My cheeks flushed at the compliment, even though I knew he was deflecting. "You mean this?" I gestured to my tailored navy dress and blazer. "This is just so I don't look like I rolled in from the grove. Like some people usually do."

"Not today, though," Nikos chimed in as we entered the office. He shot Andreas a teasing glance. "That suit? Bold choice. By the way, is anyone else still reeling from Maria's insistence on managing the investors' transfer? That was... unexpected."

I groaned, sinking into a chair in the meeting room. "Don't remind me. I still don't know how we let her talk us into it."

"We didn't let her do anything," Andreas muttered, leaning against the window. "She just announced it and brushed off my protests like I was still twelve, asking for a second helping of cake."

"She's got a way of making refusal impossible," Nikos said with a chuckle. "What was her line again?"

"'Leave the details to me; you kids already have a lot on your plates,'" Andreas said, mimicking his mother's voice with impressive accuracy.

"She's not wrong," I pointed out. "But after her questions the other night, I'm wondering what her real plan is."

Andreas pinched the bridge of his nose. "Knowing her? It's either a perfectly orchestrated masterpiece or absolute chaos."

"Either way, it'll be memorable," Nikos added with a grin. "Let's just hope it's more of the former."

I moved to join Andreas at the window, the morning sun casting long shadows across the facility parking lot. "It's Maria," I said. "How bad could it—"

A familiar, rattling engine cut me off. My eyes widened as Yiannis' ancient, fish-scented car wheezed its way into the lot, trailing a plume of questionable-smelling smoke. It bounced into an open spot with a final shuddering clank, like it was relieved the journey was over.

"What the..." Nikos started, peering out the window.

Realization dawned, and Andreas froze. "Oh no," he muttered, his face paling. "Oh, for fuck's sake."

I couldn't help it. The laughter bubbled up uncontrollably, spilling out as I clutched the windowsill for support. "You don't think—"

"Oh, I think," Andreas said darkly, watching as Yiannis climbed out of the car, dressed in his usual mismatched clothes, his cap askew.

***

The hot sun beat down on the asphalt as Andreas and I rushed toward the parking lot, my sandals clacking against the ground in a way that perfectly matched the rhythm of my rising frustration. Yiannis' rickety car sat idling near the facility entrance, a fresh plume of smoke curling lazily from its exhaust. The smell of fish hit me like a wall before I even reached the vehicle. Andreas, his linen suit now feeling wildly out of place, muttered something under his breath that I suspected would have made a sailor blush.

As we approached, the back doors creaked open, and one by one, the passengers emerged.

The first to step out was a tall woman with sleek platinum-blonde hair that could have doubled as a mirror. She wore a tailored black dress and heels that seemed entirely impractical for navigating the facility. Despite the heat, she looked as cool and composed as if she'd stepped off the cover of a high-end magazine. She smoothed her dress, her piercing blue eyes immediately locking onto Andreas with a deadpan expression.

"Charming welcome," she said, her tone clipped yet perfectly polished. "Memorable, certainly."

I opened my mouth to respond, but nothing came out. Andreas cleared his throat, clearly trying to regroup. "We aim to leave an impression," he said dryly.

Behind her, a man in his late 50s climbed out of the car, clearly less amused. He wore a dark suit clashing spectacularly with the Greek sun, his tie already slightly loosened. His sharp, weathered face was fixed in a polite but distinctly unamused expression. You'd expect to see the kind of face at the head of a boardroom, not stepping out of Yiannis' fish-mobile.

The third passenger followed—a man in his late 30s with sandy brown hair, a neatly trimmed beard, and a pair of sunglasses that he removed as he stepped into the light. His attire was slightly more relaxed—a light grey suit sans tie—but his energy radiated something slick and professional. Unlike the others, he seemed more entertained than annoyed, brushing a smudge from his cuff with an easy smile.

"Welcome," Andreas said quickly, stepping forward to salvage the moment. "I'm Andreas Papadopoulos, and this is Eleni Katsaros."

"Isabella Hart," the woman said, stepping forward and offering Andreas her hand with a smooth, practised motion. Her handshake was firm, her piercing blue gaze steady and appraising.

Andreas, ever the polite host, took her hand and smiled faintly. "It's good to put a face to the voice," he said, his tone warm but entirely innocent.

Isabella's lips curved into a small, knowing smile as her gaze flicked over him, deliberate and unapologetic. "Likewise," she said smoothly, her voice dipping just slightly. "And unexpectedly good."

Something unpleasant and unfamiliar twisted in my stomach as I watched her obvious assessment of him. Is this... jealousy? The thought came unbidden, and I dismissed it quickly, forcing myself to focus as she released Andreas's hand, her gaze lingering just a second too long. Andreas, meanwhile, seemed oblivious and chuckled politely, brushing her comment off with a casual charm. I, on the other hand, was left wrestling with the unfamiliar twinge bubbling inside me.

The older man stepped forward next, his handshake brisk and efficient. "Edward Whitmore, CFO of Crownstone Investments," he said, his voice clipped and authoritative. "We're grateful for the invitation and eager to see what you've built here."

Standing beside him, Isabella added smoothly, "Edward and Lucas travelled with me from London. We're very much looking forward to today's presentation."

The younger man stepped forward next, his handshake warm and accompanied by a confident smile. "Lucas Vance, Head of Marketing at Crownstone. Isabella's told us a lot about the grove and the facility." His tone was friendly, almost overly so, with the kind of polish that spoke of someone who knew how to charm a room when needed.

As we began walking toward the entrance of the facility, our unlikely entourage in tow, I couldn't shake the faint smell of bait still clinging to the air. The conversation between Isabella, Edward, and Lucas hummed lightly in the background, their crisp British accents contrasting with the gentle hum of cicadas around us.

***

The meeting room was exactly how I'd envisioned it: spotless, professional, and basking in the glow of sunlight streaming through the large windows. A tray of refreshments sat untouched on the sideboard, and my carefully prepared slides were projected crisply onto the wall. Everything was perfect—or so I thought.

As I stood at the head of the table, my voice steady and practised, I ran through the financials and outlined the business's potential. My pitch was polished, packed with data points, growth projections, and an impassioned explanation of our planned upgrades to the facility. Nikos, seated beside Andreas, nodded occasionally in quiet encouragement.

But the response from the three across the table was... underwhelming.

Edward Whitmore leaned back in his chair, his sharp suit impeccable but his expression unreadable. He asked a few generic questions—nothing that required more than a surface-level response. "That's clear now, thank you," he said flatly after I explained a key revenue model, his tone giving no indication of whether he was impressed or bored.

Lucas offered polite smiles, occasionally jotting something down, though the way he glanced out the window suggested his mind was elsewhere. While more attentive, Isabella seemed preoccupied, her sharp blue eyes scanning the room with more interest than the presentation itself.

By the time I clicked on the final slide, the silence was deafening. My stomach churned with unease. Shouldn't Edward be grilling me by now? Shouldn't they all be asking questions about how we plan to increase production or break into more export markets? Instead, there were a few more murmurs of "I understand" and "Thank you for clarifying." Polite but utterly devoid of the enthusiasm I'd expected. Nikos cleared his throat and began answering Edward's question about sustainable agriculture in the region, launching an articulate explanation about local practices and long-term environmental benefits.

While Nikos spoke, I found myself unable to focus on his words. Instead, my gaze drifted to Isabella.

She exuded self-confidence, the kind that came with knowing you belonged wherever you chose to be. The way she moved, the way she spoke—it was all polished and deliberate, radiating the kind of entitlement that comes from spending years in high-stakes boardrooms. Her every gesture seemed to say, I've worked for this, I've earned this, and I'm untouchable.

And she was stunning. Her sleek blonde hair, perfectly applied makeup, and tailored outfit made her look like she'd stepped out of a glossy magazine. Isabella Hart was representing everything I was supposed to become when I escaped London—everything I thought I never wanted to be. Cold, distant, all about business and money and looks.

But as I watched her, a strange feeling crept over me. My father would have loved Isabella. She was the kind of person he'd always wanted me to become: clever, successful, perfectly groomed, and utterly professional. I could almost hear his voice in my head, praising her achievements, contrasting them with my own messy, unpolished life.

The thought stung. I had run away from London to escape that world. To escape the pressure to be something I wasn't. I had told myself that I wanted a different life, one that felt more meaningful and authentic. And yet... sitting here now, facing Isabella, I couldn't help but feel an unwelcome pang of underachievement. I had never been her—not in London, not anywhere. She represented everything I'd failed to become, according to my father.

The question clawed at the edges of my mind: Was my escape to Greece genuine? Or was I just running away from a fight I didn't think I could win?

I blinked, snapping out of my thoughts as Nikos finished his answer, his voice trailing into Edward's polite hum of acknowledgement. I shifted uncomfortably in my seat, forcing my focus back to the conversation, but the questions Isabella had stirred in me lingered, heavy and unresolved.

We finally moved on to the facility tour. Me and Andreas took them through every nook and cranny, explaining the upgrades we were planning, from solar-powered processing equipment to advanced quality control systems. Nikos jumped in to elaborate on the sustainability benefits, still, their reactions barely shifted.

The olive oil tasting was the final act. I watched as they sampled the oils we'd poured into pristine glass cups, Lucas offering the occasional "Hmm" and Isabella making vague comments about the flavours. Edward remained the picture of stoic disinterest.

By the time we escorted them to their waiting car—a sleek, air-conditioned company vehicle that Andreas had personally arranged—it was hard to tell if they'd been impressed, indifferent, or quietly planning their exit strategy. "We'll pick you up at your hotel for dinner in a few hours," Andreas told them, his tone polite but a touch stiff. They nodded their thanks, and then they were gone.

As the car disappeared down the road, the three of us lingered near the facility entrance, the late afternoon sun casting long shadows across the lot.

"Is it just me," I began, breaking the silence, "or are you two also finding this weird?"

"One thing's for sure," Nikos said, running a hand through his hair, "I wasn't expecting this."

Andreas crossed his arms, his linen suit no longer looking as polished as it had this morning. "They looked more like a group of tourists on an olive oil facility tour than potential investors. Weird."

"Weird, indeed," I said softly, staring after the car, my unease settling deeper in my gut.

We stood there for a moment longer, the hum of the facility behind us, before retreating inside, each of us lost in our own thoughts about what had just unfolded.

***

The company car pulled up smoothly in front of the hotel, and Andreas and I stepped out, greeted by the soft glow of the entrance lights. Edward, Isabella, and Lucas were already waiting in the lobby, their polished appearances perfectly matching the hotel's luxurious ambience. Edward's handshake was firm, his smile a touch too knowing, while Lucas's easy grin contrasted sharply with Isabella's poised, unreadable expression.

The drive to the marina passed mostly in polite small talk, with Andreas expertly steering the conversation toward light, neutral topics: the weather, the charm of Navagos, and a few humorous anecdotes about the village. I noticed Isabella's occasional glances toward Andreas in the rearview mirror, her interest thinly veiled behind casual remarks about the scenery.

The marina sparkled under the evening lights, the reflections of yachts dancing on the calm waters. The fine dining restaurant Andreas had chosen for the evening was elegant but understated, with white linens, a view of the harbour, and the hum of quiet conversations filling the air. As dinner progressed, I couldn't help but notice that Edward's tone toward me was markedly different from the morning. Where he had been distant and perfunctory earlier, now he seemed oddly warm, almost overly so. He asked about my plans for the grove with a genuine curiosity that felt entirely out of place compared to his earlier disinterest. At first, I thought it might be the wine loosening him up, but then it clicked.

He wasn't here just for business—this warmth wasn't about me or the grove. It was about my father.

"Your father and I go way back," Edward said, swirling his wine glass with the ease of someone accustomed to this kind of setting. "We worked on a few deals together years ago. A sharp man, Petros. Always a step ahead."

Andreas raised an eyebrow. "So, he's the one who encouraged you to come out here?" he said, shooting me a glance.

Edward nodded. "He certainly had... strong opinions on the matter. Told me this place had potential. And he's rarely wrong."

I smiled tightly, trying to keep my unease in check. Of course he did... He was probably hoping Edward would bring his London expertise to bear on what he likely viewed as my latest impulsive adventure.

"What do you think of Navagos so far?" Andreas asked, steering the conversation away from my father.

"It's lovely," Isabella said, her voice smooth as silk. She leaned slightly toward Andreas, her blue eyes gleaming. "Quite a change of pace from London."

"Much warmer," Lucas added with a chuckle, loosening his collar slightly.

"And there's certainly no shortage of charm here," Isabella said, her tone silky as she let her gaze drift over Andreas with deliberate slowness. "Not just the scenery, of course."

Andreas chuckled. "We do our best."

I forced a smile, though my grip on my fork tightened. She wasn't exactly subtle. The way her perfectly manicured fingers grazed her wine glass and her soft laughter at Andreas' every comment was enough to set my teeth on edge. And what made it worse was that Andreas wasn't shutting it down. If anything, he was being... nice. Polite. Charming.

"What did you think of the facility?" I asked, my tone a little sharper than I intended.

Edward glanced at me briefly, his expression unreadable. "Interesting," he said. "You've clearly put a lot of work into it."

"Very thorough," Lucas added vaguely, already distracted by the menu.

"Impressive," Isabella chimed in, her gaze flicking briefly to me before settling back on Andreas. "Though I'm sure you already know that."

I bit my lip to keep from snapping something I might regret.

The rest of the dinner passed in a blur of small talk about business in London, the intricacies of olive oil production, and Edward's mildly condescending anecdotes about his past ventures. When the check came, Andreas smoothly covered it, assuring the group that they were our guests.

As we stood to leave, Edward turned to Andreas with a wry smile. "Tomorrow, someone will pick us up at eleven, yes? Just make sure it's not the same old chap from this morning."

Andreas laughed lightly. "I'll see to it personally."

By the time we arrived at my house, exhaustion was settling into my bones. The adrenaline of the past few days had worn off, leaving me feeling drained. I sank into one of the terrace chairs, the cool night breeze brushing against my skin, too tired to even make it inside.

Andreas leaned against the railing, looking far too relaxed for someone who had endured the same day. "See? It wasn't so bad. Even with the airport transfer saga."

I raised an eyebrow, unable to resist. "For you, it was good for sure. You expanded your fan club."

He laughed, the sound low and easy in the quiet night. "Are you jealous, Katsaros?"

I glanced at him, too weary to banter or think of a clever comeback. "Should I be, Papadopoulos?"

He walked over, leaning casually against the arm of my chair, his eyes glinting with a soft warmth. "Come on, Eleni," he said, a small smile tugging at his lips. "You know you've got me wrapped around your finger, all for yourself."

The playful warmth in his voice tugged at something deep inside me, easing the tension I hadn't even realized I was holding. I managed a small smile, shaking my head lightly as his words wrapped around me, reassuring in a way only Andreas could be.

As we finally headed inside to bed, I kicked off my shoes and stretched out on the mattress. "Do you think she'll wear those heels to the grove tomorrow?" I asked, barely able to suppress a grin.

Andreas chuckled as he climbed in beside me. "If she does, I hope she's prepared to sink."

His laughter followed me into sleep, a comforting reminder that, despite everything, we were on the same side.

***

The farmhouse stood quiet in the morning sun, the light bouncing off its stone walls and terracotta roof. Andreas and I waited by the entrance, the silence between us companionable. The olive grove stretched endlessly before us, the sea glinting in the distance.

I shifted my weight, glancing at Andreas. "Do you think they'll even bother showing up? After yesterday, I wouldn't be surprised if they decided to skip straight to the beach."

He smirked, adjusting the cuff of his linen shirt. "Maybe they're curious to see if Yiannis is our chauffeur again."

The low hum of an approaching car cut through the morning stillness. A black sedan pulled up, its air-conditioned perfection at odds with the rustic charm of the grove. As the doors opened, the investors emerged one by one.

Isabella stepped out first, and I found myself studying her. "Well," I muttered to Andreas, "she's not wearing the heels."

"She wouldn't," he said, not missing a beat, his eyes scanning the group.

I kept watching Isabella. She was dressed impeccably, of course—tailored beige slacks paired with a crisp white blouse and a lightweight navy blazer that accentuated her slender frame. Flat leather sandals completed the look, practical yet refined, and she carried a sleek Hermès handbag in one hand, somehow managing to make it blend effortlessly with the rustic surroundings in a way that defied logic. It was irritating, really, how effortlessly she could look both elegant and capable, no matter the setting.

"Come on," Andreas said, gesturing to the group. "Time to impress."

He led them toward the grove, launching into an easy explanation of its history. "Some of these trees are over 500 years old," he said, gesturing to a particularly gnarled specimen. "They've weathered storms, wars, and countless harvests. This grove is as much a part of our family as any living member."

Isabella listened intently, her piercing blue eyes scanning the grove as though committing it to memory. "Remarkable," she said softly, and for a moment, her tone held something genuine.

Edward, however, glanced at his watch. "Fascinating," he murmured, though it was clear his mind was elsewhere.

Meanwhile, Lucas was a whirlwind of motion, snapping photographs of everything—the trees, the farmhouse, the sea in the distance. He crouched low, climbed onto a rock, and even asked Andreas to step aside so he could get an unobstructed view of a particularly picturesque tree.

As the tour continued, Andreas recounted anecdotes about the grove: how our grandfathers had planted certain sections by hand, how the community came together during harvest seasons, and how the sea air gave our olives their distinct flavour. Isabella nodded thoughtfully, her respect for Andreas growing with each story, but Edward remained stoic, occasionally muttering an obligatory "Interesting."

Lucas, for his part, was already at least 50 photos deep.

The atmosphere shifted when the tour ended near a rocky outcrop overlooking the sea. Gone was the detached indifference of the previous day. Now, questions came rapidly, one after another, as though the group had woken from a daze.

"How large is the property, exactly?" Edward asked his tone sharper now.

"Roughly 5 hectares," Andreas replied, though he frowned slightly at the abruptness.

"Does the land extend all the way to the beach?" Isabella added her notebook open and pen poised.

"It does," Andreas said. "About a kilometre of coastline, though it's undeveloped."

"Any water sources on the land?" Lucas chimed in, lowering his camera for once.

"There's a natural spring near the eastern grove," Andreas said, now visibly puzzled.

The questions kept coming, each more specific and less related to olive production. Edward leaned forward, suddenly animated. "And the zoning status? Is it entirely agricultural, or are there mixed-use options?"

Andreas hesitated. "It's primarily agricultural, though some sections closer to the coast have mixed-use potential."

I stood beside him, my unease growing with each passing question. These weren't the queries of investors interested in olive oil or sustainability. They were sizing up the land, the beach, the infrastructure. What is going on here?

Andreas answered patiently, though I could see the faint crease of confusion on his brow. When the barrage finally slowed, he looked at me, then back at the group. "Anything else you'd like to know about the grove? The production processes? The oil itself?"

Edward smiled faintly, his expression unreadable. "No, I think we've covered the essentials. For now."

***

Just as we were approaching the farmhouse and a semblance of calm returned to the grove, a distant rustling caught my attention. At first, I thought it was the wind, but then the sound grew louder—a frantic pattering accompanied by high-pitched bleats.

Before I could process what was happening, a herd of goats burst into view, streaming towards us like an unstoppable tide. Leading the charge was none other than Mythos, the mischievous little goat who seemed to make it his mission to wreak havoc wherever he went.

"Oh, for the love of—" Andreas groaned, cutting himself off as Mythos leapt nimbly onto a low stone wall, his tiny tail wagging like he knew exactly what he was doing.

"What on earth?" Edward exclaimed, stepping back instinctively as the goats surged forward, nibbling on olive leaves and bumping into the group with zero regard for personal space.

"This is not supposed to be happening," I muttered, already moving to intercept Mythos, who had his sights set on Isabella.

"Of course it isn't," Andreas snapped, darting after a particularly determined goat that had decided to sample the bark of one of the ancient trees. "Villagers must've sent them here. There's no way they wandered this far on their own."

As I lunged for Mythos, the little terror sidestepped me with infuriating agility and made a beeline for Isabella's handbag. He grabbed the strap in his teeth with a triumphant bleat and bolted.

"My bag!" Isabella's polished composure cracked for the first time as she pointed at Mythos, who was already running with her bag flapping wildly from his mouth.

"I've got it!" Andreas shouted, tearing after him like his life depended on it.

Meanwhile, Lucas was laughing so hard he could barely hold his camera steady, snapping photos of the chaos. "This is gold," he wheezed.

Edward, however, was less amused. In his attempt to dodge one of the larger goats, his pristine white shirt snagged on a low-hanging branch, leaving a jagged tear in the sleeve. "This is absurd!" he barked, swatting at a goat that seemed entirely too interested in his shoes.

I finally managed to corral a few of the smaller goats toward the edge of the grove, waving my arms and muttering threats that I knew they wouldn't understand. Mythos, however, remained untouchable, leading Andreas on a merry chase that ended with Andreas grabbing the handbag just as Mythos tried to leap over a stone fence.

"Got it!" Andreas called triumphantly, holding the bag aloft like a trophy. Mythos gave a defiant bleat, clearly unbothered by the loss, and trotted off to join the rest of his herd.

By the time we'd wrangled the goats, leaves were scattered everywhere, and one of the younger goats had toppled a basket of olive samples we'd prepared for the tour. I glanced over at the group, bracing for their reactions.

To my surprise, Isabella was smiling—an actual, genuine smile that transformed her usual cool appearance into something almost... human.

"I have to admit," she said, brushing a stray leaf off her blazer, "this place has... personality."

Her comment drew a laugh from Lucas, who was still snapping photos. Even Edward, despite his torn sleeve and ruffled hair, managed a grudging smirk.

Andreas walked over, handing Isabella her bag with a wry smile. "I'd apologize, but I'm not sure the goats would mean it."

Isabella chuckled softly, shaking her head. "Consider it an unforgettable experience."

"Unforgettable," Edward muttered, eyeing his sleeve with disdain. "Yes, that's one way to put it."

As we surveyed the mess, I caught Andreas's eye, and for a moment, neither of us could help but laugh. Chaos aside, the grove had certainly made an impression—just not the one we'd planned.

Once everybody seemed calmed down, Andreas and I led the group back toward the farmhouse. Despite the ruffled start, the investors seemed more relaxed now, even Edward, whose torn sleeve was the only remaining evidence of the previous pandemonium. True to form, Isabella adjusted her blazer and smoothed her hair, her composure firmly back in place.

"Why don't we head to the farmhouse for some refreshments?" Andreas suggested as we neared the stone steps. "We can wrap things up there."

The group agreed, and soon, we were gathered around the farmhouse's rustic table, sipping chilled lemonade and recapping the visit. Andreas summarized the grove's unique characteristics and history while I offered a few final details about the operations and future plans.

The atmosphere was cordial, almost friendly, but there was an undeniable sense of distance, especially when Edward finally spoke. "Thank you for your time and hospitality," he said, rising from his chair. "We'll take everything into account and send you our proposal once we're back in London."

Lucas gave his usual easy smile as he stood. "This has been... enlightening," he said, though his tone didn't quite reveal how enlightening he actually found it.

Isabella was the last to stand, her gaze lingering briefly on Andreas before she extended her hand. "Thank you for the tour," she said, her voice smooth. "It's been... memorable."

Andreas nodded with his usual politeness. "Talk to you soon, then."

Her lips curved into a faint smile. "Oh, I'm looking forward to it," she said, her tone carrying just enough warmth to make her meaning unmistakable.

I didn't trust myself to speak, so I busied myself tidying up the table as Andreas walked them to the waiting car. There were handshakes, polite farewells, and even a rare, genuine smile from Edward as the car pulled away down the dirt road.

The moment they were gone, I let out a breath I hadn't realized I'd been holding. The farmhouse seemed quieter now, the air lighter. Relief washed over me, though I wasn't entirely sure what had caused it. Was it the fact that this whirlwind investor visit was finally over? Or was it because Isabella Hart was on her way to the airport and out of Andreas's orbit?

I shook my head, chuckling softly at myself. "Look, look now, Eleni," I muttered under my breath. "Who would've thought you were the jealous type?"

***

The drive back to the village was wrapped in silence. I kept my eyes on the road, stealing the occasional glance at Andreas. His jaw was set, his knuckles tight on the steering wheel, and the faint tension radiating from him made my chest ache. The relief I'd felt earlier from seeing the investors off was now shadowed by an unsettling sense that something wasn't right.

As we pulled into the village square, a group of familiar figures stood waiting for us. Maria and Sophia were at the centre, flanked by a handful of the village elders. Their expressions ranged from stern to expectant, their collective presence leaving no doubt that this wasn't a casual gathering.

The moment Andreas stepped out of the car, his frustration spilt over. "What now?" he demanded, running a hand through his hair. "Haven't you all done enough already?"

Maria stepped forward first, her voice calm but firm. "Andreas, we need to talk."

"Talk?" he snapped. "About what? About the goats? About how you're sabotaging this whole thing?"

"We're not sabotaging anything," Sophia interjected, her tone steady, laced with quiet authority. "We're trying to protect what's ours. What's yours."

Andreas laughed bitterly. "Protect it? By unleashing goats and pulling stunts that make us look like fools?"

"Enough," Maria said sharply, her eyes flashing. "You know why we're doing this."

Andreas hesitated, his anger softening as he locked eyes with her. "You don't understand what it's like," he said, his voice quieter now, though the frustration still simmered beneath the surface. "You don't know the weight of it all. The pressure. This isn't just a grove—it's our history, our land. And we're on the brink of losing it all."

Sophia stepped forward, her dark eyes steady and filled with quiet compassion. "Andreas," she said softly, "we're not your enemy here. We're doing this because this grove—it's part of you. And so is she."

Her words lingered in the air, gentle but firm, and Andreas's gaze faltered. His shoulders sagged under the weight of it all, his frustration giving way to a weariness that spoke of burdens carried for far too long. For a moment, he looked more tired than angry, a man carrying far too much for far too long.

The group fell silent, their point made, and Andreas turned away, motioning for me to follow. We walked out of the square, the murmurs of the villagers fading behind us as we made our way down the familiar path toward my house.

For a while, I didn't say anything. I could feel the storm brewing inside him, and I wanted to tread carefully. But the nagging feeling in my chest wouldn't let me stay silent.

"Andreas," I began softly, glancing at him. "Is there something you're not telling me?"

His head snapped toward me, his face tight. "No," he said sharply.

I stopped walking, taken aback by the sudden edge in his tone. "Okay," I said slowly, "but just so you know, I think these investors are up to something very, very unpleasant. And I think you're aware of that too."

He stopped as well, turning to face me fully. "Eleni," he said, his voice low but strained. "Not now, please."

His words stung, and I stepped back slightly, swallowing hard. "Alright," I said quietly, my chest tightening.

He exhaled sharply, running a hand over his face as though trying to compose himself before speaking. "I've got some things to do in town, so I need to head back after I walk you home. I'll probably stay at my flat in Navagos tonight—I might finish late."

I blinked, caught off guard. He didn't need to walk me home—we were in Seranos, and I knew my way perfectly well. In fact, he hadn't needed to leave the car at the village square earlier; he could have told me this then and dropped me off there. This felt like a decision made on the spot, an escape rather than a plan.

I didn't press him. Maybe he needed some time alone, and now that I thought about it, I realized I might need the same. These last couple of weeks had been overwhelming, and we'd been practically living together since his so-called "love declaration." I was too tired to unpack what I was feeling, and all I wanted was a glass of wine, the sunset, and the unjudging company of Ari and Zeus to pour my frustrations onto.

I said, "Sure!" trying to sound casual, though the word felt heavier than it should have.

Once we arrived at my terrace gate, he paused briefly and gave me a smile—a smile that seemed forced, sad, and laden with unspoken regrets. Leaning in, he placed a quick peck on my lips, his movements almost mechanical, like he was already elsewhere in his mind.

"Love you, Leni," he said quietly, turning to walk away. His words, though meant to reassure me, felt more like he was reminding himself, as if he needed to hold onto something familiar before stepping into whatever storm was brewing inside him.

When the Truth Breaks

The soft hum of the office fan was the only sound, a steady rhythm that matched the faint tapping of my pen against the desk. The facility had settled back into its usual cadence in the days following the investors' visit—an odd, almost jarring return to normalcy. Paperwork, schedules, and budgets had replaced the questions, tours, and chaos.

I should have felt relief. The farm was running, the facility was productive, and the villagers were back to their routines. But something else had settled in too—something quieter, less tangible. A kind of distance I couldn't quite name.

Andreas and I had fallen into separate rhythms. I was here at the facility most days, drowning in spreadsheets and emails, while he stayed at the grove, busy with harvest preparations. It is usual for us to work apart, but this felt different. Less like a practical division of labour and more like… avoidance.

The night after his retreat to Navagos, he came back, staying at my house as if nothing had happened. For a moment, I let myself believe the distance was just in my head, a product of my overthinking. But now, a week later, the pattern was clear. Some nights, he stayed with me, slipping seamlessly back into our routine; other nights, he retreated to his flat without explanation, back to that unspoken space where he kept the things he wouldn't—or couldn't—share. And I let him.

It wasn't anything obvious. He still cracked his familiar jokes and still smiled at me in that way that felt like it was meant just for me. But I could feel it—an unnamed shift, something quiet and undefined, pulling us apart even as we moved through the same motions. We carried on as if nothing was wrong, pretending not to notice the growing void.

I sighed, dropping the pen and leaning back in my chair. Through the office window, the coastline stretched out in the distance, the sea glinting under the afternoon sun. It was serene, unwavering—a sharp contrast to the restless questions that had taken up residence in my mind.

The door to my office burst open, startling me so much that I nearly knocked over my coffee. Nikos was the first in, followed closely by Andreas, whose expression immediately set me on edge.

"Did you check your emails?" Nikos asked, his tone sharp, eyes wide with urgency.

I froze, the words sending a rush of boiling water through my veins. "What is it?" My voice barely held steady as I looked between them.

Andreas stepped forward, his jaw tight. "The offer. It's in."

I stared at him, my heart thudding in my chest as I turned to my laptop, fumbling to open the inbox. The email was there, its subject line as innocuous as it was ominous: Proposal from Crownstone Investments. My hands trembled as I clicked it, revealing the attached PDF. Nikos leaned over my shoulder as Andreas perched on the desk, his arms crossed, both of them silent as I scanned the document.

The offer was staggering. Two to three times the business's value, the numbers were so generous they almost didn't feel real. But my stomach turned as I reached the terms. Full buyout. Non-negotiable. No guarantees about preserving the groves, no commitment to retaining staff, and no mention of the community's connection to the business. A clean slate, free of ties, leaving nothing behind but money.

"This is a joke," I said, my voice shaking with anger. "They don't care about the grove or anything else. They have other plans. This isn't an offer—it's an insult."

"Eleni," Andreas began cautiously, his tone far too measured for my liking. "I don't think it's that simple."

I whipped around, glaring at him. "Not that simple? They're offering to wipe us all away—our families, the staff, the village's connection to this place—and you're saying it's not that simple?"

Andreas held up his hands, his expression a mix of frustration and unease. "I'm not saying I'm thrilled about it, okay? But look at the numbers, Eleni. This is life-changing. With figures like these, we could create other opportunities for the community too."

"It's not about 'opportunities,' Andreas," I interrupted, my voice rising. "This is about legacy. About family. About this village."

He exhaled sharply, leaning back. "Eleni, I get it. But we can't ignore the reality here. The grove's struggling. The business isn't exactly thriving. If we lose everything, then we won't be able to help anyone at all."

The calmness in his voice, the logical detachment, felt like a betrayal. "You're seriously entertaining this?" I spat, my anger boiling over. "How can you even think about selling this place to people who'll probably gut it? And we won't even have any say in it."

"Because we can't keep running on sentiment alone!" he snapped, his own frustration breaking through. "This isn't just about what you want, Eleni. It's about what's possible."

"Enough," Nikos interjected, stepping between us with his hands raised. "Let's all take a breath. Eleni, I get where you're coming from. Andreas, I get where you're coming from too. But this isn't a decision to be made in five minutes."

Neither of us spoke, the tension crackling like static in the air. I turned back to the document, my vision blurred with anger and something else I didn't want to name. Disappointment? Fear?

Nikos looked between us, his tone softer now. "Let's sleep on it. Discuss it again tomorrow. This isn't the end of the world, but we need to be clear-headed about what's at stake—for everyone."

Andreas nodded curtly, standing and heading for the door without another word. I stayed seated, my fists clenched as I stared at the screen. Nikos lingered, his expression concerned but careful. "Eleni," he said gently, "just... think it over, okay? You've got time."

I didn't answer, my gaze fixed on the glowing numbers that seemed to mock everything I cared about. As Nikos left, the quiet of the office felt deafening, the space between me and Andreas growing wider than ever.

***

Andreas

I steered toward the farmhouse, the silence in the car pressing against me like a weight. The offer was repeating in my head, and each line and figure was a stark reminder of the impossible situation we were in. My heart twisted painfully as I thought of Eleni's face, the anger and disappointment in her eyes still fresh, cutting deeper than I wanted to admit.

I didn't blame her for reacting the way she had. God knows I wanted to refuse the offer as swiftly and categorically as she did. Every fibre of my being ached at the thought of selling the grove—this land, these trees—they were as much a part of me as breathing. They'd seen me grow, stumble, and rebuild.

But I couldn't ignore the reality staring me in the face. With my shares tied up in my credit debts, this grove wasn't just a legacy—it was also a burden I was struggling to carry. Trying to save it felt less like a noble fight and more like a romantic daydream, one without a miracle cash injection waiting in the wings.

I loved this land. I loved this community. Hell, more than anyone else, I knew what it meant to the people here. It wasn't just business; it was identity, pride, and survival. But love alone wasn't enough to pay the staff, repair the equipment, or keep the business afloat.

Eleni's passion for preserving it all—our history, our traditions—was one of the things I admired most about her. But I couldn't afford to think like her, not entirely. Not when the stakes were this high. If there was a way to turn this offer into something that helped the village—if selling meant giving these people a real chance at something better—wasn't that worth considering?

I turned into the farmhouse driveway, parking beneath the shadow of the ancient olive tree at its entrance. The sunlight filtered through its branches, casting dappled patterns on the ground. I sat there for a moment, staring at the house, the fields, the sea just visible in the distance. God, how I wanted to find a way to save this place.

I killed the engine, my chest tightening with every passing second. The only thing heavier than the silence was the weight of knowing there was no easy way out of this.

The next morning, my phone buzzed on the farmhouse's table. I glanced at the screen and frowned. Isabella Hart.

I hesitated for a moment before picking up. "Hello," I answered, leaning back in my chair and bracing myself for whatever smooth London line she was about to throw my way.

"Hello, Andreas," came Isabella's voice, polished and poised as ever. "I trust you've had a chance to review our offer?"

Straight to the point. No pleasantries, no small talk. Typical.

"We received it," I said carefully, running a hand over my jaw. "But it's not quite what we were expecting."

There was a slight pause, her silence heavy with unspoken analysis. "Not what you were expecting, or not what you were hoping for?"

I leaned forward, resting my elbows on the table. "Let's just say it's different from what we had in mind. No decisions have been made yet."

"Understandable," she replied smoothly, her tone unbothered. "These things take time. I'm back in Navagos now if you need a face-to-face meeting to discuss this further. I just wanted to ensure everything was clear on your end."

"Crystal," I said dryly, my eyes narrowing as I stared out the window at the grove. The way she spoke—calm, detached, unflappable—it only made me more curious. "Why are you back, Isabella?"

Her laugh was light, almost amused, but it didn't quite mask the calculation behind it. "I'm here to oversee the legal checks and paperwork," she said, her voice slipping into the polished professionalism she wielded like armour. "But I hardly need you to chaperone me if that's what you're worried about."

"Not worried," I said, though the knot in my stomach told a different story. "Just wondering why someone like you would bother coming back for what seems like a done deal on your end."

"Maybe I like to be thorough," she replied, her tone softening slightly. "Or maybe," she added, her voice dipping just enough to hint at something more, "I thought we might take the opportunity to catch up while I'm here. It'd be a shame to waste the chance."

I stiffened, her words landing somewhere between playful and deliberate. "I'm sure you've got plenty to keep you busy," I said, keeping my tone even.

"Oh, I do," she replied smoothly, "but one must balance work with pleasure, wouldn't you agree?"

I tightened my grip on the phone, my mind racing. She wasn't just playing games—she was testing the waters, probing for leverage, or maybe something else entirely.

"I'll think about it," I said finally, my voice clipped.

"Do," she said, her voice as smooth as the olive oil she seemed entirely uninterested in. "You have my number."

The line went dead, but her words lingered, curling around my thoughts like smoke. Isabella Hart didn't look like someone who did anything without purpose. And as much as I didn't like it, she wasn't leaving anytime soon.

I was midway through daily work when my phone buzzed. Dimitris' name lit up the screen.

"We need to talk, Andreas. Urgently," Dimitris said, his voice unusually tense.

I frowned, wiping my hands on my jeans. "What's going on?"

"Not over the phone," he replied sharply. "Where are you?"

"At the grove, but I can drive to Navagos if—"

"No, stay put," he interrupted. "Better we meet there. Full privacy. Call Eleni too."

Eleni? My chest tightened slightly, but I didn't argue. "Fine. I'll call her now."

The call ended abruptly, leaving me staring at my phone for a moment. Dimitris rarely sounded this serious unless it was something big. And if it involved Eleni, it couldn't be good news.

I dialled her number, keeping my voice neutral. "Dimitris needs to meet us. He's coming to the grove. Says it's important."

"Alright," she said simply, and I could sense her hesitation, the undercurrent of tension we hadn't yet addressed. "I'll be there soon."

***

Eleni arrived first, her car pulling up in a cloud of dust. She stepped out, her posture as poised as ever, but the stiffness in her movements betrayed the unease between us.

"Hey," I said, leaning against the farmhouse's stone wall.

"Hey," she replied, her tone clipped but polite. She glanced around the grove, avoiding my eyes.

"How's the facility?" I asked, breaking the silence with the safest small talk I could muster.

"Fine," she said, crossing her arms.

I nodded, the weight of unsaid words pressing down on us. The seconds stretched painfully, and we lapsed into an awkward silence.

I glanced at her, unable to help myself. She looked tired, her shoulders slumped in a way that seemed so unlike her usual poised self. Dark shadows smudged beneath her eyes, and I could tell she probably hadn't slept much last night. The fire in her gaze—the one that always gave her this untouchable strength—was dimmer, replaced by something raw and uncertain. It wasn't just exhaustion. It was sadness, an insecurity she didn't want me to see, though it sat there in plain view.

It hit me harder than I expected. This woman, who had spent months fighting for this place with everything she had, now looked like she was barely holding herself together. And all I wanted to do was pull her into my arms, to tell her that somehow, everything would be okay. That we'd figure it out. But the truth was, I had no good words to offer, no promises I could keep. The weight of my own doubts and the unspoken truth about my debts kept me rooted in place.

Her body language told me everything I needed to know: "Don't touch me." She kept her arms crossed, her gaze flitting toward the grove like it might give her answers. The distance between us wasn't just physical—it was palpable, heavy with things we weren't saying. And I hated it. Hated that I couldn't fix this for her, for us. So, I stayed silent, my hand rubbing the smooth surface of the pebble inside my pocket, hoping Dimitris would arrive soon and break the unbearable tension.

The sound of a car broke the tense silence, and I turned toward the dirt path just as Dimitris' shiny sedan rumbled up, kicking up a trail of gravel and dust. He stepped out, grinning like he didn't have a care in the world, his tan blazer and polished shoes sticking out like a sore thumb against the grove.

"Eleni!" he called out, his arms wide as he approached her. His voice was annoyingly cheerful. "You look stunning."

I watched Eleni smile politely at him, but I could tell the compliment barely registered. "You're too kind, Dimitris. How are you?" she asked, her tone distant but polite.

"Better now," he replied, throwing in a wink for good measure. "It's been too long. You should've visited me at the townhouse. You're missed, you know."

I cleared my throat loudly, leaning against the wall to make it obvious I wasn't in the mood for small talk. "Dimitris," I said, sharper than I intended.

He turned to me, "Relax, Papadopoulos, I'm getting to it." Then, as if I wasn't even there, he turned back to Eleni, his voice softening. "But it really is good to see you."

My jaw tightened. My patience was running on fumes. "You said it was urgent," I snapped, folding my arms.

Finally, Dimitris straightened up, the grin slipping from his face. "It is," he said, his eyes darting between me and Eleni. "But you're not going to like it."

"Then just spit it out," I said, the tension in my voice thick enough to cut through the air.

"I was at the townhouse earlier," he began, finally locking eyes with me. "Spotted that blonde bombshell from the investors—what's her name? Isabella."

Eleni stiffened beside me, and my stomach dropped like a lead weight.

"She was meeting with some municipal staff," Dimitris continued, "Caught my attention, so I decided to dig around a bit."

"And?" I pressed, the words heavy in my throat. I already knew I wasn't going to like where this was headed.

Dimitris glanced briefly at Eleni, then back at me, "Turns out those investors don't give a damn about the grove or the olive oil business. Their real plan is to flip the land for a luxury villa development. They're planning to gut the whole operation."

The words slammed into me like a gut punch. Villas? My mind raced, trying to piece together the implications, but the nausea rising in my chest made it impossible to think clearly. "You're sure about this?" I asked, though I already knew the answer.

"Positive," Dimitris said grimly. "The permits they're quietly inquiring about have nothing to do with olive oil production and everything to do with private beachfront properties."

"I knew it!" Eleni's voice rang out beside me, sharp and cutting. I could hear the anger beneath her words, but I couldn't bring myself to look at her.

The weight of it all pressed down on me like a vice. The grove, the community, my family—it wasn't just at risk. It was being dismantled before we even had a chance to fight back. And now, I had no idea how to stop it.

As Dimitris finished recounting the troubling news, he glanced at his watch, his expression apologetic but hurried. "I'd love to stay and talk more, but I'm drowning in work right now," he said, rising to his feet. "I just thought you needed to know this as soon as possible."

Eleni nodded, her face set with determination despite the flicker of weariness in her eyes. "Thank you for telling us, Dimitris. This changes everything."

Dimitris placed a hand on her shoulder, his tone warm. "You'll figure it out." Then he turned to me, his usual easy charm giving way to something more serious. "I'll call you later, Andreas. We need to talk more about this."

As Dimitris drove away, leaving behind a trail of dust and a weighty silence, I stood rooted in place, staring at the retreating car. My mind raced, the implications of his words colliding with the knowledge I'd been carrying alone for far too long. I stole a glance at Eleni, who hadn't moved from her spot.

She stood with her arms crossed, her eyes fixed on the grove, but it was clear her focus was elsewhere. The tension in her shoulders, the furrow in her brow, the way her fingers tapped against her elbow—she was wound as tightly as I'd ever seen her. She looked so damn vulnerable it hurt to look at her.

"Eleni," I said finally, my voice breaking the silence between us. She turned toward me, her expression guarded but curious.

"There's... more we need to talk about," I said, each word dragging like lead.

Her brows knit together. "What do you mean? What's going on?"

"Let's go inside," I said, trying to keep my tone even.

She hesitated, clearly searching my face for answers, but when she didn't find any, she sighed and nodded. "Alright."

She started toward the farmhouse, her steps deliberate but slower than usual, as if she were bracing herself. I followed, the knot in my chest tightening with every step. Once we were inside, there'd be no more hiding, no more stalling. It was time to lay everything bare—and I had no idea what it would cost me.

***

Eleni

The farmhouse door creaked open, and I stepped inside ahead of Andreas. I glanced back at Andreas as he followed, shutting the door behind him. His shoulders were hunched, his movements slow and deliberate, like he was dragging an invisible weight behind him. He didn't look at me, his focus fixed somewhere ahead, though his expression was distant—hollow, almost. He looked like a man on the brink; the fight drained out of him.

It wasn't just exhaustion. It was something deeper. The same look he'd worn when I first came back to Seranos. Back then, I'd thought of him as a man hardened by life, guarded and bitter, with walls so high they seemed impenetrable. Over the past few months, those walls had come down, little by little. I'd seen glimpses of the lighter, kinder Andreas hidden beneath them. But now, standing here, he looked just as he had back then—closed off, detached, and battered by things he wouldn't share.

It hurt to see him like this. He was angry at the world, at life, at whatever had brought us to this moment. I could see it in the way his fists curled and uncurled at his sides.

But mostly, I saw the sadness—an ache he tried to bury beneath frustration and silence.

I stayed quiet, my chest tightening. Whatever he was about to say, I knew it wouldn't make things easier. But I needed to hear it. I needed to know.

He finally turned, his face a mask of exhaustion and something darker—shame. "There's no point in delaying this," he said quietly, his voice rough. "You need to know the truth."

The following words hit me like a series of punches, each harder than the last. The debts. The credit. The bad harvests. The shares tied to the bank. By the time he was done, I was struggling to breathe, the weight of it crushing.

I shook my head, the room spinning. "You needed credit to pay for your divorce? How is that even possible without George's approval? He was your partner back then. He would never—"

"He did," Andreas interrupted, his tone sharp but laden with something that looked too much like shame. "He gave his authorization."

"What?" I could barely force the word out. "George knew? He knew about all of this, and he just—"

"He was the only one who knew. He agreed because he believed in me!" Andreas snapped, his voice cracking under the weight of the confession. "He said this was family. That we'd find a way out together."

Those words struck a deep chord within me—this was the George I remembered.

"The debts," Andreas said, his voice rough, like the admission was tearing something out of him. "They've been hanging over us for a couple of years."

I frowned, trying to grasp the timeline. "And the bad harvest? Callie told some things, but why didn't anyone----"

"It was before you came back, Eleni. Half the olives were ruined, and what we managed to press wasn't enough to cover costs. The grove's finances were already fragile, and that tipped everything over the edge."

I stepped forward, my voice trembling. "How could you not tell me this? How could you—"

"I didn't want to burden you," he interrupted, his tone defensive. "I didn't think you needed to—"

"Didn't need to know?" My voice rose, sharp and unsteady. "Andreas, I'm your partner. Or at least, I thought I was. But clearly, you don't see me that way."

He flinched, his jaw tightening, but his eyes betrayed a flicker of pain. "Eleni, it wasn't about not trusting you. It was about protecting you."

"Protecting me?" I scoffed, the bitterness in my voice cutting like shattered glass. "Do you even hear yourself? Protecting me from what? The truth? The reality? I don't need protection, Andreas—I need honesty. I need respect. I need a partner who sees me as an equal, not some delicate little porcelain doll you keep on a shelf and feed half-truths to."

His face hardened, the rising tension palpable between us. "That's not fair," he shot back, his voice louder now, his frustration barely restrained. "You think I wanted this? You think I wanted to lie to you?"

"Yes!" I shouted, taking a step closer, my anger blazing now. "Because God forbid Andreas Papadopoulos shows a crack in his armour. God forbid I see the man I love as anything less than indestructible. Your pride can't handle being vulnerable with me, but it's perfectly acceptable to stop fighting and put a goddamn price tag on your roots? On everything you say you love?"

His expression twisted, a mix of anger and something deeper—something raw and wounded. "Don't you dare question my fight, Eleni," he said, his voice breaking with emotion. "You think this is easy for me? You think I don't care? About this land? About this community? About you?"

"Do you?" I shot back, the words cutting even as I said them. "Because if you did, you wouldn't have kept this from me. You wouldn't have pushed me out."

"You don't get it," he snapped, his voice shaking with frustration, his eyes flashing. "You come here for a few months, and suddenly you think you care more than I do? That you cherish this community more than me? You don't have a clue, Eleni. This isn't a side project for me. This isn't some dream I woke up to one day. This is my life. My entire goddamn life."

"And you think it's a game to me?" I yelled back, my voice raw. "Do you think I'm here for fun? For some romantic little adventure?"

"You're here because you can be," he shot back, the bitterness in his tone cutting like a blade. "Because when this all falls apart—and it will—you can pack your bags, run back to London, and pretend this never happened. You can go back to your cosy, privileged life. Not all of us have rich fathers and backup plans, Eleni. Some of us don't have a safety net. Some of us don't have anywhere else to go."

The words hit me like a physical blow, knocking the air from my lungs. "That's what you think of me?" I asked, my voice trembling. "That I'll just leave? That I don't care enough to stay and fight?"

"You don't know what it means to fight," he spat, his frustration boiling over. "Not when it means choosing between pride and survival. Not when it means losing everything you've ever known. This isn't a goddamn fantasy, this is the reality. And I can't afford to fight like you do—not with ideals and dreams and solar panels. I have to fight with numbers, with facts, with compromises I hate. That's what survival looks like."

The room fell silent, his words echoing in the space between us. My breath caught, and I stared at him, the ground shifting beneath me.

"Andreas..." I started, but the lump in my throat choked the rest of the words.

His shoulders slumped, the anger draining from his face, replaced by something heavier. Regret. Pain. He turned back to the window, his voice quiet now. "I didn't mean that."

"Yes, you did," I whispered, my voice breaking. "And maybe... maybe you're right."

He turned toward me, his expression stricken, but he didn't move. He didn't speak. He just stood there, rooted in place, as if the weight of what we'd said had drained him of the will to even try.

The silence between us was deafening, thick with everything we'd torn open and left raw. For the first time, I felt like we were no longer reaching for each other, like the distance between us was no longer something either of us knew how—or wanted—to close.

"I need some air," I said, my voice hollow and brittle. He didn't respond, didn't so much as flinch.

I walked out, the door clicking softly behind me, the sound quiet but final. Like the closing of something we'd never reopen.

***

I sat outside the farmhouse for a few minutes, the afternoon air heavy on my skin, every breath feeling like it scraped my throat raw. Continuing to talk now would only tear us apart more, and I didn't trust myself to speak without causing more damage. With a sharp exhale, I got to my feet and headed to the car.

The drive back to Seranos blurred into one restless thought after another, the tightness in my chest refusing to ease. By the time I pulled into the village parking lot, the square was quiet, save for the hum of cicadas and the occasional distant chatter of a passing villager. The weight of the fight still pressed down on me as I locked the car and started walking toward home, my steps slow and heavy, each one crunching softly against the cobblestone path.

I don't even remember turning down the street that led to Sophia's house. But suddenly, I was standing at her door, my hand hesitating just long enough for doubt to creep in before I knocked. The door creaked open, and Sophia appeared, her small frame wrapped in a loose, earthy shawl, her sharp eyes studying me in a way that made me feel like she already knew why I was there.

"Eleni, my dear," she said, her voice as soothing as it was piercing. She stepped aside without another word, gesturing for me to enter.

The inside of her house smelled of herbs and aged wood, the kind of warmth that reminded me of my grandmother's home when I was a child. I sank into a chair by her kitchen table, my hands shaking slightly. Sophia moved unhurriedly, pouring tea into mismatched cups before sitting across from me, her expression patient.

"I don't even know where to start," I admitted, my voice barely a whisper.

Sophia tilted her head, the corner of her mouth twitching as though she wanted to smile but didn't. "The beginning is always a good place, dear," she said simply, her words carrying that maddening, sage-like quality that both calmed and frustrated me.

And so I began, haltingly at first, then with a torrent of words—about the fight, about Andreas, about the offer, the debts, the lies. By the time I was done, my tea had gone cold, and my throat felt as raw as my heart.

Sophia didn't speak immediately, letting the quiet settle over us. When she finally did, her words came slowly, deliberately. "George was behind that boy, you know," she said, her voice carrying an unexpected weight. "He believed in Andreas, not just because of the business, but because he saw him as family. And family... family isn't about perfection, Eleni. It's about the fight."

I swallowed hard, the lump in my throat refusing to budge. "How can I fight when he doesn't trust me?" I asked, my voice cracking. "When he shuts me out?"

Sophia leaned forward, her eyes gleaming with a knowing light. "Because some fires are worth feeding," she said, her voice low and measured. "You don't need to forgive every wound, nor let it fade like it never was. But silence, Eleni, is a drought. It withers everything in its path. You must speak. You must fight—not just for the land or for him, but for the truth of what you believe."

She paused, letting the weight of her words settle before continuing. "Anger, child, is a wild flame. It can burn everything to ash, or it can temper steel. The difference lies not in the fire but in the hands that shape it.

Her words hit me like a wave, heavy and undeniable. I nodded slowly, though my mind still raced, trying to piece together what fighting even meant now. Sophia didn't push me for an answer. She simply patted my hand, the warmth of her touch grounding me as she sent me off with a cryptic "The night always knows how to listen."

I walked back to my house feeling marginally steadier, though my heart still felt raw and tender. The shadows of the setting sun were on the terrace, the quite broken only by the soft padding of Ari and Zeus as they trotted over to greet me. I sat on one of the chairs. Zeus pressed his head into my lap, his warmth soothing, while Ari rubbed against my legs with a faint purr, which was very unlikely of him.

"I don't know what to do," I whispered, stroking Zeus's fur as he blinked up at me with those impossibly understanding eyes. "I don't even know if I can fix this." Zeus didn't answer, of course, but his steady presence offered the kind of compassion I couldn't seem to find anywhere else. I sat there with them for what felt like hours, the weight of Sophia's words mingling with my own swirling thoughts.

***

I was staring blankly at the horizon as the sun dipped lower in the sky. The air was still, heavy with the kind of silence that felt louder than any sound. My thoughts were a jumbled mess, looping back to the same questions, the same ache. When I heard the gate creak open, I barely turned my head, the numbness too thick to break.

"Don't even start," Callie said as she stepped into view, her arms clutching two bottles of wine. She plopped down on the chair next to me, pulling me into a tight, wordless hug in a way I didn't realize I needed.

I managed a weak laugh, though it sounded foreign to my ears. "Two bottles? Did you think one wouldn't do the job?"

Callie leaned back, her eyes scanning me like a doctor assessing a patient. "One's for me," she said lightly, cracking open the first bottle. "I'm not dealing with your drama sober."

I smirked faintly, though the effort felt exhausting. "Fair enough. How did you even hear about the 'drama'?"

"Dimitris called Nikos, Nikos called me, and I called Andreas," she said with a shrug as if her information network working at warp speed was the most natural thing in the world. "Never mind all that—I know enough."

"Of course you do." I sighed deeply, swirling the wine in my glass once she poured it. "He told you everything?"

Callie shook her head. "Not directly. But I pieced it together. Nikos said Dimitris overheard some things. And, well, Andreas isn't exactly subtle when he's upset."

For a moment, we sat in silence; the quiet between us was heavy but not uncomfortable. Finally, Callie broke it.

"I'm shocked too," she admitted, her voice softer now. "I don't understand how he kept this from everyone—especially you."

"Apparently, George knew," I said bitterly, unable to keep the edge out of my voice. "He worked with Andreas to sort it out. Decided not to tell anyone."

Callie's brow furrowed as she tilted her glass. "George? I guess that makes sense. He was like a second father to Andreas."

I nodded, the sharp sting of emotion welling up in my chest. "He stood by Andreas through everything, didn't he? Even this. He trusted him to figure it out, to fix it." My voice cracked slightly. "And that's part of what hurts so much. He didn't give us the chance to deal with this together."

Callie reached across the small table and rested a hand over mine. "Eleni, you're not wrong to feel angry. He should've told you. But you've got to understand—Andreas isn't wired like that. Especially since our father died, he's always carried this ridiculous burden of protecting everyone. Me, Mum... even people who didn't ask for his help. He thinks asking for support is a weakness."

I frowned, staring into my glass. "But why? Why would he think I need protecting? I'm not some damsel in distress."

"Because he loves you," Callie said simply, her voice tinged with both warmth and exasperation. "And love makes people stupid. Andreas? He's been acting like this his whole life. He puts himself in front of every problem, every fight, and takes the hits so no one else has to. It's how he's built."

I bit my lip, my thoughts racing. "It's not fair."

"No, it's not," Callie agreed, draining her glass and pouring herself another. "But it's how he's survived. And now? He's trying to figure out how to let someone else in. That's hard for him, especially with you. He doesn't want you to see him as weak."

I snorted bitterly. "What's weak about being honest?"

"That's a question you should ask him," Callie said, giving me a knowing look. "And you should. Soon."

We sat together in comfortable silence for a while, the kind that only someone like Callie could make feel natural. Just having her beside me brought a strange sense of reassurance, as if her mere presence had the power to convince me that things couldn't be as bad as they seemed. That was Callie's gift—she could bring a sliver of light to the darkest situations without even trying. Eventually, she broke the quiet with easy chatter about the villagers, the flowers on the terrace, and Nikos. Bit by bit, her words smoothed the jagged edges of my thoughts like a balm I hadn't realized I needed.

She stood, smoothing her dress. "What are you going to do?"

I hesitated, the words catching in my throat before I finally spoke. "I'll talk to him. Tomorrow morning. I just… I need to sleep on it first."

Callie nodded approvingly. "Good. But don't let him off easy."

I managed a faint smile. "When have I ever let Andreas off easy?"

She laughed, leaning down to kiss the top of my head. "Get some rest, Eleni. You look like you're carrying the weight of the world."

As Callie disappeared down the path, I let out a long sigh, the ache in my chest still lingering. Heading inside, I found Zeus curled up on the couch, his tail thumping lazily at the sight of me. Ari perched on the windowsill, staring out at the window.

When I finally crawled into bed, the weight in my chest felt heavier than ever. My body ached—not from physical exertion, but from the deep, bone-deep pain of a heart that didn't know how to heal.

Shattered Trust, Silent Reckonings

Andreas

The dim hum of voices and clinking glasses filled the air of the modest taverna near my flat in Navagos. It was a place I hadn't visited in months, yet tonight, it felt like the only place I belonged. My usual restraint was gone, drowned somewhere in the bottom of the second—or was it the third?—glass of ouzo.

Eleni's voice still echoed in my mind, sharp and cutting in ways I hadn't imagined possible. Irreversible, I thought, swirling the liquid in my glass. That was the word. It hung there, unspoken yet palpable. Whatever we'd been building together—at the grove, with the village, with each other—felt like rubble now. And wasn't that just fitting? Everything I touched eventually crumbled.

"Drowning your sorrows, Andreas?" The voice was smooth, confident, and far too familiar.

I didn't need to look up to know it was Isabella. Here she was, standing in the dim light with that same unshakable composure. Her sharp, tailored blazer stood out against the taverna's rough-hewn tables, a queen amidst peasants.

"What do you want?" My voice was low and flat. The words came out more slurred than I intended.

She didn't answer immediately, sliding onto the stool beside me and signalling to the bartender with a simple tilt of her head. "You looked like you could use some company."

"I don't need your kind of company," I muttered, gripping the glass tighter. "Or your lies. Did Crownstone think I'd just roll over when I found out about the villas?"

Her lips curled into the faintest smile as the bartender set down her drink. "I see you've been doing your homework. Impressive." She took a sip, calm as ever. "But, Andreas, I think you're giving me too much credit. I don't make the decisions—just help facilitate them."

"Facilitate," I scoffed. The word tasted bitter. "You mean destroy. You and your investors want to tear apart everything that matters to people like me. Like Eleni."

Her name slipped out before I could stop it, and I hated the way Isabella's eyes flickered with interest. She leaned in slightly, her voice softening. "And what exactly does matter to you, Andreas? The grove? The village? Eleni?" She tilted her head, studying me with those piercing eyes. "You don't seem so sure yourself."

I glared at her but said nothing, my jaw tight. She took it as an invitation to continue.

"You're not the villain here, you know," she said, her tone shifting to something almost sympathetic. "You've been dealt a bad hand. You're trying to keep a sinking ship afloat, but no one can blame you for wanting something more. Something... easier."

Her words slithered in, wrapping around the cracks in my armour. My grip on the glass loosened. "What do you know about what I want?"

"I know more than you think." Her smile was faint but confident, and the way she held my gaze made it impossible to look away. "You're tired. Of fighting. Of pretending you can fix everything. Why not let someone else carry the burden for once?"

The bartender set down another glass, and I drained it without hesitation. The alcohol burned, but not enough to numb the weight in my chest. She was wrong—completely wrong. But in that moment, it didn't matter.

"Come on," she said, her voice dipping into something playful. "You look like you could use a break. There's a place I know—music, drinks, no responsibilities. Just for tonight."

I should have said no. I knew better. But the thought of returning to my empty flat was unbearable. "Fine," I muttered, standing too quickly and feeling the room tilt slightly. "Lead the way."

The nightclub was loud and chaotic, the pulsing music drowning out my thoughts in a way that felt almost merciful. Isabella stayed close, her touch lingering just enough to keep me tethered. Drink after drink passed between us, her laughter breaking through my defences.

By the time she leaned in, brushing her lips against mine, I didn't resist. Her presence felt... uncomplicated. No expectations, no history, no heartbreak. Just a fleeting escape from everything that was falling apart.

"Let's go," she whispered, her breath warm against my ear.

We stumbled into my flat hours later, the door slamming shut behind us with a sound that seemed louder than it should have been, cutting through the haze of alcohol and noise still pounding in my head. My breath came ragged, more from the weight pressing down on my chest than from the night's excesses. Isabella's hands were on me before I could think, her touch firm and certain like she had already decided what came next.

Her fingers traced my jaw, guiding my face to hers, her lips brushing mine in a way that demanded surrender. And for once, I didn't resist. My body responded before my mind could intervene as if I had been waiting for something—anything—to quiet the storm raging inside me.

Her mouth was warm, insistent, and I kissed her back harder than I meant to, a mixture of anger, desperation, and the need to feel something—anything—that wasn't this endless, gnawing ache. She tasted like whiskey, sharp and bitter, and it felt wrong, so wrong, but I didn't stop. I couldn't. I let her lead me, let her hands slip beneath my shirt, her nails raking over my skin, every move was deliberate, her control absolute, and I let myself drown in it because control was the last thing I wanted tonight.

Her blazer hit the floor first, then my shirt; the cool air against my skin felt like a slap—just enough to make me falter, to think. Eleni. Her name cut through the fog like a shard of glass, sharp and painful. My breath hitched, my body tensing for a split second, and Isabella pulled back just enough to look at me.

Her eyes searched mine, intense and unyielding, and when she spoke, her voice was low, almost a whisper. "Stop thinking, Andreas. Just… let go."

Let go. The words hit harder than they should have. At that moment, that fight felt like a line drawn in stone, irreversible. Eleni was already gone, wasn't she? And maybe I deserved it. Maybe this—her—was all I deserved.

Isabella kissed me again, and this time, I kissed her back without hesitation. The tension in my chest gave way to something darker and heavier as we moved toward the bedroom, shedding layers of clothing like a trail of discarded choices I couldn't take back.

Her skin was smooth, her movements calculated but not unkind, and as we fell onto the bed, her hands slid over me with a confidence that felt foreign. She pulled me closer, her lips tracing my neck, my shoulders, and I gave in completely. The rational part of my mind had already shut down, replaced by something primal, self-destructive. I moved with her, against her, letting the rhythm of our bodies drown out the screaming in my head. For a moment, it worked. For a moment, there was only the sound of her breath, the weight of her body, the warmth of her skin. But it didn't last.

Even as I reached for her and buried myself in the simplicity of the act, the emptiness crept in, cold and unrelenting. This wasn't solace. This wasn't an escape. It wasn't even comfort. It was punishment—a way to confirm what I already believed: that I was irreparably broken, that I'd already lost the one thing that mattered, and that there was no coming back from it.

When it was over, the silence was deafening. Isabella lay beside me, her breathing steady. I stared at the ceiling, the darkness pressing down on me harder than her weight ever could. My body was exhausted, my mind numb, but the guilt had already begun to take root, twisting in my gut like a knife.

I turned my head slightly, catching the faint outline of Isabella's face in the moonlight spilling through the window. She looked serene and content, and I envied her for it: for her ability to live in the moment, to take what she wanted without the crushing weight of consequences. For a fleeting second, I almost hated her for it. But how could I? This wasn't her fault. She hadn't forced me into this. I'd walked willingly into the fire. I closed my eyes, the ache in my chest sharper than ever.

***

The sound of running water stirred me from sleep, a steady hiss cutting through the fog in my head. My eyes blinked open to a room drenched in grey morning light. The headache hit me next—a dull, throbbing reminder of the drinks, the night, and... her.

The sheets beside me were empty and rumpled. My heart sank as the memories clawed their way to the surface. Isabella. Her lips, her hands, her voice—laced with temptation and everything I should have resisted. I sat up abruptly, my breath catching as guilt and nausea churned in my stomach.

What the hell have I done?

The sound of the shower stopped, the faint creak of pipes giving way to silence. My body felt heavy as I pushed myself out of bed, grabbing a discarded t-shirt and pulling it over my head. In the kitchen, I poured a glass of water, staring blankly at the sink as I tried to piece myself together. But no matter how hard I tried, the answers wouldn't come. There was no justification. No excuse.

When Isabella emerged from the bathroom, she was dressed, perfectly composed, as if the night had meant nothing. Her hair was slicked back, her makeup immaculate, every inch of her polished and unbothered. She gave me a faint smile as she picked up her bag from the counter.

"Good morning," she said, her tone casual, almost detached.

I didn't respond, setting the glass down with more force than I intended.

She raised an eyebrow. "Regret already? That's fast, even for you."

"Don't," I said, my voice hoarse. "Don't make this into something it's not."

Her smile widened, cool and calculated. "Relax, Andreas. I'm not expecting a love letter. Last night was… fun. You needed it. I needed it. That's all." She adjusted the strap of her bag, her eyes flicking to the door. "Now, if you'll excuse me, I have a meeting to get to."

The words stung more than they should have, her indifference a mirror to my own failure. I followed her to the door, desperate to end the interaction and the suffocating tension that lingered in the air. But as I opened it for her, the view of Eleni froze me in place.

She was standing there reaching for the doorbell, clutching her bag with a quiet determination that broke the moment her eyes landed on us. Her gaze darted between Isabella and me, her expression shifting from confusion to something raw and uncontainable.

Isabella, ever composed, gave her a faint smile. "Good morning," she said breezily, stepping past Eleni with practised ease.

Eleni didn't move, her eyes fixed on me as Isabella disappeared down the hall.

"Eleni..." I began, my voice cracking under the weight of her silence.

She stepped closer, her eyes burning with an intensity that made me want to look away but left me rooted to the spot. "Tell me," she said, her voice low, trembling. "Tell me I didn't just see what I think I saw."

I opened my mouth, but no words came. The truth was there, hanging heavy between us, undeniable and unforgivable.

Her breath hitched, and when she spoke again, her voice broke. "How could you? After everything... after us."

"Eleni, it's not what you think—"

"Not what I think?" Her laugh was sharp, bitter. "Then explain it to me, Andreas. Because from where I'm standing, it looks a hell of a lot like you sleeping with someone else the moment we hit a wall."

Her words cut deeper than I thought possible, each one a blade carving into the cracks I'd tried to ignore. I reached for her, but she stepped back, shaking her head.

"You don't get to do this," she said, her voice rising. "You don't get to tell me you care, you love me, to let me believe in you, in us, and then throw it all away the moment things get hard. I gave you my heart, Andreas, and you threw it to the floor and kicked it repeatedly. You were my home, which you burnt to ashes."

Her tears began to fall quietly at first, pooling in her eyes before streaking down her cheeks. Her voice trembled, raw with disbelief. "I believed in you, Andreas. I came here ready to tell you I would fight—for the grove, for us—that I was here for us no matter what. And this… this is what I walk into?"

"I'm sorry," I said, the words hollow and inadequate even as they left my mouth.

She stepped back, her eyes blazing with fury. "Go to hell, Andreas. Just—fuck off!"

"Eleni, please—"

"No," she snapped, her voice trembling with anger and heartbreak. "I'm done. You don't get to fix this with an apology. You've destroyed everything, Andreas. Everything. And you know what hurts the most? After my father pushing me around since my mum died, treating me like one of his projects, and Archie cheating on me over and over while planning to propose—the moment I finally started to put the pieces back together, to trust, to love you unconditionally—you joined the ranks of men who make me feel disposable. That's what hurts the most, Andreas."

I reached for her again, desperate, but she was already walking to the stairs, her tears falling freely now as she stumbled into the hallway.

I followed her to the door, torn between chasing her and knowing I had no right to. Her sobs echoed in the stairwell as she descended, the sound tearing through me like a storm. I stood there, frozen, my body heavy with guilt and shame.

When I reached the street below, I saw her through the windshield of her car, her face buried in her hands as she wept. My feet wouldn't move. My breath caught in my throat.

I wanted to run to her, to say something, anything, to fix the broken pieces I'd caused. But what could I say? What could I possibly do to undo the damage?

I stayed where I was until the car's engine roared to life, and Eleni drove away.

***

I sat in the car, gripping the steering wheel so tightly my knuckles turned white. My chest heaved, my breath coming in shallow, shaky bursts. I couldn't process it. Any of it.
The image of Andreas standing there—dishevelled, barely dressed, and with her—was burned into my mind like a cruel, vivid nightmare. My heart felt like it was on fire, a searing, unbearable pain that spread through my chest, tightening, suffocating.
So, this was heartbreak. Not just some poetic phrase but a real, physical ache. It clawed at me, twisting, burning. I didn't know it could feel like this.
With Archie, when I found out about his affairs, my pride was wounded more than anything else. That was anger, betrayal, but it didn't feel like this. This was something else entirely. Like there was a hand inside my chest, squeezing my heart until it threatened to burst.
My tears blurred my vision as I gripped the wheel harder, pressing my forehead against it. "Here I am again," I muttered bitterly, my voice shaking with the weight of it all. "The woman you can so easily cheat on." A harsh laugh escaped my lips, but it quickly turned into a sob. "Well, Eleni, life is full of lessons, and you always manage to choose the short stick."
I closed my eyes as if shutting out the world would dull the ache, but it didn't. If anything, it sharpened it. Because this wasn't just about Andreas. It wasn't just about him sleeping with someone else.
It was everything.

My breath hitched as the realization swept over me, a new wave of despair crashing down. Everything I built since coming here… every decision, every fragile routine I'd carefully pieced together—it all shattered in front of me.
I thought about the home I'd created, the tentative hope I'd started to feel, the belief that I was building something solid, something that mattered. And now? It was like watching a house of cards come crashing down, one betrayal after another knocking it over.
My father, hiding the investors' true intentions, treating me like a pawn in his plans. Andreas, hiding the extent of his debts, then turning to someone else the moment things got hard. How could I not see it coming? How could I be so naïve?
I cried harder, my hands trembling as they gripped the wheel. The rawness of it all was unbearable as if the weight of my own failures was pressing down on me. And yet, amid the storm of emotions, anger began to rise.
Not at them. Not entirely.
At myself.
I slammed my palm against the steering wheel, a sharp, hollow sound that reverberated through the car. "Come on, Eleni," I muttered, my voice hoarse and choked. "What now? Are you going to give up everything you've built because Andreas couldn't keep his promises and your father couldn't see you for who you are?"
The words hung in the air, their truth settling over me like a cold, hard slap. I thought about all the months I'd spent rebuilding my life in Seranos, the small victories that had started to add up.
I remembered a moment not long ago thinking about the time I first came to Seranos, when I felt that flicker of purpose for the first time in years. Back then, I was a mess, I'd told myself. Panicked, unsure of what to do or where to start. But now, as frustrating as everything was,

I was facing it with a sense of purpose I hadn't known I had. I wasn't just reacting anymore—I was stepping up and taking ownership, even if it scared me.

That resolution now felt shattered, broken like everything else. But as the memory lingered, a flicker of determination stirred within me.

"Are you seriously going to let two men define you?" I whispered bitterly, fresh tears spilling down my cheeks. "Your father, walking all over you? Andreas, betraying you?" My voice grew firmer, though it trembled under the weight of my pain. "You came here to build a life for yourself, Eleni. And now you're making it all about them."

I straightened, wiping at my face even as fresh tears fell. "Get it together. Take the ropes of your life in your own hands."

The anger didn't replace the hurt—not by a long shot. The burning ache in my chest was still there, cutting into me with every breath. But it was joined now by something else, something stronger.

I turned the key in the ignition while I wiped at my tears again. The road to Seranos stretched out ahead of me, and I felt the smallest glimmer of clarity for the first time in hours.

I wouldn't let Andreas' betrayal or my father's lies derail me. The grove, my family's legacy, my dignity—they were mine to protect.

As I drove, the pain lingered, searing and relentless, but I let it drive me forward instead of pulling me under. The tears kept falling, silent and unyielding, but I gripped the wheel tighter, my resolve hardening with each passing mile.

I wouldn't fall apart. Not this time.

***

By the time I parked my car at the square, the strength I had found earlier had already begun to slip away. Each step toward home felt heavier than the last. The late-morning sun bathed Seranos in golden light, but the village felt far too bright, far too alive for the dull ache inside me.

The cobbled streets seemed narrower today, the bougainvillea more vivid, as if mocking my inability to appreciate them. Every so often, I'd catch a sympathetic glance from a villager, their knowing expressions only deepening the pit in my stomach. Seranos was a place where nothing stayed secret for long.

I spent the day wandering from room to room, trying to distract myself, talking to Zeus and Ari. I cleaned the terrace and scrubbed the kitchen counters, but nothing seemed to quiet the storm raging inside me. My chest burned with every shallow breath, the pain sharp and unrelenting, like it was feeding off my thoughts.

Every now and then, a fresh wave of tears would hit, leaving me curled up on the sofa. By evening, my resolve had crumbled entirely.

As the sun began its slow descent, Yiannis appeared on his side of the garden. I hadn't even heard him approach. He leaned against the low wall separating our houses.

"You've been quieter than usual today," he called out, his voice carrying just enough humour to make me roll my eyes. "I was starting to wonder if you'd been swallowed up by one of those city-sized emotions of yours."

I sighed, wiping my face and stepping outside. "I'm fine, Uncle Yiannis. Just tired."

He squinted at me, his blue eyes sharp, as if he could see straight into the mess inside my chest. "You're a terrible liar, my daughter. Come on, spit it out. What's got you tied up like a fish in a net?"

I hesitated, but to my surprise, the words spilt out before I could stop them. I told him everything—Andreas, Isabella, the grove, my father. Every frustration, every betrayal.

When I finished, Yiannis nodded slowly as if he'd heard this story a thousand times before.

"Why does everything have to be so complicated?" I asked, my voice trembling. "The moment I feel excited and happy, I always end up with a broken heart or my self-esteem shattered. It's like every bit of confidence I build is just waiting to fall apart. Why is life so... complicated?"

He chuckled, a sound that somehow didn't diminish the seriousness of the moment. "Life isn't complicated, Eleni. You're born, you live, and you die. It's as simple as that. It only gets 'complicated,' as you call it, when you forget the living part. You youngsters love using fancy words to describe what's really just a miserable existence."

"Thank you," I said dryly, crossing my arms. "That's exactly what I needed—to be reminded I have a simply miserable existence."

He grinned, undeterred. "Ah, Eleni, you're missing the point. Let me ask you something. You came here to find yourself, didn't you? You fell in love, you felt alive—excitement, happiness, all those wonderful emotions. You poured yourself into the grove, into saving George's legacy. Am I right?"

I shrugged, biting my lip. "Maybe. But that doesn't change what happened. Andreas lied to me, then slept with someone else. He broke my heart, Yiannis. And now even the grove is falling apart."

"That's irrelevant," he said simply as if the words weren't absurd.

"Irrelevant?" I shot back, glaring at him. "How can you say that?"

"Let me put it this way," he said, leaning closer. "Imagine we could turn back time to the day you first came here. You know everything that would happen—every high and every low. Would you still come? Or would you stay in London and let a solicitor handle it all?"

I froze, the question hanging heavy in the air. My mind flashed back to the grove, the moments of laughter and triumph, the way my heart had raced with hope and love. "No," I said softly. "I wouldn't give any of it up."

He smiled knowingly. "There you go. So, you agree the ending is irrelevant."

I groaned. "If I have to… fine. But why does every good thing in my life have to end in drama? Why couldn't I have a happy ending, even if it's irrelevant?"

Yiannis' expression softened. "Sometimes things end well, Eleni. Sometimes they don't. That's why the ending doesn't matter. All that matters is that you live—one day at a time. Enjoy the good while it's there, and don't miss it trying to avoid bad endings. Now," he added, standing and gesturing to the house, "feed Zeus, water the plants, and pour yourself a glass of ouzo when the sun sets. Watch those oranges and purples you love so much, and just live, Eleni. Life is simple—you just have to remember to live it."

I stared at him for a long moment before stepping forward and wrapping him in a tight hug.

"Thank you, Uncle Yiannis. You should write a book on mindfulness. You'd be a bestseller."

"I don't even know what that means," he said with a laugh.

That evening, I did as he told me. The sunset was breathtaking, and the ouzo was bittersweet on my tongue. The ache in my chest didn't disappear, but for a moment, it felt bearable. As the waves lapped at the shore, I cried—just a little—but even the tears felt alive.

I didn't expect tomorrow to be anything extraordinary when I went to bed. It would just be another day; I would still hurt. But maybe, just maybe, I could remember to live it.

***

The villagers surprised me over the next few days. Kindness came in ways I didn't expect—Maria and Sophia showing up uninvited to help at the facility, their constant bickering somehow soothing the silence I'd been trying to escape. Yiannis dropping off fresh fish with a gruff, "You'll need this more than I do." A basket of figs was left on my doorstep, no note, just the unspoken understanding that someone cared.

These small gestures rooted me in Seranos more deeply than ever before. They reminded me that this wasn't just a place I'd come to out of obligation; it was becoming my home. Their support became the fuel I needed to keep going. I threw myself into the work, exhausting my body so my mind wouldn't have the energy to wander.

Still, the ache lingered, sharp and relentless, like a wound that refused to heal.

Late one afternoon, my phone buzzed.

"Eleni," Callie's voice came through brisk and determined. "We're meeting at Theo's tonight. Don't argue."

"I don't want to," I said, already dreading the thought of conversation.

"I wasn't asking. Be there at eight."

"Callie, I really—"

"You've had a terrible week. Theo's has ouzo and grilled fish. I have gossip. And you need to get out of that house before Zeus starts giving you pep talks."

Despite myself, I laughed, something I hadn't done in days. "Fine. Eight."

Theo's was alive with the usual evening bustle. Lanterns and string lights cast a warm glow over the shack and its scattered tables, the sound of the waves blending with laughter and the clinking of glasses. Callie was already there, seated at a table close to the shore.

I slid into the seat across from her, the scent of grilled fish mingling with the salt in the air.

"So," she said, "When were you going to tell me?"

My stomach twisted. "Tell you what?"

She raised an eyebrow. "That my idiot brother slept with someone else."

The words hit me like a punch to the gut. I'd been so careful not to mention it, not wanting to put her in the impossible position of choosing sides. "Callie, I—"

"He told me," she said, cutting me off. "And before you say anything, yes, I practically had to beat it out of him. He's been hiding like a wounded animal since it happened. I knew it couldn't just be about debts."

"Callie, I didn't want to put you in a difficult position. He's your brother—"

"And you're my sister," she said firmly, her eyes locking onto mine. "By choice, not blood. You should've told me."

Her words cracked something inside me, breaking through the walls I'd been holding up. "I'm sorry," I said quietly. "I just… I didn't want to make you choose."

Callie's expression softened. She reached across the table, squeezing my hand. "You don't have to protect me from Andreas. I can love him and still tell him when he's being a complete idiot. And right now? He's being a complete idiot."

The ouzo began to flow freely, loosening the knot in my chest. I told Callie everything—how I'd felt seeing

Isabella, the betrayal that had gutted me, the endless ache I couldn't shake.

"I came here for some grand journey of self-discovery," I said bitterly, swirling my drink. "And what does it end with? A cheated-woman tragedy."

Callie smirked, her gaze steady. "Eleni, stop giving him the starring role in your life story."

"I'm trying," I said, exasperated. "But why does it always come back to a man? To love? Why does it always have to be about that?"

"Because you're human," Callie said simply. "We're wired to connect. To want. But don't let it get stuck there. Love's not the whole story."

Her words settled over me, not a solution but a salve.

We laughed. We cried. The heaviness I'd been carrying felt lighter by the time the stars dotted the dark sky above us. As we hugged goodbye, Callie whispered, "You've got this, Eleni. Don't let him—or anyone else—define you."

***

Andreas

The days since that night blurred into a haze of guilt and self-loathing. I hadn't been to the grove or the facility, avoiding the world as if hiding could erase what I'd done. My flat had become my prison, the walls closing in tighter with every hour.

I spent most of my time staring at the ceiling, replaying the moment Eleni saw me with Isabella. The look on her face was burned into my memory—the shock, the betrayal, the heartbreak. Each time I closed my eyes, it came back sharper and more painful.

When Callie knocked on my door, I almost didn't answer. "Andreas," she called, her tone brisk. "We need to talk."

I sighed, dragging myself to the door. "Callie, please," I said as I opened it, unable to meet her eyes. "I know what you're going to say. What a horrible person I am, how I ruined Eleni's life, how I'm a monster, and that you hate me. I really can't take any of it right now."

"Hold your horses," she said, brushing past me and settling herself on the couch like she owned the place. "First of all, you're my big brother, and I love you with all my heart. Nothing can change that, and you should know better. Second, yes, I am very angry at you—for what you did to Eleni, but even more for what you're doing to yourself."

I sank into the chair across from her, burying my face in my hands. "How is she? Have you seen her?"

"She's a wreck," Callie said bluntly. "But she's going to survive it. You broke her heart in the most horrible way, Andreas. It probably scarred her for life and ruined her trust in herself and her feelings. She's in a lot of pain and hasn't figured out how to deal with it yet. But she's strong—amazingly strong. She'll survive. Eventually, she'll fall in love again, trust again, be loved and appreciated again. She'll heal her wounds, make peace with the scars you've left behind, and find the happiness she deserves."

The thought twisted my gut. "If only there was a way to take it all back," I said, my voice cracking. "To make things better, to go back to the way things were. To make her forget this and forgive me…"

Callie leaned forward, her expression softening but not losing its edge. "I'll be honest with you, Andreas. I know you love her like you've never loved anyone before. I know she's the love of your life. But you did what you did. I don't know if she'll ever want to give you a second chance, and I don't know if she should, considering the self-destructive path you've been on. She'll never forget what happened, but maybe one day, she'll forgive you.

"But," she added firmly, "for that to even be possible, you must forgive yourself first. You need to stop destroying everything good around you. And if you want to make things better, there's something you can do—for her and for yourself."

"What's that?" I asked, my voice barely above a whisper.

"Help her save the farm," she said simply. "She's working herself to the bone trying to protect it. You can't let her lose it. You can't let bulldozers sting those olive trees and pour concrete over our heritage. If you let that happen, no matter where you go or what you do, you'll never forgive yourself.

"This isn't something either of you can survive. Save the farm with her. Once it's safe, do whatever you want—sell your shares to her, move away—but not now. Not like this. Pull it together, Andreas. For God's sake, fight for something good."

The weight of her words settled over me, cutting through the fog in my mind. I felt the faint stirrings of clarity for the first time in days. I crossed the room and pulled her into a hug.

"Oh, Callie," I said, my voice breaking. "I'm so, so sorry. And I love you so much."

"I know," she said, her arms tightening around me.

"And I don't know when you became the big sibling in this relationship," I added with a weak smile.

"Oh, that," she said with a laugh. "I don't know either, but it's not something I enjoy. I love our little-sister-big-brother dynamic, so don't get used to it."

I managed a chuckle, the first in what felt like forever. "You know I'm going to make her forgive me, right? There's no 'eventually finding love again' as long as I'm around."

Callie smirked, shaking her head. "The 'village golden boy' attitude is back faster than the speed of light. It won't be easy, big brother. But I really, really hope you're right. And that girl has been stupidly in love with you her whole life, so your odds aren't zero."

The next morning, I woke with a renewed sense of purpose. For the first time in days, I left my flat. I threw myself into the work, spending hours at the grove, determined to support Eleni's fight in any way I could.

A couple of days later, we crossed paths at the facility during a meeting about harvest preparations. It was mid-morning and Eleni was addressing a group of workers with her usual determination.

I couldn't take my eyes off her. Despite everything, she was so strong, so composed, her resilience shining through. Her voice was steady, her commands clear. She carried herself like someone who refused to be broken.

The sight deepened my regret—and my admiration.

Our eyes met briefly as the meeting ended, and she acknowledged me with a polite nod. Her professionalism was flawless, but there was no warmth, no trace of the Eleni who had once looked at me with love.

It stung, but I couldn't blame her.

As I left the facility, I resolved to work even harder, fight for the grove, for our grandfathers' legacy, and for Eleni's dream. I didn't know if it would ever be enough to win her back. But it was the least I could do.

***

Eleni

The house was quiet, save for the rhythmic crash of waves against the rocks below. I stood in the kitchen, pouring a glass of wine, the red liquid swirling like my restless thoughts. It had been a week since everything fell apart, but the ache in my chest hadn't dulled. If anything, it had sharpened, cutting more profound with each passing day. The image of Andreas at the facility earlier this week lingered in my mind. He'd looked exhausted, his usual confidence replaced with something almost hollow. For a fleeting moment, our eyes had met, and I thought I saw a flicker of regret, but I refused to dwell on it. Regret wasn't enough to undo what he'd done.

I lifted the glass to my lips, the wine warming my throat, when Zeus' growling jolted me from my thoughts. It was low and unfamiliar, a sound I didn't think he was capable of making. His barking followed, sharp and unrelenting, coming from the terrace.

I rushed outside, the cool evening air hitting me as I spotted the reason for his outburst. Standing at the gate, looking startled and amused, was the last person I wanted to see.

"Isabella Hart," I said flatly, crossing my arms.

"Hi, Eleni," she replied, her voice calm, though Zeus' growls made her flinch.

I glanced at Zeus, debating whether to encourage his instincts or calm him down. "Good boy, Zeus," I said, stroking his head. "Now calm down, it's okay." He settled reluctantly, his eyes still fixed on her.

"I must congratulate you, Isabella," I said with a bitter edge. "You've managed to be the first living creature Zeus growls at. That's quite an accomplishment, even for you. What do you want?"

"Just to talk," she said, her tone measured.

"No," I replied immediately, turning back toward the house.

"Come on, Eleni," she called after me. "I just need to say a couple of things. You don't even have to respond. Please."

I froze at the doorway, her persistence grinding against my already frayed nerves. She was here to ease her conscience, no doubt, to unload her guilt and leave me to carry it.

Andreas' voice echoed in my mind: What's the harm in listening? I mentally punched him. That exact phrase had led to this mess in the first place.

After a long, internal battle, I sighed. "Fine. Come in. But be quick."

She stepped onto the terrace, looking different than usual. The sharp suits and high heels were replaced by jeans, a plain t-shirt, and flat shoes.

Her eyes flicked to the glass of wine in my hand. "Relax," I snapped. "We're not here to socialize. Don't push your luck."

She chuckled, genuinely this time, and took a seat as if she owned the place. "Very nice view," she remarked. "And a very... mmm... cute house."

I clenched my jaw. "We're not here for small talk either," I said coldly. "Say what you came to say and leave."

"Fine," she said, raising her hands. "I'm here to say I'm sorry."

"For what?" I cut in, my tone sharp.

"For Andreas, of course."

I raised a hand, stopping her. "You have nothing to apologize to me for when it comes to Andreas. You're no one to me, Isabella. You slept with someone, and that's your business. You can do whatever you want."

Her eyes widened in surprise, but I didn't let her speak. "Andreas, on the other hand—that's a different story. That's between me and him, and it has nothing to do with you. So don't flatter yourself."

For the first time since we'd met, her expression shifted. Gone was the smug superiority. Instead, there was a flicker of respect.

"It was just fun, you know," she said carefully. "I was drunk, he was very drunk, and one thing led to another. I've never seen anything like the love in that man's eyes when he looks at you. Don't lose that over one night."

Anger bubbled to the surface. "Isabella," I said, my voice trembling, "as I've already told you, it's none of your fucking business what happens between me and Andreas.

"And another thing," I continued, the words pouring out. "The world isn't your playground, and people aren't your toys. You don't get to bulldoze relationships, lives, history, and nature for your amusement or profit, then shrug it off as 'just business', 'just fun'. You're a self-centred bitch with no respect for anyone or anything, you know that, right?"

Her shock was brief. "Oh, come on, Eleni," she snapped. "Don't start with the I'm better than you crap. You don't know where I come from or what I've been through.

"I wasn't born into a cosy middle-class family with private school and an olive grove to inherit. I've fought tooth and nail for everything I have. So don't act like you're some virtuous heroine while I'm the villain. You're just a spoiled, ungrateful bitch playing at a simpler life, you know that, right?"

Her words hit harder than I wanted to admit. For the first time, I saw her differently—as someone who had fought battles I didn't know about. My grandfather echoed in my mind: You never know what people are going through. Don't judge too quickly.

She exhaled deeply, her tone softening. "I spent the day at the grove," she admitted. "Don't worry, I didn't see Andreas."

I shot her a glare, but she ignored it.

"There's something about that place," she continued. "The air, the trees… They mess with your head.

Reminded me of my past. Those trees—they're magical or something?"

We talked for hours after that, our defences slowly lowering. She told me about her childhood, her struggles, and the loneliness her success had brought. She was just as lost as I was, trying to make sense of a life that didn't always make sense.

When she finally stood to leave, she gave me a small smile. "I'm heading back to London tomorrow. You're rid of me. But, Eleni… about Andreas. He's an amazing man. Don't lose him over one mistake."

"That's none of your business," I replied firmly.

She laughed softly, shaking her head as she walked away. After she was gone, I sat on the terrace, staring out at the sea. The ache in my chest remained, but something had shifted. Maybe it wasn't forgiveness, but it was a step toward understanding—of her, and maybe even myself.

From Chaos to Collaboration

The first light of dawn filtered through the sheer curtains, painting the room in muted hues of pink and gold. I sat on the edge of my bed, staring at the day ahead with a mix of dread and determination.

The past week had been a whirlwind—one I hadn't quite caught my breath from. My mornings had become an almost meditative routine: I rise early, sip my coffee on the terrace, and mentally brace myself for the day.

The grove had become a hive of activity. Everyone—myself included—was pouring every ounce of energy into preparing for the harvest. The grove's survival had become the village's collective mission, and their support, though overwhelming at times, had kept me moving forward.

I couldn't help but think of Andreas. Despite the tension between us, he'd thrown himself into the work as if trying to atone. I'd caught glimpses of him in passing—his broad shoulders bent over a piece of damaged equipment, grease staining his shirt as he worked alongside one of the workers. His quiet efficiency was hard to ignore, and it stirred something in me I wasn't ready to confront.

But even as he worked tirelessly, the space between us felt insurmountable. The unspoken words, the pain, and the betrayal lingered like a shadow between us, ever-present and unrelenting.

I turned my attention to the coffee cup in my hands, the warmth grounding me. My thoughts drifted to the villagers—their determination was a bright spot in an otherwise dark week. With his dry humour, Nikos had rallied a group to clear the eastern grove after a storm had left debris scattered. Callie had become my rock, her sharp wit cutting through my spiralling thoughts with ease.

Even Yiannis, with his cryptic wisdom, had played his part, reminding me that life wasn't about avoiding pain but about living through it. The memory of his words brought a faint smile to my lips.

As I stood to begin the day, a sense of resolve settled over me. The grove was more than a business—it was the heart of Seranos, my grandfather's legacy, and a testament to resilience. There was no room for doubt, not now.

The clock on the wall caught my eye, pulling me from the fog of my thoughts. I sighed and reached for my phone, ready to dive into the next task of the day, when it buzzed in my hand. The name on the screen froze me for a second.

"Dad," I said, answering quickly, my voice neutral.

"Hi, Eleni. How are you?"

I let out a dry laugh. "I think you know how I am, Dad."

There was a pause on the other end, just long enough for me to brace myself.

"I have some things to talk to you about," he said finally. "Are you available?"

"Yes, Dad, I'm available," I replied, already defensive. "But if this is another lecture about how unrealistic I am, how I should come back to London, and how you have job interviews lined up for me—then no. I'm very busy."

To my surprise, Petros chuckled. "Oh, I gave up on that a while ago. Don't worry. I have something else to discuss. Please, just listen."

The unexpected warmth in his tone threw me off balance. "Okay," I said cautiously.

He cleared his throat. "Isabella came to me after she returned from Seranos. She told me about the luxury villas and the proposal. Eleni, I didn't know. I swear to you, I had no idea what the plan was. Cutting all those trees for villas…" His voice trailed off, heavy with something I rarely heard from him—regret. "I know I've always seen the farm as a burden, but I would never support destroying it like that. I'm truly sorry. I should have been more thorough."

The sincerity in his words was disarming. For a moment, I thought I heard disappointment—not in me, but in himself. Petros Katsaros, disappointed in himself? It was almost unbelievable.

"It's okay, Dad," I said softly, unsure of how else to respond. "We refused the proposal anyway. We don't know how we're going to save the business, but selling it to them is off the table."

"That's what I wanted to talk to you about," he continued. "After speaking with Isabella, something happened. Apparently, she was affected by the grove—and as she already had a good understanding of the business from the investors, she reached out to one of her contacts in a major supermarket chain. She brought back olive oil samples, and they might be interested in a deal."

I blinked, stunned. "A deal?"

"Yes," he said, his voice steady. "They're proposing two product lines. One would be a premium line under the Seros brand. The other would carry their branding but come with an exclusive distribution agreement for the UK market."

I struggled to process his words. This was the kind of breakthrough we'd been chasing for months. Every time we approached a major supermarket, we couldn't get past junior procurement managers. Now, here was an opportunity served on a silver platter.

"That's… incredible," I stammered. "But, Dad, I don't know if we can handle a contract like that. Their demand would be huge, and we don't have the cash to expand production. We're barely paying workers for the next harvest. And then there's Andreas' debt—"

"I know," Petros interrupted. "I've already looked into it. I spoke with an old friend of mine, who is a director of international corporate credits with a major bank. We prepared a preliminary business plan, and Isabella drafted legal terms for the supermarket deal. He's given verbal approval for a loan—better terms than Andreas has now. The credit would cover his debt and give you the cash to expand operations."

I was beyond shocked. "How… How do you know all this? Andreas' debt? The financials?"

"I called him," he admitted. "Isabella already had a lot of the details, but Andreas filled in the gaps. He said I should talk to you first—he insisted, actually. I didn't want to bring this up until there was something worth discussing."

His words hit me like a double-edged sword. Relief and frustration battled within me. "So, again, everything's orchestrated behind my back. Some things never change, do they?"

"Eleni, no one is orchestrating anything," he said firmly. "These are just preliminary steps. Right now, I'm telling you because it's your decision. Nothing is finalized. And, for what it's worth, Andreas wanted you to be the one to decide."

"Well, from where I stand, it sounds like plans have already been made—agreements arranged. Even Isabella knows more about my business than I do. Do you think I can't handle this on my own?"

"Don't be dramatic," he said with a sigh. "We drafted some documents and tested the waters. That's it. If you decide to proceed, the hard work will fall on you. Negotiating with the supermarket, preparing the business plans, convincing the bank—it's all on you. I'm here if you need help, but this is your show. And, Eleni, be careful—nothing is guaranteed. This might work, or it might not. You and Andreas need to be at the top of your game for this to succeed."

Something in his tone shifted, a faint note of pride breaking through. It softened me, and guilt for snapping at him crept in.

"I'm sorry, Dad," I said quietly. "It's just… it's been a difficult couple of weeks. I feel like I'm stuck in an impossible situation, and this all feels too good to be true. Coming from you, I went on the defensive automatically. I thought you were pushing me into something again."

"It's okay," he replied, his voice gentler now. "Let me make one thing clear, though. I'm not thrilled about this situation—about you staying there, choosing this life over what London could offer. But I accept that this is what you want. And, Eleni, as long as I'm alive, I'll do whatever I can to help you succeed and be happy."

The weight of the week finally broke me. Tears welled up, spilling over as I sank into my chair. The exhaustion, frustration, and unexpected relief all collided in a tidal wave of emotion.

"I wish you'd come to visit," I blurted through the tears, surprising myself.

The line was silent for a moment before Petros responded, his voice steady but tinged with something softer. "Maybe I will, Eleni. Maybe I will."

***

I ended the call with my father and exhaled deeply, letting the weight of the conversation settle over me. The idea of a breakthrough deal was exhilarating, but the way it had come together left me reeling. My father's rare display of trust and pride had been unexpected, leaving me both comforted and unsettled. And then there was Isabella—of all people, she had taken it upon herself to push this forward. That was the real shock of the day. The same woman who had seemed indifferent, even destructive, had not only recognized the grove's value but acted to protect it in her own way. I didn't know whether to be grateful, suspicious, or just utterly confused.

I stood by the terrace railing, the sea breeze brushing my skin as I let the new possibilities sink in. This was big—bigger than I could have imagined—and it would require everyone working together. That meant facing Andreas.

My stomach tightened at the thought, but I shoved the hesitation aside. Whatever was happening between us couldn't overshadow the importance of the grove.

As I slid into the car, I dialled Callie.

"Morning, sunshine," she answered, her tone as brisk as ever. "What's got you calling this early? Don't tell me Zeus finally convinced you to adopt his exercise routine."

"Funny," I said dryly. "I have news. Big news. Can you and Nikos meet me at the grove later?"

"Hold on, let me check Nikos' schedule," she said with exaggerated seriousness. "Oh wait, he's standing right here eating feta out of the fridge like a savage. Hang on."

I heard muffled voices in the background before Nikos came on the line.

"Morning, Eleni. What's this about?"

"I was going to make you wait until we met to hear this, but I can't keep it in. My father called this morning. Isabella brought olive oil samples back to London, and a major supermarket chain is interested in a distribution deal. It's huge."

There was a pause on the other end, and then Nikos let out a low whistle. "You're kidding."

"I'm not," I said, the excitement creeping into my voice. "It's real. They're talking about two product lines—one premium under the Seros brand, the other under theirs.

But there's more. My father's already lined up a preliminary credit offer to help us scale production."

"Eleni!" Callie's voice came through, unmistakably thrilled. "This is massive! Like, actually massive! What's the catch?"

"No catch. Yet," I said cautiously. "We'd need to handle the negotiations, secure the credit, and increase capacity—which is going to be a challenge with where we're at financially. But this could change everything."

Callie's enthusiasm was palpable even through the phone. "I cannot meet with you during the day as I have the "harvest fest of the year" organizations, but we meet at our place all together as soon as possible. We need to talk strategy!"

"Perfect," I said, my voice steadier now.

As I hung up, the knot of anxiety in my chest loosened ever so slightly. This was a big step forward, and I felt a flicker of real hope for the first time in weeks.

***

The grove buzzed with activity when I arrived. Workers moved among the rows of trees, their voices carrying through the warm morning air. It didn't take long to spot Andreas. He stood near a group of workers, his shirt soaked through with sweat. His focus was unwavering, his movements efficient, his tone encouraging but firm as he gave instructions.

I watched from a distance for a moment, taking in the way the team naturally gravitated toward him. They respected him—not just as a boss, but as someone who understood the intricacies of the land better than anyone else. It stirred something in me I couldn't quite name, a mix of admiration and frustration.

He looked up, sensing my presence. Our eyes met, and for a brief moment, the tension that had hung between us softened.

"Eleni," he said, walking toward me. His tone was cautious, his posture uncertain, as if he wasn't sure how close he could get.

"Andreas," I replied, nodding in acknowledgement.

He wiped his hands on a rag and gestured toward the rows of trees. "We're making good progress. The machinery issue from last week is fixed, and we've started clearing the southeast section for the next planting phase."

His professionalism was disarming, and I found myself responding in kind. "Good. That's great."

A moment of silence stretched between us before he offered a faint smile. "You showing up like this caught us off guard. I think Stephanos nearly dropped his rake."

I laughed despite myself, the tension easing just slightly. "Well, I hope I didn't cause too much chaos."

"Nothing we can't handle," he said, his smile lingering for a moment before his expression turned serious. "What brings you here?"

I hesitated, then launched into the story. "I just got off the phone with my father. He told me about the supermarket deal Isabella facilitated and the credit proposal from his contacts."

Andreas' brow furrowed, his posture stiffening. "I was going to tell you, but—"

"But you didn't," I interrupted, my tone sharper than I intended. "Again, I had to hear about this from someone else."

He sighed, running a hand through his hair. "I didn't plan to keep it from you, Eleni. Your father called me first, and I gave him the information he needed. That's it. The rest—Isabella's contacts, the bank—I didn't know much about them."

I studied him, searching for any hint of dishonesty, but his sincerity was clear.

His eyes lit up slightly, a glimmer of hope breaking through his guarded appearance. "So this is a thing now if Petros called you...This could change everything," he said softly. "If the deal comes through, it could save the grove."

I nodded; my emotions conflicted. "It's promising," I admitted. "But there's a lot of work ahead, and nothing's guaranteed."

"Then we'd better get to it," he said simply.

I caught the way the workers glanced at him as they passed, their respect and trust evident in every gesture. Despite everything that had happened between us, Andreas was still the heartbeat of this place.

"I'll see you later," I said, turning toward my car.

"Eleni," he called after me. I paused but didn't turn back. "Thanks for telling me in person."

I nodded and kept walking, the mixture of emotions swirling in my chest as I climbed into the car.

The drive to the facility was a blur. My mind buzzed with conflicting thoughts—about Andreas, the business, and the tenuous hope this new opportunity brought. The tension between us remained, but so did his unwavering dedication.

As I parked and stepped into the cool air of the facility, I resolved to focus on what mattered most. The grove's future was still uncertain, but I started to feel the faintest flicker of optimism.

***

The facility meeting room buzzed with quiet intensity, sunlight streaming through the open windows as papers rustled and voices overlapped in spirited debate. Around the long wooden table sat Andreas, Nikos and a few of our most experienced managers. The air was thick with both pressure and possibility as we hammered out the details of the supermarket proposal.

"Logistics are key," Andreas said, his voice steady but firm as he leaned over the table, gesturing toward the distribution plan sketched out on a sheet of paper. "We need to make sure we can meet their volume demands without compromising the premium quality of the Seros brand."

"Agreed," I said, matching his intensity. "But we also need to lean hard into the grove's history and the community behind it. That's what makes us different. It's not just about numbers—it's about identity."

Andreas straightened, his brow furrowing. "Eleni, identity won't matter if we can't deliver the product on time. Supermarkets don't buy stories; they buy reliability."

My eyes narrowed as I shot back, "You think customers don't care about where their food comes from? They'll pay more for authenticity, Andreas. That's what sets us apart."

The room grew quiet as our voices clashed, the weight of unresolved emotions adding an edge to the exchange. Nikos cleared his throat, breaking the tension.

"She's got a point, Andreas," he said diplomatically. "But so do you. We need both. Let's highlight the legacy in the branding while making sure we have the supply chain to back it up."

Andreas exhaled, rubbing the back of his neck, his shoulders relaxing slightly. "Fine. Let's focus on making both sides work. But it's going to take more than a story to convince them."

"It's not just a story," I muttered under my breath, though I dropped the argument, choosing to redirect the discussion toward the next agenda item.

For the next two hours, we dug into every aspect of the proposal—pricing models, packaging designs, and delivery logistics. Ideas flew back and forth, scribbled notes piling up as the meeting room turned into a whirlwind of collaboration. Despite the friction, it felt like progress. Andreas and I were working in sync again, if only for the sake of the grove.

People dispersed in small clusters when the meeting wrapped up, murmuring about the next steps. Nikos lingered behind as I gathered my papers, his expression thoughtful.

"Eleni," he said, his voice low but warm as he approached me. "Can I steal you for a second?"

"Of course," I said, curious as he led me toward the open window at the room's far end.

He leaned against the windowsill. "I just wanted to say... you're doing an incredible job. The way you handled that meeting—it's no small thing, keeping everyone focused with so much at stake."

I felt a flush rise to my cheeks but managed a small smile. "Thanks, Nikos. That means a lot. But it's not just me. Everyone's pulling together."

"True," he said with a nod. "But you're the one holding the reins. And the villagers see that. You should hear the things they're saying—about how proud they are of you, how they're ready to help however they can. Sophia's already organizing an additional group to help with the harvest. Even Yiannis is pitching in, though he'd never admit it outright."

A laugh escaped me at the thought of Yiannis grumbling his way through olive picking. "That's... incredible. I don't even know what to say."

"You don't need to say anything," Nikos said, his voice gentle but firm. "Just know that we're all behind you and Andreas, Eleni. No matter what happens, you're not alone in this."

The weight of his words settled over me, not as a burden but as a reassurance. "Thank you, Nikos," I said, my voice catching slightly. "That means everything."

As I left the facility, my heart swelled with gratitude—for the villagers, for Nikos and Callie, Maria and even for Andreas, despite everything.

The road ahead was far from easy, but my resolve grew stronger with every step. For the first time in a long while, I felt like we just might have a chance.

***

Before leaving the facility, Maria called to invite me to a gathering at the village square that evening. She and Sophia, unsurprisingly, were behind the plans for a casual get-together with the villagers. Naturally, it seemed every living soul in Seranos was already buzzing about the supermarket deal.

The village square was alive with the golden glow of lanterns strung between trees. Laughter and the hum of conversation filled the air as Maria and Sophia bustled about, ensuring every table was laden with food and drink. It was one of those spontaneous gatherings the village was so adept at orchestrating—equal parts celebration and rallying cry, meant to remind us of the community's strength.

The warmth of the villagers' smiles and greetings was genuine, but I felt a flicker of unease. Everyone here knew the stakes, and their hopefulness weighed heavy on me.

Maria appeared at my side, her hands on her hips, surveying the crowd like a general. "Look at them," she said with a grin. "Every man, woman, and goat ready to save this grove of ours. Even Yiannis put on a clean shirt. Miracles, Eleni. They're happening."

I couldn't help but laugh. "I'll believe it when I see Yiannis."

"That old goat cares about this village more than anyone. Speaking of goats, you've got an entire herd behind you, so don't forget that," Maria said with a nudge and a wry smile. Then, with a quick shift in tone, she added, "And do you know where that wild boy of mine has disappeared to?"

I told her I hadn't seen Andreas since the meeting at the facility earlier that afternoon—he was probably back at the grove. Maria's expression softened as she looked at me, her eyes holding a mix of admiration, love, and a touch of sadness if that combination was even possible.

"Well," she said after a pause, "the two of you being in the same room is all I can ask for... for now." Her voice was quiet but firm. "And don't think I don't know Eleni," she added gently. "I haven't brought it up because I knew you'd come to me if you needed to. But don't forget what I told you before—whatever happens between you two, I'm your mother too."

The tenderness in her words hit me hard, and my emotions spilt over. I hugged her tightly, overwhelmed by the warmth and comfort she offered when I needed it most.

I made my way through the crowd, stopping to greet familiar faces. People shared their memories of the grove—weddings, harvest festivals, moments of joy and hardship. A younger couple, Yianni and Aliki, told me about how their grandparents had met picking olives there, the grove serving as the backdrop to a lifetime of love.

By the time Yiannis stood to speak, a quiet hush fell over the gathering.

"The grove isn't just trees," he began, his voice gruff but steady. "It's not just olives, or oil, or money. It's history. It's the reason this village survived the hard years—wars, droughts, poverty. Those trees fed our children; they gave us something to believe in when the world seemed determined to take everything away."

A cheer erupted, the tension of the moment breaking as Maria raised her glass. "And it will be as long as we have every man, woman, and goat pitching in!" she declared, drawing laughter from the crowd.

The mood lifted, the villagers toasting to the grove and to each other. But even as I joined in the smiles and laughter, a weight pressed on me. This wasn't just about me or Andreas anymore. It was about them—all of them.

I was refilling my glass when Andreas arrived, the murmurs of his name rippling through the crowd. He was late, his shirt rumpled and his hands still streaked with dirt from the day's work. Yet the villagers greeted him warmly, clapping him on the back, pulling him into their conversations.

I watched from the edge of the square as he shook hands, exchanged smiles, and even endured a teasing jab from Maria about his tardiness. He kept a respectful distance from me, his eyes flickering in my direction only briefly before he turned his attention back to the villagers.

Seeing him like this was strange—immersed in the community, his guardedness easing as he laughed and listened to their stories. For a moment, I almost forgot the hurt between us. Almost.

As the night wore on, I slipped away, the weight of the evening pressing too heavily on my chest. I paused at the edge of the square, looking back at the lantern-lit faces of the villagers who had placed their hopes in us.

The supermarket pitch wasn't just an opportunity—it was our lifeline. Failure wasn't an option.

I turned toward home, the mix of hope and pressure swirling in my mind. For their sake, for the grove, we couldn't let them down.

***

Callie called The next afternoon and insisted we meet at their place for "strategizing." I agreed without hesitation—my mind had been running in overdrive every evening anyway. Being with them and working together seemed far better than sitting alone, endlessly cycling through plans in my head.

The glow of Callie and Nikos' house came into view as I drove along the winding road that hugged the coast. Perched just on the outskirts of Seranos, the house stood out against the deepening twilight, its whitewashed walls catching the last rays of the sun and glowing faintly under the first hints of moonlight. The garden that surrounded the house was alive with soft, fragrant movement—a gentle breeze carrying the scent of thyme, lavender, and Nikos' cherished lemon trees.

Pulling into their small gravel driveway, I parked and stepped out, taking in the sight of the house bathed in the warm glow of its exterior lights. Even after all these years, their home had an almost magnetic charm, blending tradition with a sense of ease that reflected Callie and Nikos perfectly.

The sound of laughter carried out to meet me as I approached the front door, which swung open just as I reached it. Callie stood there, apron still tied around her waist.

"Finally!" she exclaimed, ushering me inside. "We were about to send out a search party—or worse, let Andreas take over your part of the presentation."

Inside, the open-plan living area felt as inviting as ever. The honey-coloured wood beams crisscrossed the high ceilings, and the stone accents around the doorways lent a rustic charm. The large windows facing the sea were dark now, reflecting the warm glow of the pendant lights above the dining table, where Nikos and Andreas were already seated amidst a clutter of notebooks, printouts, and an assortment of snacks.

"You've been warned," Nikos said with a grin, gesturing toward Andreas, who was scribbling something in his unmistakably terrible handwriting. "Callie wasn't kidding. He's tried to sabotage the presentation with his chicken scratch."

"Don't listen to them," Andreas said, not looking up. "This is all strategy."

"Chaos is not a strategy," Callie shot back as she joined us at the table. "Let's get to work."

The four of us reviewed every detail of the supermarket pitch for the next couple of hours. The dining table transformed into a war room—papers spread out in every direction, a laptop propped up on a stack of books, and pens and highlighters scattered like ammunition. We debated pricing models, dissected the logistics of scaling production, and scrutinized the branding strategies.

"Why do we even need a branding expert?" Callie teased, twirling a pen. "Eleni's planning alone deserves a whole marketing campaign. 'The Olive Queen of Seranos.'"

Nikos chuckled, raising his glass in mock toast. "To her majesty and her spreadsheets!"

Andreas glanced at me then, a flicker of amusement in his eyes. "She does have a talent for pulling things together," he said, his voice quieter but sincere.

It was moments like that—a look, a word, a brief touch as we reached for the same piece of paper—that seemed to suggest something unspoken between us. Yet, we both avoided lingering on them too long. There was too much at stake.

By the time we wrapped up, a cautious optimism hung in the air. The proposal felt solid, and Callie, the eternal pragmatist, nodded approvingly as she surveyed the plans.

"Not bad," she said, stretching. "Now, all we need is a miracle or two."

"Or three," Andreas muttered, though his smirk betrayed a hint of hope.

As we packed up, Andreas offered to walk me to my car. I hesitated for only a moment before nodding, the soft click of the front door behind us breaking the hum of conversation inside.

The garden was quiet, the air cool against my skin. Neither of us spoke at first, the silence stretching between us like a fragile thread.

"Good work tonight," he said finally, his voice low.

"Yeah," I replied, glancing at him. "It feels... good, having a plan."

His eyes lingered on me for a second longer than necessary, his usual guarded expression softened by something I couldn't quite place. "We've got this, Eleni. I know we do."

I swallowed hard, nodding. "Goodnight, Andreas."

"Goodnight," he said, stepping back as I climbed into the car.

As I drove away, I couldn't help but replay the evening in my mind—the camaraderie, the shared purpose, and the subtle, unspoken connections that still lingered in the spaces between us.

***

The following days blurred into a whirlwind of work, the weight of the supermarket pitch pressing down on all of us. The air at the facility buzzed with urgency as we finalized financial projections, polished branding visuals, and hammered out logistics.

Late into the night, I found myself hunched over my laptop, reviewing email threads and spreadsheets, my eyes burning with exhaustion. The office was quiet except for the hum of electronics and the faint sound of Andreas outside, coordinating with workers to ensure the grove's operations were seamless and aligned with the proposal's requirements.

Callie became our unofficial morale officer, bursting in with plates of food and sharp quips. "Here's some fuel for your overachieving brains," she declared, setting down sandwiches and coffee. "Try not to die before the proposal is submitted—I don't have time to organize funerals."

Moments of frustration erupted, tempers flaring as we debated numbers or wording, but the shared sense of purpose always pulled us back together. Nikos joked about instituting a "no yelling after midnight" rule, while Andreas, surprisingly calm amidst the chaos, diffused arguments with quiet logic or a well-timed sarcastic comment.

By the time we submitted the proposal, exhaustion weighed heavily on all of us. The email left my outbox with an almost audible finality, and I leaned back in my chair, staring at the screen as though expecting an immediate answer. The room was silent, save for the soft sighs of relief as we exchanged weary glances.

"We did it," Andreas said, his voice quiet but resolute. His words hung in the air, a fragile thread of hope binding us as we waited for the verdict that could change everything.

Later that night, I sat on my terrace, Zeus curled at my feet, and Ari perched lazily nearby. The sea murmured softly in the background, its rhythm almost lulling me into calm. Almost.

The weight of the past week settled on my shoulders as I stared out at the dark horizon. We had given everything we had to the proposal, but doubts lingered, clawing at the edges of my mind. Had we done enough? Was it good enough? The stakes felt monumental, the grove's survival resting on the decision of distant strangers.

Andreas' face drifted into my thoughts. Despite the unresolved tension between us, we had worked together seamlessly, rebuilding a fragile rhythm that once felt effortless. His focus, his determination—it was impossible to ignore. And though I wasn't ready to admit it aloud, the slow thaw in our dynamic gave me a flicker of hope. Reconciliation felt like a distant star—far away but not entirely out of reach.

I let out a breath, tilting my head back to gaze at the scattered stars above. "Focus on the grove," I whispered to myself. Personal feelings could wait. The grove had to come first.

As Zeus stirred at my feet, I reached down to scratch his ears, a faint smile tugging at my lips. "If the grove can survive," I murmured, my voice barely audible, "maybe we can too."

One Step at a Time

The facility's office hummed with nervous energy, the walls echoing the occasional buzz of phones and the rhythmic click of laptop keyboards. It was mid-morning, and the team gathered around the large wooden conference table, now nearly invisible under piles of paper, coffee cups, and stray pens.

I sat at the head of the table, meticulously reviewing the presentation slides on my laptop. My pulse was steady but quick, my concentration razor-sharp. Andreas leaned over my shoulder, pointing out a minor adjustment in the financial chart displayed on the screen. His voice was calm, even as the tension gripped the room.

"Slide 12," Andreas said quietly but firmly. "We need to underline the cost efficiency projections for the premium line. They'll latch onto any hint of risk."

I nodded, my fingers flying over the keyboard. "Got it. Nikos, are we set with the branding visuals?"

"Done and uploaded," Nikos replied from across the room, gesturing to the large TV screen mirroring the presentation. "Callie's genius touch is all over it."

Callie smirked, giving a thumbs-up without glancing up from her phone. "If they don't love it, they have no taste."

As the minutes ticked closer to the call, the room fell into a tense silence, even the earlier bits of humour fading away. The weight of everyone's expectations pressed down on me, but I straightened my back and took a steadying breath. On the bright side, our proposal hadn't been outright rejected—the procurement team of the supermarket chain had requested this online meeting, a sliver of opportunity. On the downside, we'd been given only 24 hours to prepare a polished presentation, one that could decide our future. I wasn't ready to throw in the towel if this deal didn't pan out, but I knew there wasn't a Plan B. The clock was ticking.

"Ready?" I asked, cutting through the quiet. Andreas glanced at me and nodded. Callie and Nikos exchanged a quick look, holding their breath.

The call began promptly at 11 a.m. The procurement director of the supermarket chain, a sharp-eyed woman named Shannon Whitmore, appeared on the screen, flanked by two other representatives. After brief introductions and pleasantries, I launched into the pitch.

I spoke with conviction, keeping my voice steady and warm as I detailed the grove's rich heritage and the collective dedication of the Seranos community. The visuals of the grove, paired with candid shots of the villagers, added authenticity. When I spoke about my grandfather's legacy and the effort to preserve it, my voice caught slightly, drawing Shannon's attention.

Shannon leaned forward, her expression softening for the first time. "Your community's story is compelling, Ms. Katsaros. But let's talk numbers."

That was Andreas' cue. He stepped in seamlessly, presenting the financial breakdown with confidence. Anticipating their concerns about profitability, he countered each one with a clear argument for long-term growth and sustainable practices. The team's polished visuals and Andreas' sharp understanding of market trends seemed to catch Shannon's interest.

The questions that followed were tough. Shannon's team grilled us on production scalability, logistics, and the risks of tying their supply chain to a single grove. Each question hung in the air like a challenge. Nikos handled one about branding, and Andreas tackled a logistics query.

Then, just as the tension reached its peak, Dimitris burst into the room, a folder clutched in his hands.

"Sorry to interrupt," he said, slightly breathless but smiling. "I have news."

I frowned, glancing at Andreas, who shrugged. "Not now, Dimitris," I whispered, motioning for him to step back.

"It's about a government grant," he pressed, lowering his voice just enough to avoid being picked up by the microphone. "Sustainable farming initiatives. It's approved."

His words jolted me. Pausing the discussion, I quickly incorporated the grant into our pitch, presenting it as a boost to our financial stability and as an attractive element of innovation and eco-consciousness. Shannon exchanged a glance with her colleagues, a flicker of intrigue crossing her face.

When we wrapped up the presentation, Shannon leaned back in her chair, tapping her pen against her lips. "This has been unexpectedly thorough," she said, her tone neutral but not dismissive. "We need time to deliberate, but your case is... compelling."

The call ended with polite goodbyes, leaving us in silence. I glanced around the room, my heart pounding. Andreas sat back in his chair, exhaling audibly, while Callie and Nikos exchanged hopeful smiles.

"Well," Callie finally said, breaking the silence. "That wasn't a no."

"Not yet," Andreas added, his tone carrying a hint of optimism.

***

The meeting room felt suffocating, the air thick with the weight of unspoken emotions as we all processed the aftermath of the pitch. The supermarket representatives listened intently, asked the hard questions, and gave no immediate clue about their decision. With the call ended, silence settled over us like a heavy blanket.

Nikos broke the quiet with a wry grin. "Well, at least nobody laughed us out of the meeting. That's got to count for something, right?" His attempt at humour drew a few weak chuckles but did little to lift the tension.

I glanced around the table, my eyes landing on Andreas. When our gazes met, a flicker of unspoken understanding passed between us. We both knew the stakes—the razor-thin line between success and failure. Inhaling deeply, I tried to steady myself as the silence stretched on.

The buzz of Callie's phone shattered the quiet. She glanced at the screen and sighed before answering. "Hi, Mum."

Maria's voice rang out, clear and direct enough for all of us to hear. "Well? How did it go?"

Callie exchanged glances with the team before responding cautiously. "We think it went okay. They're taking time to deliberate."

"Perfect," Maria replied with characteristic energy. "Now that it's done, I expect every one of you at my dinner table tonight to celebrate."

Callie hesitated, looking around at the group for confirmation. "Mum, don't you think it's a bit premature to celebrate? We don't even know their decision yet."

"Nonsense, Callie," Maria insisted, her tone unwavering. "I know how much effort you've all put into this. Tonight, we're having dinner together—no arguments. The outcome doesn't matter right now; the fight alone deserves recognition."

Callie lowered the phone, her resigned expression sweeping over the room. With a shrug, she relayed the final verdict. "Dinner at Maria's. Apparently, it's mandatory."

A small smile tugged at my lips. Maria's determination was oddly comforting. "She's right," I said softly. "We've done everything we can. We might as well take a moment to breathe."

The group nodded in agreement, murmuring about the logistics of the evening. Slowly, everyone began gathering their things, the tension easing just slightly as we prepared to leave.

As the others filtered out, I lingered, stacking papers with careful precision. When I glanced up, Andreas was still standing by the door, his expression unreadable. For a moment, it seemed like he wanted to say something, but he hesitated, the words hanging in the air between us.

"See you tonight," he finally said, his tone neutral, before turning and walking out.

I exhaled deeply, the unspoken weight of the moment pressing heavily on my chest as I watched him leave. A confusing mix of relief and frustration bubbled inside me. As the adrenaline of the day ebbed, I caught myself longing for the simplicity we used to share—the ease of being with him before everything fell apart.

But I forced myself to stop. The memory of Isabella leaving his flat still burned raw in my mind, a sharp reminder of the betrayal I couldn't forget. Every time I saw him, my heart betrayed me, skipping a beat and filling with warmth before the cold sting of reality struck. The ache of it felt endless, an unrelenting pain I didn't know how to let go.

So much between us was unresolved, tangled in a web of emotions I couldn't sort through now.

***

The warm glow of lanterns lit up Maria's courtyard, the soft murmur of conversation blending with the mouthwatering scent of grilled fish and oregano. Plates of meze lined the long table, surrounded by familiar faces that eased the day's tension. Laughter rippled through the air, carrying on the sea's salty breeze.

Maria clapped her hands to get everyone's attention, holding up her glass. "To Eleni and Andreas," she said, her voice rich with pride. "Your fight for the grove is not just about business. It's about preserving who we are as a village, as a family. No matter what happens next, you've made us proud."

Everyone raised their glasses, the clinking of cheers echoing in the courtyard. I felt my cheeks flush, the weight of Maria's words settling somewhere between gratitude and pressure.

As the laughter from Maria's toast faded, Nikos reached for the ouzo bottle to refill Dimitris' glass. A slight miscalculation sent a splash of the clear liquid straight into Dimitris' lap.

"Ah, perfect aim," Nikos quipped, his expression a mix of sheepishness and amusement. He handed over a napkin with a shrug. "I thought you looked like you needed cooling off."

Dimitris raised an eyebrow, a playful grin on his face as he stood to dab at the spill. "You know, Nikos, I've always said you have a unique way of making a toast memorable."

Nikos laughed, handing him another napkin. "What can I say? I like to keep things interesting."

Callie chuckled, shaking her head. "Interesting, indeed. Ouzo showers at the next dinner, then?"

"Don't tempt me," Nikos shot back, pouring another glass—this time safely away from Dimitris' reach.

I couldn't help but laugh softly, exchanging a glance with Andreas, who smirked and added, "If nothing else,

Dimitris, consider it a blessing. Ouzo stains build character."

Dimitris groaned theatrically, waving the napkin. "Well, if I'm the character in this story, you're all the comic relief."

The table erupted into easy laughter, the warmth of the moment spreading as the tension melted into the night air. "By the way," Callie said, shaking her head before turning her gaze to Andreas. "I didn't know you could make financial spreadsheets sound almost exciting. Truly, a man of many talents."

Andreas smirked, his tone dry. "High praise from someone who said my handwriting looked like Zeus tried to write with his paw."

"That wasn't high praise," Callie quipped, her grin widening as the group erupted into laughter.

I found myself smiling, my gaze drifting to Andreas. It was strange—this sliver of warmth between us. For weeks, it had felt like that kind of connection was impossible. As the laughter around the table began to settle, Andreas caught my eye and leaned closer, his voice low, meant only for me.

"Maria's right, you know," he said softly. "Whatever happens, this fight wouldn't have come this far without you."

I blinked, caught off guard. "It's not just me. It's everyone."

He nodded, a hint of a smile tugging at his lips. "Still. You've been the heart of it. That hasn't gone unnoticed."

For the first time in what felt like forever, we shared something real—a moment of camaraderie. It wasn't about the mess of our past or the lingering pain between us. It was about the grove, the people gathered here, and the sense of family Maria's home seemed to radiate.

As the celebration wound down, I bid everyone goodnight and stepped into the cool night air. The moon hung low, bathing the village in a soft, silver glow as I walked home. The streets were quiet, save for the distant crash of waves against the shore. But my mind refused to settle.

I couldn't stop picturing Andreas during the pitch earlier—his steady eyes, his firm voice. Yet, beneath it all, I'd caught something else: a vulnerability I hadn't seen before. That look stayed with me, threading itself into my own tangled thoughts about what lay ahead.

Once I was home, I let myself sink into the comforting familiarity of the terrace. Zeus settled at my feet, Ari perched nearby, watching me with that aloof curiosity only he could manage. Above, the stars seemed to mirror my thoughts—scattered, complex, but still beautiful. I reached down to run my fingers through Zeus' fur, speaking softly to my quiet companions.

"Today felt... different," I murmured. "Not better, not worse. Just... like maybe things are starting to shift."

Zeus let out a soft huff, his ears flicking as though he agreed. I leaned back, my gaze drifting toward the horizon, where the sea melted into the sky.

"Whatever happens," I whispered, "I just hope we're ready."

***

The days after the presentation blurred into a whirlwind of work. There was no room to dwell on the uncertainty of the supermarket's decision—the harvest couldn't wait. The grove and the facility thrummed with life, everyone throwing themselves into the tasks at hand.

I spent most of my time at the facility, buried in logistics. There were schedules to organize, workers to coordinate, and endless details to oversee. Andreas was a constant presence at the grove, a steady force amid the chaos. His voice carried through the rows of trees, firm and clear, as he directed the workers with precision. Villagers of all ages worked side by side, their hands and hearts united in the effort. Watching them filled me with a quiet pride, even as the weight of what was still unknown pressed down on me.

I couldn't avoid crossing paths with Andreas, though we kept things strictly professional. A few clipped words exchanged over schedules or updates were the most we allowed ourselves. Yet, it was the small moments that left me off balance—his hand brushing mine as we passed a clipboard, a quick glance held a second too long. Those brief touches of something unresolved felt like ripples in an otherwise steady stream, stirring up emotions I didn't have the energy to face.

By the time the day wound down, the facility was quiet, the last workers had left hours ago. I sat at my desk, bathed in the amber glow of the setting sun, trying to wrap up the day's work. My phone buzzed on the table, jolting me from my thoughts.

I glanced at the screen. The message was from Andreas.

"Can you meet me at the farmhouse tonight?"

I stared at the words, my heart skipping a beat. The farmhouse. Memories tugged at the edges of my thoughts, but I pushed them aside. Then my thoughts started spiralling. Was this about the deal? Maybe he'd heard something. Maybe it was bad news, and my dad called him first to soften the blow before I heard it directly. Or... was this about us?

What if he wanted to talk about us? My chest tightened at the thought. I wasn't ready to restart anything, not by a long shot. But was I ready to let go completely? If I wasn't ready to give up, did that mean I was ready to forgive? My mind looped through one vicious circle after another, every insecurity bubbling to the surface like a relentless tide.

Come on, Eleni. You're an adult. Just deal with it. Whatever it is. It's just Andreas.

And that's the problem, isn't it? It's not just anyone—it's Andreas.

I sat there longer than I'd like to admit, staring at the screen, knowing full well there was no point in asking what this was about. If he wanted to tell me on the phone, he would have.

Finally, I typed, Sure, I can be there in 30, and hit send.

With a deep breath, I stood, grabbed my keys, and stepped out. Whatever this was, I would face it head-on. There wasn't much choice anyway.

***

The farmhouse stood quiet under the night sky, its weathered beams illuminated by the soft glow of a single lamp spilling through the open doorway. I hesitated on the threshold, my breath catching as memories brushed against the edges of my mind. I could see Andreas inside, pacing the room with his hands shoved into his pockets, his movements restless, his posture unguarded in a way I wasn't used to.

I stepped in, the sound of my shoes on the wooden floor breaking the silence. Andreas turned, his expression flickering between relief and nervousness. For a moment, neither of us spoke.

"Thanks for coming," he said finally, his voice quieter than I expected.

I nodded, crossing my arms against the chill in the air—or maybe just against the uncertainty hanging between us. "What's this about, Andreas?"

He exhaled, running a hand through his hair. "I didn't know how else to say this, Eleni. I didn't want to keep it bottled up anymore." His voice wavered, and he looked down before meeting my eyes again. "I'm sorry. For everything. For the lies, for what I did to you… for how I let my fear ruin us."

My throat tightened, but I stayed silent, letting him continue.

"I thought I was protecting you," he said, his voice low and raw. "I thought if I carried it all—my debts, my screw-ups—you wouldn't have to. I didn't want you dragged into my mess. But in trying to shield you, I ended up shutting you out. I was so scared of losing you, of not being enough, that I ended up doing the one thing I swore I'd never do—hurt you."

His words struck something deep inside me. I wanted to lash out, to tell him how much he had hurt me, but the rawness in his voice pulled at the walls I'd built around my heart.

"You shattered my trust, Andreas," I said, my voice trembling despite my best effort to keep it steady. "You let me believe in you, in us, and then you took that belief and crushed it. Do you have any idea how hard it is for me to come back from that?"

He stepped closer, his hands still buried in his pockets, his eyes locked on mine like he was forcing himself not to look away. "I don't have the right words for this, Eleni. I'm not good at this. But what I do know? I love you. Not just 'I want you around' love. The kind that's there even when I don't want it to be. You're in my head, in every decision I make, and no matter how much I try to focus on anything else, it's always you. And yeah, I'm an idiot who ruined everything, but if there's even a small chance to fix it, I'll take it. I'd do anything for you—no second thoughts, no excuses. Just you."

His voice faltered, the weight of his words hanging in the air. "You make me want to get it right, Eleni. Not just for you—but for me. For us. I don't know if I can fix everything I've messed up, but I'm not giving up, not on you or us. I'll keep showing up every day for as long as it takes. No promises I can't keep, just the truth—I'll do the work."

My breath hitched, and my defences wavered. There was no denying the truth in his words, the vulnerability etched into every line of his face. But the pain of his betrayal still lingered, and I wasn't sure if love alone was enough to overcome it.

I took a deep breath before speaking, my words measured but honest. "I hear you, Andreas. And I believe you mean every word. But trust isn't something you just patch up—it takes time. Time for me to find my footing again, to see if we can even rebuild what we had. For now, the grove comes first. Let's focus on that and see where it takes us."

His jaw tightened briefly, and then he gave a small nod. "One step at a time," he said, his voice steady but low. "I'm here. As long as it takes."

As I turned to leave, his voice stopped me. "Eleni... just so you know, nothing's ever mattered to me as much as you do."

I didn't look back, afraid that the weight of everything between us would pull me under if I did. The drive back to Seranos was quiet, and the hum of the engine was the only sound accompanying my racing thoughts.

Andreas' words replayed repeatedly, each one as clear as if he were still standing before me. He'd been so sure of himself, so painfully direct. No grand declarations—just his raw, honest self. It caught me off guard. For someone who often used sarcasm as a shield, he'd let it drop completely tonight, leaving nothing but his truth exposed. And oh dear, how handsome he looked, even with the weight of the world etched on his face. His gaze, steady and unflinching, felt like it could see right through me. One part of me wanted to collapse into his arms, let him hold me until the hurt dissolved, forgive him, forget everything, and lose myself in his warmth.

But then there was the other part—that part clung to the pain, the blinding ache of betrayal, of knowing he'd touched someone else the way he'd once touched me. That image, unbidden and relentless, had burrowed deep into my chest, a wound that refused to close. No matter how heartfelt, it wasn't something an apology could simply erase.

One thing I knew, though, as I drove through the dark hills toward home: I loved that man. Too much. Like he was a piece of my soul, something I couldn't tear away even if I wanted to. But loving him and being ready to take him back were two entirely different things. And tonight, as much as it broke me to admit it, I wasn't ready. Not yet.

***

The morning light filtered through the facility office windows, casting long shadows on the floor as I stood by the desk, scrolling through a never-ending list of tasks on my phone. The past couple of days had been a blur of routine—overseeing the final harvest preparations, fielding endless questions from Callie about the Harvest Festival, and dodging my own swirling thoughts about the decision we were waiting for. Callie had called me at least five times already today, her voice filled with faux drama. "I need to know, Eleni," she'd declared during her last call, "Am I organizing the celebration of the century or the end of an era? Not that I'm being dramatic or anything." I could practically hear her rolling her eyes on the other end of the line, but I knew the tension was getting to her as much as it was to the rest of us.

Now, as the time for the video call drew closer, the air in the office seemed to thicken. Andreas, Nikos, and our core team sat around the table, reviewing notes one last time. I leaned against the desk, arms crossed tightly, trying to keep my face neutral. It wasn't working.

Finally, the screen flickered to life, and the familiar faces of the procurement managers filled the frame. The room stilled, the sound of our collective breath held hanging heavy in the air.

The lead manager, a middle-aged woman with sharp eyes and a clipped tone, greeted us briskly. "Good morning. Thank you for waiting."

"Good morning," I managed, my voice steadier than I felt. Andreas nodded beside me, his posture rigid but composed.

The woman glanced down at her notes before looking directly into the camera. "We've reviewed your proposal thoroughly, and after much deliberation, we've reached a decision."

I gripped the edge of the desk so tightly that my knuckles turned white.

"We are pleased to inform you that we will proceed with the partnership," she said, her voice measured. "However, there are conditions. Your production and distribution capacity must be scaled to meet our standards within a year. Additionally, we'll require quarterly updates to ensure compliance. We will send you a detailed report shortly, and we can start working from there."

The words lingered for a moment before their meaning fully sank in. It wasn't an outright triumph—there was still a monumental amount of work ahead—but it was a yes. Securing the bank credit would be the next hurdle, though my father had assured me it would fall into place with the supermarket deal in hand. For now, one thing was clear: the grove was safe.

The room erupted. Andreas let out a low exhale, a genuine smile breaking through his usual stoicism. I didn't realize I was smiling too, until I caught Andreas' gaze. In a rare moment of unguarded emotion, we exchanged a brief hug, the warmth of his arms calming me before we quickly stepped apart.

As the others began to disperse, buzzing with excitement and murmuring about the next steps, Andreas and I lingered by the meeting room window. The view stretched down to the Navagos port, where the sunlight glinted off the water in the distance.

"We did it," I said quietly, my voice carrying a mix of relief and trepidation.

Andreas nodded, his hands stuffed in his pockets as he leaned slightly against the window frame. "We did. But this is just the beginning. One year to scale up… it's going to take everything we've got."

I let out a soft laugh, shaking my head. "You could've at least let us have five minutes to celebrate before pulling out the doomsday reminders."

His lips quirked into a smirk. "Just keeping expectations realistic. You wouldn't want me getting soft, would you?"

"Oh, perish the thought," I said, rolling my eyes. "Next thing you know, you'll start using words like 'team spirit' and 'positive vibes.'"

He chuckled, his shoulders relaxing slightly. "Don't push it, Eleni."

I nodded, my gaze shifting back to the distant waves. "Still, it's daunting. But for the first time in a while, I feel… hope."

His expression softened as he glanced at me. "We'll make it work. For the grove, for the village. For everything it means to everyone."

"And for your pride, of course," I teased lightly, my smile widening just a fraction. "Can't forget that."

"Well, naturally," he said, his smirk returning. "What would this world be without my infallible sense of pride?"

Our eyes met then, and for a moment, the weight of the past weeks seemed to dissolve. It wasn't resolution—not yet—but it was understanding. We both knew the road ahead wouldn't be easy, but for the first time in what felt like forever, it felt like we were facing it together.

I turned back to the window, a faint smile tugging at the corners of my lips. "One year," I murmured. "Let's see what we can do."

***

We were at Theo's for a small celebration between ourselves, the cosy taverna glowing warmly under the soft light of hanging lanterns. Tonight was light-hearted—something we all needed after weeks of relentless tension and uncertainty.

Callie and Nikos sat across from Andreas and me, their faces animated as they recounted a disastrous childhood attempt at climbing the old sycamore tree by the church. "Nikos insisted he could jump to the next branch like a monkey," Callie said, barely able to contain her laughter. "Spoiler alert: he couldn't."

Nikos feigned offence, dramatically clutching his chest. "I fell with style, thank you very much."

Andreas chuckled beside me, his deep laugh sending a ripple of warmth through me. I wasn't sure if it was the laughter, the ouzo, or just the sheer relief of the evening, but the atmosphere at the table was alive with camaraderie. Occasionally, Andreas' arm brushed mine, or our knees touched under the table. Each fleeting contact sent a jolt through me, though I couldn't tell if it was unintentional on his part—or very much intended. His subtle smirk when I glanced at him made me suspicious.

Throughout the night, villagers wandered over to offer their congratulations. The warmth and pride in their voices reminded me why we'd worked so hard. By the time the plates were cleared and Theo himself filled our glasses for a final round on the house, the evening had taken on the glow of nostalgia. Callie sighed contentedly. "We needed this," she said, "Laughter and no spreadsheets."

As we stood to leave, Callie grinned mischievously as she caught Andreas standing next to me instead of taking the path to the village parking with them. "Oh, look at that. Andreas, the gentleman. Walking Eleni home, are we?"

"I'm just making sure she gets back safely," Andreas said smoothly, his tone neutral but his eyes sparkling with amusement.

"Oh, how noble," Callie quipped, nudging Nikos as they waved us off.

The walk back to my house was quiet. Andreas kept a step behind me, his hands in his pockets, his usual self-assured presence muted by the tranquillity of the night.

When we reached my terrace entrance, I hesitated, my hand resting lightly on the gate. I wasn't ready for the evening to end—not yet. The thought surprised me, but the words were out before I could second-guess myself. "Would you like a nightcap? Just a quick drink on the terrace."

Andreas' smirk was immediate and infuriating. "Of course," he said, his tone low and entirely too smug.

I groaned inwardly. "Don't flatter yourself, Papadopoulos," I said, trying to regain my composure. "It's just a final celebration drink between business partners. No touching involved."

Andreas laughed, the sound rich and unbothered. "Whatever you say, Eleni. Whatever you say."

On the terrace, the conversation stayed light about the grove, the pitch, and some village gossip that made us both laugh. The tension that had hovered between us for weeks seemed to ease, replaced by something softer, more familiar.

When Andreas finally left, the silence of the night felt heavier than before. I sat for a while, watching the stars as Zeus rested his head on my lap. My thoughts circled back to the warmth of the evening—the laughter, the stories, the ease of being surrounded by people who felt like family. And Andreas.

He'd been different tonight. Relaxed, sure of himself, but without the walls he so often kept up. I found myself smiling at the memory of his smirk, his quick retorts, and how he listened when I spoke as if every word mattered.

But then came the ache, sharp and sudden. As much as I enjoyed tonight, I couldn't ignore the lingering pain, the cautious wall I'd built around myself. I loved him—deeply, maddeningly—but the hurt was still there, refusing to fade.

I sighed, running a hand through Zeus' fur. "One step at a time," I murmured, echoing Andreas' earlier words.

Festivities, Lanterns, and a Dark Lane

I sat at the terrace table, nursing my coffee and watching Zeus lounge by my feet, paws twitching in some dream-induced chase. The Aegean glittered in the distance, calm and utterly unconcerned about the fact that my father was on his way here. To this house. For the Harvest Festival.

I would've suggested a medical check-up if someone had told me six months ago that Petros Katsaros would voluntarily spend a week in Seranos. Or maybe an exorcism. Yet here I was, waiting for him, my stomach doing little flips that had nothing to do with the three cups of coffee I'd already inhaled.

Margaret was coming too, which, admittedly, softened the whole ordeal. Margaret was… Margaret. Warm, patient, and completely unfazed by my father's occasionally frosty demeanour. If anyone could navigate this village's quirks, it was her. They were staying in a hotel in Navagos; he said they would be more comfortable there, but nevertheless, this was big.

I glanced at the empty chair across from me, imagining Petros sitting there, telling me what I was doing wrong. Would he criticize the house too? Would he find fault in the cracked paint or the slightly wobbly terrace railing? Of course, he would. Petros didn't come to relax; he came to observe, evaluate, and—most importantly—judge.

The crunch of their footsteps on gravel broke my spiral of self-pity. I stood, smoothing my dress like I was about to greet royalty. Zeus perked up, his tail thumping against the stone floor as he ran to the gate. I walked to greet them and heard Margaret's unmistakable voice.

"Oh, Eleni, this is absolutely beautiful!" she exclaimed as she stepped through the gate, arms outstretched. "I've seen photos, but they don't do it justice."

I hugged her tightly, her enthusiasm disarming me as always. "Welcome to Seranos," I said, trying not to sound too awkward. "It's... different from London."

"It's perfect," Margaret said firmly, taking in the terrace and the sea, "I can't wait to see the rest of it."

Then there was Petros, as precise and composed as ever, his expression unreadable as he stepped to the terrace. "Eleni," he said, his voice gruff but—was that a faint smile? "You look well."

"Thanks, Dad," I said, bracing myself for the follow-up critique.

"You've gotten some colour," he added, his gaze sweeping over me. "You're starting to look like a proper Greek woman."

I blinked at him, startled. Was that... a compliment? From Petros?

Margaret immediately fell in love with everything, the view, the house, the weather. Even the cat. "Ari!" she exclaimed, crouching down to scratch his ears. "He's magnificent! Oh, I've missed having animals around."

Margaret turned her attention to the house, stepping inside with wide-eyed wonder. "It's so charming! The woodwork, the stone floors, the history—Eleni, this must feel so special."

I hesitated, unsure how to respond. Did it feel special? Yes. And no. And complicated. But Margaret didn't need to hear all that. "It's home," I said simply.

While Margaret settled on the terrace, Petros wandered. He circled the terrace like he was inspecting a job site, his movements slow and deliberate. His hand brushed the railing, pausing as if he could feel the decades embedded in the wood. Then, without a word, he stepped inside.

I watched from the doorway as he moved through the house, his fingers trailing along a bookshelf, a table, and the kitchen counter. He lingered near a framed photo of my grandfather, George, his expression softening for a moment before he caught himself.

When he reappeared, he'd changed into swimming shorts. I was beyond surprised. "Are you… going swimming?"

"It's tradition," he said matter-of-factly, stepping past me toward the rocky path that led down to the water.

"It's the end of October, Petros!" Margaret called after him, half-laughing, half-alarmed. "Are you sure the water isn't freezing?"

He waved her off. "We used to swim until mid-November. The sea here doesn't get cold; it just clears your head."

I followed his movements as he made his way down the familiar rocky path to the sea. He moved so knowingly, with a certainty that startled me. He knew every dip, every step, every curve of those rocks. For the first time, it truly hit me: this house wasn't just where my grandfather lived. This was my father's home. He belonged here in a way I'd never fully grasped before.

After what felt like an eternity in the water, Petros emerged, his hair dripping and his expression calm. He towelled off, and as he made his way back, Yiannis called out from the terrace next door.

"Oh, I thought it was Petros when I saw someone swimming like that," Yiannis exclaimed, grinning as he leaned on the railing. "You still have the speed, boy. How are you?"

Petros laughed warmly, shaking Yiannis' hand. "Still faster than you, Yiannis. How have you been?"

They chatted for a while, their conversation filled with nostalgia and familiarity. Watching them interact, I felt a strange sense of pride—and a little awe. Here was a version of my father I didn't recognize: relaxed, unguarded, at home.

By the time he stretched out on the low stone wall, Ari had somehow decided he was the day's sunbathing companion and perched next to him. Petros, of all people, was lazily scratching behind Ari's ears with the air of a man who'd spent his life doing nothing but this. Margaret, meanwhile, was the picture of tranquillity, her legs tucked under her as she flipped a page in her book, the sea breeze rustling the corner of her shawl.

The whole scene was absurd. Absurd. Like some alternate reality had folded itself into my terrace, where Petros Katsaros—the man who once scolded me for "wasting time" by sitting in a park for too long—was now lying in the sun like a lazy housecat, completely at peace. This was a man who thrived on structured days, schedules, and his perpetually ticking mental to-do list. And now, here he was, sprawled out like he'd spent every afternoon of his life doing exactly this.

I just stood there for a moment, utterly frozen by the sheer impossibility of it all. My logical part insisted that this was some elaborate ruse or an uncharacteristic one-off. But another part—a quieter, softer part—wondered if this was who my father had been before. Before London, before finance, before… everything.

And in that absurdity, I felt something unexpected: a thread of closeness, faint but unmistakable. Not from words—we hadn't exchanged many—but from the silence, the ease, the sheer ridiculousness of this moment that felt somehow real.

After some time, he stood and stretched, the picture of ease. "I'll head to the village square," he said casually. "Say hello to a few people. Maybe you can show me the facility and the grove afterwards, Eleni?"

"Of course," I replied. Margaret, still absorbed in her book, glanced up briefly. "I think I'll stay here," she said. "Petros, you can pick me up later."

A little while later, I walked to the square to meet him, expecting him to be finishing up his greetings. Instead, I found him at one of the café tables, engrossed in a game of backgammon with an elderly villager. The scene stopped me in my tracks. Petros laughed as he slapped a piece onto the board, his opponent grumbling good-naturedly.

The shock of it lingered as I watched him: my father, sitting comfortably in the heart of Seranos, joking and playing as though he'd never left. For the first time, I wondered if perhaps this village wasn't just my home—it was his too, in a way I'd never understood.

***

After a whirlwind of a few days split between the facility, the grove, and managing my father, the harvest festival finally arrived—and it was not a moment too soon. I found myself longing for it all to be over so I could return to the comfort of my routine: my work and my quiet evenings with Zeus and Ari by my side.

The village square was a swirling hive of activity, a symphony of chaos and charm that somehow managed to teeter on the edge of disaster without completely falling apart. At the centre of it all stood Callie, her hands on her hips and a clipboard clutched like a weapon of mass coordination.

"I said lanterns, not Christmas lights, Giorgos! Do you see a sleigh and reindeer here?" Callie's voice rang out, sharp enough to make Giorgos jump and mumble something about the only lights he could find in storage.

"Fix it," she barked, not missing a beat before turning to a group of kids who were supposed to be rehearsing their dance routine. "And you lot—what is this? A zombie shuffle? Put some life into it! Aunt Maria is watching, and if you bore her, you'll never hear the end of it."

The kids exchanged panicked glances before leaping into a spirited rendition of a traditional dance. I couldn't help but laugh as Callie turned her focus on me, her sharp eyes narrowing.

"Eleni! Make yourself useful!" She gestured to the stack of mismatched tablecloths on the steps of the café. "Sort those out before the elders decide to stage a coup over clashing patterns."

"Yes, ma'am," I saluted her with mock seriousness. She rolled her eyes, muttering something about city girls and their theatrics before storming off to tackle another crisis.

I made my way to the tablecloths, weaving through a landscape that could only belong to Seranos. Maria and her nemesis, Katerina, were locked in a heated debate over the correct number of sesame seeds for the festival bread.

"Anything more than a sprinkle is vulgar," Katerina declared, her arms crossed.

"And you, Katerina, wouldn't know proper bread if it danced on your table singing hymns!" Maria shot back, waving a rolling pin in the air like a sceptre.

Nearby, Theo was trying to hang a banner across the square with the help of two teenagers who were apparently allergic to competence. The ladder wobbled precariously as Theo bellowed, "Carefully! If I fall, you're explaining it to my wife, and she'll make you wish you hadn't been born!"

Despite the madness, there was something endearing about the whole scene. These were my people now—chaotic, opinionated, and utterly irreplaceable.

As I finished sorting the tablecloths into "acceptable" and "absolutely not" piles, I spotted Andreas across the square, unloading boxes of decorations from a truck. His broad shoulders flexed under the weight; he moved with purpose, but his expression was softer than usual—focused but not weighed down. He didn't see me at first, focused on his task, but when our eyes met, he paused.

I hesitated for a moment before walking over. "Need a hand?" I asked, my voice deliberately casual.

He glanced up, surprised. "Thought you were busy keeping Callie from terrorizing the children."

"She's got that under control," I said, smirking. "Apparently, threatening to ban them from the dessert table works wonders."

Andreas let out a soft chuckle, wiping his hands on a rag as he leaned against the truck. "Noted. I'll remember that for the next village crisis."

We stood in companionable silence for a moment, the bustle of the preparations carrying on around us. The sound of laughter and the clinking of tools filled the air, but here, beside the truck, it felt strangely calm.

"How's everything coming along on your end?" I asked finally, gesturing to the crates.

"Almost done," he said, his tone practical but lacking its usual edge. "It's shaping up. Callie's got the whole village running like a well-oiled machine."

"Callie has the patience of a saint and the attitude of a drill sergeant," I quipped. "A dangerous combination."

"Well," he said, straightening up and grabbing another crate. "If you're offering help, these decorations aren't going to hang themselves."

I rolled my eyes, but I grabbed the nearest crate anyway. "You know, I didn't come here to play your assistant, Andreas."

"Could've fooled me," he shot back, his smirk softening into something almost playful. "But thanks." We worked side by side for a while, and the silence between us was less charged than before and more comfortable.

***

The evening finally arrived. The square glowed under a canopy of lanterns, their soft light swaying gently in the evening breeze. Strings of tiny golden bulbs crisscrossed above us, competing with the stars that were just starting to wink into the velvet sky. The hum of a bouzouki floated through the air, weaving its way through bursts of laughter, clinking glasses, and the happy chaos of children darting between tables.

If someone had told me when I first arrived that I'd be standing here, not just part of the village but at the heart of it, I would've laughed. And yet, here I was—dusting powdered sugar off my dress from a sneak attack by Theo's granddaughter, who had taken her role as the "dessert distributor" far too seriously.

Tables groaned under the weight of food—baskets of crusty bread, plates piled high with dolmades, bowls of tzatziki, and precariously stacked platters of loukoumades. It was a feast so decadent it would've made the gods themselves jealous, and the villagers were digging in like there was no tomorrow.

Across the square, near the makeshift dance floor, Andreas was surrounded by a swarm of giggling children. He crouched low, pretending to lose a game of "catch the ball," his exaggerated defeat earning shrieks of triumph. One particularly daring boy threw his arms around Andreas' neck, and he swung the kid onto his shoulders, laughing in a way I hadn't seen before.

I leaned against one of the long tables, watching him as he joined a group of men clapping along to the music. They coaxed him into the dance circle, and he reluctantly obliged, his moves a mix of surprising agility and awkward hesitation. The sight of him—so at ease, so alive—made something twist in my chest. This was

Andreas as he was meant to be: fully present, part of something bigger than himself. For once, he wasn't brooding, wasn't guarded. He was just... Andreas.

"Enjoying the view?" a voice teased at my elbow.

I jumped, nearly knocking over a bowl of olives. Margaret's face was all mischief as she leaned closer, her wineglass precariously balanced between her fingers.

"No one told me your business partner was that handsome," she said, her tone conspiratorial. "I mean, if I'd known, I might've volunteered to come here a little sooner."

"Margaret!" I hissed, my face flaming as I tried—and failed—not to glance back at Andreas.

"Oh, don't 'Margaret' me," she said, waving her glass dismissively. "You're not fooling anyone, dear. The way you two look at each other? It's like watching a poorly disguised love story unfold."

"It's complicated," I said, with defeat in my voice; there was no point in arguing with her.

"Love always is," she said with a shrug, her expression softening.

With that, she sauntered off, leaving me to stew in my embarrassment as she joined Nikos and Callie, who were locked in a heated debate over who had been the more dramatic child. Judging by the grin on Margaret's face, she was having the time of her life.

A cheer went up as Theo climbed onto a chair, raising a glass high above his head. "To the grove!" he boomed, his face ruddy from both the ouzo and his unshakable enthusiasm. "May it thrive for another hundred years—and may our children and grandchildren work it so we don't have to!"

Laughter rippled through the crowd, followed by a round of applause. Nearby, Nikos took the opportunity to tell the crowd an utterly humiliating story about Callie's childhood attempt at "training" a goat to pull a wagon, which apparently ended with her riding the goat into the village fountain. Callie turned a shade of red, which I didn't know was possible, but her laughter was genuine as she threw a piece of bread at his head.

Maria, always the wise matriarch, took the moment to share a story of her own. Her calm and steady voice carried easily over the noise as she spoke about the grove's history—how it had weathered wars, storms, and countless challenges. "It's not just the land we're saving," she said, her words striking a deep chord. "It's who we are."

The hum of the festival was briefly interrupted as Dimitris strolled into the square, hand in hand with a woman who seemed to embody an effortless grace. She wasn't flashy or overdone—just strikingly natural, with a quiet beauty that caught your attention without demanding it. Her simple dress swayed lightly as she walked, her understated elegance a stark contrast to the usual whirlwind of sequins and sky-high heels Dimitris usually paraded around.

The whispers started immediately, low and buzzing like bees through the crowd. Heads turned, and even Maria paused mid-toast, her sharp eyes narrowing in appraisal. Callie nudged me with a poorly concealed grin. "Who's this?" she murmured her tone a mix of curiosity and amusement. "And since when does Dimitris bring someone like her to the village?"

I leaned closer, keeping my voice low. "I don't know, but this might be the first time he's introduced someone who looks like she'd survive a second round of questions from Maria."

Callie snorted into her wine as Dimitris and the woman made their way toward us. When they stopped, Dimitris flashed his usual roguish grin, but his tone was softer than usual. "Ladies, meet Anna," he said. "She works in sustainable tourism at the town hall. And yes, before you ask, I've already been lectured on my ecological footprint."

Anna rolled her eyes good-naturedly, offering us a warm smile. "It wasn't a lecture. Just… gentle encouragement." Her voice was calm, confident, and disarming. Within moments, she had us at ease, chatting about her ideas for promoting the region's natural beauty without compromising its integrity. As she spoke, it became clear that Anna wasn't just Dimitris' latest distraction—she was sharp, thoughtful, and, quite frankly, amazing.

"I like her," Callie whispered to me under her breath, her tone laced with genuine surprise. "How did Dimitris manage this?"

"No idea," I whispered back. "But I think she might actually like him, too."

Andreas clapped Dimitris on the back a few feet away, his tone teasing but sincere. "She's a keeper," he said with a smirk, and for once, Dimitris didn't argue.

I spotted my father in a corner, surrounded by a group of old friends. His glass was perpetually full, and his laughter boomed above the music as he recounted stories from their youth. By the way he swayed slightly in his chair, he'd clearly had more than his fair share of ouzo. Margaret caught my eye from across the square, her expression half amused, half resigned.

"Looks like Petros remembered he is Greek", Callie commented, smirking.

I chuckled, shaking my head. "He's probably giving them a detailed analysis of ouzo production costs, but at least now he's doing it in Greek."

As the festival continued into the night, I found myself stepping away from the crowd, drawn to the edges of the square where the noise softened and the lanterns cast long, golden shadows. From here, I could see the village in its entirety—a tapestry of laughter, music, and connection. It wasn't perfect. It was messy and loud and wonderfully alive.

And somehow, without me even realizing it, it had become home.

***

Out of the corner of my eye, I saw Zeus trotting toward me, tail wagging with the kind of enthusiasm only he could muster. Of course, he couldn't miss the festivities—he was acting like a kid in a candy store, stealing food from every table he passed. I groaned inwardly, already dreading the inevitable aftermath.

"Zeus, you should stop eating, or you'll be sick," I murmured as I bent down to scratch behind his ear. That's when I noticed something dangling from his collar—an envelope.

"What did you steal this time?" I asked, tugging it loose. But as I unfolded it, I froze. My nine-year-old handwriting stared back at me: "Very Important Document."

The flood of memories hit me instantly. It was the marriage certificate I'd crafted for Andreas and me when I was a kid. I'd entrusted it to Maria all those years ago, solemnly swearing her to secrecy until Andreas signed it—a promise she, of course, didn't keep, as it quickly became the centrepiece of every family dinner's laughter. Yet, somehow, she'd held onto it all this time. But why was Zeus parading around with it now?

I opened the envelope, a laugh bubbling out when I saw the childish scrawl, bright doodles and hearths. But as my eyes drifted to the bottom of the page, the laughter died.

There, next to my own signature, was Andreas'. My breath caught, and I stared at it in disbelief.

When I finally looked up, he was there, leaning against the far wall of the square, hands in his pockets, watching me with an infuriating and devastatingly charming smile. I walked toward him without thinking, the paper clutched tightly in my hand. My emotions swirled—shock, confusion, and something else I wasn't ready to name.

"That," I said, stopping just short of him, "was a blow below the belt, Papadopoulos."

His grin widened, eyes sparkling with mischief. "Anything to see you walk toward me with that look in your eyes."

I couldn't help the smile tugging at my lips. "Plus, using Zeus? That was low."

"I know," he admitted, his tone teasing. "I had to bribe him with two sausages."

The warmth in his voice softened something inside me. He stepped closer, and suddenly, the space between us felt far too small and impossibly vast at the same time. I could feel the heat radiating from his body, and his scent—sandalwood, sun, and something inherently him—clouded my thoughts. He was looking at me like I was the only thing in the world that mattered, and my heart clenched.

For the first time since that horrible day, I felt like I could breathe again—deep, unhindered breaths without the sting of pain in my chest. The weight I'd been carrying for weeks began to lift, just enough for me to feel it.

While I was lost in my own thoughts, Andreas reached out, gently taking my wrist and pulling me into the shadowed lane between two houses. I let out a startled squeal, followed by an embarrassing giggle that sounded like it belonged to a teenager.

"Andreas," I hissed, my back pressed to the cool stone wall, "what are you doing?"

His face was close to mine, so close I could feel the rough stubble of his jaw brushing against my cheek as he whispered, "I missed you, Eleni. Terribly."

The huskiness of his voice sent shivers down my spine. "Someone will see us! My father is sitting just around the corner."

"No one will see us," he murmured, his lips brushing against my ear. "Don't worry." He punctuated his reassurance with soft kisses along my jawline, and my resolve wavered.

"Oh, so this isn't your first time, then?" I teased, trying to keep my composure.

He smirked—actually smirked—and replied, "I grew up in this village. I know all the dark lanes."

"You're an idiot, you know that?" I said, playfully swatting his arm. But the words barely made it out before his lips found my neck, each kiss sending my pulse racing.

In one smooth motion, he lifted me, and my legs wrapped instinctively around his waist. One hand clutched the back of his neck, my fingers tangling in his hair, while the other still gripped the "very important document". Our noses brushed, his forehead resting lightly against mine.

"Now," he whispered, his voice low and deliberate, "if you're finished talking, I'm going to kiss you."

That was it. Whatever hesitation lingered evaporated in an instant. Before he could move, I closed the distance, finding his lips with mine. The kiss started slow, deliberate, his hands under my thighs, keeping me securely against him as our bodies aligned. The world outside the narrow lane disappeared, leaving only the rhythm of his touch, the soft heat of his lips, and the faint hum of distant music in the background.

His hand moved with a deliberateness that sent shivers through me, settling beneath my breast while his thumb traced over the sensitive peak, his touch light but maddeningly precise. A soft moan escaped my lips before I could stop it; my body responded instinctively, arching into him, silently pleading for more. His fingers moved with confident precision, tracing over my most sensitive places, igniting a fire with every deliberate stroke. His body was rubbing against mine, moving slowly and deliberately, the heat of his skin against mine unravelling every last thread of restraint. He unearthed desires I hadn't realized I craved, leaving me breathless, trembling, and utterly consumed by his touch. It was as if our bodies had been holding onto this moment, waiting for the perfect alignment of emotion to finally move together in a rhythm that felt inevitable, unspoken, and completely consuming.

And then, as if on cue, footsteps echoed down the street, followed by Dimitris' unmistakable voice. "Oi, Papadopoulos! Get a room! How old are you, fifteen?"

Andreas pulled away, laughing as I buried my face in my hands, mortified. I adjusted my dress, muttering as I started to walk away. "You're such a bad influence, Andreas. Don't follow me. We can't enter the square together."

"Why?" he called after me, amusement lacing his voice. "Afraid people will think you're sneaking into dark lanes with boys?"

"You're a jerk," I shot back, not turning around. But I couldn't stop the ridiculous smile spreading across my face as I made my way back to the table.

The second I sat down, Callie caught my eye and burst into laughter. "You're kidding me," she said, her voice carrying over the music. "Not in the dark lane by Old Christos' house? That's too cliché even for Andreas!"

"Shut up, Callie," I muttered, though my grin gave me away.
"If those walls could talk," she continued, shaking her head, "the village would burn from shame."
"I'm officially tuning you out," I said, my cheeks burning, though the smile on my lips refused to fade.

***

The music shifted, the familiar notes of an old folk melody rising into the air. It was the kind of song that carried memories with it, a tune passed down through generations that spoke of resilience and hope. Slowly, villagers began to gather in the square, forming a circle. Young and old joined hands, their laughter and chatter fading into a shared rhythm as they began to dance.
I stood on the sidelines for a moment, watching the scene unfold. The children who had been darting around all night were now clinging to their parents, swaying sleepily to the music.
It wasn't long before Callie grabbed my hand, pulling me into the circle. "No hiding," she said, her grin wide. "This is your moment too."
Before I could protest, I was swept into the flow, spinning and stepping in time with the others. I caught glimpses of Margaret laughing with Nikos, her cheeks flushed with wine and joy. Petros, leaning heavily on a friend for balance, was bellowing along with the lyrics he likely hadn't sung in decades. And somewhere near the far side of the square, Andreas was clapping along, his eyes finding mine across the crowd, his expression soft and full of something I couldn't quite name.
As the song ended and the dancers began to drift back to their tables, I found myself standing at the edge of the square, watching as the glow of the festival started to

fade. I thought about how far I'd come since I arrived—how far we'd all come. From the chaos of the grove to this night of celebration, it hadn't been easy, but it had been worth it. And my family, fractured and complicated as it was, felt closer now than I ever thought possible.

Zeus trotted up to me, his tail wagging lazily as he plopped down at my feet, his belly full and his mischief spent. I reached down to scratch behind his ears, the simple gesture grounding me.

"Hey," Andreas' voice came from beside me, soft and unassuming. I hadn't heard him approach, but I wasn't surprised. He had a way of finding me when I needed it most.

"Hey," I replied, glancing up at him. The square behind us was still alive with music and laughter, but it felt quiet and peaceful here, on the outskirts.

"Some night, huh?" he said, his hands tucked into his pockets.

"Some night," I agreed, my gaze drifting back to the square. "It feels… different."

He didn't respond immediately; he just stood there, letting the silence stretch between us. When he finally spoke, his voice was low, almost reverent. "It's good, though. The kind of different that makes you want to see what's next."

I smiled, the warmth of his words settling over me like a blanket. "Yeah," I said softly.

For a moment, we stood there together, Zeus shifted at my feet, his head resting heavily on my shoe, and I felt a quiet contentment settle over me. The road ahead wasn't clear, but it didn't feel daunting this time. It felt full of promise.

One Year Later…

The comforting aroma of slow-cooked lamb and rosemary drifted from the kitchen, wrapping the farmhouse in a warmth that made it feel alive. I adjusted the place settings for the third time, trying to keep my hands busy while Maria worked her magic in the kitchen. She'd arrived hours ago, arms full of fresh herbs and spices, waving off my half-hearted offer to help with a smile.
"Eleni, you're good at many things," she'd said kindly, "but tonight, let me take care of this. You've done enough already."
And she meant it. As pots clanged and her familiar hum floated into the room, I felt a pang of gratitude—not just for her cooking but for her. For being the steady presence we all needed, the heart of so many meals that turned into memories.
"She kicked you out of the kitchen again, didn't she?" Andreas asked as he stepped onto the terrace, two bottles of wine in hand, his smirk both teasing and fond.
"She said I'd done enough already," I replied, smoothing out the tablecloth. "Which is her polite way of saying I'm better off not burning the lamb."
Andreas laughed softly, setting the bottles down. "She's not wrong."
"She's never wrong," I admitted, glancing toward the kitchen, where Maria was orchestrating her feast like a symphony conductor.

***

The table was alive with chatter and clinking glasses, a mosaic of voices weaving together in celebration. Callie sat with Nikos at one end, her hand resting lightly on his, the excitement in her eyes a mix of nerves and anticipation. Across from them, Anna, as polished and poised as ever, leaned toward Dimitris, whispering something that made him grin like a schoolboy. The two of them were still together—a miracle in itself—and Dimitris had even started talking about the future in ways that didn't involve vague deflections. It still felt surreal that they'd be leaving for a year—a whole year in Barcelona, working with the mayor's office as part of a program to exchange knowledge about sustainable agriculture.

"So," Callie said, raising her glass with a teasing smile. "One year in Barcelona. Nikos, are you sure you can survive without the village gossip?"

Nikos chuckled, slipping an arm around her shoulders. "Oh, I'll manage. But the real question is, how will Seranos survive without you?"

"I'm sure they'll struggle," she said with mock seriousness, "but it's about time I see what's out there. Besides, someone needs to make sure you don't embarrass us in front of an international audience."

The table burst into laughter as Dimitris raised his glass. "To Nikos and Callie," he said, his voice unusually earnest. "For showing the world that this village can produce more than olives—and for coming back with stories that make our lives sound boring."

"And," he added, looking pointedly at Andreas and me, "to Seros Olive Groves, which, if I may say, is thriving thanks to these two. Who knew a Londoner and a brooding farmer could turn this place around?"

"Don't forget yourself," Andreas said, lifting his glass in return. "We wouldn't have half the connections we do without your 'charm,' Dimitris."

"Ah, my charm," Dimitris said with a grin. "A valuable resource."

As the meal went on, the conversation turned to lighter topics. Dimitris, ever the entertainer, regaled us with stories of village escapades we hadn't heard before—or perhaps he'd made up on the spot. Maria fussed over whether Nikos and Callie would have access to proper ingredients in Spain, insisting that they take a stash of oregano and olive oil with them "so they don't ruin perfectly good food with strange new flavours."

Callie rolled her eyes, laughing. "Mum, I promise you, Barcelona has plenty of good food. It's the Mediterranean, after all."

Maria fixed her with a look of mock gravity. "Yes, but it's not the Aegean," she replied, her tone so serious it sent us all into fits of laughter.

As the laughter rose and the food disappeared, I let myself sit back for a moment, letting the scene unfold around me. Callie and Nikos, preparing for their next great adventure. Dimitris and Anna, surprisingly grounded and in sync. Maria, keeping all of us together no matter what. And Andreas, catching my eye across the table with that quiet smile of his—the one that said everything without saying anything at all.

The farm was thriving. The village had grown stronger and more connected, embracing a future that honoured its past. And me? I'd found my place here, in the lives of the people who sat at this table. They were my roots, my foundation, as much a part of me as the soil beneath the olive trees.

***

The drive back to Seranos was quiet; the full moon hung low in the sky, casting a silver glow over the sea, so bright that it almost felt like daylight. As we reached the house, Andreas gave me a sideways glance. "One last drink on the terrace?" he asked, his voice soft. I nodded, smiling. Zeus greeted me with his usual enthusiasm, his tail wagging in an erratic rhythm as Ari perched on the windowsill, casting us a glance of indifference—until Andreas walked in. Ari hopped down instantly, brushing against Andreas' leg and purring as if he were some kind of feline deity. "Traitor," I muttered at him, and Andreas smirked, scratching behind her ears.

Andreas headed to the kitchen to pour our drinks, and I stepped out onto the terrace, the cool sea breeze brushing against my skin. This house—the one I'd inherited, the one I'd fought so hard to keep—wasn't just mine anymore. It was ours. Andreas had sold his flat in Navagos months ago, moving in with me, Zeus, and Ari. Now, this place felt fuller, richer, alive in a way I never could've imagined a year ago.

As I waited, I found myself reflecting on the year we'd shared. It hadn't been a bed of roses for Andreas and me—not even close. That lingering pain of betrayal I'd carried didn't vanish overnight, no matter how much love or effort we poured into our reconciliation. At every bump in the road, it found a way to resurface, threatening to pull us apart. For a long time, it lingered between us like a shadow. I could see it in Andreas' eyes—the way he carried the weight of my hurt. Deep down, I knew it wasn't fair to keep bringing it up, to let it resurface again and again, but sometimes I couldn't stop myself.

When I first came back to Seranos, we were completely different people. I was flailing, trying to find my footing, acting like a fish out of water. And Andreas? He was like a wounded animal, retreating into himself, his walls so high I wondered if anyone could scale them. But somehow, we healed each other. Not in grand, sweeping gestures but in slow, steady moments that built a foundation we didn't even realize we were creating.

When we first got together, I think we were still trapped by the past—by what we used to be to each other. The little sister's best friend. The boy I'd once idolized. Our banter, our fights, the way we saw each other—it was all rooted in who we'd been. But since our reconciliation, everything has shifted. We became something entirely new. A couple who loved each other as much as we respected each other. And somewhere along the way, I learned to make peace with that pain. Not because it stopped hurting but because I realized I couldn't let it define us anymore. I had to stop punishing Andreas—and myself—for something we'd already fought so hard to overcome. Slowly, I accepted it as part of our story, not the whole of it.

This past year has tested us in every way. We worked tirelessly, facing stress and deadlines that sometimes felt impossible. But somehow, we managed. The grove was thriving, the business on track, and yes, we were even making good money. Of course, some things stayed the same. I was still making Andreas do all the heavy lifting, and he still turned my head like the very first day. No matter how hard I tried, I couldn't get enough of him. And, true to form, he was still a sexy, smug jerk who knew exactly how to drive me crazy. We never talked about getting married; my childhood "marriage certificate" hung proudly on our bedroom wall, and somehow, that felt like all we ever needed.

At Christmas, we visited my father and Margaret in London, cleared out my old basement flat, and put it on the market. Spending time with Andreas in London felt surreal—a world he'd never been part of—but I was glad he could catch a glimpse of the life I'd left behind.

Petros and Margaret returned for this year's harvest festival, staying for two weeks this time. I had a feeling this was becoming a tradition. They still chose to stay in Navagos, but it was nice to have my father nearby.

Of course, he couldn't resist "helping the kids," as he put it, spending a couple of days at the facility and the grove, sweating everyone with his endless questions and thorough inspections. He found plenty to critique and warn us about—because that's who he is—but I could see it in his eyes: pride. Pride in me, pride in Andreas, and pride in the life we were building together.

Andreas stepped out onto the terrace, carrying two glasses of wine, his presence as grounding as ever. He set one down in front of me before taking a seat next to me. Zeus curled up at our feet, his soft snores blending with the rhythmic crash of the waves. For a long while, we just sat there, watching the moonlight dance on the water, the silence between us warm and easy.

I reached over, letting my hand rest on his. He glanced at me, his lips curving into the kind of smile that still sent butterflies fluttering through my stomach. At that moment, I didn't need words. We'd come so far—individually, together—and the future didn't seem daunting anymore. It felt full of promise and possibility, as infinite as the sea stretching before us.

Printed in Great Britain
by Amazon